SHARPE'S REVENGE

BERNARD CORNWELL was born in London and
raised in Essex, and now lives mainly in the
USA, with his wife. In addition to the hugely
successful Sharpe novels, Bernard Cornwell is
the author of the highly praised Starbuck
Chronicles, the acclaimed Warlord trilogy, and
the recent bestseller *Stonehenge*.

By *Bernard Cornwell*

The Sharpe novels
(in chronological order)

BERNARD CORNWELL

Sharpe's Revenge

Richard Sharpe and
the Peace of 1814

HarperCollins*Publishers*

HarperCollins*Publishers*
77–85 Fulham Palace Road,
Hammersmith, London w6 8jb

www.fireandwater.com

This paperback edition 1997
7 9 8

Previously published in paperback by HarperCollins in 1994
(reprinted four times)
and by Fontana in 1990 (reprinted four times)

First published in Great Britain by
Collins 1989

Copyright © Rifleman Productions Ltd 1989

ISBN 0 00 766010 3

Set in Baskerville

Printed and bound in Great Britain by
Bookmarque Ltd, Croydon, Surrey

FOREWORD

This book encompasses the end of the Peninsular War. The army that was chiefly responsible for that victory, Wellington's army, marched across France to embark for home from the quays of Bordeaux and there occurred one of the most horrid and shameful moments of the whole war.

Thousands of men had contracted wives on the long campaign. They were, mostly, Portuguese or Spanish, and those women had marched every step of the way. They had carried muskets and packs for the weak, done the officers' laundry, baked bread, foraged for food, suffered every hardship and contributed significantly to the army's string of victories. Yet, at Bordeaux, the order was given that such wives, unless they could produce proof that the regimental commanding officer had sanctioned the marriage, were to be abandoned. Very few could produce such proof, and so husbands, wives and children were forcibly torn apart. The men sailed away, while the women and children were left to cope as best they could in a foreign port. It was not the British army's finest moment.

Life, of course, is not fair, and in this novel no one suffers more from its unfairness than William Frederickson. I wanted to reward him for his long service to the Sharpe novels and so introduced him to a delicious French lady, Lucille, fully expecting that they would live happily ever after, but things, as will become apparent, turned out very differently. It is always a pleasure when that happens, not for Frederickson perhaps, but for the author. The characters dictate their own lives and, manipulate them as I might, their wishes forced the story to an unexpected conclusion. Thus, at the book's end, Sharpe has made the decision to live in France. Live in France? I never expected that. I always assumed Sharpe would retire to some green and pleasant corner of England, probably in Dorset, and become a grumpy justice of the peace. Looking back on his career, it now makes sense that he does not live in England. But all the same, France? That was his choice, not mine.

Lucille is one of those characters who become unexpectedly important. Another, one of my favourites, is Major General Nairn who first crossed Sharpe's path in *Sharpe's Enemy*. Nairn had a very simple job to do in that book: merely give Sharpe some orders and then gracefully retire from the series, but he had other ideas and, within half a page of meeting him, I knew I was stuck with another character that was going to muscle in on every page he could. That, however inconvenient, is one of the delights of writing. I never know when a book begins how it is going to end, so writing it is not unlike reading it, in the sense that I want to know what happens. But even so, France?

Sharpe, alas, is not perfect.

Nor, though he does not know it, has his war against Napoleon ended.

But that is another story.

Part One

PROLOGUE

Major Richard Sharpe had made every preparation for his own death. His horse, Sycorax, and his fine French telescope would go to Captain William Frederickson, his weapons would become the property of Sergeant Patrick Harper, while everything else would belong to his wife Jane. Everything, that was, except for the uniform in which Sharpe always fought. That uniform consisted of knee-high riding boots, French cavalry overalls, and a faded green jacket of the 95th Rifles. Sharpe had asked to be buried in that uniform.

'If you weren't buried in those rags,' Frederickson observed disdainfully, 'they'd be burned anyway.'

It was true that the leather boots had been deeply scarred by knives, bayonets and sabres, and that the overalls were so patched with brown homespun that they looked more like a ploughman's cast-off breeches than the plundered uniform of a Chasseur Colonel of Napoleon's Imperial Guard, and that the green jacket was so faded and threadbare that even a moth could not have made a decent meal from it, but the clothes were still those in which Sharpe fought and were therefore dear to him. He might have looked like a scarecrow in the old uniform, but wearing it for battle was one of his obsessive superstitions, which was why, on a cold March morning in 1814, and despite being miles from any enemy soldier, Sharpe wore the old clothes.

'You'll have to take off the jacket,' Frederickson, who understood Sharpe's superstitious attachment to the uniform, warned his friend.

'I know.' There was no detail of this morning that Sharpe had not rehearsed again and again in his mind. What would happen this morning was called 'grass before breakfast'. It sounded innocuous, but it could well mean death.

The two men stood on a low grassy bluff above a grey and sullen Atlantic. A long and heaving swell was running from the west to break against the rocks beneath. To the north of the bluff was the French port of St Jean de Luz that was crammed with merchant shipping and fishing boats, while in the harbour's outer roads a small Royal Navy flotilla lay at anchor. The flotilla consisted of three sloops, two frigates, and a great chequer-sided battleship, the *Vengeance*.

It was a shivering dawn, yet spring was coming and with the spring would come a resurgence of battle. The Emperor Napoleon had refused the peace terms offered by his enemies, so now the French armies would have to fight to defend their homeland. Their enemies were now all Europe. Wellington's army of Britons, Spaniards and Portuguese had captured the south-western corner of France and would soon strike yet further into the heartland, while, far to the north, the Prussians, Austrians and Russians skirmished across Napoleon's northern frontiers.

None of which seemed immediately important to Major Richard Sharpe as he began to pace the frosted grass on the bluff's flat summit. A cold wind was gusting from the ocean and William Frederickson took shelter from it in the lee of some bent and stunted pines. Sharpe, pacing up and down, was oblivious of the wind, obsessed instead with the thought of his own death. The most important thing, he decided, was that Jane was well taken care of. She already had the piece of paper which gave her authority over Sharpe's money; which money was the profit of the plunder he had taken from the French baggage after the battle at Vitoria. Many soldiers had become rich that day, but few

8

as rich as Major Richard Sharpe or Sergeant Patrick Harper.

Sharpe paced close to Frederickson. 'Time?'

Frederickson fumbled with gloved hands to open his watch's lid. 'Twenty minutes past six.'

Sharpe grunted and turned away. The dawn had made the grey clouds palely luminous, while the sea was so dark that it seemed to be made of a liquid and sluggish slate. A small, high-prowed fishing boat was perilously close to the rocks beneath Sharpe. The fishermen were heaving lobster-pots overboard. Perhaps, Sharpe thought, his enemy would be eating one of those lobsters this very night, while Sharpe would already be as cold as stone and lying six feet under French soil. Grass before breakfast.

'God damn it,' he said in sudden irritation, 'why can't we fight with swords?'

'Because Bampfylde chose pistols.' Frederickson had just lit a cheroot and the wind whirled its smoke quickly away.

'God damn it.' Sharpe turned away again. He was nervous, and he did not mind showing his nervousness to Frederickson. The Rifle Captain was one of Sharpe's closest friends and a man who understood how nerves could make the belly into a tight cold knot before a fight. Frederickson, half English and half German, was a fearsome looking man who had given up most of his teeth and one of his eyes on Spanish battlefields. His men, with clumsy affection, called him after a homely flower, Sweet William, though on a battlefield he was anything but sweet. He was a soldier, as tough as any in the army, and tough enough to understand how a brave man could be almost paralysed by fear.

Sharpe understood that too, yet even so he was surprised by the fear he felt in this cold morning. He had been a soldier ever since he had joined the 33rd as a sixteen-year-old recruit. In the twenty-one years since, he had clawed

9

his way through defended breaches, he had stood in the musket line and traded death with an enemy not forty paces away, he had shattered cavalry charges with volley fire, he had fought the lonely fight of a skirmisher ahead of the battle line, he had watched the enemy's artillery tear his men to red ruin, and he had done all of those things more often than he could remember. He had fought in Flanders, India, Portugal, Spain and France. He had risen from the red-coated ranks to become one of His Majesty's officers. He had taken an enemy standard, and been captured himself. He had been wounded. He had killed. Other men had spent their lives mastering the skills of peace, but Richard Sharpe had become a master of war. Few men had fought so often, few men had fought so well, and now, Sharpe thought, the lumpen memories of those many fights were gnawing at his confidence. He knew the luck of the long bloody years could not hold, or perhaps it was that now, better than most men, he understood the danger and therefore feared it. That a man who had fought across the foulest battlefields could be killed by grass before breakfast seemed an appropriate twist of fortune. 'Why do they call it "grass before breakfast"?' he demanded of Frederickson who, knowing that Sharpe already knew the answer and that the question had sprung only from his friend's irritation, did not bother to answer.

'It's a ridiculous name,' Jane had said two weeks before, 'a stupid, stupid name.' 'Grass before breakfast' simply meant a duel which, traditionally, was fought at dawn and usually on some sward of lawn which gave the pistols or swords room for their work. 'If you insist on fighting this stupid duel,' Jane had continued, 'I shall return home. I won't permit you to destroy yourself, Richard.'

'Then you had better go home,' Sharpe had said, 'because I'm fighting it.'

The disagreement had started as a skirmish, but developed into a searing, exhausting argument that had soured the last two weeks. Jane's reasons for not wanting Sharpe to eat grass before breakfast were entirely good. For a start he might very well be killed, which would leave Jane a widow, but even if he won, he would still be a loser. Duelling had been banned in the army, and if Sharpe insisted on fighting, then his career could be undone in a single moment. Her husband's career was precious to Jane and she did not want it risked; neither by a duel, nor even by the skirmishes of a war's ending. Jane said it was time for Sharpe to go back to England and take the plaudits for his achievements. In England, she said, he would be a hero and he could take a hero's reward. Had he not been given an audience by the Prince of Wales, and would not that Prince now make certain that Major Sharpe became Sir Richard? Jane wanted Sharpe to abandon the army, to forget the duel, and to sail home, but instead, like the stubborn fool he was, he would stay to eat grass before breakfast and Jane could see all that future eminence, and all those princely rewards, fading like pistol smoke in a wind. Thus she had tried her ultimatum: that if Sharpe insisted on fighting, she would publicly shame him by going home. Sharpe had successfully called her bluff, but at the price of a fortnight's cold and silent misery.

Frederickson fumbled with his watch again. 'Half past six.'

'It's cold.' Sharpe seemed to notice the temperature for the first time.

'In an hour,' Frederickson said, 'we'll be breakfasting on chops and pease pudding.'

'You might be.'

'We will be,' Frederickson insisted patiently, then turned to watch a small black carriage which appeared at the foot of the low hill. The coachman whipped the horses up the rutted earth track, then steered towards the bent pine trees where he stopped with a clatter of trace chains and squealing brake blocks. Sergeant Harper, looking indecently cheerful, unfolded himself from the cramped interior and offered Sharpe a confident grin. 'Good morning, sir! A bit chilly.'

'Morning, Sergeant.'

'I've got the bugger, sir.' Harper gestured at a black-dressed man who had shared the coach.

'Good morning, Doctor,' Sharpe said politely.

The doctor ignored the greeting. He was a thin elderly Frenchman who stayed inside the small carriage. He had a black bag which doubtless contained knives, bonesaws, gouges and clamps. The doctor had been reluctant to come to this dawn slaughter, which was why Frederickson had charged Harper with the duty of making sure the man was up and ready. No British doctor, either of the Navy or Army, had been willing to serve at this illegal ceremony which could well lead to courts-martial for everyone involved.

'He was drunk last night, sir.' Harper, wearing a Rifleman's green jacket as faded as either Sharpe's or Frederickson's, confided to Sharpe.

'Who was drunk? The doctor?'

'No, sir. Captain Bampfylde was drunk. He stayed ashore, you see, and I saw him in the yard of that big inn back of the ropewalk.' Harper laughed with a scornful pleasure. 'Pissed as a bishop, he was. He's as twitchy as a cat, I reckon.'

'I'm nervous, too,' Sharpe snapped. 'I hardly slept last night.' Or the night before, because the anticipation of this duel had kept him awake as he tried to foresee what might happen in this cold morning. Now he would discover what was ordained, and the closeness of the discovery only added to the fear. He confessed as much to Harper, and was glad to make the confession, for the big Irishman was Sharpe's closest friend and a man who had shared all of the battles since Wellington's army had first landed in Portugal.

'But you weren't drunk, sir. Bampfylde's going to have

the bloody shakes this morning. They'll be pouring eggs into him, they will.' Harper, four inches taller than Sharpe's six feet, seemed amused at the impending confrontation. Harper had no doubt that Sharpe would despatch Captain Bampfylde's loathsome soul to eternal damnation.

And Sharpe had no doubt that Bampfylde deserved such a fate. Bampfylde was a Naval officer, Captain of the great *Vengeance* which was anchored in the outer roads, and, just weeks before, he had led an expedition north to capture a French coastal fort. Sharpe had been the senior land officer and, once the fort was captured, Sharpe had marched inland to ambush the French supply road. He had returned to the captured Teste de Buch fort to find Bampfylde gone. Sharpe, with two companies of Riflemen and a force of Marines, had been stranded in the fort, where he had been besieged by a French brigade led by a General called Calvet. By the grace of God, the luck of the Rifles, and the help of an American privateer, Sharpe had saved his men. But not all of them; too many had died in the fort, and Bampfylde was to blame. Sharpe, returning from the savagery of the battle against Calvet, and lethal with indignation, had challenged the Naval officer to this confrontation. 'I wish we were fighting with swords.'

'Swords or guns, who cares?' Harper said blithely.

'I care.'

'He's a dead bastard either way.'

'He's a late bastard.' Frederickson swung his arms to generate warmth, then, apparently oblivious to the gnawing tensions in Sharpe, asked Harper if the company was ready to march.

'Aye, sir.'

'Good.' For as soon as this duel was fought, Frederickson would take his prime company of the 60th Rifles eastwards to join the army. Sergeant Harper would go with Frederickson for, just like Sharpe, he had become detached from his old battalion. That battalion, the Prince of Wales's Own Volunteers, had a new Colonel who had appointed his own Majors and a new Regimental Sergeant-Major, which had left Sharpe and Harper adrift.

Harper had been eagerly recruited by Frederickson who, in turn, had been just as eagerly snapped up by Major-General Nairn, a Scotsman who at long last had been given his own fighting brigade and wanted Frederickson's men to add a lethal sting to his skirmish line. Nairn also wanted Sharpe, not for the skirmish line, but to be his chief of staff.

'But I've never been a staff officer,' Sharpe had protested.

'I've never commanded a brigade before,' Nairn had replied cheerfully.

'I must talk with Jane,' Sharpe had said, and had then gone back to his lodgings where he broke a week's chill silence, but their discussion about Nairn's offer had been no happier than the tearful, rage-shredding arguments about the duel. Jane still insisted that they go home, and this time added a new reason for Sharpe to desert the army. Once peace came, she averred, the price of property in England would rise steeply, which made it all the more sensible to sail home now and find a London house. Sharpe had violently protested at such a notion, claiming that he would never live in London; that it was a vile, dirty, crowded and corrupt city, and while he was not averse to buying a house, that house should be in the country. For no very good reason he wanted to live in Dorset. Someone had once extolled that county, and the idea had lodged irreversibly in his head.

In the end, exhausted by the arguments, a reluctant compromise had been agreed. Jane would go home to take advantage of the existing prices of property, but she would seek a country house in Dorset. In the meantime, and if he survived the duel, Sharpe would serve Major-General Nairn.

'But why?' Jane had pleaded tearfully. 'You said yourself

14

you feared fighting more battles. You can't fight and live for ever!' But Sharpe could not really tell her why he refused to go home before the war's ending. He certainly did not want to be a staff officer, and he readily acknowledged his reluctance to face more battles, but there was a deeper reason that fought those urges and which tugged at his soul like a dark and torrential current. His friends would be in Nairn's brigade; Nairn himself, Frederickson, and Harper. So many friends had died, and so few were left, and Sharpe knew he would never forgive himself if he deserted those good friends in the last weeks of a long war. So he would stay and fight. But first he would kill a Naval officer, or else be killed himself.

'I spy the bastards,' Frederickson said happily.

Three horsemen were spurring along the road from the town. All wore dark blue naval cloaks and had fore-and-aft cocked hats. Sharpe looked past the three Naval officers to see if any mounted provosts were riding from the town to stop the duel and arrest the participants. The duel was not exactly a secret, indeed half the depot officers in St Jean de Luz had wished Sharpe luck, so he could only assume that the provosts had chosen to be deaf and blind to the duel's illegality.

The Naval officers walked their horses up the hill and, without an apparent glance at Sharpe, dismounted fifty yards away. One of the officers held the horses' reins, one paced nervously, while the third walked towards the three Riflemen.

Frederickson, who was Sharpe's second, went to meet the approaching Naval officer. 'Good morning, Lieutenant!'

'Good morning, sir.' Lieutenant Ford was Bampfylde's second. He carried a wooden case in his right hand. 'I apologise that we're late.'

'We're just pleased that you've arrived.' Frederickson glanced towards Captain Bampfylde who still paced nervously behind the three horses. 'Is your principal prepared to make an apology, Lieutenant?'

The question was asked dutifully, and just as dutifully answered. 'Of course not, sir.'

'Which is regrettable.' Frederickson, whose company had suffered at the Teste de Buch fort because of Bampfylde's cowardice, did not sound in the least regretful. Indeed his voice was positively gleeful in anticipation of Bampfylde's death. 'Shall we let the proceedings begin, Lieutenant?' Without waiting for an answer he beckoned to Sharpe as Ford signalled to Bampfylde.

The two principals faced each other without speaking. Bampfylde looked deathly pale to Sharpe, but quite sober. He was certainly not shaking. He looked angry, but any man who had been accused of gross cowardice should look angry.

Ford opened the wooden case and produced two duelling pistols. Bampfylde, because he had been challenged, had been offered the choice of weapons, and he had chosen a pair of long-barrelled French-made percussion pistols. Frederickson weighed them in his hands, inspected their hammers, then pulled the ramrod from one of the guns and probed both barrels. He was checking that neither pistol had concealed rifling in the rear part of their barrels. Both were smooth-bore. They were, so far as a craftsman's high skill could make them, identical weapons.

The doctor was leaning forward in the carriage to watch the careful preparations. His coachman, swathed in a cloak, stood by the horses' heads. Harper waited by the pine trees.

Ford loaded both pistols, carefully watched by Frederickson. The Lieutenant used fine black powder that was dispensed from a small measuring cup. Ford was nervous, his hand quivered, and some of the powder was wisped away by the wind, but he carefully took an extra pinch to compensate for the loss. The powder was tamped down with the ramrod, then each lead ball was wrapped in an oiled leather patch. Bullets, however carefully cast, were never quite of a perfect calibre, but the leather patch made the fit as true as was possible, and thus gave the pistols added accuracy. Greater accuracy would have been achieved if the weapons' barrels had been rifled, but that was thought to be unsporting. The balls were rammed down the barrels, then the ramrod was struck with a brass hammer to make sure that the missiles were sitting hard against the powder charge.

Once the barrels were charged Ford opened a small tin case which contained the percussion caps. Each cap was a wafer of paper-thin copper enclosing a tiny charge of black powder. When the pistol's hammer struck the copper wafer the hidden powder exploded to lance a tiny jet of flame down the touch-hole to the compacted charge in the barrel. Such guns were finicky, expensive, and much more reliable than the old-fashioned flintlock that was so prone to dampness. Ford carefully pressed the caps into the tiny recesses beneath the two hammers, then gently lowered the hammers so the guns were safe. Then, with a curiously diffident air, he offered both butts to Frederickson.

Frederickson, thus given the choice, looked at Sharpe.

'Either,' Sharpe said curtly. It was the first word either principal had spoken since they had met. Bampfylde glanced at Sharpe as the Rifleman spoke, then quickly looked away. The Naval officer was a plump young man with a smooth face, while Sharpe had a tanned, scarred skin and angular bones. A scar on the Rifleman's left cheek distorted his mouth to give his face an unwitting look of mockery that only disappeared when he smiled.

Frederickson chose the right-hand gun. 'Coats and hats, gentlemen, please,' he said solemnly.

Sharpe had anticipated this ritual, yet it still seemed strange and clumsy as he threw down his shako, then as he took off the threadbare rifleman's jacket. On the jacket's sleeve was a dirty cloth badge; a wreath of oak leaves that proved he had once led a Forlorn Hope into a breach that had been savage with fire and steel. He gave the coat to Frederickson who, in return, handed the loaded pistol to Sharpe. The wind stirred Sharpe's black hair that he irritably pushed away from his eyes.

Bampfylde shrugged off his boat-cloak, then undid the buttons of his blue and white jacket. Beneath it he wore a white silk shirt that was tucked into a sash about the waistband of his white uniform breeches. It was said to be easier, and thus much safer, to remove shreds of silk from a bullet wound, which was why many officers insisted on wearing silk into battle. Sharpe's shirt was of stained linen.

Ford took Captain Bampfylde's hat, cloak and jacket, then cleared his throat. 'You will take ten paces, gentlemen, to my count –' Ford was very nervous; he swallowed phlegm, then cleared his throat once more – 'after which you will turn and fire. If satisfaction is not given with the first exchange, then you may insist on firing a second time, and so forth.'

'You're happy with your station?' Frederickson asked Bampfylde who gave a start at being thus addressed, then looked around the bluff as if seeking a safer place to fight.

'I am content,' he said after a pause.

'Major?' Frederickson asked Sharpe.

'Content.' The butt of the pistol was made of cross-hatched walnut. The gun felt heavy and unbalanced in Sharpe's hand, but that was only because he was not used to such weapons. It was undoubtedly a gun of great precision.

'If you'll turn, gentlemen?' Ford's voice was shaking.

Sharpe turned so that he was staring out to sea. The freshening wind had begun to fleck the slaty swell with rills of white foam. The wind, he noted, was coming straight into his face so he would not have to aim the pistol off to compensate for a cross-breeze.

'You may cock your weapons,' Frederickson said. Sharpe pulled back the hammer and felt it click into place. He was besieged by a sudden worry that the percussion cap would fall out of its recess, but when he looked he saw that the wafer's copper edges were so crimped by the tight fit that the cap was effectively wedged tight.

'Ten paces, gentlemen,' Ford announced. 'One. Two . . .'

Sharpe walked his normal paces. He held the gun low. He did not think he had shown any fear to Bampfylde, but his belly was like knotted ice and a muscle was trembling in his left thigh. His throat was dry as dust. He could see Harper out of the corner of his eye.

'Seven. Eight.' Ford had raised his voice so it would carry above the sound of the sea wind. Sharpe was close enough to the bluff's edge to see the French lobstermen pulling on long oars to escape the sucking undertow at the cliff's ragged base.

'Nine,' Ford shouted, then a perceptible and nervous pause before the last word, 'ten.'

Sharpe took the last pace, then turned his back to the Atlantic wind. Bampfylde was already raising his pistol. He looked very near to Sharpe who suddenly seemed unable to raise his right arm. He was thinking of Jane who he knew was waiting in horrid suspense, then he jerked his arm into motion because Bampfylde's pistol was already nothing but a round black hole pointing straight between Sharpe's eyes.

He watched the black hole and suddenly felt the warm calm of battle. The reassurance was so unexpected, yet so familiar, that he smiled.

And Bampfylde fired.

Flame pierced at Sharpe through the billowing smoke, but he had already heard the ball go past his head with a crack like a leather whip snapped hard. The bullet could not have been more than six inches from his left ear, and

Sharpe wondered if both pistols pulled to the right. He waited, wanting the smoke of Bampfylde's pistol to dissipate in the wind. He was still smiling, though he did not know it. Bampfylde, doubtless from nerves, had fired too quickly and thus had wasted his shot. Sharpe now had all the time he needed to take revenge for the men who had died in the fortress of Teste de Buch.

The wind shredded the smoke, revealing a Bampfylde who stood in profile to Sharpe. The Naval Captain was sucking in his belly to make his body into a smaller target. Sharpe had the blade of the pistol's foresight outlined against the white silk shirt, and now he lined the back notch with the blade foresight, then he edged the pistol a fraction to the left just in case the weapon did pull to the right. He would aim low, for most guns fired high. If this one did not fire high then he would give Bampfylde a belly wound. That would kill, but slowly; as slowly as some of Sharpe's men had died after Bampfylde had abandoned them behind the enemy's lines.

His finger curled round the trigger. The smoke was entirely gone from Bampfylde now and was nothing more than a tenuous scrap of distant mist that was being whirled high off the bluff's edge to sail inland.

'Fire, damn you!' Bampfylde blurted the words aloud, and Sharpe, who had been about to fire, saw that the Naval Captain was visibly shaking.

'Fire, God damn you!' Bampfylde called again, and Sharpe knew he had won utterly, for he had reduced this proud man to a quivering coward. Sharpe had accused Bampfylde of cowardice, and now he was proving the allegation.

'Fire!' Bampfylde called the word in despair.

Sharpe lowered the pistol's muzzle to compensate for the upward pull, then fired.

Sharpe's pistol did not pull up at all, but had a slight tendency to fire leftwards, rather than right, and the result, instead of a belly shot, was to sear the ball through both cheeks of Bampfylde's bottom. It ripped his white naval breeches open, then scored bloody gouges in his flesh. Bampfylde squealed like a stuck pig and lurched forward. He dropped his pistol, fell to his knees and Sharpe felt the exultation of a job well done. He could see blood bright on the white breeches. The doctor was running clumsily with his black bag, but Ford was already kneeling beside the wounded Bampfylde. 'It's only a flesh wound, sir.'

'He's broken my back!' Bampfylde hissed the words as evidence of his pain.

'He's creased your arse.' Frederickson was grinning.

Ford looked up at Frederickson. 'You agree honour is served, sir?'

Frederickson was finding it hard not to laugh. 'Eminently served, Lieutenant. I bid you good day.'

The doctor knelt beside the Naval Captain. 'A flesh wound, nothing more. It will only need a bandage. There'll be some bruising and soreness. You're a lucky man.'

Ford translated for the distraught Bampfylde, but the Naval Captain was not listening. Instead he was staring through angry and shameful tears at the black-haired Rifleman who had come to stand over him. Sharpe said nothing, but just tossed down the smoking pistol and walked away. He had failed to kill the man, which angered him, but honour had been served on the dead of the Teste de Buch. He had eaten his grass before breakfast, and now Sharpe must cement his fragile peace with Jane, send her away with his love, then go back to the place he knew the best and feared the most: the battlefield.

*   *   *

Bordeaux still belonged to the Emperor, though for how long no one could tell. The river wharfs were empty, the warehouses bare and the city's coffers dry. A few men still proclaimed their loyalty to Napoleon, but most longed for the peace that would revive trade and, as a symbol of that longing, they made themselves white cockades that were the badge of France's royal house. At first the cockades were kept hidden, but as each day passed more were worn in open defiance of the Bonapartist troops that remained. Those imperial defenders were few, and pitifully weak. Some crippled veterans and pensioners manned the river forts, and a half battalion of young infantrymen guarded the prefecture, but all the good troops had marched south and east to reinforce Marshal Soult and, encouraged by their absence, the hungry city grumbled with disaffection and rebellion.

On a March morning, brisk with a cold wind and wet with rain that swept from the Atlantic, a single wagon arrived at the city's prefecture. The wagon held four heavy crates and was escorted by a troop of cavalrymen who, oddly, were commanded by an infantry Colonel. The wagon stopped in the prefecture's yard and its Dragoon escort, on weary and muddied horses, slouched empty-eyed in their saddles. They wore their hair in *cadenettes*; small pigtails which hung beside their cheeks and were a mark of their élite status.

The infantry Colonel, elderly and scarred, climbed slowly from his saddle and walked to the porticoed entrance where a sentry presented his musket. The Colonel was too weary to acknowledge the sentry's salute, but just pushed through the heavy door. The cavalry escort was left under the command of a Dragoon Sergeant who had a face that was the texture of knife-slashed leather. He sat with his heavy straight-bladed sword resting across his saddle bow and the nervous sentry, trying not to catch the Sergeant's hostile eyes, could see that the edge of the dulled blade was brightly nicked from recent battle.

'Hey! Pigface!' The Sergeant had noted the sentry's surreptitious interest.

'Sergeant?'

'Water. Fetch some water for my horse.'

The sentry, who was under orders not to stir from his post, tried to ignore the command.

'Hey! Pigface! I said get some water.'

'I'm supposed to stay . . .'

The sentry went silent because the Sergeant had drawn a battered pistol from a saddle holster.

The Sergeant thumbed back the pistol's heavy cock. 'Pigface?'

The sentry stared into the pistol's black muzzle, then fled to get a bucket of water while, upstairs, the infantry Colonel had been directed into a cavernous room that had once been gracious with marble walls, a moulded plaster ceiling, and a polished boxwood floor, but which was now dirty, untidy and chill despite the small fire that burned in the wide hearth. A small bespectacled man was the room's only occupant. He sat hunched over a green malachite table on which a slew of papers curled between the wax-thick stumps of dead candles. 'You're Ducos?' the infantryman demanded without any other greeting.

'I am Major Pierre Ducos.' Ducos did not look up from his work.

'My name is Colonel Maillot.' Maillot seemed almost too tired to speak as he opened his sabretache and took out a sealed dispatch that he placed on the table. Maillot deliberately placed the dispatch on top of the paper upon which Ducos was writing.

Pierre Ducos ignored the insult. Instead he lifted the dispatch and noted the red seal that bore the insignia of a bee. Other men might have shown astonishment at receiving a missive with the Emperor's private seal, but Ducos's attitude seemed to express irritation that the Emperor should aggravate him with further work. Nor, as other men would have done, did Ducos immediately open the dispatch, but instead he insisted on finishing the work that the Colonel had interrupted. 'Tell me, Colonel,' Ducos had an extraordinarily deep voice for such a puny man, 'what would your judgement be on a General of Brigade who allows his command to be defeated by a handful of vagabonds?'

Maillot was too tired to express any judgement, so said nothing. Ducos, who was writing his confidential report to the Emperor on the events at the Teste de Buch fort, dipped his nib in ink and wrote on. It was a full five minutes before Ducos deigned to close his inkwell and slit open the Emperor's dispatch. It contained two sheets of paper that he read in silence, and afterwards, in obedience to an instruction contained on one of the sheets, he threw the other on to the fire. 'It's taken you long enough to reach me.'

The words were ungracious, but Maillot showed no resentment as he walked to the fire and held chilled hands to the small warmth generated by the burning page. 'I'd have been here sooner, but the roads are hardly safe, Major. Even with a cavalry escort one has to beware bandits.' He said the last word mockingly for both men knew that the 'bandits' were either deserters from Napoleon's armies or young men who had fled into the countryside to avoid conscription. What Maillot did not say was that his wagon had been attacked by such bandits. Six of the Dragoons had died, including Maillot's second-in-command, but Maillot had counter-attacked, then released the surviving Dragoons to pursue and punish the brigands. Maillot was a veteran of the Emperor's wars and he would not be insulted by mere vagabonds.

Ducos unhooked the spectacles from his ears and wiped the round lenses on a corner of his blue jacket. 'The consignment is safe?'

'Downstairs. It's in an artillery wagon that's parked in the yard. The escort need food and water, and so do their horses.'

Ducos frowned to show that he was above dealing with

such humdrum requirements as food and water. 'Do the escort know what is in the wagon?'

'Of course not.'

'What do they think it is?'

Maillot shrugged. 'Does it matter? They simply know they have fetched four unmarked crates to Bordeaux.'

Ducos lifted the dispatch's remaining sheet of paper. 'This gives me authority over the escort, and I insist upon knowing whether they can be trusted.'

Maillot sat in a chair and stretched out his long, weary and mud-spattered legs. 'They're commanded by a good man, Sergeant Challon, and they'll do nothing to cross him. But can they be trusted? Who knows? They've probably guessed what's in the crates by now, but so far they've stayed loyal.' He stifled a yawn. 'What they're more concerned about now is food and water.'

'And you, Colonel?' Ducos asked.

'I need food and water, too.'

Ducos grimaced to show that his question had been misunderstood. 'What do you do now, Colonel?'

'I return to the Emperor, of course. The consignment is your responsibility. And if you'll forgive me, I'm damned glad to be shot of it. A soldier should be fighting now, not acting as a baggage-master.'

Ducos, who had just been given the responsibilities of a baggage-master, restored the polished spectacles to his face. 'The Emperor does me great honour.'

'He trusts you,' Maillot said simply.

'As he trusts you,' Ducos returned the compliment.

'I've been with him many years.'

Ducos glanced at the grey-haired Maillot. Doubtless Maillot had been with the Emperor for many years, but he had never been promoted above the rank of Colonel. Other Frenchmen had risen from the ranks to command whole armies, but not this tall, scarred veteran with his doggedly trustworthy face. In brief, Ducos decided, this

25

Maillot was a fool; one of the Emperor's loyal mastiffs; a man for errands; a man without imagination. 'Bordeaux is not a safe place,' Ducos said softly, almost as if he was speaking to himself, 'the mayor has sent a message to the English, asking them to come here. He thinks I don't know of the message, but I have a copy on this table.'

'Then arrest him,' Maillot said casually.

'With what? Half the town guard wears the white cockade now, and so would the other half if they had the guts.' Ducos stood and crossed to a window from which he stared at the rain which swept in great swathes across the Place St Julien. 'The wagon will be safe here tonight,' he said, 'and your men can take some of the empty billets.' Ducos turned, suddenly smiling. 'But you, Colonel, will do me the honour of taking supper at my lodgings?'

All Maillot wished to do was sleep, but he knew in what favour the Emperor held this small bespectacled man and so, out of courtesy and because Ducos pressed the invitation so warmly, the Colonel reluctantly accepted.

Yet, to Maillot's surprise, Ducos proved a surprisingly entertaining host, and Maillot, who had snatched two hours' exhausted sleep in the afternoon, found himself warming to the small man who talked so frankly of his services to the Emperor. 'I was never a natural soldier like yourself, Colonel,' Ducos said modestly. 'My talents were used to corrupt, outguess and cheat the enemy.' Ducos did not talk of his past failures that night, but of his successes such as the time when he had lured some Spanish guerrilla leaders to truce talks, and how they had all been slaughtered when they trustingly arrived. Ducos smiled at the memory. 'I sometimes miss Spain.'

'I never fought there,' Maillot helped himself to more brandy, 'but I was told about the *guerilleros*. How can you fight men who don't wear uniforms?'

'By killing as many civilians as you can, of course,' Ducos said, then, wistfully, 'I do miss the warm climate.'

Maillot laughed at that. 'You were evidently not in Russia.'

'I was not.' Ducos shivered at the very thought, then twisted in his chair to peer into the night. 'It's stopped raining, my dear Maillot. You'll take a turn in the garden?'

The two men walked the sodden lawn and their cigar smoke drifted up through the branches of the pear-trees. Maillot must still have been remembering the Russian Campaign, for he suddenly uttered a short laugh then commented how very clever the Emperor had been in Moscow.

'Clever?' Ducos sounded surprised. 'It didn't seem very clever to those of us who weren't there.'

'That's my point,' Maillot said. 'We heard about the unrest at home, so what did the Emperor do? He sent orders that the female dancers of the Paris ballet were to perform without skirts or stockings!' Maillot laughed at the memory, then turned to the garden's high brick wall and unbuttoned his breeches. He went on talking as he pissed. 'We heard later that Paris forgot all about the deaths in Russia, because all they could talk about was Mademoiselle Rossillier's naked thighs. Were you in Paris at the time?'

'I was in Spain.' Ducos was standing directly behind Maillot. As the older man had talked, Ducos had drawn a small pistol from his tail pocket and silently eased back its oiled cock. Now he aimed the pistol at the base of Maillot's neck. 'I was in Spain,' Ducos said again, and he screwed his eyes tight shut as he pulled the trigger. The ball shattered one of Maillot's vertebrae, throwing the grey head back in a bloody paroxysm. The Colonel seemed to give a remorseful sigh as he collapsed. His head jerked forward to thump against the brickwork, then the body twitched once and was quite still. The foul-smelling pistol smoke lingered beneath the pear branches.

Ducos retched, gagged, and managed to control himself.

27

A voice shouted from a neighbouring house, wanting an explanation for the gunshot, but when Ducos made no reply there was no further question.

By dawn the body was hidden under compost.

Ducos had not slept. It was not conscience, nor disgust at Maillot's death that had kept him awake, but the enormity of what that death represented. Ducos, by pulling the trigger, had abandoned all that had once been most dear to him. He had been raised to believe in the sanctity of the Revolutionary ideals, then had learned that Napoleon's imperial ambitions were really the same ideals, but transmuted by one man's genius into a unique and irreplaceable glory. Now, as Napoleon's glory crumbled, the ideals must live on, only now Ducos recognized that France itself was the embodiment of that greatness.

Ducos had thus persuaded himself in that damp night that the irrelevant trappings of Imperial France could be sacrificed. A new France would rise, and Ducos would serve that new France from a position of powerful responsibility. For the moment, though, a time of waiting and safety was needed. So, in the morning, he summoned the Dragoon Sergeant Challon to the prefecture where he sat the grizzled sergeant down at the green malachite table across which Ducos pushed the one remaining sheet of the Emperor's dispatch. 'Read that, Sergeant.'

Challon confidently picked up the paper, then, realizing that he could not bluff the bespectacled officer, dropped it again. 'I don't read, sir.'

Ducos stared into the bloodshot eyes. 'That piece of paper gives you to me, Sergeant. It's signed by the Emperor himself.'

'Yes, sir.' Challon's voice was toneless.

'It means you obey me.'

'Yes, sir.'

Ducos then took a risk. Spread on the table was a newspaper which he ordered Challon to throw to the floor.

The Sergeant was puzzled at the order, but obeyed. Then he went very still. The newspaper had hidden two white cockades; two big cockades of flamboyant white silk.

Challon stared at the symbols of Napoleon's enemies, and Ducos watched the pigtailed Sergeant. Challon was not a subtle man, and his leathery scarred face betrayed his thoughts as openly as though he spoke them aloud. The first thing the face betrayed to Ducos was that Sergeant Challon knew what was concealed in the four crates. Ducos would have been astonished if Challon had not known. The second thing that the Sergeant betrayed was that he, just like Ducos, desired those contents.

Challon looked up at the small Major. 'Might I ask where Colonel Maillot is, sir?'

'Colonel Maillot contracted a sudden fever which my physician thinks will prove fatal.'

'I'm sorry to hear that, sir,' Challon's voice was very wooden, 'as some of the lads liked the Colonel, sir.' For a second, as he looked into those hard eyes, Ducos thought he had wildly miscalculated. Then Challon glanced at the incriminating cockades. 'But some of the lads will learn to live with their grief.'

The relief washed through Ducos, though he was far too clever to reveal either that relief or the fear which had preceded it. Challon, Ducos now knew, was his man. 'The fever,' Ducos said mildly, 'can be very catching.'

'So I've heard, sir.'

'And our responsibility will demand at least six men. Don't you agree?'

'I think more than that will survive the fever, sir,' Challon said as elliptically as Ducos. They were now confederates in treachery, and neither could state it openly, though each perfectly understood the other.

'Good.' Ducos picked up one of the cockades. Challon hesitated, then picked up the other, and thus their pact was sealed.

Two mornings later there was a sea-fog that rolled from the Garonne estuary to shroud Bordeaux in a white, clinging dampness through which nine horsemen rode eastwards in the dawn. Pierre Ducos led them. He was dressed in civilian clothes with a sword and two pistols at his belt. Sergeant Challon and his men were in the vestiges of their green uniforms, though all the troopers had discarded their heavy metal helmets. Their saddle bags bulged, as did the panniers of the pack horses that three of the troopers led.

To deceive, cheat, disguise, and outwit; those were the skills Ducos had given to his Emperor; which skills must now serve his own ends. The horses clattered through the city's outer gate, stirred the fog with their passing, and then were gone.

CHAPTER 1

'Of course the Peer knew about it,' Major-General Nairn was speaking of the duel, 'but between you and me I don't think he was unhappy about it. The Navy's been rather irritating him lately.'

'I expected to be arrested,' Sharpe said.

'If you'd have killed the bugger, you would have been. Even Wellington can't absolutely ignore a deceased Naval Captain, but it was clever of you just to crease the man's bum.' Nairn gave a joyful bark of laughter at the thought of Bampfylde's wound.

'I was trying to kill him,' Sharpe confessed.

'It was much cleverer of you to give him a sore arse. And let me say how very good it is to see you, my dear Sharpe. I trust Jane is well?'

'Indeed, sir.'

Sharpe's tone caused Nairn to give the Rifleman an amused look. 'Do I detect that you are in marital bad odour, Sharpe?'

'I stink, sir.'

It had taken Sharpe three days to catch up with the advancing army, and another half-day to find Nairn, whose brigade was on the left flank of the advance. Sharpe had eventually discovered the Scotsman on a hilltop above a ford which the British had captured that morning and through which a whole Division now marched. The French were only visible as a few retreating squadrons of cavalry far to the east, though a battery of enemy artillery occasionally fired from a copse of trees about a mile beyond the river.

'You brought Frederickson?' Nairn now asked.

'His men are at the foot of the hill.'

'Creased his bum!' Nairn laughed again. 'Can I assume from your marital odour that Jane is not with you?'

'She sailed for home two days ago, sir.'

'Best place for a woman. I never really did approve of officers carrying wives around like so much baggage. No offence, of course, Jane's a lovely girl, but she's still baggage to an army. Hello! Christ!' These last words were a greeting for a French cannonball that had thumped across the river and bounced uphill to force Nairn into a frantic evasion that almost spilled him from his saddle. The Scotsman calmed his horse, then gestured over the river. 'You can see what's happening, Sharpe. The bloody French try to stop us at every river, and we just outflank the buggers and keep moving.' At the foot of the slope Nairn's brigade patiently waited their turn to cross the ford. The brigade was composed of one Highland battalion and two English county battalions.

'What exactly do you want me to do?' Sharpe asked Nairn.

'Damned if I know. Enjoy yourself. I am!' And indeed the Scotsman, who had endured years of dreary staff work for Wellington, revelled in his new command. Nairn's only regret was that so far there had been no battle in which he could demonstrate how foolish Wellington had been in not giving him a brigade much earlier. 'God damn it, Richard, there's not much of the war left. I want one crack at the garlic-reekers.'

Sharpe might have been ordered to enjoy himself, but he soon discovered that being chief of staff to a brigade entailed enormously long days and seemingly endless problems. He worked wherever Nairn's headquarters happened to be; sometimes in a sequestrated farmhouse, but more usually in a group of tents pitched wherever the brigade happened to bivouac. Sometimes Sharpe would hear the thump of guns to the east and he would know that a French rearguard was in action, but Sharpe had neither the time, nor the responsibility, to join the fighting. He only knew that every river crossed and every mile of country captured meant more work for the harried staff officers who had to marry men to food, weapons to ammunition, and Divisional Headquarters' orders to a baser reality.

It was a salutary job. Sharpe had always expressed a combat soldier's scorn for most staff officers, believing that such arrogant creatures were overpaid and under-worked, but as Sharpe discovered the problems of organizing a brigade, so he learned that it was his job, rather than Nairn's, to solve those problems. Thus one typical day, just two weeks after his arrival at the brigade, began with an appeal from the commander of a battery of horse artillery whose supply wagon had become lost in the tangle of French lanes behind the British advance. Retrieving the errant wagon was no part of Sharpe's duties, except that the gunners were detailed to support Nairn's forward positions and Sharpe knew that field guns without roundshot were useless, and so he sent an aide in search of the missing supplies.

At breakfast a patrol of the King's German Legion light cavalry fetched a score of French prisoners to the farmhouse that was Nairn's temporary headquarters. The cavalry commander bellowed for a competent officer and, when Sharpe appeared, the man waved at the frightened enemy soldiers. 'I don't want the buggers!' He and his men galloped away and Sharpe had to feed the Frenchmen, guard them, and find medical help for the half-dozen men whose faces and shoulders had been slashed by the German sabres.

A message arrived from Division ordering Nairn to move his brigade three miles eastward. The brigade was supposed to be enjoying a rest day while the southern divisions caught up, but evidently the orders had been changed. Sharpe sent an aide in search of Nairn who had snatched the opportunity to go duck-shooting, then, just as he had all the clerks, cooks, prisoners, and officers' servants ready to move, another message cancelled the first. The mules were unloaded and urgent messages sent to countermand the march orders which had long gone to the battalions. Another aide was sent to tell Nairn he could continue slaughtering ducks.

Then three provosts brought a Highlander to head-quarters. They had caught the man stealing a goose from a French villager and, though the Scotsman was undoubt-edly guilty, and the goose indisputably dead, Sharpe had no doubt that Nairn would find some reason for sparing a fellow Scotsman's life. Two Spanish officers arrived asking for directions to General Morillo's Division and, because they were in no hurry, and because Wellington had stressed how vital it was that the Spanish allies were treated well, Sharpe pressed them to stay to lunch which promised to be hastily cooked stolen goose and hard-baked bread.

A village priest arrived to seek assurances that the women of his parish would be safe from the molestation of the British, and in the very next breath mentioned that he had seen some of Marshal Soult's cavalry to the north-west of his village. Sharpe did not believe the report, which would have implied that the French were attempting an outflanking march, but he had to report the sighting to Division who then did nothing about it.

In the afternoon there were a dozen new standing orders for the clerks to copy and send to Nairn's three battalions. Sharpe wondered if he would now have time to join the Spaniards who were lingering over the lunch table, but then the problem of the brigade's cattle landed on his lap.

'They're just no damned good, sir.' The head drover, a Yorkshireman, stared gloomily at the beasts which had been driven into a pasture behind the headquarters. These animals had been sent as the brigade's walking larder

34

which the Yorkshireman was supposed to herd forward as the army advanced. 'It's the wet that's done it, sir.'

'They look plump,' Sharpe said, hoping that optimism would drive the problem away.

'They're fleshy, right enough,' the Yorkshireman allowed, 'but you should see their hooves, sir. It's fair cruel to do that to a beast.'

Sharpe stooped by the nearest cow and saw how the hoof had separated from the pelt. The gap was filled with a milky, frothy ooze.

'Once they start seeping like that,' the drover said grimly, 'then you've lost the beasts. They've walked their last mile, sir, and I can't understand the nature of a man who'd do this to a creature. You can't walk cattle like men, sir, they have to rest.' The Yorkshireman was bitter and resentful.

Two hundred cattle stared reproachfully as Sharpe straightened up. 'Are they all like it?'

'All but a handful, sir, and it'll mean a killing. Nothing else will serve.'

So butchers had to be fetched, ammunition authorised, and barrels and salt found for the meat. All afternoon the sound of bellowing and musket shots, mingling with the stench of blood and powder smoke, filled headquarters. The sounds and smells at least served to drive away the two Spaniards who otherwise seemed intent on draining away Nairn's precious hoard of captured brandy. An aide arrived from Division demanding to know what the firing was, and Sharpe sent the man back with a curt complaint about the quality of the cattle. The complaint, he knew, would be ignored.

At the day's end, and despite its unrelenting activity, Sharpe felt that most of his work was still unfinished. He said as much to Nairn when they met before supper in the farm's parlour. The Scotsman, as ever, was ebullient. 'Four brace of duck! Almost as satisfying as a good battle.'

'I've got enough work without fighting battles,' Sharpe grumbled.

'There speaks the true staff officer.' Nairn stretched out his legs so his servant could tug off his muddied boots. 'Any important news?' he asked Sharpe.

Sharpe decided not to worry Nairn with the problem of the cattle. 'The only remarkable aspect of today, sir, is that Colonel Taplow didn't make any trouble.'

Lieutenant Colonel Taplow commanded one of Nairn's two English battalions. He was a short and choleric man with a manner of astonishing incivility who perceived slights to his dignity in every order. Nairn rather liked the foul man. 'Taplow's easy enough to understand. Think of him as typically English; stubborn, stupid, and solid. Like a lump of undercooked pork.'

'Or salt beef,' Sharpe would not rise to the Scotsman's bait, 'and I hope you like salt beef, sir, because you're going to get a damned lot of it.'

Next day the advance continued. Every village greeted the British with a sullen curiosity that later turned to astonished approval when the villagers discovered that, unlike their own armies, this one paid for the food they took from barns and storehouses. Soldiers found French girls who then joined the Spanish and Portuguese wives who straggled behind the advancing battalions. The women were more trouble than the soldiers, for many of the Spanish wives had an ineradicable hatred of the French that could lead to quick savage knife fights. Sharpe once had to kick two women apart, then, when the Spanish girl turned from her French enemy and tried to stab Sharpe, he stunned her with his rifle butt before spurring his horse onwards.

Sergeant Harper, before leaving St Jean de Luz, had sent his own Spanish wife home. She and the baby had gone to Pasajes, just across the French border, with orders to wait there for Harper. 'She'll do just fine, sir,' Harper said to Sharpe. 'She's happier with her own people, so she is.'

'You don't worry about her?'

Harper was astonished at the question. 'Why should I? I gave the lass money, so I did. She knows I'll fetch her and the child when it's time.'

Harper might not have worried about his Isabella, but Sharpe found Jane's absence hard to bear. He persuaded himself that it was unreasonable to expect any letters to have yet reached him from Britain, but he still eagerly searched each new bag of mail that came to the brigade. At other times he tried to imagine where Jane was and what she did. He constructed a dream in his head of the house she would buy; a gracious stone house set in a placid gentle countryside. There would be a place in the house where he could hang up his ugly heavy sword, and another place for his battered rifle. He imagined friends visiting, and long conversations by candlelight in which they would remember these lengthening spring days as they pursued an army across its homeland. He imagined a nursery where his children would grow up far from the stink of powder smoke.

They were a soldier's dreams of peace, and peace was in the air like the smell of almond blossom. Each day brought a new rumour of the war's ending; Napoleon was confidently said to have taken poison, then a contrary rumour claimed that the Emperor had broken a Russian army north of Paris, but the very next day a Spanish Colonel swore on the six bleeding wounds of Christ that the Prussians had trounced Bonaparte and fed his body to their hunting dogs. An Italian deserter from Marshal Soult's army reported that the Emperor had fled to the United States, while the chaplain of Colonel Taplow's fusiliers was entirely certain that Napoleon was negotiating a personal peace with Britain's Prince Regent; the chaplain had heard as much from his wife whose brother was a dancing-master to a discarded mistress of the Prince.

Fed by such rumours the talk of the army turned more and more to the mysterious condition of peacetime. Except for a few months in 1803, most men had never known Britain and France to be at peace. These men were soldiers, their trade was to kill Frenchmen, and peace was as much a threat as a promise. The threats of peace were very real, unemployment and poverty, while the promises of peace were more tenuous and, for most men in the army, non-existent. An officer could resign his commission, take his half pay, and chance his arm at civilian life, but most of the soldiers had enlisted for life, and peace for them would simply mean their dispersal to garrisons across the world. A few would be discharged, but without pension and with a bleak future in a world where other men had learned useful skills.

'You'll get me papers?' Harper nevertheless asked Sharpe one night.

'I'll get you papers, Patrick, I promise.' The 'papers' were the certificate of discharge that would guarantee that Sergeant Patrick Harper had been retired because of wounds. 'What will you do then?' Sharpe asked.

Harper had no doubts. 'Fetch the wife, sir, then go home.'

'To Donegal?'

'Where else?'

Sharpe was thinking that Donegal was a long way from Dorset. 'We'll miss our friends,' he said instead.

'That's the truth, sir.'

Sharpe was visiting Captain William Frederickson's company that had taken over a windmill on a shallow hill above a wide, tree-bordered stream. The Riflemen's supper was roast pork, a dish that Captain Frederickson was very partial to and which meant that no sow or piglet was safe if it was close to his line of march. Sharpe was given a generous helping of the stolen meat, after which Frederickson led him up the dizzying cradle of ladders which climbed to the mill's cap. There Frederickson opened a small door and the two officers crawled out on to a tiny platform that gave access to the mill's big axle. A spitting rain was being gusted by an east wind. 'There,' Frederickson pointed eastwards.

Beyond the stream, and beyond the dark loom of some further woods, there was a glimmering smear of light in the night sky. Only one thing could make a light such as that: the flames of an army's bivouac fires reflecting off low clouds. The two Rifle officers were looking towards the French.

'They're camped around Toulouse,' Frederickson said.

'Toulouse?' Sharpe repeated vaguely.

'It's a French city, though I wouldn't expect anyone as exalted as a staff officer to know that. It's also the place where Marshal Soult doubtless hopes to stop us, unless the war ends first.'

'Perhaps it's all wishful thinking.' Sharpe took the bottle of wine that Frederickson offered him. 'Boney's escaped from disaster before.'

'There'll be peace,' Frederickson said firmly. 'Everyone's tired of the fighting.' He paused. 'I wonder what the devil we'll all do in peacetime?'

'Rest,' Sharpe said.

'In your Dorset home?' Frederickson, knowing that Jane had gone home to purchase a country property, was amused. 'And after a month of it you'll be wishing to hell that you were back here in the rain, wondering just what the bastards are planning, and whether you've got enough ammunition for the morning.'

'Have you?' Sharpe asked with professional concern.

'I stole four cartridge boxes from Taplow's quarter-master.' Sweet William fell silent as a billow of wind stirred the furled and tethered mill-sails.

Sharpe gazed towards the French encampment. 'Is it a big city?'

'Big enough.'

'Fortified?'

'I would imagine so.' Frederickson took the wine bottle back and tipped it to his mouth. 'And I imagine it will be a bastard of a city to take.'

'They all are,' Sharpe said drily. 'Do you remember Badajoz?'

'I doubt I'll ever forget it,' Frederickson said, though nor would any man who had fought across that ditch of blood.

'We took that at Eastertime,' Sharpe said, 'and next week is Easter.'

'Is it, by God?' Frederickson asked. 'By God, so it is.'

Both men fell silent, both wondering whether this would be their last Easter. If peace was a promise, then it was a promise barred by that great red smear of light for, unless the French surrendered in the next few days, then a battle would have to be fought. One last battle.

'What will you do, William?' Sharpe took the bottle and drank.

Frederickson did not need the question explained. 'Stay in the army. I don't know another life and I don't think I'd be a good tradesman.' He fumbled with flint and steel, struck a spark to his tinder box, then lit a cheroot. 'I find I have a talent for violence,' he said with amusement.

'Is that good?' Sharpe asked.

Frederickson hooted with laughter at the question. 'Violence solved your problem with bloody Bampfylde! If you hadn't fought the bugger then you can be certain he'd even now be making trouble for you in London. Violence may not be good, my friend, but it has a certain efficiency in the resolution of otherwise insoluble problems.' Frederickson took the bottle. 'I can't say I'm enamoured of a peacetime army, but there'll probably be another war before too long.'

'You should get married,' Sharpe said quietly.

Frederickson sneered at that thought. 'Why do condemned men always encourage others to join them on the gallows?'

'It isn't like that.'

'Marriage is an appetite,' Frederickson said savagely, 'and once you've enjoyed the flesh, all that's left is a carcass of dry bones.'

'No,' Sharpe protested.

'I do hope it isn't true,' Frederickson toasted Sharpe with the half empty wine bottle, 'and I especially hope it isn't true for all of my dear friends who have pinned their hopes of peacetime happiness on something as wilfully frail as a wife.'

'It isn't true,' Sharpe insisted, and he hoped that when he returned to headquarters he would find a letter from Jane.

But there was none, and he remembered their arguments before the duel and he wondered whether his own peacetime happiness had been soured by his stubbornness.

And in the morning the brigade was ordered to advance eastwards. Towards Toulouse.

*   *   *

In finding Sergeant Challon, Major Pierre Ducos had unwittingly found his perfect instrument. Challon liked to have a woman in his bed, meat at his table, and wine in his belly, but most of all Challon liked to have his decisions made for him and he was ready to reward the decision maker with a dogged loyalty.

It was not that Challon was a stupid man; far from it, but the Dragoon Sergeant understood that other men were cleverer than himself, and he quickly discovered that Pierre Ducos was among the cleverest he had ever known. That was a comfort to Challon, for if he was to survive his treachery to the Emperor's cause, then he would need cleverness.

The nine horsemen had travelled eastwards from Bordeaux. Their route took them far to the north of where Marshal Soult retreated in front of the British army, and far to the south of where the Emperor protected Paris with a dazzling display of defensive manoeuvres. Ducos and his men rode into the deserted uplands of central France. They lived well on their journey. There was money for an inn room each night, and money for those men who wanted whores, and money for food, and money for spare horses, and money for good civilian clothes to replace the Dragoons' uniforms, though Ducos noted that each man saved his green uniform coat. That was pride; the same pride that made the Dragoons wear their hair long so that, one day, they might again plait it into the distinctive *cadenettes*. Their possession of money also made the nine men ride circumspectly, for the forests were full of dangers, yet by avoiding the main roads they travelled safely around the places where hungry brigands laid desperate ambushes.

Ducos, Sergeant Challon, and three of the troopers were Frenchmen. One of the other Dragoons was a German; a great hulking Saxon with eyes the colour of a winter's sky and hands that, despite the loss of two fingers on his right hand, could still break a man's neck with ease. There was a Pole who sat dark and quiet, yet seemed eager to please Ducos. The other two Dragoons were Italians, recruited in the early heady days of Napoleon's career. All spoke French, all trusted Challon and, because Challon trusted Ducos, they were happy to offer allegiance to the small bespectacled Major.

After a week's eastward travel Ducos found a deserted upland farm where for a few days the nine men lay up in seclusion. They were not hiding, for Ducos was happy to let the Dragoons ride to the nearby town so long as they fetched him back whatever old newspapers were available. 'If we're not hiding,' one of the Italians grumbled to Challon, 'then what are we doing?' The Italians disliked being stranded in the primitive comforts of the turf-roofed farmhouse, but Challon told them to be patient.

'The Major's sniffing the wind,' Challon said, and Ducos was indeed sniffing the strange winds that blew across France, and he was beginning to detect a danger in them. After two weeks in the farm Ducos told Challon of his fears. The two men walked down the valley, crossed an uncut meadow and walked beside a quick stream. 'You realize,' Ducos said, 'that the Emperor will never forgive us?'

'Does it matter, sir?' Challon, ever the soldier, had a carbine in his right hand while his eyes watched the forest's edge across the stream. 'God bless the Emperor, sir, but he can't last for ever. The bastards will get him sooner rather than later.'

'Did you ever meet the Emperor?' Ducos asked.

'Never had that honour, sir. I saw him often enough, of course, but never met him, sir.'

'He has a Corsican's sense of honour. If his family is hurt, Sergeant, then Napoleon will never forgive. So long as he has a breath in his body he will seek revenge.'

The grim words made Challon nervous. The four crates that Challon had escorted to Bordeaux had contained property that belonged to the Emperor and to his family, and soon the Emperor would have all the leisure in the world to wonder what had happened to that precious consignment. 'Even so, sir, if he's imprisoned, what can he do?'

'The Emperor of France,' Ducos said pedantically, 'is the head of the French State. If he falls from power, Challon, then there will be another head of state. That man, presumably the King, will regard himself as

Napoleon's legitimate heir. I presume that you would like to die of a peaceful old age in France?'

'Yes, sir.'

'So would I.' Ducos was staring over the stream and dark trees towards a tall crag of pale rock about which two eagles circled in the cold wind, but Ducos was not seeing the rock, nor even the handsome birds, but instead was remembering the Teste de Buch fort where, once again, he had been humiliated by an English Rifleman. Sharpe. It was odd, Ducos thought, how often Sharpe had crossed his path, and even odder how often that crude soldier had succeeded in frustrating Ducos's most careful plans. It had happened again at the benighted fort on the French coast and Ducos, seeking some clever stroke that would give himself and Sergeant Challon freedom, had found himself thinking more and more about Major Richard Sharpe.

At first Ducos had resented the intrusion of Sharpe into his thoughts, but in these last two days he had begun to see that there was a possible purpose to that intrusion. Perhaps it would be possible for Ducos to take revenge on his old enemy as a part of the concealment of the theft. The plan was intricate, but the more Ducos tested it, the more he liked it. What he needed now was Challon's support, for without the Sergeant's physical courage, and without the loyalty that the other Dragoons felt for Challon, the intricacy was doomed. So, as they walked beside the stream, Ducos spoke low and urgently to the Sergeant, and what he said revealed a golden bridge to a wonderful future for Sergeant Challon.

'It will mean a visit to Paris,' Ducos warned, 'then a killing somewhere in France.'

Challon shrugged. 'That doesn't sound too dangerous, sir.'

'After which we'll leave France, Sergeant, till the storm blows out.'

'Very good, sir.' Challon was quite content so long as

his duties were clear. Ducos could do the planning, and Challon would doubtless do the killing. Thus, in Challon's world, it had ever been; he was content to let the officers devise their campaign plans, and he would cut and hack with a blade to make those plans work.

Ducos's clever mind was racing backwards and forwards, sensing the dangers in his ideas and seeking to pre-empt those risks. 'Do any of your men write?'

'Herman's the only one, sir. He's a clever bugger for a Saxon.'

'I need an official report written, but not in my own handwriting.' Ducos frowned suddenly. 'How can he write? He's had two fingers chopped off.'

'I didn't say he wrote so as you can read it, sir,' Challon said chidingly, 'but he's got his letters.'

'It doesn't matter,' for Ducos could even see a virtue in the Saxon's illegible handwriting. And that, he realized, was the hallmark of a good plan, when even its apparent frailties turned into real advantages.

So that night, under a flickering rushlight, the nine men made a solemn agreement. The agreement was a thieves' pact which pledged them to follow Ducos's careful plan and, to further that plan, the Saxon laboriously wrote a long document to Ducos's dictation. Afterwards, as the Dragoons slept, Ducos wrote his own long report which purported to describe the fate of the Emperor's missing baggage. Then, in the morning, with panniers and saddle-bags still bulging, the nine men rode north. They faced a few weeks of risk, a few months of hiding, then triumph.

CHAPTER 2

Over the next few days it seemed as if Wellington was offering peace an opportunity, for he broke off his direct advance on Toulouse and instead ordered the army into a confusing series of manoeuvres that could only delay any confrontation with Marshal Soult's army. If the manoeuvres were designed to offer the French a chance to retreat, they did not take it, but just waited at Toulouse while the British, Spanish and Portuguese forces made their slow and cumbersome advance. One night Nairn's brigade was marched through pelting rain to where Engineers were laying a pontoon bridge across a wide river. Sharpe knew the river was the Garonne, for his orders said as much, but he had no idea where in France the Garonne ran. Nor did it much matter for the night became a fiasco when the Engineers discovered their bridge was too short. Nairn's men slept by the roadside as the Engineers swore and wrestled with the clumsy tin boats that should have carried the wooden roadway. Eventually the crossing was abandoned.

Three days later a bridge was successfully laid elsewhere on the river, troops crossed, but it seemed the bridge led to nothing but swampland in which the artillery floundered up to its axles. In Spain no such mistake would have happened, for in Spain there had always been willing local guides eager to lead the British army towards the hated French, but here, on the Emperor's own soil, there was no such help. Neither was there any opposition from the local population who merely seemed numbed by the years of war.

The troops who struggled in the swamps were called back and their bridge was dismantled. There had been no interference from Marshal Soult's army that was entrenched about the city's outskirts. A German deserter reported on the enemy dispositions, and also said that the Emperor Napoleon had committed suicide. 'A German soldier will say anything to get a decent meal,' Nairn grumbled, 'or an English one to get a bottle of rum.'

No confirmation came of the Emperor's death. It seemed that Napoleon still lived, Paris was uncaptured, and so the war went on. Wellington ordered a new bridge made and this time almost the whole army crossed to find itself north of Toulouse and between two rivers. They marched south and by Good Friday they were close enough to smell the cooking fires of the city. Next day the army marched even closer and Sharpe, riding ahead with Nairn, saw what obstacles protected the city. Between the British and Toulouse there lay a long hog-backed ridge. Beyond the ridge was a canal, but the ridge provided the city's real protection for it was the high ground, and whoever possessed it could pour a killing fire down on to their enemies. Sharpe drew out his telescope and gazed at the ridge's summit where he saw fresh scars of newly dug earth which betrayed that the French, far from being ready to surrender, were still fortifying the hill's top. 'I hate God-damned bloody trenches,' he said to Nairn.

'You've faced them before?'

'In the Pyrenees. It wasn't pleasant.'

It began to rain as the two men rode back to the British lines. 'Tomorrow's Easter Day,' Nairn said moodily.

'Yes.'

Nairn took a long swig of rum from his flask, then offered it to Sharpe. 'Even for a disbeliever like me it's a bloody inappropriate day to fight a battle, wouldn't you say?'

Sharpe did not reply for a gun had boomed behind him. He twisted in his saddle and saw the dirty puff of smoke on the crest of the ridge and, just a second later, he saw a spurt of water splash and die in the western marshes. The French were sighting in their twelve-pounders; the killing guns with their seven foot barrels.

The thought of those efficiently served weapons gave Sharpe a quick sudden pain in his belly. He had somehow convinced himself that there would be no fight, that the French would see how hopeless their cause was, yet the enemy gunners were even now ranging their batteries and Sharpe could hear the whining scrape of blades being whetted on stones in the British cavalry lines. At luncheon, which Nairn's military family ate inside a large tent, Sharpe found himself hoping that peace would be announced that very afternoon, yet when a message arrived it proved to be orders for the brigade to prepare itself for battle the next day.

Nairn solemnly toasted his aides. 'An Easter death to the French, gentlemen.'

'Death to the French,' the aides repeated the old toast, then stood to drink the King's health.

Sharpe slept badly. It was not work that kept him awake, for the last marching orders had been copied and dispatched well before nightfall. Nor was it the supper of salt beef and sour wine that had made him restless. It was the apprehension of a man before battle; that same apprehension which had kept him awake on the nights before the duel with Bampfylde. The apprehension was fear; pure naked fear, and Sharpe knew that battle by battle the fear was getting worse for him. When he had first joined the army as a private he had been young and cocksure; he had even felt exhilarated before a fight. He had felt himself to be immortal then, and that had made him confident that he could maul and claw and kill any man who opposed him. Now, as an officer, and married, he possessed more knowledge and so had more fear. Tomorrow he could die.

He tried the old tricks to conquer the knowledge; attempting to snatch an augury of life or death from the commonplace. If a sparrow alighted this side of a puddle, he would live. He despised such superstitious obsessions, yet could not help but indulge them, though he had made the attempt too often in the past to believe in any such trivial portents. Indeed, every man in both armies, Sharpe knew, was trying to snatch just such prophecies from their fears, but there were few who would allow themselves to see death written in their stars, yet many must die. The eve of battle was a time for talismans and amulets and charms and prayers, but the dawn would bring the kick of musket-butts, the hiss of sabres and the skull-shattering sound of artillery firing. So Sharpe shivered in the night and hoped his death would be quick, and that he would not scream beneath the surgeon's knife.

By dawn the rain had stopped and a drying wind blew across the countryside. High clouds scudded away from the sun's rising as Sharpe walked through the smoking bivouac fires in search of a cavalry armourer who could put an edge on to his sword. It was the sword of a trooper of the Heavy Cavalry; a long-bladed, heavy, and unbalanced weapon. It was far too unwieldy for most men, even for the burly men who rode the big horses and trained with dumb-bells to give strength to their sword arms, but Sharpe liked the sword and was strong enough to make it into a responsive and murderous weapon.

He found an armourer who ran the blade up his treadled wheel and afterwards stropped it on his leather apron. Sharpe gave the man a coin, then shared a tin mug of tea. Afterwards, with the oiled sword-blade safe in its scabbard, he went back to Nairn's tent outside of which he found the old Scotsman breakfasting on bread, cold salt-beef, and strong tea. Nairn watched with amusement as Sharpe unrolled the ancient and threadbare jacket from his pack.

'While you were gone,' Nairn said, 'I was vouchsafed a new glimpse of our noble Colonel Taplow.'

Sharpe was grateful for the distraction from his fears. 'Tell me, please?'

'He's holding a service of Holy Communion, for officers only, mark you, behind the latrines in ten minutes. You are invited, but I took the liberty of declining on your behalf. And on mine, as it happens.'

Sharpe laughed. He sat opposite Nairn and wondered whether his right hand was shaking as he reached for a slice of twice-baked bread. The butter was rancid, but the salt on the beef smothered the sour taste.

Nairn picked a shred of salt-beef from his teeth. 'The thought of Taplow at his sacred offices is quite loathsome. Do you think God listens to such a man?' Nairn poured rum into his tea.

'I don't know, sir.'

'You're not a believer, Sharpe?'

'No, sir.'

'Nor am I, of course, but I was still half tempted to attend Taplow's magical incantations. Just in case they helped. I'm damned nervous, Sharpe.'

Sharpe felt a sudden strong surge of affection for Nairn. 'Me too, sir.'

'You? Truly?'

Sharpe nodded. 'Truly. It doesn't get easier.'

'How many battles have you fought?'

Sharpe was dunking a lump of hard bread into his tea. He left it there as he thought, then shrugged. 'God knows, sir. Dozens of the damn things. Too many.'

'Enough to entitle you to be cautious, Richard. You don't have to be heroic today. Leave that to some wet-behind-the-ears Lieutenant who needs to make his name.'

Sharpe smiled his thanks. 'I'll try, sir.'

'And if I do anything foolish today, you will tell me?'

Sharpe looked up at the Scotsman, surprised by this confession of uncertainty. 'You won't need that, sir.'

'But you'll tell me?' Nairn insisted.

'Yes, sir.'

'Not that I'll share any of the glory with you, Sharpe, you mustn't think that, though I might say afterwards that you were moderately useful.' Nairn laughed, then waved a greeting to two of his other aides who came to the breakfast table. 'Good morning, gentlemen! I was thinking last night that perhaps Paris doesn't count.'

'Paris?' One of the puzzled aides asked.

Nairn was evidently thinking of the war's ending. 'Perhaps the northern allies will take Paris, but Napoleon might just fall back and fall back, and we'll keep marching on, and someday this summer the whole damned lot of us will meet in the very middle of France. There'll be Boney himself in the centre, and every French soldier left alive with him, and the rest of Europe surrounding him, and then we'll have a proper battle. One last real bastard of a killing. It seems unfair to have come this far and never actually fought against Napoleon himself.' Nairn gazed wistfully across the bivouacs where the smoke of the cooking fires melded into skeins like a November mist. 'I'll keep the Highlanders in reserve, Sharpe. That way no one can accuse me of showing them favouritism.'

It was a strange world, Sharpe thought, in which to keep a battalion out of the battle line was construed as an insult. 'Yes, sir.'

'I suppose there's no point in giving Captain Frederickson direct orders?'

'Not if you want those orders obeyed, sir. But he knows what to do, and his men would appreciate a visit from you.'

'Of course, of course.' Nairn added more rum to his tea, then frowned. 'Frederickson's Rifles are the only men in this brigade who eat properly. They never have salt beef! Why do we never catch them looting?'

'Because they're Riflemen, sir. They're much too clever.'

Nairn smiled. 'At least there'll be no more salt beef once this battle's won. We'll have French rations.'

The other aides arrived, faces gleaming from their razors. Sharpe had still not shaved, and he had a sudden irrational conviction that he would survive the day if he did not shave, then another equally strong impulse said that he would only live if he did shave, and he felt the reptilian squirm of fear in his belly. He stared up at the long, long ridge that, just like the British bivouacs, was topped by a shifting layer of smoke. The smoke was thick enough to suggest the large numbers of Frenchmen who would be defending the high ground this day. Sharpe thought of Jane and suddenly longed for the Dorset house with its implicit promise of a nursery. He was about to ask whether any·mail had arrived when a light flashed from the ridge top and Sharpe knew it was the sun reflecting from a telescope as an enemy officer gazed down at the British lines. The fear stirred in Sharpe. He was tempted to take some of Nairn's rum, but resisted.

The waiting abraded the fear. The first Spanish, Portuguese and British brigades had marched long before dawn, their long lines uncoiling from the encampment in a slug- gishly macabre motion, but Nairn's brigade would be one of the last to leave the lines. They could only wait, pretending confidence, as the minutes wore on. Nairn inspected his battalions and tossed gruff encouragement to the soldiers. Some of the Highlanders sang psalms, but their tunes were so dirge-like that Sharpe went out of earshot. He had decided that his survival lay in not shaving.

It took another half hour before the orders came from Division and Nairn at last could order his men forward. Taplow's battalion led, and the Highlanders marched at the rear. The brigade followed the other battalions who were already marching to the ridge's southern slopes. Sharpe, mounted on his mare Sycorax, could see the

Spanish Divisions that waited at the ridge's northern end. Today those Spaniards had the place of honour, for they would comprise the major attack up the ridge's spine. They had asked for the honour. As they attacked, so the British and Portuguese, under Marshal Beresford, would assault the ridge's southern end to split the French defences. Other British troops were ringed about the city to make threatening feints designed to stop Marshal Soult concentrating his army on the ridge.

The French, secure on their heights, could see all that Wellington planned. There could be no deception this day, no sleight of arms to blind the enemy and cheat him. This would be work, hard work, work for the bayonet and the bullet, work for the infantry.

The southward march was not easy for the ground was soft. Nairn's brigade, among the last in Beresford's long column, found the tracks churned into a morass. At first that clinging mud was their only problem, but as their route angled ever closer to the ridge the brigade came within range of the French gunners. Nairn ordered his men to march through the marshy fields to the west of the tracks, but still the roundshot slashed into his battalion columns. The British artillery tried to reply, but they were shooting uphill at enemy batteries well dug in behind thick emplacements.

'Close up, you scum!' Lieutenant-Colonel Taplow bellowed at his leading company after a cannonball had crashed through a file to leave three men bloody and twitching on the soaking ground. 'Leave them there!' he shouted at two men who stooped to help the victims. 'Leave them, I say, or I'll have you flogged!' At the rear of Taplow's fusiliers a band played, their music made ragged by their stumbling progress over the tussocky soft ground. Drummer boys were ordered to attend to the three men, but two were already dead and the third had not long to live. The battalion surgeon finished the man with a quick knife cut, then, shrugging, wiped his bloody hands on his grey breeches.

The French artillery pumped smoke from the ridge crest. Sharpe, staring eastwards, could sometimes see the trace of a dark line in the sky and he knew he watched a cannonball at the top of its arcing flight, and he also knew that such a pencil line was only visible in the sky when the ball was coming straight at the observer. At those moments he felt a temptation to spur Sycorax onwards, feigning some urgent duty, but he restrained himself in case any man should think him cowardly. Instead he rode steadily, flinching inwardly, and hid his relief as the balls missed. One roundshot thumped into the mud just ahead of Sycorax, making the mare rear frantically. Somehow Sharpe kept his feet in the stirrups and his arse on the saddle as the gobbets of wet mud fountained about him. The mare was not properly trained to battle, but she was a good steady horse. She had been a gift from Jane, and that thought gave Sharpe a sentimental longing to see his wife. He wondered if her mail had become lost, because no letter had yet arrived, then a cannon-ball went just over his shako to decapitate a redcoat marching to Sharpe's left and he forgot his wife in the sudden surge of fear.

'Close up!' a Sergeant shouted. 'Close up!' It was the litany of battle and the only obituary of the common soldier.

'You're used to this, I suppose?' A Lieutenant, one of Nairn's junior aides, spurred alongside Sharpe. Ahead of them a man's entrails were being trodden into the mud, but either the Lieutenant did not notice or did not recognize what he saw.

'I don't think you ever get used to it,' Sharpe said, though it was not true. One did get used to it, but that did not help the fear. The Lieutenant, who was new to the war, was clearly terrified, though he was trying hard not

54

to show it. 'It's better,' Sharpe said truthfully, 'once you can fire back. It's much less frightening then.'

'Bless you, sir, I'm not frightened.'

'I am.' Sharpe grinned, then looked to his right and saw that Frederickson's men were so far unscathed. Frederickson had taken his Riflemen closer to the enemy, which had been a shrewd move for the Greenjackets made a small and seemingly negligible target compared to the long and cumbersome column of redcoats. The French were firing over the Riflemen's heads.

A cavalry officer galloped past Frederickson's men towards the head of Beresford's column. Sharpe recognized the man as one of Wellington's aides, and assumed from his haste that he carried an urgent message. A clue to the message came when the ridge's northern end suddenly exploded with cannon fire. Sharpe twisted in his saddle and saw that the French had unmasked a dozen batteries that were hammering their missiles down the hill at the attacking Spaniards.

The Lieutenant frowned. 'I thought we were supposed to attack at the same time as the Dagoes, sir?'

'We were.'

God only knew what had gone wrong, but gone wrong it had. The Spaniards, instead of waiting until Beresford's diversionary attack was in position to the south, had precipitately charged up the ridge's northern slopes. Their bright uniforms and gaudy colours made a brave show, but it was a gallant display being eviscerated by the concentrated fire of the deadly twelve-pounders.

'Halt! Halt!' Divisional officers were galloping back down Beresford's column. 'Face right! Face right!'

Battalion officers and sergeants took up the cry and the great column halted and clumsily turned to face the bleak, steep slope at the ridge's centre.

Nairn, who had been riding at the head of his brigade, spurred back. 'Column of half companies!' he ordered. It seemed that Marshal Beresford must be contemplating an immediate assault on the ridge. Certainly, if Beresford was to divert attention from the Spanish attack then he could not wait till he reached the gentler slopes at the ridge's southern end, but would be forced to launch his eleven thousand men on a desperate uphill scramble against the French entrenchments.

The French batteries, seeing the British and Portuguese battalions shake into their attack columns, kept firing. 'Lie down!' Nairn shouted. 'Lie down!'

The battalions dropped, making themselves a smaller and lower target for the enemy gunners, but leaving the officers on horseback feeling horribly exposed. Sharpe stared at the ridge and feared its muscle-sapping steepness. The sun, just rising above the summit, was suddenly dazzling.

'Wait here, Sharpe!' Nairn was excited. 'I'll discover what's happening. You wait here!'

Sharpe waited. After breakfast he had pushed some bread and beef into a saddle bag and now, suddenly hungry, he gnawed at a lump of the meat.

'They've cocked it up!' Colonel Taplow, his red face as bad-tempered as ever, rode to Sharpe's side. 'The Spanish have cocked it up, Sharpe!'

'So it seems, sir.' A cannonball thumped the earth to Sharpe's left. Sycorax skittered sideways until Sharpe soothed her.

'Seems?' Taplow was incensed by the mild word. 'They've cocked it up, that's what they've done. Cocked it up!' He gestured to the north where a new sound erupted as French musketry began flaying the Spaniards. The crackle of musketry was a thick, splintering sound that gave witness to just how many defenders had been waiting for the Spanish. 'They went too early.' Taplow seemed to revel in the Spanish mistake. 'They couldn't keep their breeches up, could they? Too much damned eagerness,

Sharpe. No whippers-in, that's their problem. No bottom. Not like the English. It'll be up to us now, Sharpe, you mark my words. It'll be up to us!'

'Indeed it will, sir.'

The musketry was unending; a sustained terror of sound just like a million snapping rails of wood. And every snap meant another lead bullet flicking down the slope to strike home in the bunched Spanish ranks.

'Ah ha! Told you so! No bottom!' Taplow crowed triumphantly for the Spanish had begun to retreat. The movement was slow at first, merely a slight edging backwards, but it swiftly turned into a quick scramble to escape the flailing bullets. Sharpe was astonished that the Spaniards had climbed as far as they had, and he doubted whether any troops in the world could have gone further, but Colonel Taplow was not so generous. 'All priming and no charge, that's the Dago's problem. No bottom, Sharpe, no bottom. Have a boiled egg.'

Sharpe accepted a hard-boiled egg which he ate as Beresford's column patiently waited. The sun's warmth was detectable now, and the small mist that had cloaked the western marshes was quite gone. A heron flapped clumsily into the air and flew southwards. A cannonball struck into Taplow's bandsmen and Sharpe watched a blood-spattered trumpet fly into the air.

'It'll be up to us now!' Taplow said with immense satisfaction. 'It's no good relying on foreigners, Sharpe, they only cock things up. Let me salute you.'

Sharpe suddenly realized that the irascible Taplow was offering a hand. He shook it.

'Good man!' Taplow said. 'Proud to know you! Sorry you didn't take communion, though. A fellow ought to square things with the Almighty before he kills the King's enemies. Only decent thing to do. Had you realized that your servant forgot to shave you this morning? Flog the fellow. Let me wish you well of the day now!' Taplow galloped southwards towards his men while Sharpe sighed. The egg had taken the edge from his hunger, so he pushed the lump of salt beef back into his pouch. Sycorax dropped her head to crop at the trampled grass.

New orders came. The southwards march was to resume, for there was clearly no advantage to be gained in assaulting the ridge's centre now that the Spanish attack had been repulsed. Nairn said there was a hope that the Spanish would re-form and attack again, but he could offer no explanation as to why their first attack had been premature. 'Perhaps they wanted to end the war without us?'

Beresford's column re-formed and trudged onwards. The French long-range cannonade continued. The men marched silently, not even singing, for they all knew that they would soon have to turn eastwards and assault the ridge. They had seen one attack bloodily repulsed, and they could guess that Marshal Soult was even now reinforcing the ridge's southern slopes. From the city's north and east came the dull crump of gunfire as allied cannon fired at the defences, but it was doubtful if the French would be fooled by such obvious feints. They knew the importance of the ridge, which was doubtless why its summit would prove a hellish place of trenches and batteries. The fears writhed in Sharpe, made worse by the cannonade that echoed in the sky like giant hammer blows.

Beresford's infantry marched for one more hour before they turned to their right to face the ridge's southern slopes. The long march across the enemy's front had at least brought Beresford's men to a place that the French had not fortified. No cannons faced down these southern slopes which stretched invitingly up to the bright, pale sky. What lay beyond the horizon, though, was another matter.

The brigades were ordered to form into three vast lines; each line consisting of two brigades arrayed just two men deep. Nairn's men would form the right hand end of the second line. It took time to make the formation, which was a job best left to Sergeants, and so the officers stared at the empty skyline and pretended they felt no fear. The only enemy in sight, besides the occasional glimpse of an officer riding forward to stare down the slope, was a force of cavalry that spilt right down the ridge's centre. The enemy cavalry had been sent to threaten the right flank of Beresford's assault, but an even larger cavalry force of British and German horsemen rode to block them.

'Skirmishers forward!' An aide cantered down the first line.

'I think we'll put our light chaps on the flank,' Nairn said. 'Will you see to it, Sharpe?'

'Can I stay with them, sir?'

Nairn hesitated, then nodded. 'But let me know if anything threatens.' He held out his hand. 'Remember you're dining with me tonight, so take care. I don't want to write a sad letter to Jane.'

'You take care as well, sir.'

Sharpe collected the brigade's three Light Companies and sent them running to the right flank where they would join Frederickson's Riflemen. As the attack advanced those skirmishers would scatter to fight their lonely battles with the French light troops. Sharpe, a skirmisher by nature, wanted to fight with them and, as ever, he wanted to fight on foot. He summoned a headquarters' clerk and gave the man Sycorax's reins. 'Keep her out of trouble.'

'Yes, sir.'

A drummer made a flurry of sound as Taplow uncased his battalion's colours. Sharpe, walking past the colour party, took his shako off in salute to the two heavy flags of fringed silks. A French roundshot, fired blind and at extreme range from one of the ridge's centre batteries, smacked into the wet ground and, instead of bouncing, drove a slurry-filled furrow across Sharpe's front. He wiped the mud from his face and unslung his rifle.

The rifle was another of Sharpe's eccentricities. Officers

might be expected to carry a pistol into battle, but not a longarm, yet Sharpe insisted on keeping the ranker's weapon. He loaded it as he walked, tested the flint's seating in its leather-lined doghead, then slung it back on his shoulder.

'A nice day for a battle.' Frederickson greeted Sharpe cheerfully.

'You think Easter is an appropriate day?'

'It has an implicit promise that we'll rise from the grave. Not that I have any intention of testing the promise.' Frederickson turned his one eye to the skyline. 'If you were Marshal Soult, what would you have waiting up there?'

'Every damned field gun in my army.' The knot was tying itself in Sharpe's belly as he imagined the efficient French twelve-pounders lined wheel to wheel.

'Let us hope he doesn't have sufficient guns.' Frederickson did not sound hopeful. He, like Sharpe, could imagine the horse-teams dragging the field guns from where the Spanish had been repulsed to where they could decimate this new attack.

Trumpet calls sounded far to Sharpe's left, were repeated ever closer, and the first line of Beresford's attack started forward. The second line was held for a moment before it too was ordered into motion. Almost at once the careful alignments of the thin lines wavered because of the ground's unevenness. Sergeants began bellowing orders for the men to watch their dressing. The officers' horses, as if sensing what waited for them, became skittish.

'Are you here to take command?' Frederickson asked Sharpe as the skirmishers started forward.

'Are you the senior Captain?'

Frederickson cast a dour look at the Captains of the three redcoat Light Companies. 'By a very long way.'

The sour tone told Sharpe that Frederickson was resenting the lack of promotion. Rank was clearly more important

60

to a man who planned to stay in the army, and Frederickson well knew how slow promotion could be in peacetime when there were no cannons and muskets to create convenient vacancies. And Frederickson, more than any man Sharpe knew, deserved promotion. Sharpe made a mental note to ask Nairn if he could help, then smiled. 'I won't interfere with you, William. I'll just watch, so fight your own battle.'

'The last one,' Frederickson said almost in wonder. 'I suppose that's what it will be. Our last battle. Let us make it a good one, sir. Let's send some souls to hell.'

'Amen.'

The three advancing lines seemed very fragile as they climbed upwards. The sweep of the lines was interrupted by the battalions' colours; splashes of bright cloth guarded by the long, shining-bladed halberds. Following the three lines were the battalion bands, all playing different tunes so that the belly-jarring thump of their big drums clashed. The music was jaunty, rhythmic and simple; the music for death.

Frederickson's Riflemen were mingled with the redcoats of the other three Light companies. Those redcoats carried the quick-firing but short-ranged muskets, while the Greenjackets had the more accurate, longer-ranged rifle that was slow to reload. The mixture of weapons could be lethal; the rifles killed with precision and were protected by the muskets. The men were scattered now, making a screen to repel the attack of any French skirmishers.

Yet so far no enemy had threatened the cumbersome advance. Even the ridge's centre batteries had ceased their speculative firing. Sharpe could see nothing but the empty skyline and a wisp of high cloud. The thin turf on the slope was dryer than the bottom-ground. A hare raced across the advance's front, then slewed and scampered downhill. A hawk hovered for a few seconds above Taplow's colours, then slid disdainfully westwards. From beyond the crest came the sound of a French band playing a quick march; the only evidence that a real enemy waited for Beresford's thin lines.

The slope steepened and Sharpe's breath shortened. The enemy's invisibility seemed ominous. Marshal Soult had been given three hours to observe the preparations for this attack; three hours in which he could prepare a devil's reception for the three lines that struggled up the ridge. Somewhere ahead of the attack, beyond the empty skyline, the enemy waited with charged barrels and drawn blades. The old game was about to be played once more; the Goddamns against the Crapauds. The game of Crecy and Agincourt, Ramillies and Blenheim. The air was very clear; so clear that when Sharpe turned he could see a woman driving two cows to pasture a half mile beyond the western river. The sight of the woman made Sharpe think of Jane. He knew that he could have accompanied Jane home without any shame, and that even now he could be sitting in England, but instead he was on a French hillside and on the brink of battle's horror.

He turned back to the east just in time to see a redcoat among Frederickson's flank skirmishers bend double, clutch his belly, and start gasping for breath. At first Sharpe thought the man was winded, then he saw the puff of dirty white smoke higher on the slope. The redcoat toppled backwards, blood drenching his grey breeches. More French skirmishers fired from positions that had been concealed in a tumble of rocks. The enemy would soon be on the flank of the advance unless they were shifted.

'We're going to clear those scum out of there!' Frederickson had seen the danger just as soon as Sharpe. He had a company of redcoats offer rapid fire to keep the enemy subdued while Sergeant Harper led a squad with fixed sword-bayonets in a flanking charge. The Frenchmen did not stay to contest the rocks, but retreated nimbly up

towards the empty skyline. One of the retreating Frenchmen was hit in the back by a rifle bullet, and Marcos
Hernandez, one of Frederickson's Spanish Riflemen,
grinned with pleasure at his own deadly marksmanship.

'Cease fire!' Frederickson called. 'Well done, lads. Now
don't bunch up! You're not in love with each other, so
spread out!' Sweet William had taken off his eye-patch
and removed his false teeth so that he looked like some
monstrous being from the grave. He seemed much happier
now that the first shots had been fired. Hernandez reloaded, then scored a line on the butt of his rifle to mark
another hated Frenchman killed.

The surviving French skirmishers ran over the skyline
from where, though the source of the noise stayed hidden,
came the sudden sound of massed French drums. The
instruments rattled the sky. Sharpe had first heard that
malicious sound when he was sixteen and he had heard
it on unnumbered battlefields since. He knew what it
portended. He was listening to the *pas de charge*, the heartbeat of an Empire and the sound that drove French infantry
to the attack.

'D'you see guns, Sergeant?' Frederickson shouted to
Harper who was some yards further up the slope.

'Not a one, sir!'

Then the skyline, as though sown by dragon's teeth,
sprouted men.

* * *

'Christ in his Scottish heaven.' Major-General Nairn, surrounded by his junior aides, sounded disgusted with the
enemy. 'You'd have thought the woollen-headed bastards
would have learned by now.' He sheathed his sword and
glowered dour disapproval at the two enemy columns.

'Learned, sir?' the young aide, whose first battle this
was, asked nervously.

'You are about to see the God-damned Frogs damned

63

even further.' Nairn took a watch from his fob pocket and snapped open the lid. 'Good God! If they're going to offer battle, then they might as well do it properly!'

The aide did not understand, but every veteran in the British attack knew what was about to happen and felt relieved because of it. They had climbed in fear of waiting artillery that would have gouged bloody ruin in the three attacking lines. Even more they had feared the conjunction of artillery and cavalry, for the cavalry would have forced the attacking infantry into protective squares that would have made choice targets for the French gunners. Instead they were faced with the oldest French tactic; a counter-attack by columns of massed infantry.

Two such columns were advancing over the skyline. The two columns were immense formations of crammed soldiers, rank after rank of infantrymen assembled into human battering rams that were aimed at the seemingly fragile British lines. These were the same columns that the Emperor Napoleon had led across a continent to smash his enemies' armies into broken and panicked mobs, but no such column had ever broken an army led by Wellington.

'Halt!' All along the British and Portuguese lines the order was shouted. Sergeants dressed the battalions while the skirmishers readied themselves to beat off the French light troops who, advancing in front of the columns, were supposed to unsettle the British line with random musketry.

The French light troops offered no threat to Beresford; instead it was the momentum of the two great columns that was supposed to drive his men into chaos. Yet, like Wellington, Beresford had faced too many columns to be worried now. His first line would deal with their threat, while his second and third lines would merely be spectators. That first line stood to attention, muskets grounded, and gazed up the long sloping sward over which the two giant formations marched. The French columns looked irresistible, their weight alone seeming sufficient to drive them through the thin skeins of waiting men. Above the Frenchmen's heads waved their flags and eagles. In the centre of the formations the drummer boys kept up the *pas de charge*, pausing only to let the marching men shout '*Vive l'Empereur!*' between each flurry of drumbeats. The veterans among the waiting British and Portuguese battalions, who had seen it all before, seemed unmoved.

The skirmishers fell slowly back before the weight of enemy light troops, but they had done their job which was to keep the French skirmish fire off the waiting line. French officers, swords drawn, marched confidently ahead of the columns. Major-General Nairn gazed at the closest column through a telescope, then slammed the tubes shut. 'Not many moustaches there!' The old moustached veterans, the backbone of France, were in their graves, and Nairn had seen how young these counter-attacking Frenchmen were. Perhaps that was why Soult had launched them in column, for raw green troops took courage from the sheer closeness of their comrades in the tightly packed mass of men. It was a formation suited to a conscripted, citizen army, but those citizen conscripts were now closing on the professional killers of Britain and Portugal.

When the columns were eighty paces from Beresford's forward line, the British and Portuguese officers stirred themselves to give a single laconic order. 'Present!'

Four thousand heavy muskets came up in a single rippling movement. The leading ranks of the two French columns, seeing their death, checked their pace, but the weight of men behind forced them onwards.

'Hold your fire!' Sergeants warned redcoats who dragged back the cocks of their weapons. The French, made nervous by the silent threat, opened fire as they marched. Only the men in the first two ranks could actually fire, the rest were there merely to add weight. Here and there along the red-coated line a man might fall, but the French aim was spoiled by the need to fire while marching.

'Close up!' A British Sergeant dragged a dead man back from the line.

'Hold your fire!' An officer, slim sword drawn, watched the blue-coated French column come closer. Four thousand muskets were aimed at the heads of the two columns.

A rattle of drums, a pause, *'Vive l'Empereur!'*

One heartbeat. The British muskets were steady, the officers' swords raised, while the men in either army were close enough now to see the expressions on the others' faces.

'Fire!'

Like a great cough, or like a gigantic throttling explosion, four thousand muskets flamed smoke and lead, and four thousand brass-bound butts mule-kicked back into men's shoulders. The smoke spewed to hide the French.

'Reload!'

Sharpe, still off to the right flank, saw the nearer enemy column quiver as the heavy bullets struck home. Blue coats were speckled by blood. The whole front rank crumpled and fell, and most of the second rank too. Only one officer was left standing, and he was wounded. The succeeding French ranks were baulked by the barrier of their own dead and wounded, but then the sheer mass of the deep column forced the new front rank to clamber over the bodies and continue the advance. *'Vive l'Empereur!'*

'Fire!'

Now it was the deadly platoon fire that rippled out of the British and Portuguese lines. Hours of training had made these men into clockwork killers. Each platoon of a battalion fired a couple of seconds after the platoon on its left, and so the bullets seemed never ending as they flicked through the screen of smoke to strike at the French. The fire flayed at the enemy, flensing men off the front and flanks of the column, so that it seemed as if the enemy marched into an invisible mincing machine. The French survivors, inexorably forced to the front ranks, tried to struggle into the storm of musketry, but no man could live against that fire. In the past, in the glorious days when the Emperor's name struck fear into Europe, the columns had won by overaweing their enemies, but Wellington's men had long mastered the grim art of bloodying French glory. They did it with musket-fire, the fastest musket-fire in the world. They blackened their faces with the explosions of the priming in their weapons' pans, they bruised their shoulders with the slamming kicks, and they broke the enemy. Cartridge after cartridge was bitten open, loaded and fired, while in front of the British line the musket wadding burned pale in the scorched grass.

The columns could not move. A few brave men tried to advance, but the bullets cut them down. The survivors edged back and the drumroll faltered.

'Cease fire!' a British voice called. 'Fix bayonets!'

Four thousand men drew their seventeen-inch blades and slotted them on to hot muzzles.

'Present!' The voices of the officers and sergeants were calm. Most of these men were veterans and they took pride in sounding unmoved by the carnage of battle. 'Battalions will advance! Forward!'

All along the front line the battalions marched stolidly into their own fog of smoke. They had fired blind through the choking screen, but a column could hardly be missed even by men obscured by smoke. Now, at last, they broke through the smoke to see what carnage their disciplined fire had done.

Officers' swords swept downwards. 'Charge!'

Now, and only now, did the British and Portuguese soldiers cheer. Till this moment they had kept silent, but now, with blackened faces and bayonets levelled, they cheered and broke into a quick march.

The French broke. They ran. They left two blood-soaked

67

heaps of dead, dying and wounded men behind and raced back towards safety. A drummer boy wept because a bullet was in his guts. He would die before noon, and his drum would be chopped up for firewood.

'Halt!' The British did not press their charge home. There was no need, for the columns had fled in panic.

'Dress ranks! Unfix bayonets! Skirmishers forward! Reload!'

Major-General Nairn looked down at his watch and noted that it had taken precisely three minutes and twenty seconds to break the French attack. In the past, he reflected, when more moustaches had filled the enemy ranks, it would have taken about six minutes longer. He put the watch away. 'Advance the brigade.'

'Battalion will advance!'

'Silence in the ranks!'

'Forward!'

The seemingly tenuous lines started forward again. In two gory places the men stepped clumsily over the piles of enemy dead. The men, long practised in the art, dragged their enemies' bodies with them for a few paces; giving themselves just enough time to loot the pockets and pouches of the dead or wounded. They took food, coins, talismans and drink. One redcoat kicked the wounded drummer boy's instrument downhill. The drum's snares twanged as it bounced and rolled down the long hill.

'Looks like it's going to be an easy Easter!' Frederickson said happily.

But then the skyline was reached, and the plateau of the ridge's summit was revealed, and nothing looked easy any more.

CHAPTER 3

The battle, as if by mutual consent, stopped to draw breath.

Beresford used the lull to divide his attack. His left hand division would now slant away to threaten the land between the ridge and the city, while the right division, in which Nairn's Brigade marched, would advance northwards along the ridge's summit. Horse artillery was being dragged up the slope to thicken Beresford's attack. The morning passed. Many of the waiting men fell asleep with their heads pillowed on their packs and their faces shaded by mildewed shakoes. Some ate, and a few just stared emptily at the sky. Some men gazed along the ridge towards the fearful French defences. Every few minutes a random French cannonball bounded through the somnolent lines, provoking an irritated scramble from its bouncing path. Sometimes a howitzer shell banged a sharp explosion on the turf, but the fire was sporadic and allowed most of the waiting men to ignore the enemy. Sharpe watched one fusilier patiently hammer the soft lead of a musketball into a perfect cube, then prick its faces with a touch-hole spike to make a dice. No one would gamble with the man who, disgusted, hurled the lead cube away.

In the early afternoon the battalions which had broken the twin French columns were moved to the rear of Beresford's new formations. Nairn's brigade now formed the right flank of the first line. He had his two English battalions forward, and his Highlanders in reserve. The horse gunners stacked their ready ammunition alongside the advanced positions, while the skirmishers deployed as a protective screen even further forward.

Sharpe strolled forward to join Frederickson who offered a piece of French garlic sausage. 'I suppose,' Frederickson was staring at the ridge's plateau, 'that this would be a good moment to resign from the army?'

Sharpe smiled at the grim joke, then drew out his telescope which he trained on the nearest French fortification. He said nothing, and his silence was ominous.

'The bloody French must know the war's lost,' Frederickson said irritably, 'so why prolong the killing?'

'Pride,' Sharpe said curtly, though why, for that matter, were his own countrymen insisting on taking Toulouse if it was really believed that the Emperor was doomed? Perhaps peace was a chimera. Perhaps it was just a rumour that would fade like the stench of blood and powder-smoke from this battlefield.

And, as Sharpe well knew, there would be much blood and smoke on this high ridge. The French were waiting, prepared, and Beresford's infantry must now advance through a series of strong fortifications that ran across the ridge's spine. There were gun batteries and entrenchments, all bolstered by earthen redoubts which, topped by palisades, stood like small fortresses athwart the line of attack. One redoubt, larger than the rest, dominated the ridge's centre and, like its smaller brethren, was faced with a ditch above which its wooden palisade was embrasured for artillery. It was no wonder that Beresford's climb up the southern slope had not been opposed by French gunfire, for all the enemy cannons were now dug safe into the small forts.

Frederickson borrowed Sharpe's glass and stared for a long time at the awesome defences. 'Easter's meant to be a day for miracles, is it not?'

Sharpe smiled dutifully, then turned to greet Sergeant Harper. 'We'll be earning our crust today, Sergeant.'

'Aye, sir, we will.' Harper accepted Frederickson's offer of the telescope and made a quick scrutiny of the great redoubt in the ridge's centre. 'Why don't we just beat the bastards to jelly with gunfire?'

'Can't get the big guns up here,' Frederickson answered cheerfully. 'We've only got galloper guns today.'

'Peashooters.' Harper spat scornfully, then handed the telescope to Sharpe. 'Do you know where our boys are, sir?'

'Our boys' were the Prince of Wales's Own Volunteers, the battalion that Sharpe and Harper had fought in for so many years. 'They're off to the east.' Sharpe vaguely waved in that direction. He could still not see the city of Toulouse, which was hidden by a shoulder of the ridge, but gunsmoke showed in the far distance to betray where Wellington's feint attacks threatened Toulouse's eastern suburb.

'They shouldn't be taking much of a beating today, then,' Harper said hopefully.

'I suppose not.' Sharpe suddenly wished he was back with the Prince of Wales's Own Volunteers who, under their new Colonel, did not have to face this devil's ridge of forts, trenches and guns. They would be safe, while Sharpe was foully aware of the symptoms of terror. He could feel his heart thumping, sweat was chill on his skin, and a muscle in his left thigh was twitching. His throat was parched, his belly felt hollow, and he wanted to vomit. He tried to smile, and sought for some casual words that would demonstrate his lack of fear, but he could think of nothing.

Hooves sounded behind, and Sharpe turned to see Major-General Nairn cantering towards the skirmish line. The General curbed his horse, then grimaced at the landscape ahead. 'We've got the right flank, so we'll be attacking the batteries.'

That was a brighter prospect than assaulting the larger redoubts. The batteries, constructed on the edge of the ridge, were the positions from which the long approach march had been cannonaded, and they had been built purely to defend the gunners from counter-battery fire. Thus there were no fortifications facing the ridge's centre, so Nairn's brigade would only have to deal with the flanking trenches and the batteries' guns which had been dragged from their embrasures and arrayed like ordinary field artillery. Those nearest guns were supported by at least two battalions of French infantry who waited in three deep lines to add their volley fire to the gunnery.

Nairn seemed to shiver as he stared at the ridge's summit, then he asked to borrow Sharpe's glass through which he gazed long and hard at the enemy positions. He said nothing when he closed the tubes, except to express surprise at the evident quality of the spyglass. 'Where did you get it?'

'Vitoria,' Sharpe said. The telescope had been a gift from the Emperor Napoleon to his brother, King Joseph of Spain, who had lost it when his baggage had been captured by the British after the battle at Vitoria. A small brass plate, let into the ivory of the barrel, recorded the gift.

Nairn held the glass out to Sharpe. 'I hate to spoil your enjoyment, Major, but I need you.'

Sharpe retrieved his horse. His task, once the advance began, would be to relay Nairn's orders. The junior aides would be doing the same thing, but Sharpe's rank and reputation would give him an authority that could be useful to Nairn. At times, Sharpe knew, he would have to use his own judgement, then claim that his decision was a verbal order from Nairn himself.

It was another hour before the order to advance was given. The French had spasmodically shelled the waiting men during the prolonged delay, but the very sparseness of the cannonade was evidence that the real artillery effort would wait until the British and Portuguese troops had marched closer to the guns. Some men grumbled at the wait, others averred that it was necessary so that the Spanish could regroup and attack again from the ridge's far end. Two chaplains led mules loaded with spare water canteens around the waiting troops. The Irishmen in the ranks crossed themselves. The loudest noise on the ridge, apart from the occasional bang of a French gun, were the pipes of the Highland Regiments.

'It's going to be a bloody business, right enough. A bloody, bloody business,' Nairn said for the fourth or fifth time to Sharpe. The Scotsman was nervous. He knew this would be his one chance to fight his brigade in battle, and he feared he would be found wanting.

Yet the true responsibility did not lie with Nairn, nor even with Wellington who commanded the battle from its northern flank, but with the ordinary soldier. It was the redcoat and greenjacket who had to march forward in the certain knowledge that the best artillery in Europe waited to decimate his ranks. A shilling, a third of a pint of rum and two pounds of twice baked bread each day were the wages for this moment, and in return they must march into hell and come out victors.

'It won't be long now,' Nairn said, as if to comfort the aides who bunched around him.

Divisional aides were galloping across the ridge's southern spur. Bands were forming into ranks and colours were being hoisted. The British gunners gave their cannon trails a last adjustment.

'The General's compliments, sir,' a cavalry Captain reined in close to Nairn, 'and if you are ready?'

'My compliments to the General.' Nairn drew his sword. No actual order to advance had been given, nor was it necessary, for as soon as the leading battalions saw the arrival of the Divisional aide, they were ordered to their feet. What waited for them on the ridge was a foretaste of hell, so it seemed best to get it done fast.

'My compliments to Colonel Taplow,' Nairn said to

Sharpe, 'and tell him not to let his men fall off to the right.'

'Indeed, sir.' Sharpe put his spurs to Sycorax's flanks. Nairn's concern about the right flank was justified for, as the attack met opposition, there would be a temptation for the right-hand men to seek safety down the ridge's western slope.

Taplow did not wait for Sharpe's arrival, but had already ordered his men forward. They advanced in two lines behind their chain of skirmishers. The front line was composed of five companies, and the rear of four. The battalion's bayonets were fixed, and their colours lofted between the two lines. Sharpe found Taplow on a grey horse just in front of the colour party. 'The General's compliments, sir.'

'He'll not find us wanting!' Taplow interrupted Sharpe. 'I told you it would be up to us!' Taplow was in high spirits.

'He's eager, sir, that your men don't deviate too far to the right.' Sharpe phrased Nairn's warning as tactfully as he could.

'Damn your eyes! Does he think we're amateurs?' Taplow's rage was instant and overwhelming. 'Tell him we shall march to the guns. Direct to the guns! We'll die like Englishmen, not like skulking Scotchmen. Damn your eyes, Major, and good day to you.'

The other English battalion of Nairn's brigade marched on Taplow's left, while behind came the Highlanders who advanced to the eerie skirl of their pipers. They were a secretive, proud battalion who followed their clan chief to war. Many spoke no English, just the Gaelic. In battle they could be terrifying, while off the battlefield they had a grave courtesy. To the left of Nairn's brigade, and straddling the spine of the ridge's summit, another brigade advanced.

Frederickson, with the skirmishers of the two English battalions, was far ahead of the leading battalions. The

French gunners, waiting with smoking linstocks, ignored the skirmish line. They would wait till the plumper targets of the close-formed battalions were nearer.

The wait was not long. Sharpe, back at Nairn's side just a few paces ahead of the Highlanders, saw a French gunner give the elevating screw of his cannon one last turn, then jump clear as the linstock came down to hover near the portfire.

'God help us,' said the agnostic Nairn, then, much louder, 'steady, lads, steady!'

'*Tirez!*' shouted the battery's commander.

The ridge erupted with gunfire. Flames lanced from barrels to pump smoke thick as fog over the hilltop. The roundshot slashed through the advancing battalions. Sharpe saw one ball carve a bloody hole in Taplow's first line, kill another man in his second, then graze the turf and, on its upward rebound, strike down a file of Highlanders. The one ball had turned four men to meat and blood and splintered bone. The screams of the wounded began to rival the music of the bands and the crashing of the enemy guns. It was not just the closest battery that fired, but the gunners in the central redoubt, and other gunners too, further and higher up the ridge, who could launch their missiles over the heads of their own infantry to plunge and bounce and tear among the British troops.

'Those poor lads.' Nairn watched Taplow's battalion that was dropping dead and wounded behind its ranks.

'Close up! Close up!' the Sergeants shouted. An Ensign, fifteen years old, and proud to be in his first battle, was disembowelled. A Sergeant, marching behind and to the dead boy's flank, filched six guineas from the corpse's tail pocket without even breaking step. 'Close up, you bastards! Close up!'

A howitzer shell landed just in front of Taplow's rear line and, because its fuse still smoked, the closest men scattered. The shell exploded harmlessly as Taplow berated the men for cowards.

Frederickson's Riflemen had advanced far forward and were now trying to pick off the enemy gunners, but the cannon smoke made a perfect screen to hide the enemy. The smoke also served to obscure the aim of the French gunners, but so long as they fired level and ahead, they could scarcely miss. French skirmishers, armed with muskets, were threatening Frederickson's men, though even the bravest enemy was loath to come too close to the deadly rifles. Harper was calling targets to his men. 'See that officer, Marcos? Kill the bugger.'

'Tell Taplow to double forward at the battery!' Nairn shouted to Sharpe over the noise of the enemy guns. 'I'll put the Highlanders in behind him!'

Sharpe spurred Sycorax forward again. The mare was nervous of the horrid noises. The guns made a deep percussive, ear-thumping bang, while the passage of the roundshot overhead sounded just like heavy barrels being rolled across a wooden floor. A cannonball that came too close sounded like the tearing of cloth, but much more sudden and overwhelming, making a man flinch in the wake of its air-splitting astonishment. Behind all the noises was the sound of the bands and the gut-wrenching music of the pipes. Men screamed, Sergeants shouted, then a new ingredient joined the cacophony: the crackling thunder of an infantry volley. It was a French volley. The enemy battalion was hidden by the cannon smoke, but Sharpe, as he rode towards Taplow, saw the smoke twitch as the bullets flicked through from the ridge's centre.

'Steady now! Steady!' Taplow was riding immediately behind his front line. His horse sheered away from a wounded man who vomited blood, and Taplow slashed his crop down on to the animal's rump to keep it steady and obedient. Behind him the battalion's colours twitched from the strike of musket bullets.

'Major-General Nairn's compliments, sir . . .' Sharpe began.

'Damn Nairn!'

'If you'd double, sir, towards the battery . . .'

'In my own time, sir, in my own time. Damn you.' Taplow twisted his horse away from Sharpe. 'Well done!' he exhorted his men. 'Close up, my lads! Be steady now! Our turn will come! We'll kill the bastards in a minute! Close up! Steady now, steady!'

When the attacking line was a hundred paces from the French guns, the enemy changed from roundshot to canister. The tin encased canisters split apart in the muzzle-flames to scatter a charge of lead-balls like birdshot. Now, instead of the surgical strike of a roundshot, each discharge tore a ragged and gaping red hole in the advancing ranks. Taplow's line was shrinking fast and littering its wide path with a scatter of dead and injured. The carnage and the noise at last made the advancing battalion check, and that evidence of his men's fear spurred Taplow to ram his horse through the ranks. 'Charge, you buggers! Charge for England!'

Released, the battalion charged. They screamed in fear, but they ran forward, and the smoke of the guns served to hide them from their enemies. A small dip in the ground helped to save them from the worst of the canister as they scrambled towards the smoke and the enemy's gun line.

'Come on, you bastards! Kill the buggers!' Taplow was ahead of his men, charging like a cavalryman with his sword aloft, when two canisters exploded full in his face so that man and horse were turned instantly into scraps of bloody flesh that ribboned back in the guns' gale to spatter the ranks behind.

'Charge!' It was a Colour Sergeant who took up the cry. There was nothing left of Taplow, except blood, bones and gobbets of flesh spread across the ridge. His men charged over the ragged ruin of their Colonel and his horse then plunged into the smoke. A shell, fired from further up the ridge, exploded ten yards behind Sycorax and the mare, terrified, bolted forward into the thick fog of gunsmoke.

The smoke was acrid. Sharpe wanted to draw his sword, but he needed both hands to curb Sycorax's panic. She burst through the smoke and Sharpe saw a mass of snarling redcoats hacking and thrusting at the French gunners. This was revenge, and none of the Fusiliers would take an enemy's surrender. The gunners would pay for the damage they had done, and so the bayonets ripped and thrust.

Sycorax stopped, quivering, because a French trench blocked her path. The trench was shallow, as if it had only been half finished. A redcoat and two Frenchmen lay dead inside. Sharpe scraped his sword free and tried to make sense of the chaos beyond the trench. Taplow's men were brawling, stabbing and clawing their way through the battery while, just seventy paces to their left, a fresh enemy battalion was marching through the gunsmoke. The only man to have seen that threat was Frederickson, who had spread his skirmishers in a tenuous line to block the enemy's approach, but a handful of Riflemen could not hope to stop a determined charge by a whole battalion. Taplow's men were in utter disorder, seeking only vengeance, yet at any moment the enemy's counter-attack would come on them like thunder.

'Form companies!' Sharpe shouted at the fusiliers. He spurred Sycorax over the shallow trench, then used the flat of his sword on men hunting down the last gunners who were trying to find refuge beneath the hot barrels of their guns. 'Form companies!' He found a Major. 'Are you in command now?'

'Command?' The man was dazed.

'Taplow's dead.'

'Good God!' The Major gaped at Sharpe.

'For Christ's sake, form your men! You're about to be attacked.'

'We are?'

Sharpe twisted to his left and saw that the French battalion had checked their advance while they fixed bayonets yet, despite the small delay, there could not be more than half a minute before the French advanced into the captured battery where they would make mincemeat of the redcoats. Sharpe shouted for the men to form, and a few Sergeants saw the danger and took up the cry, but Sharpe knew it was hopeless. Taplow's men were oblivious of everything but the captured battery and its small plunder. In less than a minute they would be overwhelmed. He swore under his breath. No one had even thought to spike the enemy guns, and Sharpe wished he had remembered to put a hammer and a few nails in his saddlebag.

Then, blessedly, he heard a crashing volley and he saw the Highlanders coming out of the smoke bank. Nairn had brought them in to the left of Taplow's charge, and now the Scots fell on the flank of the advancing French battalion. It took just two Scottish volleys before the French gave up the counter-attack.

Sharpe found Taplow's senior Major. 'Form your battalion!'

'I can't . . .'

'Do it. Now! Or else I'll have you arrested! Move!'

A French gunner, wounded from a dozen blades, collapsed beside Sharpe's horse. Redcoats were drinking the powder-stained water from the gun-buckets in which the cannon swabs were soaked between shots. The English wounded were propped against the wicker baskets filled with earth that made the cannon embrasures. One such basket seemed to explode into dirty shreds under the impact of a roundshot and Sharpe realized that French guns, further up the ridge, had begun to fire into the captured battery.

'You're the reserve now!' Sharpe shouted at the Major. 'Form your men and fall in behind the Highlanders!'

79

He did not wait to see if he was obeyed, but spurred after the Scots who were marching onwards. To their left, beyond Nairn's second battalion, another brigade was going forward. The attack seemed to have broken the outer French crust, but as the British advanced so they would squeeze the French into an ever thicker and more impenetrable defence.

Sharpe rode past a dead Rifleman and was relieved to see it was not Harper. Nairn's attack, spirited and bloody, was going well. The Highlanders' Grenadier Company was in an enemy trench, led by a group of officers and sergeants who used their massive claymore swords to scour the French out. Frederickson's sharpshooters picked off the fleeing enemy. Two pipers, apparently oblivious of the horror, calmly played their instruments. There was something about that music, Sharpe thought, that suited a battlefield. The noise was like that which a man might make if he was being skinned alive, but it seemed to fill the enemy with fear just as it inspired the Scots to savagery. A riderless horse, its neck sheeted with blood, galloped in panic towards the enemy lines.

'Taplow's dead!' Sharpe found Nairn.

Nairn stared at Sharpe as though he had not heard, then he sighed. 'So much for prayer before battle. Poor man.'

The neighbouring brigade had stormed a small redoubt and Sharpe could see its ramparts swarming with British and Portuguese infantry. Bayonets rose and fell. The attack, Sharpe decided, had gone beyond the ability of any one man to control it; now it was just a mass of maddened men released to battle, and so long as they could be kept moving forward, then so long was victory possible.

Sharpe lost sense of time. The fear was gone, as it always seemed to vanish once the danger was present. Nairn's men, thinned out and bloodied, pushed forward into gunfire. Smoke thickened. Knots of men lay in blood where canister had struck. The wounded crawled for help, or vomited, or cried, or just lay softly to let death come. Order seemed to have gone. Instead of battalions marching proudly to the attack, it now seemed to Sharpe that the assault consisted of small groups of men who dashed a few yards forward, then summoned up the courage for another quick advance. Some men sought shelter and had to be rousted back into the advance. Somewhere a Colour showed through the smoke. Sometimes a cheer announced an enemy trench taken. A British galloper gun unlimbered and fired fast into the blinding fog.

The defence thickened. The enemy gunfire, which had been shattering at the start of the assault, seemed to double in its intensity. Nairn's men, broken into leaderless units, went to ground. Nairn tried to force them on, but the brigade was exhausted, yet Division judged the moment to perfection for, just as Nairn knew he could ask no more of his men, a reserve brigade came up behind and swept through the scattered remnants of his three battalions.

The Scotsman had tears in his eyes; perhaps for the dead, or perhaps for pride. His men had done well.

'Congratulations, sir,' Sharpe said, and meant it, for Nairn's men had driven deep into the horrid defences.

Nairn shook his head. 'We should have gone further.' He frowned, listening to the battle. 'Some poor bastard's fetching it rough, though.'

'The big redoubt, sir.' Sharpe pointed forward and left to where, amidst the shifting scrim of gunsmoke, there was a thicker patch of white smoke which betrayed the position of the large central redoubt. Musketry cracked about its earthen walls.

'If we take that fort,' Nairn said, 'the battle's won.'

But other men would have to take the redoubt. They were fresh men, Highlanders of the reserve brigade who marched into the maelstrom with their pipes playing. Nairn could only watch. He sheathed his sword as though he knew it would not be wanted again in this battle, nor, indeed, in this war. 'We'll advance behind the attack, Sharpe.'

'Yes, sir.'

Sharpe rode to reorganize the shattered battalions. Bullets hissed near him, a shell dropped just over his head, and once he seemed to be bracketed by a shrill whistling of canister, yet he somehow led a charmed existence. Around him an army bled, but Sharpe lived. He thought of Jane, of Dorset, and of all the pleasures that waited with peace, and he prayed that victory would come soon, and safely.

*   *   *

The French gunners ripped bloody gaps in the Highlanders who charged the redoubt. Canister coughed at point-blank range, reinforced by the musketry of infantry who lined the palisade to fire down into the swarm of men who scrambled across the dry ditch and over the bodies of their clansmen.

'Rather them than me.' Sergeant Harper stood beside Sharpe's horse.

Frederickson's company had come well through the horror. They'd lost six men only. Taplow's battalion had suffered far worse and, when Sharpe had re-formed it, there seemed only to be half as many men as had started on the attack, and that half so dazed as to be in a trance. Some of the men wept because Taplow was dead. 'They liked him,' the Light Company's Captain had explained to Sharpe. 'He flogged them and swore at them, but they liked him. They knew where they were with him.'

'He was a brave man,' Sharpe said.

'He was frightened of peace. He thought it would be dull.'

The Highlanders scrabbled at the earth wall. French muskets clawed at them, but somehow the Scotsmen hauled themselves up and thrust their bayonets over the

82

barricade. One man dragged himself to the top, fell, another took his place, and suddenly the Scots were tearing the palisade to scrap and flooding through the gaps. The cheers of the attackers sounded thin through the smoke. The supporting companies were crossing the ditch of dead men, and the redoubt was taken.

Sharpe sheathed his sword. He noted, with some surprise, that it was unbloodied. Perhaps, he thought, he would not have to kill in this last battle, then a superstitious certainty suggested that he would only survive if he did not try to kill. He touched his unshaven chin, then forgot the auguries of life and death as a massive volley hammered from the far side of the captured redoubt.

'God save Ireland.' Harper's voice had awe in it.

A French counter-attack, as desperate as the Highland assault, had been launched on the redoubt and Sharpe saw with horror how the blue-coated enemy was clearing the newly taken ramparts. Men fought hand to hand, but the French had the advantage of numbers and they were winning by sheer weight alone.

Survivors of the Scottish regiments jumped down to escape from the fort, French cheers scorned them, then the reserve battalions, more Scotsmen, were snarling forward with bayonets outstretched.

'We'll form as a reserve!' Nairn shouted at Sharpe.

'Skirmishers forward!' Sharpe shouted.

Nairn's brigade had marched three battalions strong, but now it formed in only two. The shrunken Highlanders were on the left, and the remains of the two English battalions paraded as one on the right. The men crouched, praying they would not be needed. Their faces were blackened by powder residue through which sweat carved dirty white lines.

The second Scottish attack clawed its way into the redoubt. Once again the bayonets rose and fell on the parapet, and once again the Scots drove the French out.

Smoke drifted to obscure the fight, but the pipes still played and the cheers were again in Gaelic.

Sharpe kept his sword sheathed as he rode Sycorax towards Nairn. Above him, incongruous on this day of struggle, two larks climbed high above the smoke. Sycorax shied away from a dead Scottish Sergeant. The battle had become quiet, or at least it seemed so to Sharpe. Men fought and died not two hundred paces northwards, and all around the guns still thundered their gut-thumping menace into the smoke-cloud, but it seemed unthreatening to Sharpe. He remembered the remains of the salt beef in his pouch, and was astonished to find that a French musket bullet had lodged in the tough, gristly meat. He prised the ball free, then bit hungrily into the food.

'There's another brigade a quarter mile behind us,' Nairn said. 'They'll go on to the end of the ridge if the fort falls.'

'Good.'

'Thank you for all you did,' Nairn said.

Sharpe, embarrassed by the praise, shook his head. 'I didn't even get my sword wet, sir.'

'Nor me.' Nairn stared up into the sky.

A French cannonball, fired blind from the left flank, and aimed at the Scotsmen who had captured the redoubt, flew wide. It took off the head of Sharpe's horse in an eruption of warm blood. For a second Sharpe sat on the headless mare, then the body tipped forward and he frantically kicked his feet out of the stirrups and threw himself sideways as the animal's corpse threatened to roll on to him. 'God damn it!' Sharpe sprawled in a puddle of warm horse blood, then clambered to his feet. 'God damn it!'

Nairn governed his impulse to laugh at Sharpe's undignified fall. 'I'm sorry,' he said instead.

'She was a present from Jane.' Sharpe stared at the charnel mess that had been Sycorax. The headless body was still twitching.

'She was a good horse,' Nairn said. 'Save the saddle.' He turned in his own saddle to see if one of his spare horses was in sight, but a sudden volley of musketry turned him back.

Another French counter-attack was sweeping forward, this one outflanking and assaulting the redoubt, and again the Scots were being forced backwards by a superior number of men. Blue-coated infantry swarmed at the redoubt's walls, muskets crashed, and for the second time the French retook the fort. Screams sounded as Highlanders were hunted down inside the courtyard. 'The bloody French are fighting well today.' Nairn sounded puzzled.

The enemy scrambled along the palisade, bayoneting wounded Scotsmen. These Frenchmen were, indeed, fighting with a verve that the earlier attack, in column, had not displayed. An eagle standard shone among the smoke and, beneath its brightness, Sharpe saw a French General. The man was standing with legs straddled wide on the fort's southern parapet. It was an arrogant pose, suggesting that the Frenchman was lord of this battlefield and more than equal to anything the British could throw against him. Frederickson's Riflemen must have seen the enemy General, for a dozen of them fired, but the Frenchman had a charmed life this day.

'That's Calvet!' Sharpe had trained his glass on the Frenchman and recognized the short, squat figure of the man he had fought at the Teste de Buch. 'It's bloody Calvet!'

'Let's teach the bastard a lesson.' Nairn drew his sword. It was evident that with the last repulse of the Scots there were no fresh troops to launch against the recaptured redoubt. If Calvet was given more than a few minutes he would reorganize his defences and the fort would be doubly hard to take. Now was the moment to counter-attack, and Nairn's was the closest brigade. 'Quick, Sharpe! Let's get it over!'

Calvet turned imperiously away. On either flank of the redoubt his men were marching forward. The fort's ditch was heaped with dead and dying men.

'On your feet!' Nairn had ridden to the space between his two battalions. 'Fix bayonets!' He waited till the blades were fixed, then waved his cocked hat. 'Forward! Let me hear the pipes!'

The two battalions went forward. So far they were unnoticed. The French were clearing their embrasures and firestep, while one of Calvet's battalions was being formed in three ranks in front of the shattered palisade and blood-drenched ditch. It was an officer of that battalion who first saw Nairn's threat and shouted a warning up to the fort's parapet.

No one had thought to spike the guns, and now the French artillerymen charged them with canister and crashed death out at Nairn's attack. Sharpe, hurrying to keep up with the mounted Scotsman, saw Nairn fall, but it was only Nairn's horse that had been wounded. The old Scotsman, his hat gone and his white hair disarrayed, picked himself up and brandished his sword. 'Forward!'

The fort had been captured twice, and twice recaptured. The crude earthen square, with its battered palisades, seemed to be sucking men into its horror, almost as if by mutual consent the two armies had agreed that whoever won the fort would gain the day. Sharpe could see open ground to his right, ground that would outflank the smoking redoubt, but cool sense, which might have suggested occupying the ground, had been replaced by a savage pride that would not permit General Calvet the satisfaction of holding the redoubt. Nairn, so long denied the chance to show his skills, would now prove himself the master of this battle's heart. He had more than the redoubt's guns to contend with, for the battalion of French infantry were loading their muskets in readiness for Nairn's assault.

'Steady, lads, steady!' Nairn had launched his attack on

an impulse, now he had to slow it down so that his men did not become ragged with fear or eagerness. 'Watch your dressing! Steady, lads!' He smiled as Sharpe joined him. 'One last effort, Sharpe, just one last effort!'

One of the Highlander's Colours fell, was retrieved, and hoisted again. A Sergeant's leg was sliced off at the knee by a cannonball. The pipes whipped fervour into flagging hearts.

The French infantry was loaded and their muskets were raised. There was no sign of Calvet who must have stayed inside the redoubt. Sharpe watched the Frenchmen cock their muskets. 'We'll break the bastards!' Nairn shouted. 'We'll break them!'

The French infantry fired and the air was filled with the splintering volley and the whiplash hiss of its bullets. Smoke gouted thick as blood from the cannon embrasures and Sharpe saw the ground ahead of him churn with the strike of canister. Nairn staggered backwards and Sharpe turned to him in alarm.

'It's only my leg, man! It's nothing! Go on! Go on!' Nairn was wounded, but still exultant. He limped, but would not let Sharpe stay with him. 'Give them a volley, Richard, now's your moment!'

'Brigade!' Sharpe's voice was huge. 'Brigade will halt! Present!'

The redcoats stopped. They raised their heavy muskets. The French battalion knew what was coming and frantically tried to reload. Sharpe raised his sword, paused a heartbeat, then swept it down. 'Fire!'

A crashing thunderous volley, a spew of acrid smoke, and no time to wonder what damage the bullets had done. 'Charge!'

'Take the boys home, Richard!' Nairn called. 'Take them home!'

'Charge!' Sharpe felt the rage rising, the unreasonable rage of battle, the anger that would only be slaked by

87

victory. It was this same pride and rage that had made Taplow spur ahead of his men to certain death, and which had made Nairn lead his men into the cauldron that was the redoubt's killing ground. 'Charge!' A musket ball slapped past his face. Sharpe could see the faces of the French infantry now, and they looked desperately young and desperately frightened.

'Charge!' That was Nairn, behind Sharpe now, and the word seemed to hurl the remnants of the brigade into the stench of bodies and blood among which the enemy stood. The Highlanders ran at the French infantry who had nowhere to retreat. The enemy hesitated, and were lost. Nairn's English battalion was coming at their flank.

Scottish bayonets went forward and came back bloody. The clansmen were old in war, fighting conscripts. Sharpe, on their flank, watched the enemy run, but, in their panic, the French ran towards the closing English. One youngster ran straight towards Sharpe, then, seeing the English officer, the boy raised his bayonet to strike. Sharpe disdainfully stepped to one side and tripped the boy. He left him on the ground for one of Frederickson's men to disarm or kill.

A cannon crashed canister into the mass of struggling men, killing both Scot and Frenchmen alike.

'Give them fire!' Frederickson shouted, and his skirmishers fired up at the French embrasures. A gunner was flung backwards. A voice bellowed in French from the palisade. Nairn's Highlanders were already clawing at the sloping earth wall of the fort's southern face.

'Come right! Come right!' Sharpe shouted at the makeshift English battalion to angle their advance and follow him to the redoubt's western wall.

Sharpe jumped the ditch and reached for the palisade. A musket flamed at him. His foot slipped on the wet earth and he fell back to the ditch's foot as Frederickson's men leaped past him. Sergeant Harper had his seven-barrelled gun unslung. He fired it blindly upwards and three Frenchmen were thrown back to make a space where the Riflemen could reach the top. Sharpe went after them. A man's blood soaked his face, a body fell on him, but he pushed it aside and helped another man tug at the palisade. A splinter of wood ripped his palm open as he tugged, but then the parapet cracked outwards to make a space through which a man could pass. A French bayonet reached for them, but Sharpe stabbed with his sword and raked the man's forearm so that the musket and blade dropped.

A Greenjacket went into the gap, was shot, then another man pulled him aside. Harper was wrenching at another part of the barricade, pulling out an earth-filled wicker basket that collapsed a whole section of the defences on to a wounded redcoat. Harper was screaming his own Gaelic challenge. Redcoats were mixed with the Greenjackets, the whole mass of men scrabbling and tearing at the mud bank and timber palisade. They trampled over the wounded and fought their way up to where French muskets hammered and bayonets stabbed down. One Frenchman stabbed too far, his arm was seized, and the man screamed as he was tugged down to the waiting blades. Sharpe was wedged in a gap of the palisade now, desperately trying to fend off a bayonet, when suddenly a whole section of the wall behind him collapsed inwards under the weight of attackers. There were shouts of victory, and the British were suddenly spilling on to the narrow firestep, then leaping down into the courtyard where General Calvet tried to line his men into a solid mass, but Nairn's Highlanders had already pierced the southern wall, and the first of those Scots now carried their bayonets towards Calvet's frightened men. The courtyard had been left like a slaughterhouse from the two previous attacks.

'Close on them! Close!' Sharpe shouted, then jumped down to the courtyard.

Now it was blood and stench and blades in a very small

place. A French officer tried to duel with Sharpe, but the Rifleman had no time for such heroics and simply threw himself forward, past the man's lunge, and punched the heavy sword's guard into the man's face. The Frenchman fell backwards and Sharpe kicked him in the ribs. Sharpe would have left the man there, but the French officer fumbled at his belt to draw a pistol and Sharpe forgot his superstition about killing, reversed his sword, and thrust the blade down once. A man came at Sharpe with a bayonet, but two Rifle sword-bayonets caught the Frenchman first. A Highland officer disembowelled a gunner with a sweep of the claymore, then hacked at the dead man's head to make certain of his death.

Calvet was swearing at his men; tugging them into line, cursing them for chicken-livered bastards. A Scots officer came close enough to the General to threaten him with a claymore, but Calvet almost casually parried the blow then lunged his own sword into the Scotsman's belly before turning back to shout at his men to stand fast and fight the God-damn bastards off.

Calvet's men were mostly young conscripts who had fought like demons this day, but Nairn's attack had drained their last courage. Despite their General, they edged back.

A few fought on. A French gunner swung a rammer like a great club. Sharpe ducked under the swing, then lunged. The Frenchman looked oddly surprised as the blade punctured his belly. A Highlander finished the job for Sharpe. A piper was on the southern rampart, flaying the Scots on with his wild music.

Sharpe's sword handle was slippery with blood. Calvet's men were breaking and running. The first of them were already spilling over the northern wall. Sharpe looked for Calvet and saw him in the centre of a few moustached veterans and beneath the bright eagle standard. 'Calvet!' Sharpe shouted the name as a challenge. 'Calvet!'

The Frenchman saw Sharpe. Oddly, instead of bridling at the challenge, he raised his sword in a mock salute. Sharpe struggled to get close to the man, but a sudden rush of Highlanders came between him and the group of Frenchmen. The Colours of three British battalions were in the redoubt now, the mass of men was overwhelming, and Calvet's last staunch defenders had to give way. They had fought well, but now they just wanted to be out of this courtyard of blood. They retreated calmly, firing their muskets to hold the Scots at bay, then broke to scramble across the northern parapet.

'Man the firestep!' Sharpe ran to the northern parapet. 'Spike those damned guns!' That was the Scots Colonel.

Frederickson's men were on the northern parapet, firing at the retreating French. Sharpe joined them, unslung his rifle and looked for Calvet. He saw the General walking away, not bothering to run, but just slashing at weeds with his sword as though he took a walk in the country. Sharpe aimed his rifle dead at the small of Calvet's back, but could not bear to pull the trigger. He twitched the barrel up and to one side before firing so that the bullet slapped past the French General's right ear.

Calvet turned. He saw the Riflemen lining the parapet. None fired at him, for his calm demeanour spoke of a bravery they could admire. He was a beaten man, but a brave one. He stared at the Riflemen for a second, then bowed an ironic bow. As he straightened up he made an obscene gesture, then walked quietly on. He only began to run when British troops, flooding either side of the redoubt, threatened to cut him off. Ahead of Calvet the smoke blossomed as the Spaniards renewed their assault on the ridge's northern end. That assault, and the fall of the large fort, broke what spirit was left in Marshal Soult's army.

The French ran. They ran down the ridge's eastern face and towards the bridges that crossed the canal and led to the city. Sharpe, standing on the captured firestep, could at last stare down at the spires and towers and pinnacles and roofs of Toulouse. He could see the semi-circle of smoke that marked the British positions to the city's east and south. It was like looking at a woodcut of a siege, taken from some old book about Marlborough's wars. He stared, oblivious of the sudden silence on the ridge, and all he could think of was that he was alive.

Sharpe turned away from the city and saw Sergeant Harper alive and well. The big Irishman was cutting a canteen off a Frenchman's belt. A bugle called victory. A wounded Frenchman cursed his pain and tried to stand. A Highland Sergeant was admiring a French officer's sword which he had taken as a trophy. Men were ladling water from gun-buckets and pouring it down their faces. A dog ran with a length of intestines in its mouth. A British Lieutenant was dying at the base of the empty French flagpole. The man was blinking desperately, as though he knew that if he let his eyelids stay closed he would slip into eternal night.

Frederickson came and stood beside Sharpe and the two Rifle officers turned to stare down into the enemy city. 'Tomorrow,' Frederickson said, 'I suppose we'll have to assault the damned place?'

'It won't be us, William.' Sharpe knew that bloody business would be given to other battalions. The men who had taken this ridge had earned their pay and the proof of it was in the horror all around. Dead men, wounded men, dying horses, broken gun carriages, smoke, litter; it was a field after battle, the last battle. Surely, Sharpe thought, it had to be the last battle.

Sharpe found a cannon's cleaning rag and wiped his sword clean. He had wet the blade after all, but soon, he thought, he would hang this long sword on a country wall and let it gather dust. To his north British colours advanced along the ridge as fresh battalions hunted down the last nests of stubborn defenders. The smoke was thinning to a misty haze. There were Spanish colours visible at the ridge's far crest; proof that this day's battle was won, even if the city itself had yet to fall. Sharpe suddenly laughed. 'I had a sudden urge to take Calvet's eagle. Did you recognize him?'

'I did.' Frederickson offered his canteen to Sharpe. 'Be glad you didn't try to take his bird. You wouldn't be alive if you had.'

A bagpipe suddenly sounded, and something plangent in its notes made Sharpe and Frederickson turn.

'Oh, God,' Frederickson said softly.

Four Highlanders carried a litter made of enemy jackets threaded on to enemy muskets. On the litter, his white hair hanging, was Nairn.

Sharpe jumped down to the blood-drenched earth of the courtyard. He crossed to the body just as the Highlanders lowered it to the ground. 'He's dead, sir.' One of the men saw Sharpe's face and offered the bleak news.

'He said it was his leg.' Sharpe frowned at the old man who had been his friend.

'His lung as well, sir.'

'Oh, Christ!' Tears came to Sharpe's eyes, then fell down his bloodied cheek. 'I was to have had supper with him tonight.'

'I'm sorry, sir.'

They buried Nairn in the centre of the redoubt that the Scotsman had captured. A bagpipe played a lament for him, and a chaplain said a Gaelic prayer for him, and his beloved Highlanders fired a volley towards the northern stars for him.

And in the morning, when Sharpe awoke with a parched mouth and a heart that lurched with sorrow when he recalled the Scotsman's death, it was discovered that Marshal Soult had abandoned Toulouse. He had marched through the gap in the British ring, and he had left the city that now was flaunted with white flags to welcome its enemies. Toulouse had surrendered.

* * *

Captain William Frederickson, his false teeth and eyepatch restored to give his scarred face a semblance of respectability, discovered Sharpe in a wineshop that lay close to Toulouse's prefecture. The wineshop was crowded, but something about Sharpe's scarred face had dissuaded anyone from sharing his table. It was just after dusk and two days after Soult had abandoned the city to the British. 'Have you taken to drinking alone?' Frederickson asked.

'I never abandoned the habit.' Sharpe pushed the bottle of wine across the table. 'You're looking damned cheerful.'

'I am damned cheerful.' Frederickson paused because a loud and prolonged huzza sounded from the prefecture next door. Field-Marshal the Lord Wellington was giving a dinner to celebrate his capture of the city. All the prominent citizens of Toulouse were attending, and all wore the white cockade of the French monarchy and were swearing that they had never supported the upstart Corsican tyrant. 'It makes one wonder just who it is we've been fighting all these years.' Frederickson straddled a back-to-front chair and nodded thanks for the wine. 'But we're fighting them no longer because the Emperor has abdicated. The God-damned bloody Emperor has thrown in his hand. Allow me to toast your most excellent, and now quite safe, health.'

Frederickson had spoken in a most matter-of-fact tone, so much so that Sharpe did not really comprehend what his friend had just said.

'The war, my dear friend, is over,' Frederickson insisted.

Sharpe stared at Frederickson and said nothing.

'It's true,' Frederickson said, 'as I live and breathe, and may I be cursed if I lie, but a British officer has come from Paris. Think of that! A British officer from Paris! In fact a whole slew of British officers have come from Paris!

94

Bonaparte has abdicated, Paris has fallen, the war is over, and we have won!' Frederickson could no longer contain his excitement. He stood and, ignoring the majority of the customers who were French, climbed on to the chair and shouted his news to the whole tavern. 'Boney's abdicated! Paris has fallen, the war's over, and we've won! By Christ, we've won!'

There was a moment's silence, then the cheers began. Spanish and Portuguese officers sought a hasty translation, then added their own noise to the celebration. The only men who did not cheer were the civilian-clothed and moustached French veterans who stared sullenly into their wine cups. One such man, the news interpreted to him, wept.

Frederickson shouted to a serving girl that he wanted champagne, cheroots, and brandy. 'We've won!' he exulted to Sharpe. 'The damn thing's over!'

'When did Boney abdicate?' Sharpe asked.

'Christ knows. Last week? Two weeks ago?'

'Before the battle?' Sharpe insisted.

Frederickson shrugged. 'Before the battle, yes.'

'Jesus.' Sharpe momentarily closed his eyes. So Nairn's death had been for nothing? All the blood on the high ridge had been spilt for nothing?

Then, suddenly, he forgot that irony in an overwhelming and astonishing wash of relief. The bells of Europe could ring because the war was over. There would be no more danger. No more summoning the nerve to assault an enemy-held wall, and no more standing rock still as an enemy battalion took aim. No more cannons, no more lancers, no more skirmish line. No more death. It was over. No more waking in the night sheeted with sweat and thinking of a sword blade's threat. The war was over, and the last ranks had been closed up, and the whole damn thing was done. Europe had been rinsed with blood, and it was over. He would live for ever now, and that thought made Sharpe laugh, and suddenly he was shaking hands with allied officers who crowded about the table to hear the details of Frederickson's news. Napoleon, the ogre, the tyrant, the scourge of Europe, the damned Corsican, the upstart, the beast, was finished.

Someone began singing, while other officers were dancing between the tables where the Emperor's veterans sat keeping their thoughts hidden.

Brandy and champagne arrived. Frederickson, without asking, poured the red wine from Sharpe's cup on to the sawdust covered floor and replaced it with champagne. 'A toast! To peace!'

'To peace!'

'To Dorset!' Frederickson beamed.

'To Dorset!' Sharpe wondered whether a letter had come from England, then forgot the thought to savour this astounding news. It was over! No more canister, no more bayonets, no more shivering on long night marches, no more stench of French cavalry, no more sabres chopping down, no more bullets. Easter had triumphed and death was defeated. 'I must write to Jane,' Sharpe said, and he wondered whether she was celebrating the news in some Dorset village. There would be oxen roasting, hogsheads of ale, church bells ringing. It was over.

'You can write to Jane tomorrow,' Frederickson ordered, 'for tonight we get drunk.'

'Tonight we get drunk,' Sharpe agreed, and by one o'clock they were on the city's walls where they sang nonsense and shouted their triumph towards the British bivouac fires that lay to the city's west. By two o'clock they were searching for another wineshop, but instead found a group of cavalry sergeants who insisted on sharing some plundered champagne with the Rifle officers. At three o'clock, arm in arm to keep themselves upright, Sharpe and Frederickson staggered through the abandoned French fortifications and crossed the wooden bridge over the canal where two friendly sentries prevented them from falling into the water. At four o'clock they arrested Sergeant Harper on a charge of being sober, and at five o'clock they found him not guilty because he no longer was. At six o'clock Major Richard Sharpe was being sick, and at seven o'clock he staggered to Nairn's vacant tent and gave instructions that he was not to be woken up ever again. Ever.

Because a war was over, and it was won, and at long long last there was peace.

Part Two

CHAPTER 4

Nairn's Brigade was no more. Broken by battle and leaderless, its shrunken battalions were attached to other brigades. The reason was purely administrative, for now the army was to be run by bureaucrats instead of by fighting men, and the bureaucrats had been ordered to disband the army that had fought from the Portuguese coast to deep inside France. Frederickson was curious to discover just how far the army had marched and found his answer with the help of some old maps that he uncovered in a Toulouse bookseller's shop. 'As the crow flies,' he told Sharpe in an aggrieved voice, 'it's only six hundred and sixty miles, and it took us six years.'

Or ten thousand miles as a soldier reckoned miles, which was as bad roads that froze in winter, were quagmires in spring and choked the throat with dust in summer. Soldiers' miles were those that were marched under the weight of back-breaking packs. They were miles that were marched over and over again, in advance and retreat, in chaos and in fear. Soldiers' miles led to sieges and battles, and to the death of friends, but now those soldiers' miles were all done and the army would travel the crow's one hundred and twenty miles to Bordeaux where ships waited to take them away. Some battalions were being sent to garrisons far across the oceans, some were being ordered to the war in America, and a few were being sent home where, their duty done, they would be disbanded.

Frederickson's company was ordered to England where, along with the rest of its battalion, the company would be broken up and the men sent to join other battalions of the 60th. Most of the Spaniards who had enlisted in the company during the war had already deserted. They had joined the Greenjackets only to kill Frenchmen, and, that job efficiently done, Frederickson gladly turned his blind eye to their departure. Sharpe, without a battalion of his own or even a job, received permission to travel back to England with the Riflemen and so, three weeks after the French surrender, he found himself clambering on to one of the flat-bottomed river barges that had been hired to transport the army up the River Garonne to the quays of Bordeaux.

Seconds before the barge was poled away from the wharf a messenger arrived from Divisional Headquarters with a bag of mail for Frederickson's company. The bag was small, for most of the company could not read or write, and of those who could there were few whose relatives would think to write letters. One letter was for a man who had died at Fuentes d'Onoro, but whose mother, refusing to believe the news, still insisted on writing each month with exhortations for her long dead son to be a good soldier, a fervent Christian, and a credit to his family.

There was also a packet for Major Richard Sharpe, forwarded from London by his Army Agents. The packet had first been sent to the Prince of Wales's Own Volunteers, then forwarded to General Headquarters, then to Division, and had thus taken over a month to reach Sharpe.

'So you needn't have worried,' Frederickson said, 'Jane wrote after all.'

'Indeed.' Sharpe carried the packet forward to find a patch of privacy in the barge's bows where he tore off the sealing wafer and, with a quite ridiculous and boyish anticipation, tore open the packet to find two letters.

The first was from a man in Lancashire who claimed to have invented a chain-shot that could be fired from a standard musket or rifle and which, if fired low, would be fatal against the legs of cavalry horses. He begged Major Sharpe's help in persuading the Master General of Ordnance to buy the device, which was called Armbruster's Patent Horse-Leg Breaker. Sharpe screwed the letter into a ball and threw it over the barge's gunwale.

The second letter was from Sharpe's Army Agents. They presented their compliments to Major Sharpe, then begged leave to inform him that, in accordance with his written instructions to allow Mrs Jane Sharpe authority over his account, they had sold all his 4 per cent stock and transferred the monies into the charge of Mrs Jane Sharpe of Cork Street, Westminster. They thanked Major Sharpe for the trust and privilege of handling his affairs, and hoped that should he ever need such services again, he would not forget his humble and obedient servants, Messrs Hopkinson and Son, Army Agents, of St Albans Street, London. The humble servants added that the expense of selling the 4 per cent stock and the necessary ledger work for the closure of his account amounted to £16. 14s. 4d, which sum had been deducted from the draft passed to Mrs Jane Sharpe. They wished to remind Major Sharpe that they still held his Presentation sword donated by the Patriotic Fund, and begged to remain, etc.

The bargemen hoisted a clumsy gaff-rigged sail that made the tarred shrouds creak ominously. Sharpe stared uncomprehendingly at the letter, unaware that the barge was moving. A small child on the far bank sucked her thumb and stared solemnly at the strange soldiers who were being carried away from her.

'Good news, I trust?' Frederickson clambered into the bows to interrupt Sharpe's reverie.

Sharpe wordlessly handed the letter to Frederickson who read it swiftly. 'I didn't know you'd got a Presentation sword?' Frederickson said cheerfully.

'That was for taking the eagle at Talavera. I think it was a fifty guinea sword.'

'A good one?'

'Very ornate.' Sharpe wondered how Frederickson could so completely have misunderstood the importance of the letter, and merely be curious about a blued and gilded sword. 'It's a Rinkfiel-Solingen blade and a Kimbley scabbard. Wouldn't serve in a fight.'

'Nice to hang on the wall, though.' Frederickson handed the letter back. 'I'm glad for you. It's splendid news.'

'Is it?'

'Jane's collected the money, so presumably she's off to buy your house in Dorset. Isn't that what you wanted to hear?'

'Eighteen thousand guineas?'

Frederickson stared at Sharpe. He blinked. At length he spoke. 'Jesus wept.'

'We found diamonds at Vitoria, you see,' Sharpe confessed.

'How many?'

'Hundreds of the bloody things.' Sharpe shrugged. 'Sergeant Harper found them really, but he shared them with me.'

Frederickson whistled softly. He had heard that much of the Spanish Crown jewels had disappeared when the French baggage was captured at Vitoria, and he had known that Sharpe and Harper had done well from the plunder, but he had never dared to put the two stories together. Sharpe's fortune was vast. A man could live like a prince for a hundred years on such a fortune.

'She could buy a splendid house for a hundred guineas,' Sharpe said petulantly, 'why does she need eighteen thousand?'

Frederickson sat on the stump of the bowsprit. He was still trying to imagine Sharpe as an immensely wealthy man. 'Why did you give her the authority?' he asked after a while.

'It was before the duel.' Sharpe shrugged apologetically. 'I thought I was going to die. I wanted her to be secure.'

Frederickson tried to reassure his friend. 'She's probably found a better investment.'

'But why hasn't she written?' And that was the real rub, the blistering rub that so insidiously attacked Sharpe. Why had Jane not written? Her silence was only made worse by this tantalizing evidence which suggested that his wife was a rich woman living in London's Cork Street. 'Where is Cork Street?'

'Somewhere near Piccadilly, I think. It's a good address.'

'She can afford it, can't she?'

Frederickson twisted on his makeshift seat to watch a marsh harrier glide eastwards, then he shrugged. 'You'll be home in three weeks, so what does it matter?'

'I suppose it doesn't.'

'That's what women do to you,' Frederickson said philosophically. 'They choke up your barrel and chip your flint. Which reminds me. Some of these bastards think that just because we're at peace they don't have to clean their rifles. Sergeant Harper! Weapon inspection, now!'

Thus they floated towards home.

*　　*　　*

Later that day, as the barge wallowed between sunlit meadows, Sergeant Harper sat with Sharpe in the bows. 'What will you do now, sir?'

'Resign my commission, I suppose.' Sharpe was staring at two fishermen. They wore white blouses and wide straw hats, and looked very peaceful. It was hard to imagine that a month ago this had been a country at war. 'And I suppose you'll go to Spain to fetch Isabella?'

'If I'm allowed to, sir.'

This was Harper's rub. He, like Sharpe, was a wealthy man, and a married man, too. There was no longer any need for Patrick Harper to wear the King's badge, which he had only ever assumed out of poverty and hunger. He wanted his precious discharge papers, and Sharpe had failed to secure them. Sharpe had collected all the requisite forms, but he had needed to secure the signatures of a Staff Medical Officer, a Regimental Surgeon of the 60th, and of a General Officer. He would also have needed the imprint of the regimental seal of the 60th. Sharpe had blithely assumed that such things would be easily secured, but the army's regulations had defeated him. The army was no longer run by men who understood that a favour would be repaid by victory on a battlefield, but instead by men who could only read the small print of the regulations. Those bureaucrats understood only too well how many men would try and leave the ranks, and extraordinary precautions were being taken to stop any such desertions. Harper was thus being forced to stay in the army.

'There is another way,' Sharpe said diffidently.

'Sir?'

'Become my servant.'

Harper frowned, not at the prospect of menial servitude, but because he did not see how it would achieve his ambition.

Sharpe explained. 'So long as I'm on the active list, then I'm allowed a servant. That servant can travel at my discretion. So as soon as we're in England we'll go to Dorset, I'll report that you were kicked to death by a horse, and then you just go free. The army will cross you off the list, and we won't need a Regimental Surgeon to testify that you're dead because you'll have died outside of regimental lines. We'll need a civilian doctor, and maybe even a coroner, but there's bound to be some drunkards in Dorset who'll take a bribe.'

Harper thought about it, then nodded. 'It sounds good to me, sir.'

'There is a small problem.'

'Sir?' Harper sounded guarded.

'King's Regulations, Sergeant, concerning the interior economy of a regiment, insist that no non-commissioned officer is on any account to be permitted to act as an officer's servant.'

'You looked the rules up, did you, sir?'

'I just quoted them to you.'

Harper smiled. Then he hooked his big powder-stained fingers into the frayed hems of his Sergeant's badge. 'I never wanted the stripes in the first place.'

'I seem to remember it was one hell of a struggle to make you wear them.'

'Should have saved your breath, sir.' Harper ripped the stripes off his sleeve. He stared ruefully at the patch of dirty cloth for a moment, then threw it overboard. 'Busted back to the ranks,' he said, then laughed.

Sharpe watched the drifting stripes, and he thought how many hard years had passed since he had first persuaded Harper to put up that patch of white cloth. It was all coming to an end, Sharpe thought; all that he had held most dear and known best.

And ahead of him, beyond this placid river with its fishermen, herons, moorhens, and reeds, what then? The future was like a great mist, in which even Jane was indistinct. Sharpe touched the crumpled letter in his pocket, and persuaded himself that when he found Jane all would be well. He would discover that her letters had gone astray, nothing more.

Frederickson came forward and saw the bare patch on Harper's sleeve.

'I demoted Rifleman Harper to the ranks,' Sharpe explained.

'May one ask why?'

'For being Irish,' Sharpe said, then he thought how much he would miss Patrick Harper's friendship, but consoled himself that Jane was waiting for him, and thus he had all the happiness in the world to anticipate and then to enjoy.

So they floated on.

*　　*　　*

The quays at Bordeaux were busier than they had been for years. Wharves which had been kept empty by the Royal Navy's blockade were suddenly sprouting with masts and spars. Fat-bellied merchant ships queued in the river for their turn at the stone quays where the soldiers waited between netted mounds of supplies. Cannon barrels were slung into holds, while the gun carriages were broken down to be stacked against bulkheads. Protesting horses were lowered into floating stalls. A British Army, fresh from victory, was being hurried out of France. 'The very least they could have done,' Harper grumbled, 'was let us march into Paris.'

That was a small grudge against the larger tragedies that were now the daily coin of the Bordeaux quays. Those tragedies were occasioned by an army decree which ruled that only those soldiers' wives who could prove they had married with the permission of their husband's commanding officers would be carried home. All other women, and their children, were to be abandoned in Bordeaux.

The abandoned women were mostly Portuguese and Spanish who had left their villages when the army marched through. Some had been sold to a soldier by their families. Sharpe could remember when a strong young girl could be bought for marriage for just five guineas. Most of the women had gone through a camp-marriage, which was no marriage in the eyes of the Church, but many had persuaded a village priest to give a blessing to their union. It did not matter now for, unless the regimental records confirmed a Colonel's permission, the marriage was reckoned to be false. Thousands of women were thus forcibly taken off the quays, then prevented from rejoining their men by a cordon of provosts armed with loaded muskets. The wailing of the women and their small children was ceaseless.

'How are they supposed to get home?' Harper asked.

'Walk,' Frederickson said harshly.

'God save Ireland,' Harper said, 'but I hate this damned army.'

On the morning that Frederickson's Riflemen joined the chaos on the quays three men from redcoat battalions tried to desert to join their wives. One successfully swam upstream, his dark head constantly surrounded by the splashes of musket-balls. Men already on the ships cheered him. A Naval gig, ordered to cut him off, somehow managed to tangle her oars and Sharpe guessed that the sailors had no stomach for their job and had deliberately made a nonsense of the attempt. Two other redcoats, trying to climb a wall of the docks, were caught and charged with attempted desertion.

Frederickson was busy scribbling pieces of paper which would serve as marriage certificates for the six men of his company who might otherwise lose their women. Sharpe, as the more senior officer, gladly added his own signature, then glossed his name with the description of Temporary Brigade Commander. He doubted if the papers would work, but they had to be tried.

Sharpe and Frederickson carried the papers, along with all the company's other musters, returns and order books, to an office that was guarded by provosts and administered by civilian officials of the Transport Board. Sharpe wanted to challenge their authority with his reputation, but when he reached the office the city's multitude of church clocks successively pealed midday in a cacophony of time that sounded like a celebration of victory. It was also the signal for the Transport Board officials to close their ledgers for luncheon. They would return, they said, at three o'clock. Till then the Riflemen must wait, though if the officers wished to take luncheon in the city, then they were permitted to pass the picquet-line of provosts.

Sharpe and Frederickson left the company under Rifleman Harper's command and, out of curiosity, went to find their luncheon in the city. Yet, just as soon as the two officers were beyond the barrier, they were besieged by crying women. One held up a baby as though the infant's mute appeal would be sufficient to change the heartless decision of the authorities. Sharpe tried to explain that he had no standing in the matter. This group of women were Spanish. They had no money, they were not permitted to see their men, they were just expected to walk home. No one cared about them. Some had spent five years with the British army, carrying packs and muskets like their men, but now they were to be discarded. 'Are we to be whores?' one screamed at Sharpe. 'He wants us to be a whore!' The woman pointed at a civilian who was standing a few yards away. It appeared he was a Frenchman who had come to the docks to recruit women for his house. The man, seeing Sharpe look at him, smiled and bowed.

'I don't like that man,' Frederickson said mildly.

'Nor me.' Sharpe gazed at the well-dressed Frenchman who, under the scrutiny, feigned boredom. 'Shall we let him know how much we dislike him?'

'It would probably make both of us feel a great deal better if we did. You'll cut off his retreat?'

Sharpe gently extricated himself from the women, then sauntered past the Frenchman who was content to wait until the Spanish women had finished their importuning of the Riflemen. The Frenchman had watched every British officer so besieged, and knew that the women must soon abandon their hopeless appeals and that afterwards the prettiest among them would be glad of his offer of employment. He lit himself a cigar, blew smoke towards the gulls that screamed about the ships' topmasts, and thought that never before, and perhaps never again, would whores be so cheap. Then, suddenly, he saw a one-eyed and toothless Rifleman moving fast towards him. The Frenchman twisted to run away.

He twisted to find himself facing another scarred Rifleman. 'Good afternoon,' Sharpe said.

The Frenchman tried to swerve round Sharpe, but the Rifleman reached out a hand, checked the Frenchman, then turned him and pushed him towards Frederickson. Frederickson, who had removed his eyepatch and false teeth in honour of the occasion, let the Frenchman come, then kicked him massively between the legs.

The man collapsed. Frederickson stooped and retrieved the man's fallen cigar.

The Frenchman was breathless on the cobbles, his hands clutching a pain that was like a thousand red-hot musket balls exploding outwards from his groin. For a few seconds he could not draw breath, then he gasped and afterwards screamed so loud that even the gulls seemed to be silenced. The provosts twitched towards the sound, then decided that the two Rifle officers were best left in peace.

'Shut your bloody face, you pimp.' Sharpe slapped the man's cheek hard enough to loosen teeth, then began cutting open his pockets and seams much as if the Frenchman was a battlefield corpse. He found a few coins that he distributed to the women. It was a small gesture, and one that was shrunk to nothing in the face of the women's plight. It was also a gesture that could not be repeated for the sake of every woman who accosted the two Riflemen as they crossed the city's bridge.

To escape the hopeless appeals they ducked into a wineshop where Frederickson, who spoke good French, ordered ham, cheese, bread and wine. Outside the wineshop a legless man swung himself into the gutter where he held out a French infantry shako as a begging bowl.

The weeping women, and the sight of the beggar who had once marched proudly beneath his regiment's eagle, had depressed Sharpe. Nor did the pathetic paper signs pinned to the wineshop's walls help his mood. Frederickson translated the small, handwritten notices. 'Jean Blanchard, of the hundred and sixth of the line, seeks his wife, Marie, who used to live in the Fishmongers Street. If anyone knows of her please to tell the landlord.' The next was a plea from a mother to anyone who could inform her where her son might be. He had been a Sergeant of the Artillery, and had not been seen or heard of in three years. Another family, moved to Argentan, had left a notice for their three sons in case any should ever come back from the wars. Sharpe tried to count the small notices, but abandoned the effort at a hundred. He supposed the inns and church porches of Britain would be just as thick with such small appeals. Back on the battlefield Sharpe had never somehow thought that a rifle shot could ricochet so far.

'I suspect we shouldn't have come into the city.' Frederickson pushed his plate aside. The cheese was stale and the wine sour, but it was the stench of a city's despair that had blunted his hunger. 'Let's hope they give us an early ship.'

At three o'clock Sharpe and Frederickson returned to the Transport Board offices. They gave their names to a clerk who asked them to wait in an empty counting-house where dust lay thick on the tall desks. Beneath the window one of the two men who had been caught trying to join his wife was being strapped to a triangle for a flogging. Sharpe, remembering the day when he had been flogged, turned away, only to see that a tall, thin, and pale-eyed Provost Captain was staring at him from the counting house doorway.

'You're Major Sharpe, aren't you, sir?' the Captain asked.

'Yes.'

'And you're Frederickson?'

'Captain Frederickson,' Frederickson insisted.

'My name is Salmon.' Captain Salmon took a piece of paper from his pocket. 'I'm ordered to escort you both to the prefecture.'

'Escort us?' Sharpe reached for the piece of paper which was nothing more than a written confirmation of what Salmon had just said. The signature meant nothing to Sharpe.

'Those are my orders, sir.' Salmon spoke woodenly, but there was something in his tone of voice which sent a small shiver down Sharpe's spine. Or perhaps it was the realization that in the corridor outside the empty counting-house Salmon had a squad of provosts armed with muskets and bayonets.

'Are we under arrest?' Sharpe asked.

'No, sir,' but there was a very slight hesitation.

'Go on,' Sharpe ordered.

Salmon hesitated again, then shrugged. 'If you refuse to accompany me, sir, then I'm ordered to arrest you.'

For a moment Sharpe wondered if this was some practical joke being played by an old acquaintance, yet Salmon's demeanour suggested this was no jest. And clearly the summons presaged trouble. 'For Christ's sake,' Sharpe protested, 'we only kicked a pimp in the balls!'

'I don't know anything about that, sir.'

'Then what is this about?'

'I don't know, sir.'

'Then who wants us?' Sharpe insisted.

'I don't know, sir.' Salmon still spoke woodenly. 'You're both to bring your baggage, sir. All of it. I'll have your servants fetch it to the prefecture.'

'I don't have a servant,' Frederick said, 'so you'll have to fetch my baggage yourself, Salmon.'

Salmon ignored the gibe. 'If you're ready, gentlemen?'

'I need to speak to my servant first.' Sharpe leaned on a desk to show he would not move until Harper was fetched.

113

The Irishman was summoned and ordered to bring both officers' baggage to the prefecture. A provost would show Harper the way. As soon as Harper was gone, Sharpe and Frederickson were ordered to leave. They filed out of the room, down the stairs, and into the flogging yard where Salmon's grim squad closed about them. The two Riflemen might not have been under arrest, but it felt and looked just as if they were. The man being flogged gave a pathetic moan, then the drummer boys laid on again with their whips. Beyond the wall the man's wife and children sobbed.

'Welcome to the peacetime army, sir,' Frederickson said. Then they were marched away.

CHAPTER 5

'This tribunal,' Lieutenant-Colonel Wigram solemnly intoned, 'has been convened by and under the authority of the Adjutant-General.' Wigram was reading from a sheaf of papers and did not look up to catch the Riflemen's eyes as he read. He went on to recite his own commission to chair this tribunal, then the separate authorities for the presence of every other person in the room.

The room was a magnificent marbled chamber in Bordeaux's prefecture. Four tables had been arranged in the form of a hollow square in the very centre of the room. The top table, where the tribunal itself sat, was an extraordinary confection of carved and gilded legs on which was poised a slab of shining green malachite. To its left was a humble deal table where two clerks busily recorded the proceedings, while to the right was a table for the official observers and witnesses. Completing the square, and facing the magnificent malachite table, was another cheap deal table which had been reserved for Sharpe and Frederickson. The two Rifle officers had been fetched straight up the prefecture stairs and into the room. Captain Salmon had reported to Wigram that their baggage was being fetched, then had left. Sharpe and Frederickson had still not been given any indication why they had been summoned or why this pompous tribunal had been convened.

Sharpe gazed malevolently at Wigram who, apparently oblivious of the baleful look, droned on. Wigram was a man Sharpe had met before, and had disliked mightily.

He was a staff Colonel, a petty-minded and meticulous bore; a clerk in a Colonel's uniform. Wigram, Sharpe also remembered only too well, had been an avid supporter of Captain Bampfylde in the days before the Teste de Buch expedition had sailed. Surely this tribunal could have nothing to do with the man Sharpe had fought above a dawn-grey ocean? Yet that seemed only too possible, for one of the official observers on Sharpe's left was a Naval officer.

Wigram tonelessly introduced the other two members of the tribunal; both Lieutenant-Colonels from the Adjutant-General's department. One of the two was a uniformed lawyer, the other a provost officer. Both men had sallow and unfriendly faces. The Naval officer was introduced to Sharpe and Frederickson as Captain Harcourt. The second man at Harcourt's table was, strangely, a civilian French lawyer.

'The purpose of this tribunal,' Wigram at last reached the meat of his document, 'is to enquire into certain happenings at the Teste de Buch fort, in the Bay of Arcachon, during the month of January this year.'

Sharpe felt an initial pulse of relief. His conscience was entirely clear about the fight at the Teste de Buch fort, yet the relief did not last, for the formality of this tribunal was very chilling. Papers and pens had been provided on the Riflemen's table and Sharpe wrote a question for Frederickson, 'Why a French lawyer?'

'God alone knows,' Frederickson scribbled in reply.

'I shall begin,' Wigram selected a new sheaf of paper, 'by recapitulating the events which took place at the Teste de Buch fortress.'

It had been decided, Wigram informed the tribunal, to capture the fort in an attempt to deceive the enemy into thinking that a sea-borne invasion might follow. The expedition was under the overall command of Captain Horace Bampfylde, RN. The land troops were commanded by Major Richard Sharpe. Wigram looked up at that point and found himself staring into Sharpe's unfriendly eyes. The staff officer, who wore small round-lensed spectacles, quickly looked back to his paper.

The fort had been successfully captured, Wigram went on, though there was disagreement between Captain Bampfylde and Major Sharpe as to the exact manner in which that success had been achieved.

'Wrong,' Sharpe said, and his interruption so astonished the room that no one objected to it. 'Any disagreement between Captain Bampfylde and myself,' Sharpe said harshly, 'was ended by a duel. He lost.'

'I was about to point out,' Wigram said icily, 'that all the indications reveal that the predominant credit for the fort's capture must be given to you, Major Sharpe. Or is it that you wish this tribunal to investigate a clearly illegal occurrence of duelling?'

The Naval Captain smiled, then hastily looked more solemn as Wigram continued. Among those captured at the fort, Wigram said, had been an American Privateer, Captain Cornelius Killick. Killick had been promised good treatment by Captain William Frederickson and, when it appeared that promise was being broken by Bampfylde, Major Sharpe had released the American and his crew.

'Is that accurate, Major?' It was the provost Lieutenant-Colonel who asked the question.

'Yes,' Sharpe answered.

'Yes, sir,' Wigram corrected Sharpe.

'Yes, it is accurate,' Sharpe said belligerently.

There was a pause, and Wigram evidently decided not to press the issue.

Major Sharpe, Wigram continued, had subsequently marched inland with all the army troops, plus a contingent of Royal Marines under the command of Captain Neil Palmer.

'May one enquire,' it was the army lawyer who now interrupted Wigram, 'why Captain Palmer is not here to present his evidence?'

'Captain Palmer has been sent on a voyage to Van Dieman's Land,' Wigram replied.

'He would have been,' Frederickson said loudly enough for the whole room to hear.

The lawyer ignored Frederickson. 'We nevertheless have an affidavit from Captain Palmer?'

'There was no opportunity to secure one.' Wigram was clearly discomfited by the questions.

'There wouldn't have been,' Frederickson said sardonically.

Sharpe laughed aloud. He wondered how Bampfylde had so conveniently managed to have Palmer sent all the way to Australia, then he wondered how Bampfylde had managed to have this tribunal instituted. God damn the man! He had lost a duel, but had somehow continued the fight. How? The man had lied, had been a coward, yet here, in this captured prefecture, it was Sharpe and Frederickson who were being questioned.

During Sharpe's absence from the fort, Wigram pressed on with his account, the weather conditions were such that Captain Bampfylde deemed it sensible to take his ships off shore. Bampfylde's decision was made easier by intelligence which claimed that Major Sharpe and all his men had been defeated and captured. That intelligence later proved to be false.

Major Sharpe subsequently returned to the Teste de Buch fort, defended it against French attack, and finally escaped thanks to the intervention of the American, Killick. Wigram paused. 'Is that an accurate account, Major Sharpe?'

Sharpe thought for a few seconds, then shrugged. 'It's accurate.' In fact it had been surprisingly accurate. The nature of their quasi-arrest that afternoon had convinced

Sharpe that this tribunal had been established solely to exonerate Bampfylde, yet so far he had to admit that the proceedings had been scrupulously fair and the facts not at all helpful to Bampfylde's reputation. Was it possible that this tribunal was establishing the facts to present at Bampfylde's court-martial?

Subsequently, Wigram recounted, Captain Bampfylde had accused Major Sharpe of accepting a bribe from the American, Killick. Sharpe, hearing that accusation for the first time, sat up, but Wigram anticipated his outrage by asking whether any evidence had been produced to substantiate the allegation.

'None at all,' Captain Harcourt said firmly.

Sharpe was sitting bolt upright now. Was this tribunal indeed to be Bampfylde's doom? Frederickson must have felt the same hope, for he swiftly drew a sketch of a Naval officer dangling in a noose from a scaffold. He pushed the sketch to Sharpe, who smiled.

Frederickson's sketched prognostication of Bampfylde's fate seemed accurate, for Harcourt was now invited to offer the tribunal a summary of the Navy's own investigation. That investigation, held at Portsmouth at the beginning of April, had found Captain Bampfylde derelict in his duty. Specifically he was blamed for his precipitate abandonment of the captured fort, and for not returning when the storm abated to seek news of the shore party.

'So court-martial him,' Sharpe offered harshly.

Harcourt glanced at the Riflemen, then shrugged. 'It was decided that, for the good of the service, there will be no court-martial. You may be assured, though, that Captain Bampfylde has left the Navy, and that he still has difficulty with his bowels.'

The small jesting reference to the duel passed unnoticed. If there was to be no court-martial, Sharpe wondered, then why in hell were they here? The Navy had decided to hush up an embarrassing incident, yet this army tribunal was re-opening the sack of snakes and apparently doing it with the Navy's connivance.

It would be assumed, Wigram continued, from the evidence already offered to the tribunal, that Captain Bampfylde's accusations against Major Sharpe were groundless. The army had indeed already decided as much. Major Sharpe had been faced by a French brigade commanded by the notorious General Calvet, which brigade Major Sharpe had roundly defeated. Nothing but praise could attach itself to such an action. Captain Harcourt, who seemed rather sympathetic to the two Riflemen, applauded by slapping the table top. The French lawyer, who could hardly be supposed to share Harcourt's sympathy, nevertheless beamed happily.

'Perhaps they want to give us both Presentation swords,' Frederickson wrote on his piece of paper.

'Now, however,' Wigram's voice took on a firmer tone, 'fresh evidence has been received at the Adjutant-General's office.' Wigram laid down the papers from which he had been reading and looked owlishly to his right. 'Monsieur Roland? Perhaps you would be so kind as to summarise that evidence?'

The room was suddenly expectant and quiet. Sharpe and Frederickson did not move. Even the two clerks, who had been busily writing, became entirely still. The French lawyer, as if enjoying this moment of notoriety, slowly pushed back his chair before rising to his feet.

Monsieur Roland was a fleshy, happy-looking man. He was entirely bald, all but for two luxurious side-whiskers that gave his benevolent face an air of jollity. He looked like a family man, utterly trustworthy, who would be happiest in his own drawing room with his children about him. When he spoke he did so in fluent English. He thanked the tribunal for the courtesy shown in allowing him to speak. He understood that the recent events in Europe might lead ignorant men to suppose that no Frenchman could ever again be trusted, but Monsieur Roland represented the law, and the law transcended all boundaries. He thus spoke, Roland said, with the authority of the law, which authority sprang from a ruthless regard for the truth. Then, more prosaically, he said that he was a lawyer employed by the French Treasury, and that therefore he had the honour to represent the interests of the newly restored King of France, Louis XVIII.

'Might one therefore presume,' the lawyer from the Adjutant-General's department had a silky, almost feline voice, 'that until a few weeks ago, Monsieur, you were perforce an advocate for the Emperor?'

Roland gave a small bow and a bland smile. 'Indeed, Monsieur, I had that honour also.'

The tribunal's members smiled to demonstrate that they understood Roland's apparently effortless change of allegiance. The smiles suggested that the tribunal was composed of worldly men who were above such petty things as the coming and going of emperors and kings.

'In December last year,' Roland had arranged his papers, and could now begin his peroration, 'the Emperor was persuaded to contemplate the possibility of defeat. He did not do this willingly, but was pressed by his family; chief among them his brother, Joseph, whom you gentlemen will remember as the erstwhile King of Spain.' There was a delicacy in Roland's tone which mocked Joseph Bonaparte and flattered the British. Wigram, whose contribution to Joseph's downfall had been to amass paperwork, smiled modestly to acknowledge the compliment. Sharpe's face was unreadable. Frederickson was drawing two Rifle officers.

'The Emperor,' Roland hooked his thumbs behind his coat's lapels, 'decided that, should he be defeated, he might perhaps sail to the United States where he was assured of a warm welcome. I cannot say that he was enthusiastic about such a plan, but it was nevertheless urged upon him by his brother who alarmed the Emperor by tales of the ignominy that the family would suffer if they were forced to surrender to their enemies. Happily the generosity of those enemies has made such prophecies worthless,' again Roland had flattered his hosts, 'and it is now evident that the Emperor may confidently rely on his victors to treat him with a proper dignity.'

'Indeed.' Wigram could not forbear the pompous interruption.

Frederickson, who had always had a great facility at sketching, was now surrounding his two Rifle officers with a battery of field artillery. All the guns faced the two Greenjackets.

Roland paused to drink water. 'Nevertheless,' he began again, 'at Joseph's instigation, preparations were made for an emergency flight from France. Thus, at all times, a travelling coach stood prepared for the Emperor. In its baggage were clothes, uniforms, and decorations. However, the Emperor understood that the carriage could not be too heavily burdened, or else its weight would impede his flight. He therefore arranged, and in the most solemn secrecy, to have his heavy baggage stored at a coastal fort where, in the event of flight, it could be swiftly loaded on board a ship and carried to the United States of America. The officer chosen to convey that baggage to the Atlantic coast was a Colonel Maillot. I have here copies of his orders, signed by the Emperor himself.' Roland picked up the sheets of paper and carried them to the three members of the tribunal.

'Where is this Colonel now?' the English lawyer asked sharply. Despite his unfriendly face, the lawyer seemed assiduous to ask any question that might help Sharpe and Frederickson.

'Colonel Maillot is being sought,' Roland replied suavely. 'Sadly the present confusion in France makes his whereabouts a mystery. It is even possible, alas, that Colonel Maillot was killed in the last few weeks of the fighting.'

There was silence as the tribunal scanned the papers. Frederickson, abandoning his gloomy drawing, wrote a quick question. 'Have you heard of Maillot?'

'No,' Sharpe scrawled in reply.

Roland had returned to his own table and picked up another sheet of paper. 'Colonel Maillot delivered the baggage to a trusted officer here in Bordeaux. That officer was a Major named Pierre Ducos.'

Sharpe hissed a curse under his breath. Now he understood why he was in this room. He did not know how Ducos had worked this, but Sharpe knew who his enemies were, and none was more remorseless than Pierre Ducos. Sharpe felt ambushed. He had been prepared to fight down the clumsy and untruthful attack of the disgraced Captain Bampfylde, and all the time it had been the far more dangerous, and far more cunning, Pierre Ducos who had been working for his downfall. 'I know Ducos,' he wrote.

'Major Ducos,' Roland went blandly on, 'conveyed the baggage in great secrecy to the Teste de Buch fort which covers the seaward entrance of the Bassin d'Arcachon.'

'He's lying!' Sharpe interrupted.

'Quiet!' Wigram slapped the table.

'It was that fortress, of course,' Roland was quite unmoved by Sharpe's interruption, 'which, thanks to the great gallantry of Major Sharpe,' here Roland bowed slightly towards the angry Sharpe, 'was captured shortly after the baggage had been conveyed thither. The baggage consisted of four large wooden crates that had been concealed inside the fortress.'

'How were the crates concealed?' Frederickson asked, but in such a respectful tone that no one reprimanded him for interrupting.

'I have here Major Ducos's report,' Roland held up the

sheets of paper, 'which reveals that the four wooden crates were bricked up in the fort's main magazine. The work was done by men entirely loyal to the Emperor. None of the fort's garrison was present when the work was done, and only the fort's commandant was apprised of the existence of the baggage. The tribunal already has copies of the commandant's report, and that of Major Ducos, but I now submit those officers' original documents.'

The papers were duly handed across, and again there was silence as the tribunal perused them. It was the Adjutant-General's lawyer who broke the silence with a petulant complaint that the Commandant's handwriting was almost illegible.

'Commandant Lassan explains in the final paragraph of his report that he lost two fingers of his right hand during the defence of the fort,' Roland excused the almost indecipherable scrawl, 'but you will nevertheless discover that your copy is an exact transcription of his words.'

'I assume,' the Adjutant-General's lawyer aligned the edges of the papers in front of him, 'that, if it should prove necessary, these officers can give evidence?'

'Indeed,' Roland bowed acknowledgement of the point, 'but they were unwilling to travel into British-held territory at this moment.'

'We are fortunate,' Wigram said fulsomely, 'that you yourself showed no such reluctance, Monsieur Roland.'

Roland bowed at the compliment, then explained that he had travelled with a party of British officers to London where he had taken this matter to the Judge Advocate General in Whitehall. That official had ordered the Adjutant-General to establish an investigative tribunal, and ordered the Royal Navy to bring Monsieur Roland to Bordeaux. The Frenchman picked up his papers again. 'You will notice, gentlemen, that on the final page of Commandant Lassan's account, he states that when the fortress was finally reoccupied by the French, the baggage was gone.' Roland paused to look at his copy of the report. 'You will further note from Commandant Lassan's testimony that before the fort was evacuated by the British he saw heavy objects being transported from the seaward bastions to the American's vessel.'

The Adjutant-General's lawyer frowned. 'Do we have any other evidence which confirms that the baggage was hidden in the fortress? What about this General,' he leafed through his papers, 'Calvet. He eventually reoccupied the fort, so wouldn't he have known about it?'

'General Calvet was never informed of its presence,' Roland said, 'the Emperor's instructions were adamant that as few men as possible were to know of his preparations for exile. France was still fighting, gentlemen, and it would not have served the Emperor well if men had thought he was already contemplating defeat and flight.'

'But Calvet's evidence would be instructive,' the English lawyer insisted. 'He could, for instance, confirm whether baggage was indeed removed to the American's ship?'

Roland paused, then shrugged. 'General Calvet, gentlemen, has proclaimed an unswerving loyalty to the deposed Emperor. I doubt whether he would co-operate with this tribunal.'

'I would have thought we had quite sufficient evidence anyway,' Wigram said.

Roland smiled his thanks for Wigram's help, then continued. 'The inference of Commandant Lassan's report, gentlemen, is that the Emperor's baggage was taken by the British forces under Major Sharpe's command. They had every right to do so, of course, for the baggage was properly a seizure of war.'

'Then why are you here?' the Provost officer asked in a pained voice.

Roland smiled. 'Permit me to remind you that I am here on behalf of his Most Christian Majesty, Louis XVIII. It is the opinion of His Majesty's legal advisers, myself among them, that if the seizure of the imperial baggage was a legitimate act of war, and as such was duly reported to the proper authorities, then it now belongs to the government of Great Britain. If, however,' and here Roland turned to look at the two Riflemen, 'the seizure was for private gain, and was never so reported, then our opinion holds that the said baggage is now the property of the Emperor's political successor, which is the French Crown, and that the French Crown would be justified in any attempts to recover it.'

Lieutenant-Colonel Wigram dipped a quill in ink. 'Perhaps it would help the tribunal, Monsieur Roland, if you were to tell us the contents of the Emperor's baggage?'

'With the greatest pleasure, Colonel.' Roland picked up another sheet of paper. 'There were some personal items. These were not inventoried properly, for they were packed in great haste, but we know there were some uniforms, decorations, portraits, snuff boxes, swords, candlesticks, and other keepsakes of a sentimental nature. There was also a valise of monogrammed small clothes.' He mentioned the last item with a deprecating smile, and was rewarded with appreciative laughter. Roland was making his revelations with a lawyer's innate skill, though in truth the clumsiest of speakers could have held the room spellbound. For years the Emperor Napoleon had been an apparently superhuman enemy endowed with an exotic and fascinating evil, yet now, in this magnificent room, the tribunal was hearing from a man who could provide them with an intimate glimpse of that extraordinary being. 'Some of these possessions,' Roland went on, 'belonged to Joseph Bonaparte, but the bulk of the baggage belonged to the Emperor, and the greatest part of that baggage was coin. There were twenty wooden boxes, five in each crate, and each box contained ten thousand gold francs.'

Roland paused to let each man work out the fabulous sum. 'As I said earlier,' he went on blandly, 'His Most Christian Majesty will have no claim upon this property if it should transpire that it was a seizure of war. If, however, the baggage is still unaccounted for, we shall take a most strenuous interest in its recovery.'

'Jesus Christ,' Frederickson hissed. He had written the sum of two hundred thousand francs under his drawing of the beleaguered Riflemen, and now, beside it, he wrote its crude equivalent in English pounds, £89,000, os, od. It was a fabulous sum, even dwarfing Sharpe's fortune. Frederickson seemed dissatisfied with that simple total, for he went on feverishly totting up other figures.

Wigram's twin lenses turned on Sharpe. 'I believe I am correct in saying that you reported no capture of money on your return from the Teste de Buch expedition, Major?'

'I did not, because there was none.'

'If there had been,' the provost Lieutenant-Colonel broke in, 'you would agree that it would have been your duty to hand it over to the competent authorities?'

'Of course,' Sharpe said, though he had never known a single soldier actually to surrender such windfalls of enemy gold. Neither Sharpe nor Harper had declared the fortunes they had taken from the French baggage at Vitoria.

'But you are insisting that you did not discover any money in the fort?' the provost pressed Sharpe.

'We found no money,' Sharpe said firmly.

'And you would deny,' the Lieutenant-Colonel's tone was sharper now, 'that you divided such a spoil with the American, Killick, and that, indeed, your only motive for delaying your departure from the fort, which delay, I must say, occasioned many deaths among your men, was solely so that you could make arrangements to remove the gold?'

'That's a lie.' Sharpe was standing now.

Frederickson touched a hand to Sharpe's arm, as if to calm him. 'By my reckonings,' Frederickson said calmly, 'that amount of gold would weigh somewhat over six tons.

Arc you suggesting that two companies of Riflemen and a handful of Marines somehow managed to remove six tons of gold, their own wounded men, and all their personal baggage while they were under enemy fire?'

'That is precisely what is being suggested,' the provost said icily.

'Have you ever been under fire?' Frederickson enquired just as icily.

Wigram, disliking the twist that the questions were taking, slapped the table and stared at Frederickson. 'Did you enrich yourself with captured gold at the Teste de Buch fort, Captain?'

'I emphatically deny doing any such thing, sir,' Frederickson spoke with dignity, 'and can state with certain knowledge that Major Sharpe is equally innocent.'

'Are you, Major?' Wigram asked Sharpe.

'I took no money.' Sharpe tried to match Frederickson's calm dignity.

Wigram's face flickered with a smile, as though he was about to make a very telling point. 'Yet not a month ago, Major, your wife withdrew more than eighteen thousand pounds . . .'

'God damn you!' For a second the whole tribunal thought that Sharpe was about to draw his big sword, climb the table, and cause carnage. 'God damn you!' Sharpe shouted again. 'You have the temerity to suggest I'd let men die for greed and you have spied on my wife! If you were a man, Wigram, I'd call you out now and I'd fillet you.' Such was the force of Sharpe's words, and such the anger evident on his face, that the tribunal was cowed. Monsieur Roland frowned, not with disapproval, but at the thought of facing a man like Sharpe in battle. Frederickson, sitting beside Sharpe, watched the faces of the aghast tribunal and believed that his friend had entirely pricked the ridiculous charges with his blazing anger. Wigram, accustomed to the servility of clerks, could say nothing.

128

Then the tall gilded door opened.

Captain Salmon, oblivious of the room's charged atmosphere, carried in a white cloth bag that he laid on the table in front of Colonel Wigram. He whispered something to the Colonel, then, with the obsequious step of a servant, left the room.

Wigram, with hands that almost trembled, opened the white bag. Out of it he drew Sharpe's telescope. He peered myopically at the engraved plate, then, steeling himself for the confrontation, looked up at the Rifleman. 'If you are innocent, Major, then how do you explain your possession of this glass?'

'I've owned it for months,' Sharpe snapped.

'I can vouch for that,' Frederickson said.

Wigram handed the telescope to Monsieur Roland. 'Perhaps, Monsieur, you will translate the inscription for the benefit of the tribunal?'

The Frenchman took the telescope, peered at the plate inset on the outer barrel, then spoke the translation aloud. 'To Joseph, King of Spain and the Indies, from his brother, Napoleon, Emperor of France.'

There was a murmur in the room. Wigram stilled the sound with a further question. 'Is this the sort of personal belonging, Monsieur, which the Emperor or his brother might have stored in their baggage?'

'Indeed,' Roland said.

Wigram paused, then shrugged. 'The tribunal should be apprised that the glass was discovered in Major Sharpe's baggage during an authorized search that was done on my orders during the last hour.' Wigram, buoyed up by the evidence of the telescope, had regained his former confidence and now stared directly at Sharpe. 'It is not the business of this tribunal to be a judge of the facts, but merely to decide whether a competent court-martial should be given those facts to judge. The tribunal will now make that decision, and will inform you of its findings at ten o'clock tomorrow morning. Until that hour you are forbidden to leave this building. You will discover that Captain Salmon has made adequate billeting arrangements.'

Frederickson collated his sketches and notes. 'Are we under arrest, sir?'

Wigram paused. 'Not yet, Captain. But you are under military discipline, and therefore ordered to remain in confinement until your fate is announced tomorrow morning.'

The other officers in the room did not look at either Rifleman. It had been the discovery of the telescope that had plunged their certainty of Sharpe's innocence into an assurance of the Rifleman's guilt. Sharpe stared at them one by one, but they would not look back.

Frederickson plucked Sharpe's arm towards the door. Captain Salmon and a half dozen of his men waited on the landing outside. Sharpe and Frederickson might not be prisoners, but it was clearly only a matter of time before they were formally charged and their swords were taken away.

Salmon was embarrassed. 'There's a room set aside for you, sir,' he said to Sharpe. 'Your servant's waiting there.'

'We're not under arrest,' Sharpe challenged him.

'The room's upstairs, sir,' Salmon said doggedly, and the presence of his provosts was enough to persuade the two Riflemen to accompany him to the upper floor and into a room that looked out to the city's main square. A very indignant Patrick Harper waited there. There was also a chamber pot, two wooden chairs, and a table on which was a loaf of bread, a plate of cheese, and a tin jug of water. There was a pile of blankets and a heap of baggage that Harper had fetched from the quayside. There were three packs, three canteens, but no weapons or ammunition. Salmon hesitated, as though he wanted to stay in the room with the three Riflemen, but a glare from Harper made the Captain back abruptly into the corridor.

'That bastard of a provost searched your packs.' Harper was still smarting under that indignity. 'I tried to stop him, so I did, but he threatened me with a flogging.'

'They took my rifle?' Sharpe asked.

'It's in the bloody guardroom downstairs, sir.' Harper was incensed that he, like Sharpe, had been disarmed. 'They've got my rifle and gun there as well. Even my bayonet!' Sharpe and Frederickson, because they had not been officially placed under arrest, had been allowed to keep their swords, but those were now their only weapons.

'I hate provosts,' Frederickson said mildly.

'So what the hell's happening, sir?' Harper asked Sharpe.

'We're only accused of stealing half the bloody gold in France. Jesus Christ! It's bloody madness!'

'Indeed it is.' Frederickson was placidly cutting the loaf into big chunks.

'I'm sorry, William.'

'Why should you apologize to me?'

'Because this is my battle. Goddamn bloody Ducos!'

Frederickson shrugged. 'They could hardly ignore me. They must have known I'd testify to your ignorance, which would be embarrassing for the authorities, so it's much simpler to implicate me in the crime as well. Besides, if there had been that much gold in the fort, I'd have undoubtedly helped you to steal it.' He cut the cheese with his knife. 'Pity about the telescope, though. It's just the corroborative evidence they needed.'

'They need the gold,' Sharpe said, 'and it never existed!'

'It existed all right, but not in the fort.' Frederickson frowned. 'I've no doubt there'll be a battle-royal between Paris and London as to who the money really belongs to, but the one thing they'll agree on is that we've got a damned good share of it. And who's to disprove that?'

'Killick?' Sharpe suggested.

131

Frederickson shook his head. 'The word of a confessed American pirate against a French government lawyer?'

'Ducos, then,' Sharpe said savagely, 'and I'll rip his damned bowels out.'

'Either Ducos,' Frederickson agreed, 'or the Commandant,' he looked at his notes to find the Commandant's name, 'Lassan. The problem is that it will be very difficult to find either man if we're under arrest, and I would suggest to you that we will very soon be placed under arrest.'

Sharpe went to the window and stared at the ships' masts which showed above the rooftops. 'We've got to get the hell out of here.'

'Getting the hell out of here,' Frederickson spoke very mildly, 'is called desertion.' Both officers stared at each other, appalled at the enormity of what they proposed. Desertion would invite a court-martial, loss of rank, and imprisonment, but exactly the same fate would attend them if they were found guilty of stealing the Emperor's gold and concealing it from their masters. 'And there is rather a lot of gold at stake,' Frederickson added gently, 'and unlike you, I'm a poor man.'

'You can't come.' Sharpe turned on Harper.

'Mary, Mother of God, and why not?'

'Because if you desert, and are caught, they'll shoot you. They'll only cashier us, because we're officers, but they'll shoot you.'

'I'm coming anyway.'

'For God's sake, Patrick! I don't mind taking the risk for myself, and Mr Frederickson's in the same boat as I am, but I won't have you . . .'

'And why don't you just save your bloody breath?' Harper asked, then, after a pause, 'sir?'

Frederickson smiled. 'I wasn't enjoying peace much anyway. So let's go back to war, shall we?'

'War?' Sharpe stared back at the ships' masts. He should have been on board one of those vessels, ready for the voyage up the Garonne estuary, across Biscay, around Ushant, and so home to Jane.

'Because if we're to escape this problem,' Frederickson said softly, 'then we'll have to fight, and we're rather better at fighting when we're armed and free. So let's get the hell out of here, find Ducos or Lassan, and make some mischief. And some money.'

Sharpe stared west. Somewhere out there, beneath the sinking sun, was an enemy who still skulked and schemed. So his reunion with Jane must wait, and peace must wait, for a last fight must still be fought. But after that, he prayed, he would find his peace in the English countryside. 'We'll go tonight,' he said, but he suddenly wished to the depths of his heart that he was sailing home instead. But an enemy had decreed otherwise, so Sharpe's war was not yet done.

CHAPTER 6

The Château Lassan was in Normandy. It was called a château for it had once had the pretensions of a fortress, and was still the home of a noble family, yet in truth it was now little more than a large moated farmhouse, though it was undeniably a very pleasant farmhouse. The two storeys of the main wing were built of grey Caen stone that had been quarried and dressed fifty years before the Conqueror had sailed for England. In the fifteenth century, and as a result of a fortunate marriage, the lord of the manor had added a second wing at right angles to the first. The new wing, even now in 1814 it was still known as the 'new' wing, was pierced by a high arched gate and surmounted by a crenellated tower. A private chapel with deep lancet windows completed the château that was surrounded by a moat which also protected an acre of land that had once been gracious with lawns and flowers.

It had been many years since the moat had defended the house against an enemy's attack and so the drawbridge had been left permanently down and its heavy-geared windlass had been taken away to make the upper part of a cider press. Two further wooden bridges were put across the moat; one led from the château to the dairy and the other gave quick access from house to orchards. The old moat-encircled garden became a farmyard; a compost heap mouldered warm by the chapel wall, chickens and ducks scrabbled for feed, and two hogs fattened where once the lords and ladies had strolled on the smoothly scythed lawn. The 'new' wing, all but for the chapel, had become farm buildings where horses and oxen were stabled, wains were stored, and apples heaped next to the press.

The Revolution had left the Château Lassan unscathed, though its master, dutifully and humbly serving his King in Paris, had gone to the guillotine solely because he possessed an ancient title. The local Committee of Public Safety had visited the homely château and tried to summon a fashionable and bloodthirsty enthusiasm to pillage the dead Count's belongings, but the family was well-liked and, after much harmless bluster, the Committee had muttered an apology to the dowager Countess and contented themselves with stealing five barrels of newly pressed cider and a wagon-load of the old Count's wine. The new Count, an earnest eighteen-year-old, was troubled by his conscience into the belief that the disasters of France were truly the result of social inequalities, and so told the local Committee that he would renounce his title and join the new Republic's army. The Committee, privately astonished that anyone should renounce the privileges they so publicly despised, applauded the decision, though the dowager Countess was seen to purse her lips with disapproval. Her daughter, just seven years old, did not understand any of it. There had been five other children, but all had died in infancy. Only the eldest, Henri, and the youngest, Lucille, had survived.

Now, twenty-one years later, the wars that had begun against the Republic and continued against the Empire were at last over. The Dowager Countess still lived, and liked to sit where the sun was trapped by the junction of the château's two wings and where roses grew clear up to the moss which grew on the château's stone roof. The old lady shared the château with her daughter. Lucille had been married to a General's son, but within two months of the wedding her husband had died in the snows of Russia and Lucille Castineau had returned to her mother as a childless widow.

Now, in the peace that came after Easter, the son had come home as well. Henri, Comte de Lassan, had walked up the lane and crossed the drawbridge, just as if he was returning from a stroll, and his mother had wept with joy that her soldier son had survived, and that night, just as if he had never been away, Henri took the top place at the supper table. He had quietly and unfussily folded his blue uniform away in the pious hope that he would never again be forced to wear it. He said grace before the meal, then commented that the apple blossom looked thin in the orchards.

'We need to graft new stock on to the trees,' his mother said.

'Only there isn't any money,' Lucille added.

'You must borrow some, Henri,' the Dowager Countess said. 'They wouldn't lend to two widows like us, but they'll lend to a man.'

'We have nothing to sell?'

'Very little.' The Dowager sat very straight-backed. 'And what little is left, Henri, must be preserved. It is not right that a Comte de Lassan be without family silver or good horses.'

Henri smiled. 'The titles of the old nobility were abolished over twenty years ago, Maman. I am now Monsieur Henri Lassan, nothing more.'

The Dowager sniffed disapproval. She had seen the fashions of French nomenclature come and go. Henri, Comte de Lassan had become Citoyen Lassan, then Lieutenant Lassan, then Capitaine Lassan, and now he claimed to be plain Monsieur Lassan. That, in the Dowager's opinion, was nonsense. Her son was the Count of this manor, lord of its estates and heir to eight centuries of noble history. No government in Paris could change that.

Yet, despite his mother, Henri refused to use his title and disliked it when the villagers bowed to him and called him 'my Lord'. One of those villagers had once been on the Committee of Public Safety, but those heady days of equality were long gone and the ageing revolutionary was now as eager as any man to doff his cap to the Comte de Lassan.

'Why don't you please Maman?' Lucille asked her brother. It was a Sunday afternoon soon after Henri's return and, while the Dowager Countess took her afternoon nap, the brother and sister had crossed one of the wooden bridges and were walking between the scanty blossomed apple trees towards the millstream that lay at the end of the château's orchards.

'To call myself Count would be a sin of pride.'

'Henri!' Lucille said reproachfully, though she knew that no reproach would sway her gentle, but very stubborn brother. She found it hard to imagine Henri as a soldier, though it had been clear from his letters that he had taken his military responsibilities with great seriousness, and, reading between the lines, that he had been popular with his men. Yet always, in every letter, Henri had spoken of his ambition to become a priest. When the war is over, he would write, he would take orders.

The Dowager Countess decried, disapproved of, and even despised such an ambition. Henri was nearly forty years old, and it was high time that he married and had a son who would carry the Lassan name. That was the important thing; that a new Count should be born, and on Henri's return the Dowager quickly invited Madame Pellemont and her unmarried daughter to visit the château, and thereafter harried Henri with frequent and tactless hints about Mademoiselle Pellemont who, though no beauty, was malleable and placid. 'She has broad hips, Henri,' the Dowager said enticingly. 'She'll spit out babies like a sow farrowing a litter.'

The Dowager did not extend her desire for grandchildren to her daughter, for if Lucille were to marry again her children would not bear the family name, nor would any son of Lucille's be a Count of Lassan. It was the survival of that name and lineage that the Dowager wanted, and so Lucille's marriage prospects were of no interest to the Dowager. In fact two men had proposed marriage to the widow Castineau, but Lucille did not want to risk the unhappiness of losing love again. 'I shall grow old and crotchety,' she told her brother, though the last quality seemed an unlikely fate, for Lucille had an innate vivacity that gave her face an illuminating smile. She had grey eyes, light brown hair, and a long lantern jaw. She thought herself plain, and was certainly no great beauty, yet the spark in her soul was bright, and the man who had married her had counted himself to be among the most fortunate of husbands.

'Will you marry again?' her brother asked as they walked down to the millstream.

'No, Henri. I shall just moulder away here. I like it here, and I'm kept busy. I like being busy.' Lucille was an early riser, and rarely rested in daylight. When so many men had been away at the wars it had been Lucille who ran the farm, the cider press, the mill, the dairy, and the château. She supervised the lambing, she raised calves, and fattened hogs for the slaughter. She mended the centuries old flax sheets on which the family still slept, she churned butter, made cheese, and eked out the family's tiny income in an effort to preserve the estate. She had been forced to sell two fields, and much of the old silver, yet the château had survived for Henri's return. Henri thought that the work had worn his sister out, for she was thin and pale, but Lucille denied the accusation. 'It isn't the work that's so tiring, but money. There's never enough. We have to mend the tower roof, we need new apple trees.' Lucille sighed. 'We need everything. Even the chairs in the kitchen need mending, and I can't afford a carpenter.'

They came to the millrace and sat on the stone wall

above the glistening rush of water. Henri had been carrying a musket which he now propped against the wall. His coat pockets were weighed down with two heavy pistols. He disliked carrying the weapons, but the French countryside was infested with armed bands of men who had either deserted from the Emperor's armies or else had been discharged and had no home or work. Such men often attacked villagers, and had even ransacked small towns. No such brigands had yet been seen near the château, but Henri Lassan would take no chances and thus carried the weapons whenever he left the safe area inside the moat. The château's few farmworkers were also armed, and the village knew that if the bell above the château's chapel tolled then there was danger abroad and they should herd their cattle into the château's yard.

'Not that I can promise a very successful defence,' Henri now said ruefully. 'I wasn't very good at defending my fortress.' He had commanded the Teste de Buch fort and, day after day, year after year, he had watched the empty sea and thought the war was passing him by until, in the very last weeks of the fighting, the British Riflemen had come from the landward side to bring horror to his small command.

Lucille heard the sadness in her brother's voice. 'Was it awful?'

'Yes,' Henri said simply, then fell silent so that Lucille thought he would say no more, but after a moment Henri shrugged and began to speak of that one lost fight. He told her about the Englishmen in green, and how they had appeared in his fortress as though from nowhere. 'Big men,' he said, 'and scarred. They fought like demons. They loved to fight. I could tell that from their faces.' He shuddered. 'And they destroyed all my books, all of them. They took years to collect, and afterwards there wasn't one left.'

Lucille twisted a campion's stalk about her finger. 'The

English.' She said it disparagingly, as though it explained everything.

'They are a brutal people.' Henri had never known an Englishman, yet the prejudice against the island race was bred into his Norman bone. There was a tribal memory of steel-helmeted archers and mounted men-at-arms who crossed the channel to burn barns, steal women, and slaughter children. To Henri and Lucille the English were a rapacious and brawling race of Protestants whom God had seen fit to place just across the water. 'I sometimes dream of those Riflemen,' Henri Lassan now said.

'They failed to kill you,' Lucille said as if to encourage her brother's self-esteem.

'At the end they could have killed me. I waded into the sea, straight for their leader. He's a famous soldier, and I thought I might expiate my failure if I killed him, or pay for it if I died myself, but he would not fight. He lowered his sword. He could have killed me, but he did not.'

'So there's some good in the green men?'

'I think he just despised me.' Henri Lassan shrugged. 'His name is Sharpe, and I have the most ridiculous nightmare that one day he will come back to finish me off. That is stupid, I know, but I cannot shake the notion away.' He tried to smile the foolishness away, but Lucille could tell that somehow this Sharpe had become her brother's private demon; the man who had shamed Lassan as a soldier, and Lucille wondered that a man who wanted to be a priest nevertheless should also worry that he had not been a great soldier. She tried to tell her brother that the failure did not matter, that he was a better man than any soldier.

'I hope I will be a better man,' Henri said.

'As a priest?' Lucille touched on the argument which their mother pursued so doggedly.

'I've thought of little else these past years.' And, he

could have added, he had prepared himself for little else over these past years. He had read, studied, and argued with the priest at Arcachon; always testing the soundness of his own faith and always finding it strong. The alternative to the priesthood was to become the master of this château, but Henri Lassan did not relish the task. The old building needed a fortune spent on its walls and roof. It would be best, he thought privately, if the place was sold and if his mother would live close to the abbey in Caen, but he knew he could never persuade the Dowager of that sensible solution.

'You don't sound utterly certain that you want to be a priest,' Lucille said.

Henri shrugged. 'There's been a Lassan in this house for eight hundred years.' He stopped, unable to argue against the numbing weight of that tradition, and even feeling some sympathy for his mother's fervent wishes for the family's future. But if the price of that future was Mademoiselle Pellemont? He shuddered, then looked at his watch. 'Maman will be awake soon.'

They stood. Lassan glanced once more at the far hills, but nothing untoward moved among the orchards, and no green men threatened on the high ridge where the elms, beeches and hornbeams grew. The château was calm, at peace, and safe, so Henri picked up his loaded musket and walked his sister home.

*　　*　　*

'They're scared, you see,' Harper explained, and, as if to prove his point, he wafted the chamber-pot towards the provost sentries who guarded the corridor outside the room where Sharpe and Frederickson waited.

The provost recoiled from the chamber-pot, then protested when Harper offered to remove the strip of cloth which covered its contents.

'You can't expect gently-born officers to live in a room

with the stench of shit,' Harper said, 'so I have to empty it.'

'Go to the yard. Don't bloody loiter about.' It was the Provost Sergeant who snapped the orders at Harper.

'You're a grand man, Sergeant.'

'Get the hell out of here. And hurry, man!' The Sergeant watched the big Irishman go down the stairs. 'Bloody Irish, and a bloody Rifleman,' he said to no one in particular, 'two things I hate most.'

The windowless corridor was lit by two glass-fronted lanterns which threw the shadows of the three guards long across the floorboards. Laughter and loud voices echoed from the prefecture's ground floor where the highest officials of the Transport Board were giving a dinner. A clock at the foot of the deep stairwell struck half past eight.

More than fifteen minutes passed before Harper came whistling up the stairs. He carried the empty chamber-pot in one hand. Inside the pot were three empty wine glasses, while on his shoulder was a sizeable wooden keg that he first dropped on to the landing, then rolled towards the officers' doorway with his right foot. He nodded a cheerful greeting to the Provost Sergeant. 'A gentleman downstairs sent this up to the officers, Sergeant.'

The Provost Sergeant stepped into the path of the rolling keg which he checked with a boot. 'Who sent it?'

'Now how would I be knowing that?' Harper, when it pleased him, could easily play the role of a vague-witted Irishman. That such a role, however it distorted the truth, nevertheless suited the prejudice of men like the Provost Sergeant only made it the more effective. 'He didn't give me his name, nor did he, but he said he had a sympathy for the poor gentlemen. He said he'd never met them, but he was sorry for them. Mind you, Sergeant, the gentleman was more than a little drunk himself, which always makes a man sympathetic. Isn't that the truth? It's a pity our wives don't drink more, so it is.'

'Shut your face.' The Sergeant tipped the cask on to its end, then worked the bung loose. He was rewarded with the rich smell of good brandy. He thrust the bung home. 'I've got orders not to allow anyone to communicate with the officers.'

'You wouldn't deny them a wee drink now, would you?'

'Shut your bloody face.' The Sergeant stood, reached for the chamber-pot, and took out the three glasses. 'Get inside, and tell your damned officers that if they're thirsty they should drink water.'

'Yes, Sergeant. Whatever you say, Sergeant. Thank you, Sergeant.' Harper edged past the keg, then darted through the door as though he truly feared the Provost Sergeant's wrath. Once inside the room he closed the door, then grinned at Sharpe. 'As easy as stealing a fleece off a lamb's back, sir. One keg of brandy safely delivered. The bastards just couldn't wait to take it off me.'

'Let's just hope they drink it,' Frederickson said.

'In two hours,' Harper said confidently, 'those three will be dancing drunk. I even thought to bring them some glasses.'

'How much did the brandy cost?' Sharpe asked.

'All you gave me, sir, but the fellow in the kitchens said it was the very best.' Harper, properly pleased with himself, went on to deliver the rest of his news. There were only three guards on the top landing, and he had seen no other sentries till he reached the ground floor where he saw a sergeant and two men in the guardroom by the front door. 'But they weren't provosts, sir, so they mayn't be any trouble to us. I said hello to them, and saw our guns in there.' There were another two sentries in the town square beyond the front door. 'They're giving a grand dinner downstairs, so there's a fair number of fellows wandering about looking for places to piss. Oh, and there's a bookcase on the first floor, sir, full of bloody ledgers.'

'Did you look for the stables?' Sharpe asked.

'I did, sir, but they're already locked tight, and so's the yard gate.'

'So there's no chance of stealing horses?'

Harper considered the question, then shrugged. 'It'll be hard, sir.'

'We're infantry,' Frederickson said dismissively, 'so we can damn well walk out of the city.'

'And if they send cavalry after us?'

Frederickson dismissed the fear. 'How will they know which way we've gone? Besides, the French cavalry never caught us, so what chance would you give our dozy lot?'

'We walk, then.' Sharpe stretched his arms wide as though he prepared for exercise. 'But where to?'

'That's easy,' Frederickson said. 'We go to Arcachon.'

'Arcachon?' Sharpe asked with surprise. That was the town closest to the Teste de Buch fort, but otherwise he could think of no special significance attached to the place.

But Frederickson, while Harper had been performing his charade with the chamber-pot, had been deep in thought. There never had been any gold in the fort, Frederickson now explained, at least not when the Riflemen had captured it. If that fact could be proved, then their troubles would be over. 'What we need to do,' he went on, 'is find Commandant Lassan. I don't believe he wrote that statement. I believe Ducos made it up.' Frederickson paused as a man laughed outside the door. 'I suspect your brandy is being appreciated, Sergeant.'

'Why do you think the Commandant's statement was faked?' Sharpe asked.

Frederickson paused to strike a flame in his tinderbox and to light one of his small foul cheroots. 'Do you remember his quarters?'

Sharpe thought back to the few hectic days he had spent at the Teste de Buch fortress. 'I remember the bastard had a lot of books. He couldn't fight, but he had a lot of bloody books.'

'Do you remember what the books were about?'

'I had better things to do than read.'

'I looked,' Frederickson said, 'and I remember that Commandant Lassan had a very civilized library, which made it a great pity when we turned most of it into cartridge paper and cannon-wadding. I recall some very fine editions of essays, and a large, indeed comprehensive, collection of sermons and other devotional literature. A very devout man, our Commandant Lassan.'

'Then no wonder we beat the bastard to jelly,' Harper said happily.

'And if he is devout,' Frederickson ignored Harper's cheerful comment, 'then my guess is that he may also be honest. It doesn't always follow, of course, I remember a very sanctimonious chaplain of the 60th who stole the mess ragged and then ran off with a Corporal's rather rancid woman, but I'm willing to think Lassan may be cut from a rather better cloth. Indeed, I seem to recall that the American told us he was a decent man?'

'Yes, he did,' Sharpe remembered.

'So let's hope he is decent. Let's hope that he'll deny that damned statement and ease us all off a bloody sharp hook. The trick of it is simply to find the man, then persuade him to travel to London.'

Frederickson's calm words made the task sound oddly easy. Sharpe, turning to the window, saw how the darkness was shrouding the city. There was a slender moon, sharp-edged and low above a tangle of dark masts and rigging which showed over the black rooftops. Candles showed in some windows and torches flickered where link-boys escorted pedestrians about the streets. 'Why Arcachon, though?' Sharpe turned back from the window. 'You think Lassan lives there?'

'I doubt we shall be so fortunate as that,' Frederickson said, 'but because he's an educated man, and a devout one, it's likely that he and the local priest would have been on friendly terms. It's hard to find civilized conversation in a small garrison, let alone someone to play chess with, and I recall that we kindled a fire with a very fine chess-set from Lassan's quarters. So, my suggestion is that we find the priest of Arcachon and hope he can tell us where to find Lassan. Do you agree?'

'I think it's a brilliant notion,' Sharpe said admiringly.

'I'm just a humble Rifle Captain,' Frederickson said, 'and therefore flattered by the praise of a staff officer.'

'But,' Sharpe said, 'if Lassan's an honourable man, why would Ducos falsify a statement of his? He must know that Lassan could deny it.'

'I don't know the answer to that,' Frederickson admitted, 'but we'll never know unless we find Lassan.'

'Or get out of here,' Harper said grimly. 'Can I have permission to hit a provost?'

'No killing,' Frederickson warned. 'If we kill one of the bastards then they'll have real cause to court-martial us.' He crept close to the door. 'I wonder if our brandy is working.'

The three men went silent as they tried to decipher the small sounds from beyond the door. They heard voices, and then, quite distinctly, the sound of liquid being poured. 'Another half hour,' Sharpe decided.

The half hour crept by, but at last the first of the town's clocks rang ten. Sharpe grimaced, seized the door handle, and nodded at Harper. 'You first, Sergeant.'

He snatched the door open, and their escape had begun.

*   *   *

Lieutenant-Colonel Wigram was the guest of honour at the dinner which the Transport Board was giving in the prefecture. The officials and their guests had dined well on roast mutton, roast chicken, and baked pears. Now, as the bottles of brandy thickened among the remaining bottles of claret, Wigram was invited to make a speech.

He spoke well. The vast majority of the men about the long table were civilians from London who had come to supervise the onerous task of removing an army from France. Their days were spent in settling accounts with the masters of ships, allocating hull space, and securing supplies for the army's journey home. Now, in the candlelit splendour of the prefecture's large hall, they could hear a little of what that army had achieved.

'In the darkest days of the struggle,' Wigram said, 'when every man's voice at home was raised against our endeavours, and when any prudent man might have deemed our cause lost, there would never have been a dinner as splendid as this one you have so generously provided. Then, gentlemen, we lived on very short commons indeed. Many is the night when I have given my horse the last food from my saddlebags, then slept hungry myself. The French were never far away on those cold nights, yet we survived, gentlemen, we survived.' There were murmurs of admiration, and a few guests, overcome both by Wigram's heroism and the plenitude of the wine, tapped their glasses with their spoons to make a pleasant ringing applause.

'And even later,' Wigram's glasses reflected the candlelight as he looked up to make sure his voice reached the far end of the table where the more junior guests sat, 'when fortune smiled more compassionately upon us, hardship was still our constant companion.' In fact Wigram had slept between sheets every night of his war, and had been known to have a cook flogged because his nightly joint of beef was underdone, but this was no time to quibble. This was a time for every man to garner what credit he could from the war, and Wigram could garner with the best. He bowed to Captain Harcourt, another guest at the dinner, and paid a fulsome tribute to the contribution made by the Royal Navy. Again there was applause.

Finally Wigram turned to a question he had frequently

pondered. 'I am often asked,' he said, 'what qualities are most desirable in a soldier, and I confess to cause astonishment when I reply that it is not a sturdy arm, nor an adventurous spirit which gains an army its victories. Such qualities are necessary, of course, but without leadership they will inevitably fail. No, gentlemen, it is the man who keeps his mental faculties alert who contributes most to the glorious cause. A soldier must be a thinker. He must be a master of detail. He must be a man whose precision of thinking will render him staunch and steady amidst danger and uncertainty.' It was at that point that Lieutenant-Colonel Wigram paused, his mouth dropped open, and one by one the guests turned to stare with amazement at the apparitions which had appeared in the doorway.

It was commonly said that most men only joined the British Army for drink. The French scornfully accused the British of fighting drunk, indeed of not being able to fight unless they were drunk, though if the charge was true then it was astonishing that the French did not make their own men drunk because, sober, they could never beat the British. There was, nevertheless, a great deal of truth in the charges. The British Army was notorious for drunkenness, and more than one French unit had escaped capture by leaving tempting bottles and casks to waylay their pursuers.

So it was hardly astonishing that the three provosts were drunk. Each had consumed close to a pint and a half of brandy, and they were not merely drunk, but gloriously, happily and carelessly oblivious of being drunk. They were, in truth, in a temporary nirvana so pleasant that none of the three had even noticed when a big Irishman rapped them hard on the skull to introduce a temporary unconsciousness. It was during that blank moment that each of the provosts had been stripped stark naked. Then, to make certain they stayed incapable, Sharpe and Frederickson had poured yet more brandy down their spluttering throats.

Thus it was that Lieutenant-Colonel Wigram's speech was interrupted by three deliriously drunken men who were as naked as the day on which they were born.

The Provost Sergeant stared about him in blinking astonishment as he found himself in the brilliantly lit banqueting hall. He hiccupped, bowed to the company, and tried to speak. 'Fire,' he at last managed to say, then he slid down a wall to fall asleep.

Behind him smoke seeped through the open door.

Wigram stared, aghast.

'Fire!' This time the voice came from outside, and was a huge roar of warning. Wigram panicked, but so did almost every man in the room. Glasses and plates smashed as men fought to escape the tables and cram themselves through one of the room's two doors. The naked provosts were trampled underfoot. Smoke was thickening in the corridor and billowing up the stairwell. Wigram fought to escape with the rest. He lost his glasses in his panic, but somehow managed to scramble through the door, across the vestibule, and down into the town square where the dinner guests assembled to watch the promised inferno.

There was none. A guard sergeant filled a bucket of water and doused the pile of brandy-soaked uniforms which, heavily sprinkled with gunpowder and then piled with loosely stacked, brandy soaked ledgers, had caused the pungent smoke. There was a nasty scorch-mark on the carpet, which hardly mattered for, being embroidered with the imperial initial 'N', it was due for destruction anyway. Most of the ledgers were scorched, and a few had burned to ash, but the fire had not spread and so no real harm had been done. The Sergeant ordered the three drunken provosts to be carried to the yard and dumped in a horse-trough, then, pausing only to steal half a dozen bottles of brandy from the table in the banqueting hall, he went to the front door and reported to the officers that all was well.

Except half an hour later someone thought to look on the top floor of the prefecture and discovered that three Riflemen were missing. Two rifles, a seven-barrelled gun, a bayonet, and six ammunition pouches were also missing from the guardroom.

Colonel Wigram, panicking like a wet hen, wanted to call out the guard, then send cavalry galloping all over France to discover the fugitives. Captain Harcourt was calmer. 'There's no need,' he said.

'No need?'

'My dear Wigram, there are picquets at every exit from the city, and even if Major Sharpe's party evades those sentries, we know precisely where they're going.'

'We do?'

'Naturally. That one-eyed Rifleman was entirely correct in his evidence to the tribunal. No men could have removed six tons of gold under enemy fire. Surely you understood that?'

Wigram had understood no such thing, but was unwilling to display such ignorance. 'Of course,' he said huffily.

'They could never have carried the gold away, so they must have hidden it at the Teste de Buch, and I warrant you that's where they've gone. And that's where we've had a sloop since last week. Might I trouble you for a single messenger to warn the crew that they'll have to arrest Major Sharpe and his companions?'

'Of course.' Wigram felt aggrieved that no one had told him about the Navy's precautions. 'You've had a sloop there for a week?'

'You don't want the bloody French to get the gold, do you?'

'But by law it belongs to them!'

'I've spent the last twenty years killing the bastards, and don't intend to hand them a pile of gold just because a peace treaty's been signed. If it's necessary we'll tear that damned fort apart to find the bloody stuff!' Harcourt glanced up at the stars, as if judging the weather, then grinned. 'There is one consolation in all this, my dear Colonel. By running away, Major Sharpe and Captain Frederickson have proved their guilt, so when the Navy catches them, you shouldn't have any trouble in convening a court-martial. Shall we send that messenger? And because the roads are likely to be dangerous, perhaps he'd better be given a cavalry troop as escort? Then perhaps you'd care to finish your speech? I must admit to a great fascination in your theory as to the role of the thinking man in gaining victory.'

But somehow the joy had deserted Wigram's evening. He did at least find his spectacles, but someone had trampled them in the rush and one lens was broken and an earpiece bent. So he abandoned his speech, cursed all Riflemen, then went to his quarters and slept.

CHAPTER 7

It had been easy enough to escape the prefecture by causing some small chaos, but leaving the city itself would be a harder task. Every exit was guarded by a picquet of redcoats. The soldiers were not there to guard Bordeaux against the marauding bands of the countryside, but rather to apprehend any deserter who might have evaded the provosts at the quays and be trying to take his woman back to Spain and Portugal.

Sharpe had used the stars to find a westward road through the city, but now, so close to the open country, he had been forced to stop. He was staring at a picquet of a dozen soldiers who were silhouetted about a brazier. Sharpe was too far away to distinguish their faces or see what regiment they might be from. He silently cursed the lost telescope.

'If we wait much longer,' Frederickson warned, 'they'll have men after us.'

'Surely they won't stop officers walking past?' Harper offered.

'Let's hope not.' Sharpe decided Harper was right, and that rank alone should suffice to see them past the bored guards. He nevertheless wondered just what he should do if the picquet proved obdurate. It was one thing to strip drunken provosts naked, but quite another to use force against a squad of redcoats. 'Cock your rifles,' Sharpe said as they walked forward.

'Are you going to shoot them?' Frederickson sounded incredulous.

'Threaten them, anyway.'

'I won't shoot anyone.' Frederickson left his rifle slung on his shoulder. Harper had fewer scruples and dragged back the cock of his seven barrelled gun. The monstrous click of the heavy lock made the officer commanding the picquet turn towards the approaching Riflemen.

Sharpe was close enough now to see that the picquet's officer was a tall and dandified man who, like many infantry officers who aspired to high fashion, wore a cavalryman's fur-edged pelisse over one shoulder. The officer strolled towards the three Riflemen with a languid, almost supercilious, air. The three must have looked strange for, in an army that had swiftly accustomed itself to peace, they were accoutred for war. They had heavy packs, crammed pouches, and were festooned with weapons. The sight of those weapons made the picquet's sergeant snap an order to his men who unslung their muskets and shuffled into a crude line across the road. The officer calmly waved his hand as if to suggest that the sergeant need not feel any alarm. The officer had now walked thirty yards away from the brazier. He stopped there, folded his arms, and waited for the Riflemen to reach him. 'If you haven't got passes,' he said in a most superior and disdainful voice, 'then I'll have no choice but to arrest you.'

'Shoot the bugger,' Sharpe said gleefully to Harper.

But Harper was grinning, the officer was laughing, and Fortune, the soldier's fickle goddess, was smiling on Sharpe. The tall and disdainful officer was Captain Peter d'Alembord of the Prince of Wales's Own Volunteers. He was an old friend who had once served under Sharpe and who now commanded Sharpe's old light company. d'Alembord also knew Frederickson and Harper well, and was delighted to see both men.

'How are you, Regimental Sergeant Major?' he asked Harper.

'I'm just a Rifleman again now, sir.'

'Quite right, too. You were far too insubordinate to be promoted.' d'Alembord looked back to Sharpe. 'Purely out of interest, sir, but do you have a pass?'

'Of course I don't have a bloody pass, Dally. The bastards want to arrest us.'

It had been pure good luck that had brought Sharpe to this picquet that was manned by his old battalion. He was close enough now to recognize some of the men about the brazier. He saw Privates Weller and Clayton, both good men, but this was no time to greet old comrades, nor to implicate them in this night's escapade. 'Just get us quietly out of the city, Dally, and forget you ever saw us.'

d'Alembord turned to his picquet. 'Sergeant! I'll be back in an hour or so.'

The Sergeant was curious. The picquet duty had been boring, and now some small excitement broke the tedium, but he was too far from the three Riflemen to recognize them. He took a few steps forward. 'Can I say where you'll be, sir? If I'm asked.'

'In a whorehouse, of course.' d'Alembord sighed. 'The trouble with Sergeant Huckfield,' he said to Sharpe, 'is that he's so damned moral. A good soldier, but horribly tedious. We'll go this way.' He led the three Riflemen into a foetid black alley that reeked with an overwhelming stench of blood. 'They put me next to a slaughterhouse,' d'Alembord explained.

'Is there a safe way out of the city?' Sharpe asked.

'There are dozens,' d'Alembord said. 'We're supposed to patrol these alleys, but most of the lads don't take kindly to arresting women and children. Consequently we tend to do quite a lot of looking the other way these days. The provosts, as you might imagine, are more energetic.' He led the Riflemen away from the butcher's stink and into a wider alley. Dogs barked behind closed doors. Once a shutter opened from an upper window and a face peered out, but no one called any alarm or query. The alley twisted incomprehensibly, but eventually emerged into a rutted lane edged with sooty hedges where the smell of open country mingled with the city's malodorous stench. 'The main road's that way,' Dally pointed southwards across dark fields, 'but before you go, sir, would you satisfy my curiosity and tell me just what in God's name is happening?'

'It's a long story, Dally,' Sharpe said.

'I've got all night.'

It did not take that long, merely ten minutes to describe the day's extraordinary events. Then the sound of hooves on a road to the north forced another delay, and Sharpe used it to discover how his old battalion was managing without him. 'What's the new Colonel like?'

'He's a rather frightened and fussy little man who quite rightly believes we're all wondrously expert and that he's got a lot to learn. His biggest terror is that the army will somehow post you back to the regiment and thus show up his manifold deficiencies. On the other hand he's not an unkind man, and given time, might even become a decent soldier. I doubt he's good enough to beat the French yet, but he could probably squash a Luddite riot without killing too many innocents.'

'Are they sending you to America?' Sharpe asked.

d'Alembord shook his head. 'Chelmsford. We're to recruit up to scratch ready for garrison duty in Ireland. I suppose I shall have the pleasure of knocking your countrymen's heads together, RSM?'

'Make sure they don't knock yours, sir,' Harper said.

'I'll try to avoid that fate.' d'Alembord cocked his head to the night wind, but the mysterious hoofbeats had faded to the west. 'Are you sure there's nothing I can do to help here, sir?' he asked Sharpe.

'When do you go to Chelmsford?'

'Any day now.'

'Do you have any leave owing?'

'My God, do I? They owe me half my life.'

'So you can deliver a message for me?'

'With the greatest of pleasure, sir.'

'Find Mrs Sharpe. The last address I had was in Cork Street, London, but she may have moved to Dorset since then. Tell her everything I've told you tonight. Tell her I shall come home when I can, and tell her that I need some influence on my side. Ask her to find Lord Rossendale.'

'That's a clever thought, sir.' d'Alembord recognized Lord Rossendale's name, for d'Alembord had been with Sharpe during the strange London interlude when Sharpe had been adopted as a favourite of the Prince Regent's. One result of that favouritism was the naming of Sharpe's old regiment as the Prince of Wales's Own Volunteers, and another was a distant but friendly acquaintanceship with one of the Prince's military aides, Lord John Rossendale. If any man could harness the full power of influence to clear Sharpe's name, it was Rossendale. Sharpe knew that the best method of establishing his innocence was to discover Lassan or Ducos, but if that search failed then he would need powerful friends in London, and Rossendale was the first and most approachable of those friends.

'If you can't find my wife,' Sharpe added, 'then try and see Rossendale directly. He can talk to the Prince.'

'I'll do that gladly, sir. And how do I send messages back to you?'

Sharpe had not thought of that problem, nor did he want to consider it now. The night was getting cold, and he was impatient to be on his way westwards. 'We'll probably be home within a month, Dally. It can't take much longer than that to find one French officer. But if we fail? Then for God's sake make sure Rossendale knows we're innocent. There never was any gold.'

'But if we are delayed,' Frederickson was more cautious, 'then perhaps we can send a message to you?'

'Send it to Greenwoods.' Greenwoods was another firm of Army Agents. 'And take care, sir.' d'Alembord shook Sharpe's hand.

'You haven't seen us, Dally.'

'I haven't even smelt you, sir.'

The three Riflemen crossed a rough piece of pastureland towards the embanked high road. The high road was not the most direct route to Arcachon, for it led more south than west, but it was a road that Sharpe and Frederickson had ambushed not many weeks before and, once they reached the ambush site, they knew they could find their way across country to the Teste de Buch fort.

'I'd forgotten you had such high connections,' Frederickson said with amusement.

'You mean Lord Rossendale?'

'I mean the Prince Regent. Do you think he'll help?'

'I'm sure he'll help.' Sharpe spoke with a fervent confidence, for he remembered the Prince's assiduous kindnesses in London. 'Just so long as Jane can reach Lord Rossendale.'

'Then I wish your wife Godspeed.' Frederickson climbed the turf bank and stamped his feet on the flint roadbed. He waited for his two companions to climb the embankment, then all three turned southwest. Thus, on a night road, Sharpe walked away from the army. He was a fugitive now, sought by the British authorities, by the French, and doubtless by his old enemy, Ducos. The Riflemen had become rogues, ejected from their own society, and gone to vengeance.

* * *

Jane Sharpe felt aggrieved.

Her grievance had come with the arrival of peace and her slow realization that her husband was a man who was entirely bereft of the ambitions of peace. Jane had never doubted his resolve in war, when Private Richard Sharpe had risen high by his own merits and energy, but Jane knew that her husband had no wish to transmute that wartime reputation into peacetime success. He only wanted to bury himself in the depths of rural England, there to farm and vegetate. Jane had spent most of her life in rural England, out on the cold clay marshland of Essex, and she had no wish to return to those bare comforts. She could understand that her husband might enjoy such an existence, but Jane dreaded the prospect of rural exile and foresaw that the only visitors to their country house would be old army comrades like Sergeant Harper.

Jane liked Harper, but she did not think she should mention that liking to Lady Spindacre, for it was quite clear that the Lady Spindacre would not approve of a Major's wife being fond of a mere Sergeant, and an Irish Sergeant at that. Lady Spindacre moved in altogether more exalted circles, and Jane's grievance was fuelled when she realized that those circles were now open to her, but only if Sharpe would be willing to forsake the country and use the high friendships he had made in London.

'But he won't,' she bemoaned to the Lady Spindacre.

'You must force him, dearest. He has instructed you to buy a house, so buy one in London! You say he has given you power of the money?'

The memory of that trusting gesture touched Jane with a few seconds' remorse, but then the remorse was overborne by her new and certain realization that she alone knew what was best for Richard Sharpe's career. The war had ended, yet there was still promotion to be had, but not if he resigned from the service and buried himself in some Dorsetshire hamlet. The Lady Spindacre, impressed that Jane had once been presented to the Prince Regent, and convinced that the presentation had sprung from the Prince's genuine interest in her husband, opined that there were a multitude of peacetime jobs that were in the gift of Royalty, and that such jobs, filled by military men, were not demanding of time, yet were generous in their pay, promotion, and prestige. 'He cannot retire as a Major,' Lady Spindacre said scathingly.

'And only a brevet Major, indeed,' Jane confessed.

'At the very least he should secure his Colonelcy. He could take a sinecure at the Tower, or at Windsor. My dear Jane, he should insist on a knighthood! Look how many other men, with much lesser achievements, are being deluged with rewards! All your husband needs do, my dearest, is to cultivate those high attachments. He must present himself at Court, he must persist in his acquaintances there, and he will succeed.'

This was all sweet and sensible music to Jane who, newly released from a stultifying youth, saw the world as a great and exciting place in which she could soar. Sharpe, she knew, had already had his adventures, but surely he would not deny her the opportunities of social advancement?

And Juliet, Lady Spindacre, was ideally placed to advise on such advancement. She was no older than Jane, just twenty-five, yet she had cleverly married a middle-aged Major-General who had died of the fever in southern France. Jane met the newly widowed Lady Juliet on the boat which returned them both to England, and the two girls had made an immediate friendship. 'You must not keep calling me Lady Spindacre,' Juliet had said, and Jane had revelled in the intimacy that was cemented by the similarities between the two girls. They were both women who attracted lascivious glances from the ship's officers, they shared a fascination in the feminine accoutrements of clothes and cosmetics, men and intrigue, and they were both ambitious to succeed in society. 'Of course,' the Lady Spindacre explained, 'I shall have to be reticent for a while, because of dear Harold's death, but it will only be for a short while.' Lady Spindacre was not wearing mourning for, she said, her dear Sir Harold would not have wanted it. 'He only ever wanted me to be a spirit at liberty, to enjoy myself.'

Juliet Spindacre's enjoyment of life was nevertheless threatened by her health, which was fragile, and by her constant worries about the dead Sir Harold's will. 'He had children by his first wife,' Juliet told Jane, 'and they are monsters! They will doubtless attempt to purloin the inheritance, and till the case is settled I am quite penniless.'

This penury was no immediate problem, for Jane Sharpe had the resources of her husband's great fortune that had been taken from the enemy at Vitoria. 'At the very least,' Lady Spindacre advised, 'you should establish yourself in London until the Major returns. That way, dearest one, you can at least attempt to assist his career, and if he should be so ungrateful on his return as to insist on a country home, then you can rest in the assurance that you did your best.'

Which all seemed eminently sensible to Jane who, on reaching London, and advised by the dear Lady Spindacre, withdrew all her husband's money. She disliked Messrs Hopkinson of St Alban's Street who, when she first approached them, had tried by every means possible to prevent her from closing Major Sharpe's account. They questioned his signature, doubted her authority, and it was only a visit from Lady Spindacre's lawyer that eventually persuaded them to make over a letter of credit which Jane sensibly lodged in a proper banking house where a young and elegant man seemed delighted to make her acquaintance.

Not all the money was so sensibly secured. The Lady Spindacre had much to teach Jane about the ways of society, and such lessons were expensive. There was a house in fashionable Cork Street to buy, new servants to find, and furniture to buy. The servants had to be uniformed, and then there were the necessary dresses for Jane and Lady Spindacre. They needed dresses for morning wear, for receiving, for dinners, for luncheons, for suppers, and such were the strictures of Jane's new busy life that no single dress could be worn more than once, at least, Lady Spindacre averred, not in front of the people the two friends intended to court. There were calling cards to engrave, carriages to hire, and connections to make, and Jane persuaded herself that she did it all in her husband's best interests.

Thus Jane was busy and, in her business, happy. Then, just two weeks after the bells of London had rung their joyous message of peace, the thunderbolt had struck.

The thunderbolt arrived in the form of two dark-suited men who claimed to bear the authority of the Judge Advocate General's office. Jane had refused to receive them in her new drawing-room in Cork Street, but the two men forced their way past the maid and firmly, though courteously, insisted on speaking with Mrs Jane Sharpe. They asked first whether she was the wife of Major Richard Sharpe.

Jane, pressed in terror against the Chinese wallpaper that the dear Juliet had insisted on buying, confirmed that she was.

And was it true, the two men asked, that Mrs Sharpe had recently withdrawn eighteen thousand nine hundred and sixty-four pounds, fourteen shillings and eightpence from Messrs Hopkinson and Sons, Army Agents, of St Alban's Street?

And what if she had? Jane asked.

Would Mrs Sharpe care to explain how her husband came to have so much money in his possession?

Mrs Sharpe did not care to explain. Jane was frightened, but she found the courage to brazen out her defiance. Besides, she saw how both men were attracted to her, and she had the wit to know that such men would not be personally unkind to a young lady.

The two dark-suited men nevertheless respectfully

informed Mrs Sharpe that His Majesty's Government, pending an investigation into the behaviour of her husband, would seek the return of the monies. All the monies, which, Jane knew, meant all the monies spent on powder and lace and hair-pieces and satin and champagne and the house; even the house! Her house!

She panicked when the men were gone, but dear Lady Spindacre, who had been in bed with a mild fever, rallied swiftly and declared that no dark-suited men from the Judge Advocate General's office had the right to persecute a lady. 'The Judge Advocate General is a nonentity, dearest one. Merely a tiresome civilian who needs to be slapped down.'

'But how?' Jane no longer appeared as a sophisticated and elegant beauty, but rather resembled the timid and innocent girl she had been just a year before.

'How?' The Lady Spindacre, seeing the threat to the source of Jane's money, which was also the only source of the Lady Spindacre's present wealth, was ready for battle. 'We use those connections, of course. What else is society for? What was the name of the Prince Regent's aide de camp? The one who was so solicitous of your husband?'

'Lord Rossendale,' Jane said, 'Lord John Rossendale.' So far she had been too scared to try and profit from that tenuous connection; it seemed too ambitious and too remote, but now an emergency had happened, and Jane well understood that Carlton House, where the Prince's court resided, far outranked the drab offices of the Judge Advocate General. 'But I only met Lord Rossendale once,' she said timidly.

'Was he rude to you?'

'Far from it. He was most kind.'

'Then write to him. You will have to send him some small trifle, of course.'

'What could I possibly send such a man?'

'A snuff-box is usual,' Lady Spindacre said casually.

'For a respectable favour, he'd expect one costing at least a hundred pounds. Would you like me to buy one, dearest? I am not feeling so poorly that I cannot reach Bond Street.'

A jewelled snuff-box was duly bought and, that same evening, Jane wrote her letter. She wrote it a dozen times until she was satisfied with her words then, as carefully as a child under the stern eye of a tutor, she copied those words on to a sheet of her new perfumed writing-paper.

Next morning a servant delivered the letter and the precious snuff-box to Carlton House.

And Jane waited.

* * *

The *curé* of Arcachon was hearing confessions when the ugly foreign soldier came into his church. The soldier came silently out of the night and, though he carried no weapons, other than the sword which any gentleman might wear, his eye-patch and scarred face caused a shiver of horror to go through the parishioners who waited their turn for the confessional. One of the parishioners, an elderly spinster, whispered the news to Father Marin through the muslin which served as a screen in the confessional box. 'He has only one eye, Father, and a horrid face.'

'Is he armed?'

'He has a sword.'

'What is he doing?'

'Sitting at the back of the church, Father, near the statue of St Genevieve.'

'Then he's doing no harm, and you are not to worry yourself.'

It was another hour before Father Marin had finished his task, by which time two other parishioners had come to the church to tell him that the foreign soldier was not alone, but had two comrades who were drinking in the tavern by the saddler's shop. Father Marin had learned that the strangers wore very old and faded green uniforms.

One woman was certain they were Germans, while another was equally sure they were British.

Father Marin eased himself out of the confessional and, by the light of St Genevieve's votive candles, saw the ugly stranger still sitting patiently at the back of the now empty church. 'Good evening, my son. Did you come for confession?'

'I doubt God has the patience to hear all my sins.' Frederickson spoke in his idiomatic French. 'Besides, Father, I'm a Protestant heretic rather than a Catholic one.'

Father Marin genuflected to the altar, crossed himself, then lifted his stained stole over his grey head. 'Are you a German heretic or an English one? My parishioners suspect you of being both.'

'They're right in both respects, Father, for I have the blood of both peoples. But my uniform is that of a British Captain.'

'What's left of your uniform,' Father Marin said with amusement. 'Are you anything to do with the Englishmen who are exploring the Teste de Buch fort?' The old priest saw that he had astonished the stranger.

'Exploring?' Frederickson asked suspiciously.

'English sailors have been occupying the fort for ten days. They've pulled down what's left of the internal walls, and now they're digging in the surrounding sand like rabbits. The rumour is that they're searching for gold.'

Frederickson laughed. 'The rumour's true, Father, but there's no gold there.'

'It's further rumoured that the gold was buried by the Englishmen who captured the fort in January. Were you one of those men, my son?'

'I was, Father.'

'And now you are here, in my humble church, while your companions are drinking wine in the town's worst tavern.' Father Marin rather enjoyed seeing Frederickson's discomfiture at the efficiency of Arcachon's gossips. 'How did you come here?'

'We walked from Bordeaux. It took three days.'

Father Marin lifted his cloak from a peg behind the Virgin's statue and draped it about his thin shoulders. 'You had no trouble on the road? We hear constantly of brigands.'

'We met one band.'

'Just the three of you?'

Frederickson shrugged, but said nothing.

Father Marin held a hand towards the door. 'Clearly you are a capable man, Captain. Will you walk home with me? I can offer you some soup, and rather better wine than that which your companions are presently enjoying.'

It took three hours of conversation and two lost games of chess before Frederickson persuaded the old priest to reveal Henri Lassan's address. Father Marin proved very careful of his old friend, Lassan, but after the two chess games the old priest was satisfied that this one-eyed Captain Frederickson was also a good man. 'You mean him no harm?' Marin sought the reassurance.

'I promise you that, Father.'

'I shall write to him,' Father Marin warned, 'and tell him you are coming.'

'I should be grateful if you did that,' Frederickson said.

'I do miss Henri.' Father Marin went to an ancient table that served as his desk and began sifting through the detritus of books and papers. 'In truth he was a most unsuitable soldier, though his men liked him very much. He was very lenient with them, I remember. He was also most distressed that you defeated him.'

'I shall apologise to him for that.'

'He won't bear a grudge, I'm sure. I can't swear he'll be at his home, of course, for he was intent on joining the priesthood. I constantly tried to dissuade him, but . . .' Father Marin shrugged, then returned to his slow search among the curled and yellowing papers on the table.

'Why did you try to dissuade him?'

'Henri's altogether too saintly to be a priest. He'll believe every hard luck story that's fed to him, and consequently he'll kill himself with compassion, but, if that's what he wishes, then so be it.' Father Marin found the piece of paper he sought. 'If you do him harm, Captain, I shall curse you.'

'I mean him no harm.'

Father Marin smiled. 'Then you have a very long walk, Captain.' The address was in Normandy. The Château Lassan, Father Marin explained, was not far from the city of Caen, but it was very far from the town of Arcachon. 'When will you leave?' the priest asked.

'Tonight, Father.'

'And the sailors?'

'Let them dig. There's nothing to find.'

Father Marin laughed, then showed his mysterious visitor to the door. A pale scimitar moon hung low over the church's roof-ridge. 'Go with God,' Father Marin said, 'and thank Him for sending us peace.'

'We brought the peace, Father,' Frederickson said, 'by beating that bastard Napoleon.'

'Go!' The priest smiled, then went back indoors. He fully intended to write his warning letter to Henri Lassan that very same night, but he fell asleep instead, and somehow, in the days that followed, he never did put pen to paper. Not that it mattered, for Father Marin was convinced Frederickson meant no harm to the Comte de Lassan.

And in the sand dunes, like rabbits, the sailors dug on.

CHAPTER 8

Father Marin had warned Frederickson that it might take
a full month for a man to walk from Arcachon to Caen,
but that was by daylight and without needing to avoid
either predatory bandits or patrolling provosts. There were
public coaches that could make the journey in a week, and
such coaches were well guarded by armed outriders, but
both Sharpe and Frederickson reckoned that the new
French government, believing them to be thieves, might
already be seeking them. Similarly, the news that British
sailors were searching the Teste de Buch persuaded Sharpe
that they were just as much at risk from their own countrymen as from the French. It was better, Sharpe and Frederickson agreed, to walk by night and thus to avoid all eyes.

They encountered their greatest obstacle just three
nights after leaving Arcachon. They had headed east to
meet the River Garonne south of Bordeaux. The river was
too deep and wide to be safely swum, and it took a full
night's scouting before they found a boat. It was a ferry-
man's skiff that was chained to a thick wooden post sunk
deep into the river bank. Harper spat on his hands,
crouched, then tugged the post bodily from the flinty soil.
Frederickson had already cut two branches to serve as
paddles. The river's current was so swift that Sharpe feared
their boat might be swept clear into Bordeaux itself, but
somehow they managed to steer the small craft safe to the
eastern shore.

They crossed another and smaller river the next night,
and then at last could turn north. Father Marin had given

Frederickson a route; by Angoulême, Poitiers, Tours, Le Mans, Alençon, Falaise, and thus to Caen.

All three Riflemen were accustomed to travelling by night, for the army had always marched long before dawn so that its day's journey was done before the Spanish sun was at its fiercest. Now, in the French countryside, it was doubtful whether a single soul was aware of the Riflemen's passing. The skills they used were by now innate; the skills of men who had patrolled in war for all their lives. They knew how to travel in silence and how to hunt. One night, despite the presence of three guard dogs in a farmyard, Frederickson and Harper stole two freshly farrowed piglets that were roasted the next day in a tumbledown and deserted farmhouse high on a hill. Two nights later, in a wood that was thick with wild-flowers, Sharpe shot a deer that they disembowelled and butchered. They plucked fish from streams with their bare hands. They dined on fungi and dandelion roots. They ate hares, rabbits, and squirrels, and all they missed from their diet was wine and rum.

They avoided towns and villages. Sometimes they would hear a church bell tolling in the dusk, or smell the stench of a great town, but always they looped east or west before continuing along deserted tracks or following the contour lines of great vineyards. They waded streams, climbed hills, and struggled through brackish marshland. They followed the Pole Star on clear nights, and on others they would walk a high road to find their directions from its milestones. In their tattered uniforms they looked like vagabonds, but vagabonds so well armed that they must have appeared more fearsome than the brigands they took such trouble to avoid.

On the tenth night of their journey they were forced to lay up through the darkness. All day they had watched the clouds piling up in the west, and by nightfall the whole sky was shrouded by sullen black thunderheads. The three Riflemen were snug in a ruined byre, and when the first stab of lightning flickered to earth Sharpe decided to stay put. It had already begun to rain, softly at first, but soon it began to spit malevolently, then swelled until the downpour was thrashing the earth in a sheeting and stinging deluge. The thunder cracked and tumbled across the sky, sounding just like the passage of heavy roundshot.

Harper slept while Sharpe and Frederickson crouched in the byre's entrance. Both men were fascinated by the storm's violence. Lightning twisted and split into rivulets of brilliant white fire so that it seemed as if the sky itself was in agony.

'Didn't it thunder the night before the battle at Salamanca?' Frederickson almost had to shout to be heard above the violent noise.

'Yes.' Sharpe could hear sheep bleating their panic somewhere to the west, and he was considering the prospect of mutton for breakfast.

Frederickson sheltered his tinderbox inside his greatcoat and struck a flame for one of his few remaining cheroots. 'I astonish myself by positively enjoying this life. I think perhaps I could wander in darkness for the rest of my life.'

Sharpe smiled. 'I'd rather reach home.'

Frederickson uttered a scornful bark of laughter. 'I hear an echo of a married man's lust.'

'I was thinking of Jane, if that's what you mean.' Since leaving Bordeaux, Sharpe had taken care not to mention Jane, for he knew with what small sympathy Frederickson regarded the state of marriage, but Sharpe's worries had only increased with his silence and now, under the storm's threat, he could not resist articulating those worries. 'Jane will be fretting.'

'She's a soldier's wife. If she isn't prepared for long absences and long silences, then she shouldn't have married you. Besides, d'Alembord will see her soon enough.'

'That's true.'

'And she has money,' Frederickson continued remorselessly, 'so I cannot see that she has great cause for concern. Indeed, I rather suspect that you're more worried about her than she is about you.'

Sharpe hesitated before admitting to that truth, but then, needing his friend's consolation, he nodded. 'That's true.'

'You're worried that she's tired of you?' Frederickson insisted.

'Good God, no!' Sharpe protested vehemently, too vehemently, for in truth that worry was never far from his thoughts. It was a natural concern occasioned by the unhappiness of their parting and by Jane's subsequent silence, but Sharpe had no taste to discuss such intimacies even with Frederickson. His voice sounded harsh. 'I'm merely worried because bloody Wigram knew she'd withdrawn that money. It means someone's investigated my affairs at home. What if they try to confiscate her money?'

'Then she'll be poor,' Frederickson said heartlessly, 'but doubtless she'll live until you clear your name. One presumes your wife has friends who won't allow her to slide into ignominious penury?'

'She has no friends that I know of.' Sharpe had snatched Jane from her uncle's house where she had been forced to live a reclusive life. That life had prevented her from making any close friends and, bereft of such help, Sharpe did not know how Jane would survive poverty and isolation. She was too young and innocent for hardship, he thought, and that realization provoked a surge of affection and pity for Jane. He suddenly wished he had risked the coach journey. Perhaps, by now, they could already have found Lassan and be on their way home with the proof they needed, but instead Sharpe was marooned in this water-lashed storm and he imagined a penniless Jane crouching beneath the same thunderous violence in solitary and abject fear. 'Maybe she thinks I'm already dead.'

'For Christ's sake!' Frederickson was disgusted with Sharpe's self-pity. 'She can read the casualty lists, can't she? And she must have received one of your letters. And d'Alembord will be with her soon, and you can be sure he won't permit her to starve. For God's sake, man, stop agitating about what can't be altered! Let's find Henri Lassan, then worry about the rest of our damned lives.' Frederickson paused as a shattering explosion of thunder slammed a snake's tongue of lightning into some woods on a nearby hill. Flames blazed from twisted branches after the lightning strike, but the burning leaves were soon extinguished by the numbing rain. Frederickson drew on his cheroot. 'I wish I understood love,' he said in a more conversational tone, 'it seems a very strange phenomenon.'

'Does it?'

'I remember, the last time I was in London, paying sixpence to see the pig-faced woman. Do you remember how celebrated she was for a few months? She was exhibited in most of the larger towns, I recall, and there was even talk that she might be displayed in Germany and Russia. I confess it was a most singular experience. She was very porcine indeed, with a rather snouty face, small eyes, and bristly hairs on her cheeks. It was not quite a sow's face, but a very close approximation. I rather think her manager had slit her nostrils to increase the illusion.'

Sharpe wondered what the pig-woman had to do with his friend's scepticism about love. 'And seeing an ugly woman was worth sixpence?' he asked instead.

'One received one's money's worth, as I recall. Her manager used to make the wretched creature snuffle chopped apple and cold porridge out of a feeding trough on the floor, and if you paid an extra florin she'd strip to the waist and suckle a rather plump litter of piglets.' Frederickson chuckled at the memory. 'She was, in truth, hideously loathsome, but I heard a month later that a gentleman from Tamworth had proposed marriage to her and had been accepted. He paid the manager a hundred guineas for the loss of business, then took the pig-lady away for a life of wedded bliss in Staffordshire. Extraordinary!' Frederickson shook his head at this evidence of love's irrationality. 'Don't you find it extraordinary?'

'I'd rather know if you paid the extra florin,' Sharpe said.

'Of course I did.' Frederickson sounded irritated that the question was even asked. 'I was curious.'

'And?'

'She had entirely normal breasts. Do you think the gentleman from Tamworth was in love with her?'

'How would I know?'

'One has to assume as much. But whether he was or not it's entirely inexplicable. It would be like going to bed with Sergeant Harper.' Frederickson grimaced.

Sharpe smiled. 'You've never been tempted, William?'

'By Sergeant Harper? Don't be impertinent.'

'By marriage, I mean.'

'Ah, marriage.' Frederickson was silent for a while and Sharpe thought his friend would not answer. Then Frederickson shrugged. 'I was jilted.'

Sharpe immediately wished he had not asked the question. 'I'm sorry.'

'I can't see why you should be.' Frederickson sounded angry at having revealed this aspect of his past. 'I now regard it as a most fortunate escape. I have observed my married friends, and I don't exclude present company, and all I can say, with the greatest of respect, is that most wives prove to be expensive aggravations. Their prime attraction can be most conveniently hired by the hour, so there seems little reason to incur the expense of keeping one for years. Still, I doubt you'll agree with me. Married men seldom do.' He twisted back into the byre to find Harper's sword-bayonet that he drew from its scabbard and tested against his thumb. 'I have a fancy for a breakfast of mutton.'

'I had the very same wish.'

'Or would you prefer lamb?' Frederickson asked solicitously.

'I think mutton. Shall I go?'

'I need the exertion.' Frederickson carefully extinguished his cheroot, then stored it in his shako. He stood, peered for a moment into the slashing rain, then plunged into the night.

Harper snored behind Sharpe. At the hilltop the great branches of foliage heaved and bucked in the sodden wind. Lightning sliced the sky, and Sharpe wondered what malevolent fate had brought his career to this extremity, and then he prayed that the weather would clear so that this journey could be done and an honest Frenchman found.

* * *

Henri Lassan had struggled with his conscience. He had even gone so far as to consult with the Bishop, he had prayed, until at last he had made his decision. One night at the supper table he informed his mother of that decision. The family was eating sorrel soup and black bread. They drank red wine which was so bad that Lucille had put some grated ginger in the bottle to improve its taste.

Henri sat at the head of the table. 'Maman?'

'Henri?'

Henri paused with a spoonful of soup just inches above his plate. 'I will marry Mademoiselle Pellemont, as you wish.'

'I am very pleased, Henri.' The old lady was not going to revel in her victory, but offered her response very gravely and with the smallest inclination of her head.

Lucille showed more pleasure. 'I think that's wonderful news.'

'She has excellent hips,' the Dowager said. 'Her mother had sixteen children, and her grandmother twelve, so it's a good choice.'

'A very solid choice,' Henri Lassan said with a trace of a smile.

'She has a very lovely nature,' Lucille said warmly, and it was true. There might be those who thought Marie Pellemont to have the placidity and attractiveness of a gentle and not very energetic cow, but Lucille had always liked Marie who was her own age, and who would now become the new Comtesse de Lassan.

A betrothal ceremony was fixed for a fortnight's time and, even though the château had fallen on lean times, the family tried hard to make apt provision for the occasion. All but one of the château's saddle horses were sold so that the guests could receive their traditional gifts, sword knots for the men and nosegays for the women, and so there would be lavish food and decent wine for the guests of quality. The villagers and tenantry must also be fed, and provided with great vats of cider. Lucille found herself busy baking apple-cakes, and pressing great trays of nettle-wrapped cheese. She made sure that the hams hanging in the château's chimneys were not too nibbled by bats. She cut away the worst of the ravages, then rubbed pepper into the dark hams to keep the animals at bay. It was a happy time. The days were lengthening and growing warmer.

Then, just a week before the betrothal ceremony, the first armed brigands were reported in the château's vicinity.

The report came from a man ditching the top fields above the mill-stream. He had watched as some ragged fugitives, all armed and wearing the vestiges of imperial uniforms, had skulked along the stream-bed. They had been carrying two slaughtered lambs.

That night Henri Lassan slept with a loaded musket beside his bed. He barricaded the bridges over the moat with old cider vats, then released geese into the yard to act as sentries. Geese were more reliable than dogs, but no strangers disturbed the geese, neither that night nor the

174

next, and Henri dared to hope that the vagabonds had merely been passing through the district.

Then, just the very next day, a horrific report came of a farmhouse burned beyond the next village of Seleglise. The smoke of the burning barn could be plainly seen from the château. The farmer, all his family, and both his maid-servants had been killed. The details of the massacre, brought by the miller of Seleglise, were appalling, so much so that Henri did not tell either his mother or Lucille. The miller, an elderly and devout man, shook his head. 'They were Frenchmen who did this, my Lord.'

'Or Poles, or Germans, or Italians.' Lassan knew there were desperate men of all those nationalities released from Napoleon's defeated armies. Somehow he did not wish to believe that Frenchmen could do such things to their own kind.

'All the same,' the miller said, 'they were once soldiers of France.'

'True,' and that same day Henri Lassan donned the uniform he had hoped never to wear again, strapped on a sword, and led a party of his neighbours on a hunt for the murderers. The farmers who rode with him were brave men, but even they baulked at riding into the deep forest beyond Seleglise where the murderous vagabonds had doubtless taken shelter. The farmers contented themselves with firing shots blindly into the trees. They scared a lot of pigeons and lacerated many leaves, but no shots were fired back.

Lassan considered postponing the betrothal ceremony, but his mother was adamantly against such a course. It had taken the Dowager the best part of twenty years to persuade her adult son to take a bride, and she was not about to risk that happy eventuality because of a few vagrant scum lurking five miles away. It seemed her faith was rewarded, for there were no further incidents, and every guest travelled in safety to the château.

175

The betrothal ceremony, though modest, went very well. The weather was fine, Marie Pellemont looked as beautiful as her relieved mother could make her, while Henri Lassan, in a suit of fine blue cloth that had belonged to his father, looked properly noble. The Dowager had brought out the remains of the family's silver, including a great dish, three feet across and a foot deep, which was cast in the form of a scallop shell cradling the de Lassan coat-of-arms. A flautist, violinist and drummer from the village provided the music, there was country dancing, and there was the solemn giving of pledges followed by the exchange of gifts. Mademoiselle Pellemont received a bolt of beautiful pale-blue silk from China; a treasure that the Dowager had possessed for fifty years, always meaning to make it into a gown fit for Versailles itself. Henri received a silver-hilted pistol that had once belonged to Marie's father. The village *curé* muddled the words of his blessing, while the local doctor, a widower, danced so much with Lucille that the tongues wagged happily about the château's courtyard from which the compost heap had been removed in honour of this great day. Soon, the villagers thought, the widow Castineau would also be married, and not before time, because Lucille was nearly thirty, childless, and was a woman of the most excellent kindness and disposition. The doctor, the village thought, could do far far worse, though doubtless the widow Castineau could do far better.

By midnight all the guests had gone, except for three male cousins from Rouen who would spend the night in the château. Henri put his new pistol into a drawer, then went to the kitchen where his three cousins were sousing themselves with good Calvados. Lucille and Marie, the elderly kitchen-maid, were scouring the great scallop dish with handfuls of abrasive straw, while the Dowager was complaining that Madame Pellemont had been insufficiently appreciative of the bolt of silk. 'I warrant she hasn't seen fabric of that quality since before the revolution.'

'Marie liked it,' Lucille was ever the peace-maker, 'and she's promised to make her wedding dress from it, Maman.'

Henri, reminded of that ordeal which he faced in a month's time, said he was going outside to release the geese. He did so, then, wondering whether he had made the right choice by agreeing to marry, he leaned against the château's wall and stared up at the full moon. It was a warm night, even muggy, and the moon was surrounded by a gauzy halo. He could hear music coming from the village and he supposed that the revelry was continuing in the wineshop by the church.

'It's going to rain tomorrow.' The Dowager came out from the kitchen door and looked up at the hazed moon.

'We need some rain.'

'It's a warm night.' The Dowager offered her arm to her son. 'Perhaps it will be a hot summer. I do hope so. I notice that I feel the cold more keenly than I used to.'

Henri walked his mother to the bridge which led to the dairy. They stopped on the bridge's planks, just short of the new barricade, and stared down into the still, black and moon-reflecting water of the moat.

'I see you're wearing your father's sword,' the Dowager suddenly said.

'Yes.'

'I'm glad.' The Dowager lifted her head to listen to the music which still sounded from the village. 'It's almost like the old days.'

'Is it?'

'We used to dance a great deal before the revolution. Your father was a great dancer, and had a fine voice.'

'I know.'

The Dowager smiled. 'Thank you for agreeing to marry, Henri.'

Henri smiled, but said nothing.

'You'll find Mademoiselle Pellemont is a most agreeable girl,' the Dowager said.

'She won't be a difficult wife,' Henri agreed.

'She's like your sister, in some ways. She's not given to vapours or airs. I don't like women who have vaporous souls; they aren't to be trusted.'

'Indeed not.' Henri leaned on the bridge's balustrade, then jerked upright as the geese suddenly hissed behind him.

The Dowager gripped her son's arm. 'Henri!'

The Dowager had been alarmed by footsteps which had suddenly sounded by the dairy where flagstones provided a firm footing in the sea of hoof-churned mud. There were dark shapes moving among the mooncast shadows. 'Who is it?' Henri called.

'My Lord?' It was a deep voice that replied. The tone of the voice was respectful, even friendly.

'Who is it?' Henri called again, then gently pushed his mother towards the lit door of the kitchen.

But, before the Dowager could take a single pace, two smiling men appeared from the shadows. They were both tall, long-haired men who wore green uniform jackets. They walked on to the far end of the bridge with their hands held wide to show that they meant no harm. Both men wore swords and both had muskets slung on their shoulders.

'Who are you?' Lassan challenged the strangers.

'You're Henri, Comte de Lassan?' the taller of the two men asked politely.

'I am,' Lassan replied. 'And who are you?'

'We have a message for you, my Lord.'

The Dowager, reassured by the respect in the stranger's voice, stood beside her son.

'Well?' Lassan demanded.

The two uniformed men were standing very close to the barricade, not two paces from Lassan. They still smiled

178

as, with a practised speed, they unslung the heavy weapons from their shoulders.

'Run, Maman!' Henri pushed his mother towards the château. 'Lucille! The bell! Ring the bell!' He turned after his mother and tried to shield her with his body.

The tallest of the two men fired first and his bullet entered Lassan's back between two of his lower ribs. The bullet was deflected upwards, exploding his heart into bloody shreds, then flattened itself on the inside of his breastbone. As he fell he pushed his mother in the small of her back, making her stumble down to her knees.

The Dowager turned to see the second man's gun pointed at her. She stared defiantly. 'Animal!'

The second man fired and his bullet smacked through the Dowager's right eye and into her brain.

Mother and son were dead.

Lucille came to the kitchen door and screamed.

The two men climbed the barricade and walked into the château's yard. There were other shapes in the darkness behind them.

Lucille ran back into the kitchen where her cousins were struggling to their feet. One of the cousins, less drunk than his companions, drew his pistol, cocked it, and went to the door from where he saw the dark shapes at the far side of the yard. He fired. Lucille pushed him aside and raised the great blunderbuss that was kept loaded and ready above the soap vats. She cocked it, then fired it at the murderers. The butt hammered with brutal pain into her shoulder. One of the two killers shouted with agony as he was hit. The other two cousins pushed past Lucille and ran into the darkness, but a fusillade of gunfire from beyond the moat made them drop to the cobblestones. The bullets smacked into the château's ancient stone wall. Marie, the kitchen-maid, was screaming. The geese were hissing and stretching their necks. The dogs in the barn were barking fit to wake the dead.

Lucille snatched up an ancient battered horse-pistol, dragged back its cock, and ran towards the dark shapes that crouched over the bodies of her mother and brother. 'Stop her!' a deep voice called in French from beyond the moat, and one of her cousins, as if obeying the voice, stood up and caught Lucille about the waist and dragged her down on to the cobbles just as three more weapons fired from beyond the moat. The bullets whiplashed over Lucille and her cousin. She raised her head to see the two men who had killed her family climbing back over the barricade. She had wounded one of them, but not badly. Lucille was crying, screaming for her mother, but she saw in the moonlight that the men who escaped her vengeance wore green coats. The men in green! The English devils who had haunted her brother had come back in an evil night to finish their foul work. She howled like a dog at their retreating shapes, then fired the pistol at the retreating killers. Scraps of exploding powder from the pistol's pan burned her face, and the flash dazzled her.

The dogs in the barn were scrabbling at the door. Marie was sobbing. A servant ran to the chapel bell and began to toll the alarm. Villagers, alerted by the gunfire and harried by the bell's frantic noise, swarmed through the château's main arch. Some carried lanterns, all carried weapons. Those with guns blazed to the east where the attackers had long disappeared. The villagers' gunfire did more damage to the dairy and the château's orchards than to the murderers.

Lucille, weeping helplessly, pushed through the villagers to where her mother and brother lay in a pool of lantern-light. The village priest had covered the Dowager's face with a handkerchief. The old woman's black dress was soaked with blood that shone in the yellow light.

Henri Lassan lay on his back. His fine suit of clothes had been cut with knives, almost as if his murderers had thought that he kept coins in his coat seams. His old engraved sword had been stolen. Strangest of all was the presence of a short-handled axe beside his body. The cheap axe had been used to hack off two fingers from Henri Lassan's right hand. The job had been done clumsily, so that his thumb and third finger were half severed as well. There was no sign of the two missing fingers.

The priest thought the disfigurement must have been done in the cause of Satanism. There had been an outbreak of devil worship in the Norman hills not many years before, and the Bishop had warned against a revival of the foul practice. The priest crossed himself, but kept his opinion to himself. Sufficient unto the night was the evil already done.

Lucille, already widowed, and now orphaned and denied her good brother's life, wept like an inconsolable child while the chapel bell still tolled its useless message to an empty night.

CHAPTER 9

For three days Lucille Castineau wept and would not be comforted. The *curé* tried, the local doctor tried, and her cousins tried. It was all in vain. Only after the funeral did she show some of her old spirit when she saddled her brother's horse, took his new pistol from his study, and rode to the far side of Seleglise where she fired shot after shot into the thick woodland.

Then she went home where she ordered both wooden bridges over the moat to be dismantled. It was a horrific job, for the timbers were massive, and it was even a pointless job, for the damage had already been done, but the farm workers, with help from the villagers, sawed through the great pieces of wood that were taken away to strengthen barns, byres, and cottages. Then Lucille had a notice posted on the church door, and another posted on the door of the church at Seleglise, which promised a reward of two hundred francs for information which would lead to the capture and death of the Englishmen who had murdered her family.

The villagers believed that the widow Castineau was distraught to temporary madness, for there was no evidence that the killers had been English and, indeed, the kitchenmaid swore she had heard a voice call out in French. A very deep voice, Marie remembered distinctly, a real devil's voice, she said, but Lucille insisted that it had been Englishmen who had committed the murders, and so the reward notices faded in the sunlight and curled in the night's dew. Lucille had sworn she would sell the upper orchards to raise the reward money if someone would just lead her to revenge.

One week after the funerals Madame Pellemont arrived with her family lawyer and an impudent claim that half the château's estate, and half the château itself, properly belonged to her daughter who had gone through a betrothal ceremony with the dead Comte de Lassan. Lucille listened in apparent patience, then, when at last the lawyer politely requested her response, she opened her brother's drawer, took out the silver-hilted pistol, and threatened to shoot both Madame Pellemont and her lawyer if they did not leave her home immediately. They hesitated, and it was said that Lucille's voice could be heard in the sexton's house beyond the blacksmith's shop as she screamed at them to leave the château.

Madame Pellemont and her lawyer left, and the silver-hilted pistol, which turned out to be unloaded, was thrown after them. It lay in the road for three hours before anyone dared to pick it up.

Lucille's father-in-law, old General Castineau, came all the way from Bourges to sympathize with her. The General had only one leg; his other had been lost to an Austrian cannonball. He sat for hours with Lucille. He told her she should marry again, that every woman needed a husband, and, because he was a widower, and because he was sentimental, and because he saw in Lucille what his sharp-eyed son had once seen, he offered himself. Lucille turned him down, though so gently that the old General had no chance to take offence.

General Castineau also assured her that it was most unlikely for any Englishmen to have killed Henri and the Dowager.

'I saw them,' Lucille insisted.

'You saw men in green. Every country's army has men in green coats. Our own dragoons wear green. Or wore green. God knows what they'll wear now.'

'Those men were English.'

The General tried to explain that the English were hardly likely to be in Normandy since their army had invaded the south of France and had already been evacuated from Bordeaux. A few Englishmen had been with the allies who reached Paris, but not many. And anyway, why should an Englishman seek out this family? He begged Lucille to give the question her most serious attention.

'They were English,' Lucille said stubbornly.

The General sighed. 'Marie tells me you're not eating.'

Lucille ignored his concern, preferring her own. 'I hate the English.'

'That's understandable,' General Castineau said soothingly, though from all he had heard it was better to be captured by the English than by the Russians, and he was about to expatiate on that grisly theme when he remembered that Lucille was hardly in a receptive frame of mind for such reflections. 'You should eat,' he said sternly. 'I've ordered a dish of lentil soup for you today.'

'If the Englishmen come back,' she said, 'I'll kill them.'

'Quite right, quite right, but if you don't eat you won't have the strength to kill them.'

That remark made Lucille look shrewdly at the General, almost as though he had propounded a peculiarly difficult idea, but one which made surprising sense. She nodded agreement. 'You're right, Papa,' and at lunchtime she wolfed down all the lentil soup, then carved herself a thick slice of the ham that the General had been hoping to carry off the next day in his saddlebag.

That evening the General met privately with the doctor and both men agreed that the terrible events had sadly disturbed Madame Castineau's wits. The doctor could think of no easy cure, unless Madame Castineau could be persuaded to take the waters, which sometimes worked, but which were horribly expensive. Otherwise, he said, nature and time must do the healing. 'Or marriage,' the doctor said with a certain wistfulness, 'Madame needs a man's touch, if you understand me.'

'She won't marry again,' General Castineau opined. 'She was too much in love with my son, and now she'd rather wither away than dilute his memory. It's a sad waste, Doctor.'

General Castineau left next morning, though he made certain that there would always be reliable men from the village in the château in case the brigands should return and, indeed, just two hours after the General had left, five strange horsemen approached from the northern road that dropped off the wooded ridge and the farmworkers ran to the château's entrance with loaded muskets and hefted pitchforks.

The strange horsemen approached slowly, with their hands held in clear view. They stopped a good few yards from the moat's bridge and their leader, a plump man, politely requested an audience with Monsieur the Comte de Lassan.

'He's dead.' It was the miller's son who answered truculently.

Monsieur Roland, the advocate from Paris, eyed the ancient musket in the boy's hands and chose his next words very carefully. 'Then I would like to speak with a member of his family, Monsieur? My name is Roland, and I have the honour to be a lawyer in the service of his Most Christian Majesty.'

The words, gently said, impressed the miller's son who ran to tell Madame Castineau that yet another gentleman had come to see her.

Roland, whose rump had been made excruciatingly sore by long days in the saddle, walked with Lucille in the orchards. His four men patrolled the edges of the trees with drawn pistols to deter any strangers from intruding on the discussion.

Roland explained that he was charged by the Royal Treasury with the recovery of a sum of gold stolen by the English. The coins had been deposited in the Teste de Buch fort, and Roland had come to Normandy to hear Commandant Lassan's evidence about the loss of the bullion. He was desolated, Roland repeated the word, desolated, to hear of the Commandant's death.

'Murder,' Lucille corrected him.

'Murder,' Roland humbly accepted the correction.

'The English murdered him,' Lucille said. 'The men in green coats. The Riflemen.'

Roland stopped his slow pacing and turned an astonished face on the widow. 'Are you certain, Madame?'

Lucille, galled that no one believed her, turned in fury on the plump lawyer. 'Monsieur, I am sure! I am sure! I saw them! They were men in green coats, Englishmen just like those my brother feared, and they murdered my mother and my brother. They are animals, Monsieur, animals! My brother had said they might come, and they did! He even knew the Englishman's name. Sharpe!'

'I think you are right, Madame,' Roland said quietly, and Lucille, who till now had not been taken seriously by a single person, could only stare at the Parisian lawyer. 'In fact I am sure you are right,' Roland added.

'You believe me, Monsieur?' Lucille said in a very relieved and somewhat surprised voice.

'I do believe you. These are ruthless men, Madame. Believe me, I have met this Sharpe.' Roland shuddered. 'He and his comrade have stolen a fortune that belongs to France, and now they will try to kill the men who can testify to that theft. I should have thought to warn your brother. Alas, dear lady, that I did not think to do so.'

Lucille shook her head in denial of the lawyer's self accusation. 'Henri mentioned no gold,' she said after a while.

'A soldier should carry secrets well, and the existence of this gold was most secret.' Roland, sweating profusely in the spring sunshine, turned and walked back towards the château. 'I do not think the Englishmen will return now,' he said soothingly.

'I wish they would return.' Lucille alarmed the lawyer by revealing an enormous brass-muzzled horse-pistol that lay heavy in the wide pocket of her apron. 'If they do return, Monsieur, I shall kill at least one of them.'

'Leave the killing to those who know best how to do it.' Roland, knowing this visit was wasted, was eager to return to Caen where there was at least a vestige of civilization. He feared that Lucille would invite him to luncheon, and that the château's evident poverty would provide a most meagre meal, but, to his relief, Lucille made no such offer.

Roland mounted his horse at the château's entrance. He had given Madame Castineau his address, and begged her to write to him if the Englishmen returned, though he admitted he put small faith in such a thing happening. Nevertheless, looking down at the sad Lucille, he felt a pang of sympathy. 'May I presume to give Madame advice?'

'I should be honoured, Monsieur.'

Roland collected his reins. 'Marry again, Madame. A woman such as yourself should not be alone; not in these troubled times and in this sad country. Permit me to say that I am married, Madame, and that it gives me the greatest peace and happiness.'

Lucille smiled, but said nothing.

Roland turned his horse, then, remembering one last question, turned the animal back again. 'Madame? Forgive my indelicacy, but did your brother lose two fingers of his right hand?'

'They cut them off!' Lucille wailed the words in sudden agony. 'The Englishmen cut them off!'

Roland, thinking the loss of the two fingers must have happened when Sharpe's men had captured the Teste de Buch fort, did not ask Lucille to amplify the answer which already seemed to confirm Ducos's written testimony. Instead the lawyer raised his hat. 'Thank you, Madame, and I am sorry if I have caused you distress.'

That night, in his comfortable lodgings in Caen, Monsieur Roland wrote two reports. The first would be sent to the King's Minister of Finance and it respectfully and regretfully reported the murder of Henri Lassan and the consequent lack of any new evidence that might lead to the gold's recovery. Roland added his suspicions that the two English officers, Sharpe and Frederickson, had been responsible for Lassan's death. 'They must certainly be charged with murder,' he wrote, 'and the search for them must continue, both in France and in Britain.'

Roland's second report was far more detailed. It began by saying that Pierre Ducos's written testimony had been substantially confirmed, and that it now seemed virtually certain that the two English Rifle officers had stolen the Emperor's gold. They had also killed Lassan, presumably so that he could not testify against them. The death of Lassan prompted Roland to consider the possibility that the two English officers had already murdered Pierre Ducos; how else to account for Ducos's continued silence? Roland respectfully suggested that the two Englishmen must already have left France, but hoped they might yet be found and brought to vengeance. He added the welcome news that the English Navy had been requested by the new French government to desist from their explorations in and around the Teste de Buch fort, which request had been reluctantly complied with. The English search about the fort had found none of the imperial gold or baggage.

This second report was written on fine India paper which Monsieur Roland took to a calligrapher in Paris.

The calligrapher sealed the India paper inside two sheets of thicker paper that were so cleverly pasted together that they appeared to a casual glance to be one thick sheet of paper. Then, on the thicker paper's creamy surface, the calligrapher inscribed an extremely tedious ode in praise of the Greek Gods.

The ode was briefly read by a French government censor. Two weeks later the poem was delivered to the island of Elba, off the Tuscany coast, where the creamy page was delicately peeled apart to reveal the India paper inside. Within an hour Roland's longer report was being read by an Emperor in exile, but an Emperor who still retained some sharp claws. Except that the claws could not be unsheathed, for the enemy was hidden, and so, though Monsieur Roland's report was filed carefully away, it was not forgotten. The report, after all, concerned money, and the exiled Emperor had need of money if his dreams were once again to blazon Europe with his glory. The English Riflemen might have vanished for the moment, but they would reappear, and when they did the Emperor would have them found and have them killed. For glory.

*　　*　　*

The Saxon Dragoon wished to go home. He told Sergeant Challon as much, and the Sergeant reminded the Saxon of the vow they had all taken when they had waited in the deserted farmhouse. The vow had been an agreement that all the Dragoons would remain with Major Ducos until everything was safe, but if any man did wish to leave then he must forfeit his share of the Emperor's treasure.

The Saxon shrugged. 'I just want to go home.'

Challon put his arm about the big man's shoulder. 'It won't be long, Herman.'

'Home,' the Saxon said stubbornly.

'And you'll go home without any of the money?' Challon asked enticingly. The two men were in the stableyard of a tavern in Leghorn. Challon had gone to the stables to make certain the horses were being fed, and the Saxon had followed the Sergeant in hope of finding some privacy for this conversation.

Herman shrugged. 'I deserve something, Sergeant, and you know it.' It had been the Saxon who had been slightly wounded when he crossed the wooden bridge with Sergeant Challon to kill Henri Lassan, and it had been the Saxon who had made such havoc in the Seleglise farmhouse which Ducos had ordered attacked so that the local people would believe the subsequent attack on Lassan the work of casual brigands.

'You deserve something,' Challon said soothingly. 'I'll talk to Major Ducos. He won't like it, but I'll try and persuade him to be generous. I'll tell him how loyal you've been.' Challon had smiled, begun to walk away, but then whipped back as he drew his long straight sword. The Saxon's own blade was only half out of its scabbard as Challon's sword ripped into his throat. Twenty minutes later the Saxon's naked body was left in the street outside the tavern yard where it was reckoned to be just another dead sailor.

Ducos sold the Dragoons' horses in Leghorn, then paid the captain of a *barca-longa* to take himself and the seven remaining Dragoons southwards to Naples. It was a nervous voyage, for the coast was infested by Barbary pirates, but the occasional presence of a British naval squadron cheered Ducos. Despite that naval protection, the *barca-longa*, a two-masted coastal cargo vessel, put into a safe haven each night and the consequent delays meant that the voyage to Naples took eight days.

Sergeant Challon, in a rare outburst of disagreement with Pierre Ducos, had argued against seeking refuge in Naples. The city was the capital of the Kingdom of Naples, and its King was a Frenchman who had once been a Marshal in Napoleon's armies. Surely, Challon argued,

Marshal Murat would not offer shelter to men who had betrayed Napoleon, but Ducos patiently explained that Murat had broken with his erstwhile master. Napoleon might have put Murat on the throne of Naples, but Murat could only keep that throne if he was now seen to be an enemy of the broken Emperor, to which end he was busy cultivating new alliances and his Neapolitan troops had even marched north to expel the remnants of the Imperial French Army from Rome. 'So you see,' Ducos patiently continued, 'an enemy of the Emperor's will be a friend to the Marshal.'

Not that Ducos had any intention of seeking an audience with Murat, yet he knew he must somehow secure the help of the authorities. Strangers were suspect in a place like Naples, so Ducos must not be a stranger.

Ducos established his men in a small harbour tavern, then used his old skills, and not a little money, to discover who, besides Murat, was the power in this filthy and ramshackle city beneath its smoking volcano. It took Ducos ten days, but then he found himself kneeling before an elaborate throne and kissing the plump ring of a very fat Cardinal. 'My name,' Ducos said humbly, 'is Count Poniatowski.'

'You are Polish?' The Cardinal was so fat that his breath rasped in his throat if he even waddled the short distance from his throne's dais to the door of his audience chamber. The throne itself was supposed to face the wall, unused, except during the short period between the death of one Pope and the election of the next, but the Cardinal liked to sit in its cushioned magnificence and look down on the humble petitioners who knelt before its dais.

'I am Polish, your Eminence,' Ducos confirmed.

'Perhaps you would prefer it if we spoke in Polish?' the Cardinal asked in French.

'Your Eminence is too kind,' Ducos replied in heavily accented Polish.

The Cardinal, who spoke Italian, Latin and French, but not a word of any other language, smiled as if he had understood. It was possible, he allowed to himself, that this scrawny little man was truly a Polish aristocrat, but the Cardinal doubted it. Most refugees these days were from France, but the Cardinal's first very simple trap had failed to embarrass this petitioner, so his Eminence graciously suggested that perhaps they should continue their conversation in Italian so that the Count Poniatowski could practise that language. 'And allow me to ask, my dear Count, why you have come to our humble country?'

The country might be humble, Ducos reflected, but not this monstrous Prince of the Church who employed more than a hundred and twenty servants in his own household and whose private chapel had more eunuchs in its choir than had ever sung at any one time in St Peter's. On either side of the cardinal young boys wielded paper fans to cool the great man's brow. At the foot of the dais were guards in yellow and black, armed with ancient halberds which, despite their age, could still cleave a man from skull to balls in the time it would take to cock a pistol. The room itself seemed a fantasy of decorated stone, carved into adoring angels and archangels. In truth the decorations were of *scagliola*, a false stone made of plaster and glue, but Ducos recognized the skill of the craftsmen who had made the dazzling objects. 'I have come, your Eminence, for the sake of my health.'

'You are a consumptive, my son?'

'I have a breathing problem, your Eminence, which is aggravated by cold weather.'

The Cardinal suspected that the Count's breathing problem was more likely to be aggravated by an enemy's sword, but it would be impolite to say as much. 'The city,' he said instead, and with a wave of his plump hand about his splendid audience chamber, 'will be hard on your lungs, my dear Count. There is much smoke in Naples.'

'I would prefer to live in the countryside, your Eminence, on a hilltop where the fresh air is untainted by smoke.'

And where, the Cardinal thought, enemies could be perceived at a good distance, which explained why the Count Poniatowski had so generously presented a large ruby to the Cardinal's funds as an inducement for this audience. The Cardinal shifted himself on his cushioned throne and stared over the Count's head. 'It is my experience, my dear Count, that invalids such as yourself live longer if they are undisturbed.'

'Your Eminence understands my paltry needs only too well,' Ducos said.

'His Majesty,' it was the first time the Cardinal had acknowledged the existence of a higher power in the state than himself, 'insists upon the prudent policy that our wealthier citizens, those who pay the land taxes, you understand, should live in peace.'

'It is well known,' Ducos said, 'that his Majesty pays the closest attention to your Eminence's wise advice.' Ducos doubted whether any wealthy person in the kingdom paid any tax at all, but doubtless the Cardinal was merely using the word to describe the gifts he would expect, and now was the time to make it clear that the Count Poniatowski was a man who had gifts to give. Ducos took a purse from his pocket and, closely watched by the Cardinal, poured some gems into his palm. Ducos, knowing that the sheer weight of the boxed gold would prove too heavy to carry across an embattled continent, had bought diamonds, rubies, sapphires and pearls in Bordeaux. He had purchased the gems for a very low price, for the starving merchants in Bordeaux had been desperate for trade, and especially for gold. 'I was hoping, your Eminence,' Ducos began, but then let his voice tail away.

'My dear Count?' The Cardinal waved away the small boys whose job was to fan him in the sultry months.

'It takes time for a man to settle in a foreign country,

your Eminence,' Ducos still held the handful of precious stones, 'and under the pressures of strange circumstances, and due to the necessities of establishing a home, a man might forget some civic duties like the payment of his land tax. If I were to offer you a payment of that tax now, perhaps your Eminence can persuade the authorities to take a kindly view of my convalescence?'

The Cardinal reached out a fat palm which was duly filled with some very fine gems. 'Your responsibility does credit to your nation, my dear Count.'

'Your Eminence's kindness is only exceeded by your Eminence's wisdom.'

The Cardinal pushed the gems into a pocket that was concealed beneath his red, fur-trimmed Cappa Magna. 'I have a mind, my dear Count, to help you further. Mother Church has long admired the stalwart manner in which you Poles have resisted the depredations of the tyrant Napoleon, and now it falls to my humble lot to give a proper appreciation of that admiration.'

Ducos wondered what new financial screw the Cardinal would turn, but bowed his thanks.

'You seek a house,' the Cardinal said, 'upon a hill. A place where an invalid can live in peace, undisturbed by any past acquaintances who might disturb his fragile recovery?'

'Indeed, your Eminence.'

'I know such a place,' the Cardinal said. 'It has belonged to my family for many years, and it would give me the keenest pleasure, my dear Count, if you were to occupy the house. You will need to give it the merest touch of paint, but otherwise . . .' The Cardinal shrugged and smiled.

Ducos realized that the house was a ruin which he would now have to rebuild at his own expense, and all the while he would be paying this fat man an extortionate rent, but in return Ducos was receiving the protection of the

Cardinal who, more than any other man, was the real power in the kingdom of Naples. Ducos accordingly offered the Cardinal a very low bow. 'Your Eminence's kindness overwhelms me.'

'It is a very spacious house,' the Cardinal said, thereby warning Ducos that the rent would be concomitantly large.

'Your Eminence's generosity astounds me,' Ducos said.

'But a large house,' the Cardinal said slyly, 'might be a suitable dwelling for a man who has arrived in our humble country with seven male servants? And all of them armed?'

Ducos spread his hands in a gesture of innocence. 'As your Eminence so wisely observed, an invalid needs peace, and armed servants are conducive to peace.' He bowed again. 'If I might offer your Eminence some rent now?'

'My dear Count!' The Cardinal seemed overwhelmed, but recovered sufficiently to accept the second purse which contained a handful of French golden francs.

The Cardinal was quite sure that the Count Poniatowski was neither a Count, nor Polish, but was almost certainly a wealthy French refugee who had fled the wrath of the victorious allies. That did not matter so long as the 'Count' lived peaceably in the kingdom, and so long as he was a source of income to the Cardinal who needed a very large income to sustain his household. Thus the Count was made welcome, and the very next day a lugubrious priest with an enormously long nose was instructed to lead the Count northwards to the Villa Lupighi which stood mouldering on a steep bare hill above the coast.

The villa was indeed a ruin; a vast and decaying structure which would cost a fortune to be fully restored, but Ducos had no intention of making a full restoration, only of lying low, in security, until the last question about an Emperor's missing gold had been asked and answered. He explored his new home that overlooked the astonishingly blue sea, and Ducos saw how no one could approach the villa without being seen, and so he expressed to the long-nosed priest his full and grateful satisfaction.

Ducos had found both a refuge and a powerful protector, and thus, for the first time since he had shot Colonel Maillot, Pierre Ducos felt safe.

* * *

Sharpe had to risk letting Frederickson enter the city of Caen, for the Riflemen needed detailed instructions if they were to find the village where Henri Lassan lived.

Frederickson went into the city alone and unarmed, posing as a discharged German veteran of Napoleon's army who sought his old *Chef de battalion*. No one challenged his right to be in the city, and thus he indulged himself with a tour of the great church where his namesake, William the Conqueror, lay buried. Frederickson stood for a long time in front of the marble slab, then was accosted by a cheerful priest who merrily recounted how the Conqueror's body had been so filled with putrefaction at the time of its burial in 1087 that it had exploded under the pressure of the foul-smelling gases. 'The church emptied!' The priest laughed as if he had actually been there. 'Not that our Billy's down there any more, of course.'

'He isn't?' Frederickson was surprised.

'Those Revolutionary bastards desecrated the tomb and scattered the bones. We collected a few scraps in '02, but I doubt if any of them are the real thing. On Judgement Day we'll likely find a scrofulous beggar coming out of the hole instead of the Conqueror.'

The priest gladly accepted the offer of a glass of wine, and just as gladly told Frederickson how to reach Henri Lassan's village which lay some forty miles away. 'But be careful!' The priest reiterated Father Marin's warning. 'The countryside is a dangerous place, my friend. It's full of villains and murderers! The Emperor would never have allowed such a state.'

'Indeed not,' Frederickson agreed, and the two men commiserated with each other over the sad state of France now that the Emperor was gone.

It was dusk before Frederickson rejoined his companions, and night had fallen by the time Sharpe led them away from the city's environs. The three Riflemen still planned to travel in the dark, for by daylight a man moving across country could prompt a score of telltale signs; a hare running from its lay, a pigeon startled to clatter through leaves, or even the curious gaze of somnolent cattle could alert a suspicious man to surreptitious movement. At night those dangers were lessened, for after sundown the Norman cottages were tight barred. It was easy to avoid the cottages, even in the darkness, for each one had a great manure heap piled against an outer wall and the Riflemen's sense of smell was sufficient to send them looping far from any wakeful and suspicious villagers.

They travelled west. Sometimes they would walk for miles along deep and rutted lanes like those in England's west country. At other times they struggled through high-hedged fields, or climbed to some wooded ridge from where they could judge their position by moonlight. It took two nights to find the right district, and another night to discover Lassan's château in its deep, private valley that was filled with drifts of decaying blossom. Sharpe and Harper spent the last two hours of that night scouting round the château. They saw a youth sitting in the château's gateway. Behind him, and silhouetted by a lantern, was a crude barricade of barrels. The youth was armed with what looked like an old fowling piece. He had tipped his chair back, and seemed asleep, and Sharpe had been tempted to make his entry there and then. He resisted the urge, for to have entered at that witching hour would have caused a frantic alarm. The boy was clearly posted to guard against the brigands who threatened the country-side, and Sharpe had no wish to be mistaken for such a villain. Instead he and Harper went back to the high wooded spur where Frederickson had found a hiding place.

They spent the whole of the next day on the high ground of the ridge. They were hidden by hornbeams, elms, beeches, and oaks. It was frustrating to be so close to their quarry, and yet be forced to let the daylight hours pass in inactivity, but Sharpe had decided that, in their ragged state, a daylight approach would cause suspicion and might even trigger disaster. He could see from his eyrie that every man in the valley carried a gun; even the two boys in the big orchard who laboriously ringed the trunks of the apple trees with tar carried muskets.

'We'll go just after sundown,' Sharpe decided. The dusk was a time when men were relaxing from a day's labours.

The Riflemen anticipated their success. One evening's conversation, Frederickson averred, would be sufficient to persuade Henri Lassan to travel to England. In a week, Sharpe thought, he would be back in London. Within two weeks, at the very most, he would be back with Jane.

'I'll take some leave when we're home,' Frederickson said.

'You can visit us in Dorset.' Sharpe had a homely dream of entertaining old friends in his well-deserved comfort.

Frederickson smiled crookedly. 'I have a greater yearning to visit Rome. I'd like to stand where the emperors once stood. They say an astonishing amount of the imperial city still stands, though it's evidently much decayed. Perhaps you'll come with me?' he offered to Sharpe.

'Dorset will do me well enough.' Sharpe, lying on the high ground and staring down at the moated château, envied Henri Lassan his house. Sharpe might not have rejoiced, as Frederickson did, in the ruins of the ancient world, but he perceived a great calmness in this old Norman farmhouse. He hoped Jane had found something similar in England. He suddenly did not want a modern house with its regular geometric windows and square angular lines. He wanted something calmer and older like this château which slumbered in its deep valley.

'I'll be back in Donegal,' Harper said wistfully. 'I'll buy some Protestant acres, so I will.'

'You'll be a farmer?' Sharpe asked.

'Aye, sir, and I'll have a grand house, so I will. Somewhere where the children can grow in peace.' Harper fell silent, perhaps thinking of how close that coveted heaven had become.

'Soldiers' dreams,' Frederickson said dismissively, 'just soldiers' dreams.' He rolled on to his belly, parted the leaves in front of him, and stared down the barrel of his rifle towards the distant château. Six cows were being driven to the byre for milking. He could just see a man standing in the farmyard, beyond the moat, and he wondered if that solitary figure was Henri Lassan, and Frederickson thought how many soldiers' dreams were fixed on that one man's honesty. A farm in Ireland, a house in Dorset, and a sketchbook in the Roman Forum; all would come true if only one honest man would tell the truth. He let the leaves fall slowly back, then slept, waiting for the dusk.

* * *

An hour after the sun had sunk, and when the light was still thick and gold about the lengthening shadows, the three Riflemen crept from the woods and stalked down a deep hedgerow which led to the laneway which edged the moat at the front of Lassan's château.

Sharpe reached the laneway first and saw the same young man standing guard in the château's archway. The youth was clearly bored. He thought himself unobserved and so was practising a crude arms drill of his own invention. He shouldered his fowling piece, presented it,

199

grounded it, then thrust it forward as though it was tipped with a bayonet. After a while, and tiring of his military dreams, the boy sidled past the crude barricade of barrels and disappeared into the château's yard.

Frederickson crouched beside Sharpe. 'Shall we go now?' he asked.

Sharpe stared at the crenellated tower above the gatehouse. He could not imagine why Lassan had not thought to post a sentry on that high commanding platform, but no man watched from that eyrie so Sharpe decided it was safe to go. Sharpe had decreed that just he and Frederickson would approach the château, and that neither man would carry weapons. Two unarmed men in the twilight posed no great threat. Harper would wait with all the weapons in the hedgerow, and only join the officers once Lassan had been safely reached.

The boy was still hidden inside the yard as Sharpe and Frederickson scrambled through the hedge and walked down the lane's grass verge. No one called an alarm. This façade of the château, hard on the moat and facing the village, was an almost featureless wall, betraying that the building had once been a small fortress.

'It's a very pretty house,' Frederickson murmured.

'Monsieur Lassan's a very lucky man,' Sharpe agreed.

They had to step off the verge to approach the bridge across the moat. Once on the roadbed their boots crunched on loose stone, but still no one challenged them, not even when they reached the moat and stepped on to the mossedged planks of the ancient drawbridge. They hurried into the shelter of the archway, then edged silently by the crude barricade of empty barrels. Sharpe saw a flock of geese cropping at a thin patch of grass at the far side of the château's yard.

'Back!' Frederickson hissed. He had glimpsed the boy coming back towards the arch. The lad had evidently gone to the kitchen to collect his supper that he was now carefully carrying in both hands. His long-barrelled fowling piece was slung on his shoulder.

The two Riflemen pressed themselves against the wall of the arch. The boy, intent on not spilling a drop of his soup, did not even look up as he turned into the thick shadow of the gateway.

Frederickson pounced.

The boy, in sudden terror, let the bowl fall as he twisted violently away. He was too slow. The wooden bowl spilt its contents across the cobbles as a knife jarred cold against his throat. An arm went round the boy's face, muzzling his mouth.

'Not a word!' Frederickson hissed in French. He was holding the flat of a clasp-knife's blade against the boy's adam's apple. 'Be very quiet, my lad, very quiet. You're not going to be hurt.'

Sharpe took the old fowling piece from the boy's shoulder. He opened the lock's frizzen and blew the priming powder away to make the gun safe. The boy was wide-eyed and shivering.

'We mean no harm,' Frederickson spoke very slowly and softly to the boy. 'We don't even have guns, you see? We've simply come here to talk to your master.' He took his hand from the boy's mouth.

The boy, clearly terrified out of his wits by the two scarred and ragged men, tried to speak, but the events of the last few seconds had struck him dumb. Frederickson gripped the nape of the boy's jerkin. 'Come with us, lad, and don't be frightened. We're not going to hurt you.'

Sharpe propped the fowling piece against the wall, then led the way out of the shadowed arch. He could see a lit window across the château's yard, and the shadow of a person moving behind the small panes of glass. He hurried. Frederickson kept hold of the frightened boy. Two of the geese stretched their necks towards the Riflemen.

The geese began their cackling too late, for Sharpe had

already reached the kitchen door which, because the boy had to return his soup bowl, was still unlocked. Sharpe did not wait on ceremony, but just pushed open the heavy door.

Frederickson thrust the boy away from him, then ducked under the lintel behind Sharpe.

Two women were in the candle-lit kitchen. One, an elderly woman with work-reddened hands, was stirring a great vat that hung on a pothook above the fire. The other, a much younger and thinner woman who was dressed all in black, was sitting at the table with an account book. The two women stared in frozen horror at the intruders.

'Madame?' Frederickson said from behind Sharpe who had stopped just inside the door.

'Who are you?' It was the thin woman in black who asked the question.

'We're British officers, Madame, and we apologize for thus disturbing you.'

The thin woman stood. Sharpe had an impression of a long and bitter face. She turned away from the intruders to where two water vats stood in an alcove. 'Haven't you done enough already?' she asked over her shoulder.

'Madame,' Frederickson said gently, 'I think you misunderstand us. We are only here . . .'

'William!' Sharpe, understanding none of what was being said, turned and pushed Frederickson out of the kitchen. He had seen the thin black-dressed woman turn back from the vats, and in her hands was a great brass-muzzled horse-pistol. Her grey eyes held nothing but a bitter hatred and Sharpe knew, with the certainty of the doomed, that everything had gone wrong. He pushed Frederickson desperately into the yard and he tried to throw himself out of the door, but he knew he was too late. His body flinched from the terrible pain to come. He had already begun to scream in anticipation of that pain when Lucille Castineau pulled the trigger and Sharpe's world turned to thunder and agony. He felt the bullets strike like massive blows, and he saw a sear of flame flash its light above him, and then, blessedly, as the gun's stunning echo died away, there was just nothing.

Part Three

CHAPTER 10

Captain Peter d'Alembord sat in the drawing-room of the Cork Street house and felt acutely uncomfortable. It was not that d'Alembord was unused to luxury, indeed he had been raised in an affluent family of the most exquisite tastes, but his very familiarity with civilized living told him that there was something exceedingly vulgar about this high-ceilinged room. There was, he considered, simply too much of everything. A great chandelier, much too large for the room, hung from a plaster finial, while a dozen crystal sconces crowded the walls. The sconces, like the chandelier, dripped with candle wax that should long have been scraped away. The furniture was mostly lacquered black in the fake Egyptian style that had been fashionable ten years earlier. There were three chaise-longues, two footstools, and a scattering of small lion-footed tables. The gilt-framed pictures seemed to have been bought as a job lot; they all showed rather unlikely shepherdesses dallying with very ethereal young men. A box of candied cherries lay gathering dust on one table, and a bowl of almonds on another.

Dust was everywhere and d'Alembord doubted whether the room had been cleaned for days, perhaps even weeks. The grate was piled with ashes, and the room smelt over-whelmingly of powder and stale perfume. A maid had curtseyed when d'Alembord had handed in his card at the door, but there was little evidence that the girl did any cleaning. d'Alembord could only suppose that Jane Sharpe was merely lodging in the house, for he could not believe that she would allow such slovenliness in her own home.

d'Alembord waited patiently. He could find only one book in the room. It was the first of a three volume romance which told the story of a clergyman's daughter who, snatched from the bosom of her family by brigands in Italy, was sold to the Barbary pirates of Algiers where she became the plaything of a terrible Muslim chief. By the last page of the book, to which d'Alembord had hastily turned, she was still preserving her maidenly virtue, which seemed a most unlikely outcome considering the reputed behaviour of the Barbary pirates, but then unlikely things properly belonged in books. d'Alembord doubted if he would seek out the remaining volumes.

A black and gilt clock on the mantel whirred, then sounded midday. d'Alembord wondered if he dared pull aside the carefully looped velvet curtains and open a window, then decided that such an act might be thought presumptuous. Instead he watched a spider spin a delicate web between the tassels of a table-cloth on which a vase of flowers wilted.

The clock struck the quarter, then the half, then the hour's third quarter. d'Alembord had come unannounced to the house, and had thus expected to wait, but he had never anticipated being kept waiting as long as this. If he was ignored till one o'clock, he promised himself, he would leave.

He watched the filigreed minute hand jerk from five minutes to four minutes to one. He decided it would be prudent to leave a message in writing and was about to tug the bell-pull and demand paper and pen from the maid, when the drawing-room door suddenly opened and he turned to see the smiling face of Mrs Jane Sharpe.

'It's Captain d'Alembord!' Jane said with feigned surprise, as though she had not known who had been waiting for her for so long. 'What a pleasure!' She held out a hand to be kissed. 'Were you offered tea? Or something more potent, perhaps?'

'No, Ma'am.'

'The girl is perverse,' Jane said, though d'Alembord noted that she did not ring the bell to correct the perversity. 'I didn't know the battalion had reached England?'

'Two weeks ago, Ma'am. They're now in Chelmsford, but I'm on leave.'

'A well deserved leave, I'm sure. Would you like to draw a curtain, Captain? We must not sit here in Stygian gloom.'

d'Alembord pulled back the heavy velvet, then, when Jane had arranged herself on a chaise-longue, he sat opposite her. They exchanged news, complimented London on its current fine weather, and agreed how welcome the coming of peace was. And all the time, as this small-talk tinkled between them, d'Alembord tried to hide the astonishment he was feeling at the change in Jane. When she had been with the army she had seemed a very sweet-natured and rather shy girl, but now, scarce six months later, she was a woman dressed in the very height of fashion. Her green satin gown fell in simple pleats from its high waist to her ankles. The neckline was cut embarrassingly low so that d'Alembord was treated to an ample view of powdered breasts; very pretty breasts, he decided, but somehow it seemed inappropriate for the wife of a man he liked and admired so to display herself. The shoulders of Jane's dress were puffed and the sleeves very long, very tight and trimmed at their wrists with lace frills. She wore no stockings, instead displaying bare ankles that somehow suggested the vulnerability of innocence. Her shoes were silver slippers tied with silver thongs in the quasi-Greek fashion. Her golden hair was drawn up above her ears, thus displaying her long and slender neck about which was a necklace of rubies which d'Alembord supposed must have been plundered from the French baggage at Vitoria.

The rubies suited her, d'Alembord decided. They were rare jewels for an undoubtedly beautiful woman. He saw her smiling at his inspection, and realized with embarrassment that Jane had perceived his admiration and was relishing it.

He quickly changed the subject to the reason for his visit. He had brought her, d'Alembord said, a message from Major Sharpe. He apologized that he had brought no letter, but explained the hurried circumstances of his meeting with Sharpe in Bordeaux.

'So you don't know where the Major is now?' Jane asked eagerly.

'Alas no, Ma'am, except that he's gone to find a French officer who can attest to his innocence.'

The eagerness seemed to ebb from Jane who stood, walked to the window, and stared down the sunlit street. She told d'Alembord that she already knew something of her husband's predicament, and explained how the two men from the Judge Advocate General's office had visited her with their outrageous demands. 'I've heard nothing since then,' Jane said, 'and until your visit, Captain, I did not even know whether my husband was alive.'

'Then I'm glad to be the bearer of good news, Ma'am.'

'Is it good news?' Jane turned from the window. 'Of course it is,' she added hurriedly, 'but it all seems extremely strange to me. Do you think my husband did steal the Emperor's gold?'

'No, Ma'am!' d'Alembord protested. 'The accusations against him are monstrous!'

Jane resumed her seat, thus letting d'Alembord sit again. She plucked the folds of her dress, then frowned. 'What I do not understand, Captain, is that if my husband is innocent, which of course he is, then why did he not allow the army to discover that innocence? An innocent man does not run away from a fair trial, does he?'

'He does, Ma'am, if the only evidence against him is

false. Major Sharpe is attempting to prove those falsities. And he needs our help.'

Jane said nothing. Instead she just smiled and indicated that d'Alembord should continue speaking.

'What we have to do, Ma'am, is harness what influence we can to prevent the machinery of accusation going farther. And should the Major fail to find the truth in France, then he will need the help of influential friends.'

'Very influential,' Jane said drily.

'He mentioned a Lord Rossendale, Ma'am?' d'Alembord wondered why Jane was so unresponsive, but ploughed on anyway. 'Lord Rossendale is an aide to His Royal Highness, the Prince . . .'

'I know Lord John Rossendale,' Jane said hurriedly, 'and I have already spoken with him.'

d'Alembord felt a surge of relief. He had been unsettled by this interview, both by Jane's new and languid sophistication, and by her apparent lack of concern about her husband's fate, yet now it seemed as if she had already done her duty by Sharpe. 'May I ask, Ma'am, whether Lord Rossendale expressed a willingness to help the Major?' d'Alembord pressed.

'His Lordship assured me that he will do all that is within his power,' Jane said very primly.

'Would that include presenting Major Sharpe's problem to the Prince Regent, Ma'am?'

'I really couldn't say, Captain, but I'm sure Lord Rossendale will be assiduous.'

'Would it help, Ma'am, if I was to add my voice to yours?'

Jane seemed to consider the offer, then frowned. 'Of course I cannot prevent you from trying to see his Lordship, though I'm sure he is a most busy man.'

'Of course, Ma'am.' d'Alembord was again puzzled by Jane's impenetrable decorum.

Jane turned to look at the clock. 'Of course we will all

do everything we can, Captain, though I rather suspect that the best thing to do is to allow my husband to disentangle himself.' She gave a small unamused laugh. 'He's rather good at that, is he not?'

'Indeed he is, Ma'am. Very good, but . . .'

'And in the meanwhile,' Jane ignored whatever d'Alembord had been about to say, 'my duty is to make everything ready for his return.' She waved a hand about the room. 'Do you like my new house, Captain?'

'Extremely, Ma'am.' d'Alembord concealed his surprise along with his true opinion. He had imagined that Jane was merely staying in the house, now he discovered that she owned it.

'The Major wished to buy a home in the country,' Jane said, 'but once I had returned to England I could not endure the thought of burying myself in rustic ignorance. Besides, it is more convenient to look after the Major's affairs in London than from the country.'

'Indeed, Ma'am.' d'Alembord wanted more details of how Jane was looking after Sharpe's affairs, but he sensed that further enquiries would reveal nothing. There was something unsettling in the situation, and d'Alembord did not want to provoke it.

'So I bought this house instead,' Jane went on. 'Do you think the Major will like it?'

d'Alembord was convinced that Sharpe would detest it, but it was not his place to say so. 'It seems a very good house, Ma'am,' he said with as much diplomacy as he could muster.

'Of course I share the house at the moment,' Jane was eager to stress the propriety of her situation, 'with a widow. It would hardly be proper otherwise, would it?'

'I'm sure you would do nothing improper, Ma'am.'

'It's such a pity that the Lady Spindacre is still abed, but dear Juliet's health is not of the best. You must visit us, Captain, one evening at eight. We usually receive downstairs at that hour, but if no link is lit outside, then you will know that we are not at home. If a lamp is lit then you must announce yourself, though I should warn you that London is sadly bored with soldiers' tales!' Jane smiled as though she knew her charms would ameliorate the rudeness of her words.

'I would not dream of inflicting soldiers' tales on you, Ma'am.' d'Alembord spoke stiffly.

'London has so many other fascinations to indulge besides the late wars. It will be good for the Major to come here, I think. Especially as he made some very high connections on his last visit, and it would be impossible to preserve those connections if he buries himself in Dorsetshire.'

'You refer to the Prince?' d'Alembord said in the hope that he would learn more of Jane's conversation with Lord Rossendale.

'But none of those connections, I think, will care to travel into the remote parts of the country to hear stories of war,' was Jane's only response. She looked at the clock again, then held out her hand to indicate that the conversation was over. 'Thank you for visiting me, Captain.'

'It was my pleasure, Ma'am.' d'Alembord bowed over the offered hand. 'Your servant, Ma'am.'

Once outside the house d'Alembord leaned for an instant on the black railings, then shook his head. He had a suspicion that he had achieved nothing, but he could not quite pin down the reasons for that suspicion. Yet there was one thing for which he was supremely grateful, which was that he had no address by which he could reach Sharpe. What in hell could he have written? He sighed, wondered if there was anyone else he could approach for help, then walked away.

* * *

The horse-pistol had been loaded with three small pistol bullets. The first had entered the upper part of Sharpe's left arm where it first shattered his shoulder joint, then ricocheted to crack the blade of the big bone behind. The second bullet tore off the top half of his left ear and gouged a deep cut in his scalp that bled horrifically, though the wound itself was slight enough. The impact of that second bullet had plunged Sharpe into an instant and merciful unconsciousness. The third bullet fractured Sharpe's right thigh-bone just above the knee and tore the leg's big artery. The blood puddled about the kitchen's threshold.

Lucille Castineau, once the shot was fired, had lowered the big smoking pistol and stared defiantly at Frederickson who was picking himself up from the mud outside the door. 'Now shoot me,' she said, and though her words sounded dramatic even to herself, she nevertheless felt at that moment as if her defiance embodied a prostrated and defeated France. Indeed, though she never admitted it to anyone but herself, at that proud instant she felt exactly like Joan of Arc herself.

'We don't even have weapons!' Frederickson snapped the words in French, then shouted for water and rags. 'Quick, woman!' He tore his snake-buckled belt free and twisted it as a tourniquet round Sharpe's right thigh. 'Come on, woman! Help me, damn you!'

'Why should we help you?' Lucille was finding it hard to keep her Joan of Arc poise, but she managed to put a superb scorn into her voice. 'You killed my brother!'

Frederickson twisted the tourniquet as tight as it could go, then stared in shock at the tall and oddly calm woman. 'Your brother's dead?'

'You killed him! Out there!' She pointed to the yard.

'Madame, I have never been here before.' Frederickson turned and snapped at the boy, who had plucked up courage to creep close to the door, then turned again to Lucille. 'You have my word of honour, Madame, as a

British officer, that none of us has been here before, nor did any of us kill your brother whose death, believe me, I regret to the very depths of my soul. Now, Madame, will you please give me bandages and water. We need a doctor. Hurry!' He twisted back to the door. 'Sergeant Harper!' He bellowed hugely into the night. 'Sergeant Harper! Come here! Quick!'

'Sweet Jesus.' Lucille crossed herself, stared at the great pool of blood, and at last suspected that her certainty of who had murdered her family might be wrong. Then, because she was a practical woman, and because recriminations would have to wait, she tore a linen cloth into strips and sent the boy to fetch the doctor.

While Sharpe, pale-faced and with a fluttering pulse, just groaned.

* * *

Lord John Rossendale thought of himself as an honourable man; a decent, privileged and fair man. His greatest regret was that he had never been permitted to leave the Prince's service to fight in the wars, for he suspected that in peacetime there would be an enviable reputation attached to those men who had brought their scars and swords back from Spain and France. He had asked to be allowed to join Wellington's army often enough, but the Prince of Wales, Regent of England during his father's bouts of madness, declared that he needed Rossendale's company. 'Johnny amuses me,' the Prince would explain, and he tried to compensate for Rossendale's disappointment by offering the young cavalryman promotion. Rossendale was now a full Colonel, though he was required to perform no military duties other than the elegant wearing of his dazzling uniform, which duty he could carry off to perfection.

Rossendale was, indeed, privileged, but he was not unmindful of those less exalted officers who had carried the brunt of the war against Napoleon, which was why, when

Jane Sharpe's letter had first come to his attention, he had felt a pang of guilt and a start of compassion. He had also admired the snuff-box, though the gift was quite unnecessary, for Rossendale well remembered Major Sharpe and had preserved a great admiration for the Rifleman. Rossendale had therefore returned the snuff-box to Jane, and with it he had sent a charming note which asked Mrs Sharpe to do the honour of calling on Lord Rossendale at her leisure.

Although Lord John remembered Sharpe very well, he had no exact recollection of Sharpe's wife. He did dimly recall meeting a fair-haired girl for one evening, but Rossendale met many fair-haired girls and he could not be expected to remember each of them. He fully expected to find Mrs Jane Sharpe dull, for the woman came as a petitioner which would mean that Lord Rossendale must be forced to endure the tedium of her pathetic appeal, yet, for her husband's sake, Lord Rossendale would do his decent best to oblige.

Mrs Sharpe demonstrated an ominous desperation by calling on Lord Rossendale the very morning after he had returned the jewelled snuff-box. Lord Rossendale had been at the tables the night before and had lost heavily. He could not afford to lose heavily, and so he had drowned his disappointments in drink which meant he was very late in rising, and thus kept the importunate Mrs Sharpe waiting a full two hours. He muttered an apology as he entered his drawing-room and, having apologised, he stood quite still.

Because the importunate Mrs Sharpe was undeniably lovely.

'It is Mrs Sharpe? I do have that honour?' Lord Rossendale could not imagine how he might have forgotten meeting this woman.

She curtseyed. 'It is, my Lord.'

And thereafter, like the decent fair man he perceived

himself to be, Rossendale attempted to help Mrs Sharpe out of her troubles. He did it most successfully, extracting a promise that the government would take no further interest in Mrs Jane Sharpe's finances. In the performance of that decent and fair duty, he found himself attracted to her, which was hardly surprising for she was a girl of the most provoking looks, and if she seemed to reciprocate that attraction, then that was also hardly surprising, for Lord John Rossendale was a most elegant, handsome and amusing young man, though admittedly somewhat heavily in debt. Jane, acknowledging her own debt of gratitude to his Lordship, was only too delighted to pay his gambling debts, though each of them insisted that her payments were merely loans.

There was gossip, of course, but the gossip did not hurt Rossendale. The conquest of Mrs Sharpe, if conquest it was, was seen by society as an act of great bravery, for surely the husband would exact a terrible revenge. London knew that a certain Naval officer still found it impossible to sit in comfort, and London wondered how many weeks Lord Rossendale would live once Major Sharpe returned from the wars. The wager book at Lord Rossendale's club did not give his Lordship more than three months before he was forced to eat grass before breakfast. 'And that'll be the finish of him,' a friend said, 'and more's the pity, for Johnny's an amusing fellow.'

Yet, despite the threat, neither Jane nor Lord John tried to dull the edge of the gossip by circumspection. And, as her popularity in society increased, so did people feel a growing sympathy for Jane Sharpe. Her husband, it was said, was a thief. He had deserted the army. The man was clearly no good, and Jane was plainly justified if she sought consolation elsewhere.

Jane herself never complained that Major Sharpe was a bad man. She did tell Lord Rossendale that her husband was unambitious, and proved that contention by saying he would mire her in a country village where her silks and satins must be surrendered to the moths. She allowed that he had been a magnificent soldier, but alas, he was also a dull man, and in the society amongst which Jane now moved with such assurance, dullness was a greater sin than murder. Lord Rossendale, though frequently penniless, was never dull, but instead seemed to move in a glittering whirl of crystal bright opportunities.

Yet still, like an awkward bastion that resists the surge of a victorious army, there remained the inconvenient fact of Major Sharpe's continuing dull existence, and Peter d'Alembord's visit to Jane's house was an abrupt and unwelcome reminder of that existence. It was no longer possible, after that meeting, for Jane to pretend that Sharpe had simply disappeared to leave Jane with his money and Rossendale with Jane.

So, that same evening, Jane sent a servant to fetch a carriage and, with a cloak about her bare shoulders, she was conveyed the short distance to Lord Rossendale's town house which overlooked St James's Park. The servants bowed her inside, then brought her a light supper and a glass of champagne. His Lordship, they told her, was expected home soon from his Royal duties.

Lord Rossendale, coming into the candle-lit room an hour later, thought he had never seen Jane looking so beautiful. Perturbation, he thought, made her seem so very frail and vulnerable.

'John!' She stood up to greet him.

'I've heard, my dearest, I've heard.' Lord Rossendale hurried across the room, she met him halfway, and they embraced. Jane clung to him, and Lord Rossendale held her very tight. 'I've heard the awful news,' he said, 'and I'm so very sorry.'

'He came this morning,' Jane's voice came in a breathless rush. 'I hardly credited he would ask for your help! When he said your name I almost blushed! He says he will try to see you, and I could not dissuade him. He wants you to see the Prince about it!'

'Who came?' Lord John feared the answer. He held Jane at arm's length and there was a look of real fear on his face. 'Your husband has returned?'

'No, John!' There was a note of asperity in Jane's voice at Lord Rossendale's misapprehension, though his Lordship showed no displeasure at her tone. 'It was an officer who was a friend of Richard's,' she explained, 'a Captain d'Alembord. He says he met Richard in Bordeaux, and Richard sent him to London to seek your help! Richard expects you to plead with the Prince.'

'My God, so you haven't heard?' Lord John dismissed Jane's news of d'Alembord's visit and instead, very gently, led her to a settle beside the open window. A warm breeze shivered the candle-flames that lit her face so prettily. 'I have some other news for you,' Rossendale said, 'and I fear it is distressing news.'

Jane looked up at his Lordship. 'Well?'

Lord John first poured her a glass of white wine, then sat beside her. He held one of her hands in both of his. 'We have heard from Paris today, my dearest one, and it seems that there was a French officer who could prove your husband's guilt. Or innocence, of course.' He added the last hastily. 'That officer was murdered,' Rossendale paused for a heartbeat, 'and it seems most probable that your husband committed the murder. The French have formally requested our assistance in finding Major Sharpe.'

'No.' Jane breathed the word.

'I pray the allegations are not true.' Lord John, like Jane, knew just what was proper to say at such moments.

Jane took her hand from his, stood, and walked to the room's far end where she stared vacantly into the empty grate. Lord John watched her and, as ever, marvelled at her looks. Finally she turned. 'We should not be too astonished at such news, John. I fear that Richard is a very brutal man.'

'He is a soldier,' Rossendale said in apparent agreement.

Jane took a deep breath. 'I should not be here, my Lord,' she said with a sudden formality.

'My dearest . . .' Lord John stood.

Jane held up a hand to check his protest. 'No, my Lord. I must think of your reputation.' It was very properly and very prettily said, and the inference of noble suffering touched Lord John's heart, just as it was meant to do.

He crossed the room and took a temporarily unwilling Jane into his arms. She insisted that her married name was now tainted, and that Lord John must protect himself by preserving his own good name. Lord John hushed her. 'You don't understand, my dear one.'

'I understand that my husband is a murderer,' she said into his uniform coat.

He held her very close. 'And when he is captured, my dear one, as he will be captured, what then?'

Jane said nothing.

'You will be alone,' Lord John said, then, just in case she had not worked out for herself the fate that would attend a convicted murderer, 'and you will be a widow.'

'No,' she murmured the proper protest.

'So I think it can only reflect on my reputation,' Lord John said nobly, 'if I was to offer you my protection.' And he tilted her pretty, tear-stained face to his and kissed her on the mouth.

Jane closed her eyes. She was not a bad woman, though she knew well enough that what she now did was wrong in the world's eyes. She also knew that she had behaved very ill when Peter d'Alembord had visited her at Cork Street, but she had been frightened to be thus reminded of her husband's existence and, at the same time, she had so wanted to impress d'Alembord with her new sophistication. She knew, too, that her husband was not the brutal, dull man she depicted, but her behaviour demanded an excuse beyond the excuse of her own appetites, and so she must blame Sharpe for the fact that she now loved another man.

And Jane was in love, as was Lord Rossendale. They were not just simply in love, but consumed by love, driven by it, drenched in it, and oblivious to the rest of the world in their obsession with it. And Major Sharpe, by murdering a Frenchman, had seemingly removed their last obstacle to it. And thus, in a warm and candle-shivering night, the lovers could at last anticipate their happiness.

* * *

There had been no sentry on the tower, Lucille explained to Frederickson, because the roof timbers were rotten. So, a week after their drastic arrival at the château, Harper and Frederickson repaired the tower's roof with weathered oak that they took from the disused stalls in the château's stables. They adzed the timber to size, pegged it tight into the masonry, then spread layers of tar-soaked sacking over the planks. 'You should have lead up there, Ma'am,' Frederickson said.

'Lead is expensive,' Lucille sighed.

'Yes, Ma'am.' But Harper delved among the generations of debris that had piled up in the barns and discovered an old lead water-tank that bore the de Lassan coat-of-arms, and he and Frederickson melted it down and made thin sheets of the metal which they fixed between the courses of stone so that the tower at last had a watertight roof.

'I don't know why you God-damned well bother,' Sharpe grumbled that night.

'I've nothing better to do,' Frederickson said mildly, 'so I might as well help Madame about the place. Besides, I like working with my hands.'

'Let the bloody place fall down.' Sharpe lay swathed in stiff flax sheets on the goosedown mattress of a massive wooden bed. His right leg was encased in plaster beneath which the flesh throbbed and itched, his head hurt, and his left shoulder was a nagging viper's nest of pain. The doctor had opined that Sharpe should have the whole arm off, for he doubted if he could otherwise keep the damaged flesh clean, but Harper had performed his old trick of putting maggots into the wound. The maggots had eaten the rotten flesh, but would not touch the clean, and so the arm had been saved. The doctor visited each day, cupping Sharpe with candle-flames and glasses, bleeding him with leeches, and distastefully sniffing the maggot-writhing wounds for any sign of putrefaction. There were none. Sharpe, the doctor said, might be walking again by the summer, though he doubted if the Englishman would ever again have full use of his left arm.

'Bloody God-damned French bitch,' Sharpe now said of Lucille. 'I hope her bloody house falls down around her ears.'

'Drink your soup,' Frederickson said, 'and shut up.'

Sharpe obediently drank some soup.

'It's good soup, isn't it?' Frederickson asked.

Sharpe said nothing, just scowled.

'You're very ungrateful,' Sweet William sighed. 'That soup is delicious. Madame made it specially for you.'

'Then it's probably bloody poisoned.' Sharpe pushed the bowl away.

Frederickson shook his head. 'You should be kinder to Madame Castineau. She feels very guilty about what she did.'

'She bloody well should feel guilty! She's a murderous bloody bitch. She should be hanged, except hanging's too good for her.'

Frederickson paused, then blushed. 'I would be deeply obliged, my friend, if you would refrain from insulting Madame Castineau in my presence.'

Sharpe stared aghast at his friend.

Frederickson straightened his shoulders as though bracing himself to make a very shameful confession. 'I have to confess that I feel a most strong attachment towards Madame.'

'Good God.' Sharpe could say nothing else. This misogynist, this hater of marriage, this despiser of all things female, was in love?

'I understand how you feel about Madame Castineau, of course,' Frederickson hurried on, 'and I cannot blame you, but I think you should know that I have the warmest of feelings towards her. Towards,' he paused, tried to meet Sharpe's gaze, failed, but then, with the coyness of a lover, said the widow's Christian name fondly, 'towards Lucille.'

'Bloody hellfire!'

'I know she isn't a great beauty like Jane,' Frederickson said with an immense but fragile dignity, 'but she has a great calmness in her soul. She's a very sensible woman, too. And she has a sense of humour. If I had not met her I would scarcely have believed that so many excellent qualities could have been combined in one woman.'

Sharpe blew on a spoonful of soup and tried to accustom himself to the thought of Sweet William in love. It was like discovering a wolf purring, or learning that Napoleon Bonaparte's favourite occupation was embroidery. 'But she's French!' Sharpe finally blurted out.

'Of course she's French!' Frederickson said irritably. 'What possible objection can that be?'

'We've been killing the buggers for twenty years!'

'And now we're at peace.' Frederickson smiled. 'We might even make an alliance to mark that peace.'

'You mean you want to marry her?' Sharpe stared at his friend. 'I seem to remember that you thought marriage was a waste of money. Can't you hire its pleasures by the hour? Isn't that what you said? And do I remember you telling me that marriage is an appetite and that once you've enjoyed the flesh you're left with nothing but a dry carcass?'

'I might have questioned the validity of marriage once,' Frederickson said airily, 'but a man is permitted to reconsider his opinions, is he not?'

'Good God Almighty. You are in love!' Sharpe was flabbergasted. 'Does Madame Castineau know how you feel?'

'Of course not!' Frederickson was profoundly shocked at the thought.

'Why ever not?'

'I have no wish to embarrass her by a precipitate declaration of my feelings.'

Sharpe shrugged. 'Love is like war, my friend. Victory goes to those who pounce first and pounce hardest.'

'I can hardly imagine myself pouncing,' Frederickson said huffily, but then, because he had a desperate need to share his feelings with a friend, he coyly asked Sharpe whether his looks would be a barrier to his suit. 'I know myself to be ugly,' Frederickson touched his eye-patch, 'and fear it will be an insuperable difficulty.'

'Remember the pig-woman,' Sharpe advised.

'My feelings in no way resemble the transactions of that squalid tale,' Frederickson said sternly.

'But if you don't confess your feelings,' Sharpe said, 'then you'll get nowhere! Do you sense her feelings in this matter?'

'Madame behaves very properly towards me.'

Sharpe reflected that proper behaviour was not what his friend sought, but thought it best not to say as much. Instead he wondered aloud whether Frederickson would take a letter to the carrier who risked the dangers of the country roads by travelling once a week to Caen.

'Of course,' Frederickson agreed, 'but may I ask why?'

'It's a letter for Jane,' Sharpe explained.

'Of course.' Frederickson sought to turn the subject back to Lucille Castineau, but did so in such a roundabout way that Sharpe might not suspect the deliberate machination.

'It occurs to me, my friend, that there have been times when I might have been a trifle unsympathetic towards your marriage?'

'Really?' Sharpe flinched as a stab of pain went from his shoulder down to his ribs.

Frederickson did not notice Sharpe's discomfort. 'I assure you that I jested. I see now that marriage is a very fortunate state for mankind.'

'Indeed.' Sharpe resisted discussing Frederickson's new devotion to the married state. 'Which is why I would like Jane to travel here.'

'Is that safe for her?' Frederickson asked.

'I thought you and Patrick might meet her at Cherbourg and escort her here.' Sharpe had resumed drinking the soup which, despite his earlier boorish verdict, was quite delicious. 'And once she's here we can all rent a house while I recover? Maybe in Caen?'

'Maybe.' It was clear that Frederickson had no wish to leave the château, yet he agreed to deliver Sharpe's letter to the village carrier.

But, as it happened, there was no need for the letter to go to the postal office in Caen, for the very next night Patrick Harper offered to carry the letter clean into London itself. 'You're not going to be fighting fit, sir, not for a month or two, and I'm worried about Isabella, so I am.'

'She's not in London,' Sharpe said.

'Mr Frederickson thinks it'll be quicker to get a ship for Spain out of England, sir, than it will be from France. So I'll go to England, see Mrs Sharpe, then fetch my own lass back from Spain. Then I'll take her to Ireland.' Harper smiled and suddenly there were tears in his eyes. 'My God, sir, but I'll be going home at last. Can you believe it?'

Sharpe felt a moment's panic at losing this strong man. 'Are you going home for ever?'

'I'll be back here, so I will.' Harper tossed the seven-barrelled gun on to Sharpe's bed. 'I'll leave that here, and my uniform too. It's probably best not to travel in uniform.'

'But you will be back?' Sharpe eagerly sought the re-assurance. 'Because if I'm going to find Ducos I'll need you.'

'So you are going to find him, sir?'

'If I have to go to the end of the bloody earth, Patrick, I'll find that bastard.' It was obvious now, from the evidence of the two fingers that had been hacked off Lassan's dead body, that it must have been Pierre Ducos who had killed Madame Castineau's brother. Lucille herself had accepted that verdict, and her acceptance had only increased the remorse she felt for her precipitate shooting of the Rifleman. Sharpe did not care whether she felt remorse or not, nor did he much care that her brother was dead, but he did care that he should find Ducos. 'I'll get well first,' he now told Harper, 'then I'll hunt the bugger down.'

Harper smiled. 'I'll be back here to help you, sir, I promise.'

'It would be harder without you,' Sharpe said, which was his way of saying that he could not bear it if Harper deserted him now. Sharpe had always known that peace might separate their friendship, but the immediate prospect of that separation was astonishingly hard to bear.

'I'll be back by the summer, sir.'

'So long as the provosts don't catch you, Patrick.'

'I'll murder the bastards before they lay a hand on me.'

Harper left the next morning. It seemed strange not to hear his tuneless whistle or his loud cheerful voice about the château. On the other hand Sharpe was pleased that the Irishman was carrying the letter to Jane for she had always liked Harper and Sharpe was certain she would respond to the big man's plea that she travel quickly into Normandy where her husband lay ill.

A week after Harper had left, Frederickson carried Sharpe downstairs so he could eat at a table which had been placed in the château's yard. Madame Castineau, knowing that Sharpe disliked her, had kept a very politic distance from the Rifleman since the night when she had shot him. This night, though, she smiled a nervous welcome and said she hoped he would eat well. There was wine, bread, cheese, and a small piece of ham that Frederickson unobtrusively placed on Sharpe's plate.

Sharpe looked at Frederickson's plate, then at Madame Castineau's. 'Where's yours, William?'

'Madame doesn't like ham.' Frederickson cut himself some cheese.

'But you like it. I've seen you kill for it.'

'You need the nourishment,' Frederickson insisted, 'I don't.'

Sharpe frowned. 'Is this place short of money?' He knew that Madame Castineau spoke no English, so had no qualms about talking thus in front of her.

'They're poor as church mice, sir. Rich in land, of course, but that doesn't help much these days, and they rather emptied the coffers on Henri's betrothal party.'

'Bloody hell.' Sharpe sliced the ham into three ludicrously small portions. His actions were very clumsy for he could still not use his left arm. He distributed the meat evenly between the three plates. Madame Castineau began to protest, but Sharpe growled her to silence. 'Tell her my wife will bring some money from England,' he said.

Frederickson translated, then offered Lucille's reply which was to the effect that she would accept no charity.

'Tell the bloody woman to take what's offered.'

'I'll hardly tell her that,' Frederickson protested.

'Damn her pride, anyway.'

Lucille blanched at the anger in Sharpe's voice, then hurried into a long conversation in French with Frederickson. Sharpe scowled and picked at his food. Frederickson tried to include him in the conversation, but as it was about the château's history, and the styles of architecture that history reflected, Sharpe had nothing to offer. He leaned his chair back and prayed that Jane would come soon. Surely, he persuaded himself, her previous silence had been an accident of the uncertain delivery of mail to the army. She would have already spoken to d'Alembord, and would doubtless welcome Harper's arrival. Indeed, it was probable that Harper was already in London and Sharpe felt a welcome and warm hope that Jane herself might arrive at the château in less than a week.

Sharpe was suddenly aware that Frederickson had asked him a question. He let the chair fall forward and was rewarded with an agonizing stab of pain down his plastered right leg. 'Jesus bloody Christ!' he cursed, then, with a resentful glance at the widow, 'I'm sorry. What is it, William?'

'Madame Castineau is concerned because she told the Paris lawyer that we murdered her brother.'

'So she damn well should be.'

Frederickson ignored Sharpe's surly tone. 'She wonders whether she should now write to Monsieur Roland and tell him that we are innocent.'

Sharpe glanced at the Frenchwoman and was caught by her very clear, very calm gaze. 'No,' he said decisively.

'*Non?*' Lucille frowned.

'I think it best,' Sharpe suddenly felt awkward under her scrutiny, 'if the French authorities do not know where to find us. They still believe we stole their gold.'

Frederickson translated, listened to Lucille's response, then looked at Sharpe. 'Madame says her letter will surely persuade the authorities of our innocence.'

'No!' Sharpe insisted a little too loudly.

'Why not?' Frederickson asked.

'Because the damned French have already faked evidence against us, so why should we trust them now? Tell Madame I have no faith in the honesty of her countrymen so I would be most grateful if, for so long as we are in her house, she would keep our presence a secret from Paris.'

Frederickson made a tactful translation, then offered Sharpe Lucille's reply. 'Madame says she would like to inform the authorities who was responsible for the murder of her mother and brother. She wants Major Ducos punished.'

'Tell her I will punish Ducos. Tell her it will be my pleasure to punish Ducos.'

The tone of Sharpe's voice made any translation unnecessary. Lucille looked at Sharpe's face with its slashing scar that gave him such a mocking look, and she tried to imagine her brother, her gentle and kind brother, facing this awful man in battle, and then she tried to imagine what kind of woman would marry such a man. Frederickson began to interpret Sharpe's reply, but Lucille shook her head. 'I understood, Captain. Tell the Major that I will be for ever grateful if he can bring Major Ducos to justice.'

'I'm not doing it for her,' Sharpe said in curt dismissal, 'but for me.'

There was an embarrassed pause, then Frederickson studiedly returned the conversation to the château's history. Within minutes he and Lucille were again absorbed, while Sharpe, warm in the evening sun, dreamed his soldier's dreams that were of home and love and happiness and revenge.

CHAPTER 11

Patrick Harper liked London's cheerfully robust chaos. He could not have contemplated living there, though he had relatives in Southwark, but he had enjoyed his two previous visits, and once again found an endless entertainment in the hawkers and street-singers. There were also enough Irish accents in the capital to make a Donegal man feel comfortable.

Yet he was not comfortable now. He should have been for he was sitting in a tavern with a pot of ale and a steak and oyster pie, yet a very unhappy Captain d'Alembord was threatening to capsize Harper's well-ordered world.

'I think I can understand why it has happened,' d'Alembord said painfully, 'I just don't want to believe that it's true.'

'It's not true, sir,' Harper said stoutly, and in utter defiance of all Captain d'Alembord's evidence. 'Mrs Sharpe's good as gold, so she is. Take me round there, sir, and she'll be as happy as a child to see me.'

d'Alembord shrugged. 'She quite refused to receive me again, and Lord Rossendale has ignored all my letters. I finally went to see Sir William Lawford. Do you remember him?'

'Of course I remember One-armed Willy, sir.' Sir William Lawford, now a member of Parliament, had commanded the Prince of Wales's Own Volunteers until the French had removed one of his arms at Ciudad Rodrigo.

d'Alembord shook his head sadly. 'Sir William assured

me that Mrs Sharpe and Lord Rossendale are,' d'Alembord paused, then said the damning word, 'intimate. It could just be ill-natured gossip, of course.'

'It must be nothing but gossip.' Harper's world was bounded by certainties, one of which was that a pledge of love was entirely unbreakable, which was why, though he was made very uncomfortable by these speculations about Jane Sharpe, he still refused to give them any credit. 'I expect they're just trying to help Mr Sharpe, sir, so it stands to reason that they have to spend a bit of time together. And you know how tongues start flapping when a man and woman spend time together. So why don't we just walk round there and I'll give her the Major's letter, and I'll warrant she'll be as happy as a hog in butter when she reads it. I'll just finish the pie first, if I might. Are you sure you wouldn't want a bite of it yourself?'

'You finish it, Sergeant-Major.'

'I'm not a soldier any more, sir,' Harper said proudly, then plucked at the hem of his new coat as proof. He had discarded the old clothes Madame Castineau had given him, and replaced them with a suit of thickly woven wool, stout boots, gaiters, and a neckcloth which he had purchased with part of the money he had left in London where, like Sharpe, he had sold his Vitoria jewels. He was clearly pleased with his purchases, which made him look like a prosperous farmer come to town. His only weapon now was a thick and ungainly cudgel. 'I haven't got my papers yet,' he admitted to d'Alembord, 'but once Mr Sharpe's off the hook then I dare say he'll get them.'

'Be careful you're not arrested.'

'Who'd dare?' Harper grinned and gestured towards the cudgel.

The pie finished and the ale drunk, the two men walked slowly westwards. It was a lovely spring evening. The sky was delicately veined with thin cloud beyond the gauzy pall of London's smoke, and the new leaves in the squares and wider streets had still not been darkened by soot and so looked spring-bright and full of hope. The beauty of the evening infused Harper with a quite unwarranted optimism. 'It's going to be all right, sir, so it is,' he insisted. 'Just wait till Mrs Sharpe sees me! It'll be grand to see the lass again!' He dropped a coin into the upturned shako of a legless beggar. d'Alembord did not have the heart to tell Harper that the vast majority of wounded indigents were not, despite their remnants of army uniforms, veterans of the war, but were merely taking advantage of the generosity of officers home from France. 'Have you thought,' Harper went on, 'of writing to Nosey?'

'Nosey' was the newly created Duke of Wellington who, for lack of any better government appointment in London, had just been made Ambassador to Paris. 'I've written to him,' d'Alembord said, 'though I've had no reply.'

'Nosey won't let Mr Sharpe down, sir.'

'He won't defend him if he thinks he's a murderer.'

'We'll just have to prove he isn't.' Harper tossed another penny, this time to a man with empty eye-sockets.

They turned into Cork Street where Harper sniffed his disapproval for the elegant houses. 'Mr Sharpe will never live here, sir. She'll have to change her tune a bit smartish, I can tell you! He's set on the countryside, so he is.'

'And I tell you she's set her heart on London.'

'But she's the woman, isn't she? So she'll have to do what he wants.' That was another of Harper's unshakeable certainties.

'Hold hard.' d'Alembord put a hand on Harper's arm. 'That's the house, see?' He pointed to the far end of the street where a varnish-gleaming phaeton was drawn up outside Jane's house. A pair of matching chestnuts were in the carriage shafts and an urchin was earning a few coins by holding the horses' heads. 'See her?' d'Alembord was unable to hide the disgust he felt.

Jane was being handed down the steps by a very tall

and very thin young man in the glittering uniform of a cavalry Colonel. He wore pale blue breeches, a dark blue jacket, and had a fur lined pelisse hanging from one shoulder. Jane was in a white dress covered by a dark blue cloak. The cavalryman helped her climb into the high, perilous seat of the phaeton which was an open sporting carriage much favoured by the rich and reckless.

'That's Lord Rossendale,' d'Alembord said grimly.

For the first time since meeting d'Alembord, Harper looked troubled. There was something about Jane's gaiety which contradicted his pet theory that, at worst, she and Rossendale were mere allies in their attempt to help Sharpe. Nevertheless it was for this meeting with Jane that Harper had come to London, and so he took Sharpe's letter from a pocket of his new coat and stepped confidently into the roadway to intercept the carriage.

Lord Rossendale was driving the phaeton himself. Like many young aristocrats, he held the professional carriage-drivers in great awe, and loved to emulate their skills. Rossendale tossed the urchin a coin, climbed up beside Jane, and unshipped his long whip. He cracked the thong above the horses' heads and Jane whooped with feigned and flattering alarm as the well-trained and spirited pair started away. The carriage wheels blurred above the cobbles.

Harper, standing in the roadway, raised his right hand to attract Jane's attention. He held Sharpe's letter aloft.

Jane saw him. For a second she was incredulous, then she assumed that if Harper was in Cork Street, her husband could not be far away. And if her husband was in London then her lover was threatened with a duel. That prospect made her scream with genuine fright. 'John! Stop him!'

Lord Rossendale saw a huge man holding a cudgel. It was early in the day for a footpad to be on London's more fashionable streets, but Rossendale nevertheless assumed that the big man was attempting a clumsy ambush. He flicked the reins with his left hand and shouted at the horses to encourage them to greater speed.

'Mrs Sharpe! Ma'am! It's me!' Harper was shouting and waving. The carriage was twenty yards away and accelerating fast towards him.

'John!' Jane screamed with fright.

Lord Rossendale stood. It was a dangerous thing to do in so precarious a vehicle, but he braced himself against the seat, then slashed the whip forward so that its thong curled above the horses' heads.

'Sergeant!' d'Alembord shouted from the pavement.

The whip's thong cracked, and its tip raked Harper's cheek. If it had struck him one inch higher it would have slashed his right eye into blindness, but instead it merely cut his tanned face to the bone. He fell sideways as the horses' hooves crashed past him. Harper rolled desperately away, yet even so the phaeton's wheels were so close that he saw their metal rims flicking sparks up from the flint in the cobbles. He heard a whoop of joy.

It was Jane who had made the triumphant sound. Harper sat up in the road and saw her looking back, and he saw, too, the excitement in her eyes. Blood was streaming down Harper's face and soaking his new neck-cloth and coat. Lord Rossendale had sat again while Jane, her face turned back towards Harper and still registering a mixture of relief and joy, was gripping her lover's arm.

Harper stood up and brushed the roadway's horsedung off his trousers. 'God save Ireland.' He was disappointed and astonished, rather than angry.

'I did warn you.' d'Alembord picked up Harper's cudgel and restored it to the Irishman.

'Sweet Mother of God.' Harper stared after the carriage until it slewed into Burlington Gardens. Then, still with an expression of incredulity, he stooped to pick up the fallen letter that was spattered with his blood.

'I'm sorry, Sergeant-Major,' d'Alembord said unhappily.

'Mr Sharpe will kill the bastard.' Harper stared in the direction the carriage had taken. 'Mr Sharpe will crucify him! As for her?' He shook his head in wonderment. 'Has the woman lost her wits?'

'It all makes me believe,' d'Alembord steered Harper towards the pavement, 'that the two of them are hoping the Major never does come home. It would suit them very well if he was arrested and executed for murder in France.'

'I would never have believed it!' Harper was still thinking of Jane's parting cry of triumph. 'She was always kind to me! She was as good as gold, so she was! She never gave herself airs, not that I saw!'

'These things happen, Sergeant-Major.'

'Oh, Christ!' Harper leaned on an area railing. 'Who in heaven's name is to tell Mr Sharpe?'

'Not me,' d'Alembord said fervently, 'I don't even know where he is!'

'You do now, sir.' Harper tore open Sharpe's letter and gave it to the officer. 'The address is bound to be written there, sir.'

But d'Alembord would not take the letter. 'You write to him, Sergeant-Major. He's much fonder of you than he is of me.'

'Jesus. I'm just a numbskull Irishman from Donegal, sir, and I couldn't write a letter to save my own soul. Besides, I'm going to Spain to fetch my own wife home.'

d'Alembord reluctantly took the letter. 'I can't write to him. I wouldn't know what to say.'

'You're an officer, sir. You'll think of something, so you will.' Harper turned again to stare at the empty street corner. 'Why is she doing it? In the name of God, why?'

d'Alembord had pondered that question himself. He shrugged. 'She's like a caged singing bird given freedom.

The Major took her out of that awful house, gave her wings, and now she wants to fly free.'

Harper scorned that sympathetic analysis. 'She's rotten to the bloody core, sir, just like her brother.' Jane's brother had been an officer in Harper's battalion. Harper had killed him, though no one but he and Sharpe knew the truth of that killing. 'Christ, sir.' A foul thought had struck Harper. 'It'll kill Mr Sharpe when he finds out. He thinks the sun never sets on her!'

'Which is why I don't want to write the news to him, Sergeant-Major.' d'Alembord pushed the letter into his coat's tail pocket. 'So perhaps it's better for him to live in ignorant bliss?'

'Christ on His cross.' Harper brushed at the blood on his cheek. 'I don't want to be the one who has to tell him, sir.'

'But you're his friend.'

'God help me, that I am.' Harper walked slowly down the street and dreaded the moment when he would go back to France and be forced to break the news. 'It'll be like stabbing him to his heart, so it will, to his very heart.'

* * *

By the end of May Sharpe could walk to the château's mill and back. He had made himself a crutch, yet still he insisted on putting his weight on to his right leg. His left arm was stiff and could not be fully raised. Doggedly he persisted in exercising it, forcing the joint a fraction further each day. The exercise was horribly painful, so much so that it brought tears to his eyes, but he would not give up.

Nor did he give up hope of Jane's arrival. He liked to sit in the château's archway and stare up the village street. One day an impressive carriage did appear there, and Sharpe's hopes soared, but it was only a church dignitary visiting the priest. No message came from Harper, nor from d'Alembord who surely must have learned of Sharpe's whereabouts from the Irishman. 'Perhaps Harper was arrested?' Sharpe suggested to Frederickson.

'He's a very hard man to arrest.'

'Then why . . .' Sharpe began.

'There'll be an explanation,' Frederickson interrupted curtly. Sharpe frowned at his friend's tone. In these last weeks Frederickson had seemed very content and happy, undoubtedly immersed in his courtship of Lucille Castineau. Sharpe had watched the two of them walking in the orchards, or strolling beside the stream, and he had seen how each seemed to enjoy the other's company. Sharpe, though he was besieged by worry over Jane, had been glad for his friend. But now, in the evening light, as the two Riflemen lingered in the château's archway, there was a troublesome echo of Frederickson's old asperity. 'There'll be a perfectly simple explanation,' Frederickson reiterated, 'but for now I'm more worried about Ducos.'

'I am, too.' Sharpe was prising at the edge of the ragged plaster which still encased his thigh. The doctor insisted that the plaster should stay another month, but Sharpe was impatient to cut it away.

'You shouldn't think about Ducos,' Frederickson said airily, 'not while you're still peg-legging. You should be intent on your recovery, nothing else. Why don't you let me worry about the bastard?'

'I rather thought you had other concerns?' Sharpe suggested carefully.

Frederickson pointedly ignored the comment. He lit a cheroot. 'I rather suspect I'm just wasting my time here. Unless we believe that Ducos will simply walk down that road and ask to be arrested.'

'Of course he won't.' Sharpe wondered what had gone wrong between his friend and the widow, for clearly something had gone badly awry for Frederickson to be speaking in such an offhand way.

'One of us should start looking for him. You can't, but I can.' Frederickson still spoke sharply. He did not look at Sharpe, but rather stared aloofly towards the village.

'Where can you look?'

'Paris, of course. Anything important in France will be recorded in Paris. The Emperor's archives will be kept there. I can't say I'm enamoured with the thought of searching through old ledgers, but if it has to be done, then so be it.' Frederickson blew a cloud of smoke that whirled away across the moat. 'And it'll be better than vegetating here. I need to do something!' He spoke in sudden savagery.

'And you'll leave me alone here?'

Frederickson turned a scornful eye on Sharpe. 'Don't be pathetic!'

'I don't mind being alone,' Sharpe's own anger was showing now, 'but no one speaks English here! Except me.'

'Then learn French, damn it!'

'I don't want to speak the bloody language.'

'It's a perfectly civilized language. Besides, Madame Castineau speaks some English.'

'Not to me, she doesn't,' Sharpe said grimly.

'That's because she's frightened of you. She says you scowl all the time.'

'Then she's hardly likely to want me here on my own, is she?'

'For Christ's sake!' Frederickson said with disgust. 'Do you want Ducos found or not?'

'Of course I do.'

'Then I'll damned well go to Paris,' Frederickson said in a tone of hurt finality. 'I'll leave tomorrow.'

Sharpe, who truly did not want to be left alone in the widow's household, sought another reason to dissuade his friend. 'But you promised to escort Jane from Cherbourg!'

'She hasn't sent for that service yet,' Frederickson said caustically, and suggesting what Sharpe did not want to believe, which was that Jane would not now be coming at all. 'But if she does come,' Frederickson continued, 'she can do what other people do: hire guards.'

Sharpe tried another tack. 'The French authorities must still be looking for us, and you're rather a noticeable man.'

'You mean this?' Frederickson flicked a corner of his mildewed eye shade. 'There must be twenty thousand wounded ex-soldiers in Paris. They'll hardly notice one more. Besides, I won't be so foolish as to travel in my uniform. I'll leave it here, and you can bring it to Paris when I send for you. That is, of course, if I succeed in getting a sniff of Ducos.'

'What do you mean? Bring it to Paris?'

'That's perfectly coherent English, I would have thought, but if you need a translation it means that you can bring me my jacket when you come to Paris.' Frederickson stared at the birds wheeling about the church steeple. 'I mean that when I've discovered some trace of Pierre Ducos I will send you a message and, should you be sufficiently recovered, and should Sergeant Harper have returned, you can come and join me. Is that so very hard to comprehend?'

Sharpe did not say anything until Frederickson turned and looked at him. Then, staring into the single truculent eye, Sharpe asked the feared question, 'Why are you not coming back here, William?'

Frederickson looked angrily away. He drew on the cheroot. For a long time he said nothing, then, at last, he relented. 'I asked Madame Castineau for the honour of her hand this afternoon.'

'Ah,' Sharpe said helplessly, and he knew the rest of the story and he felt a terrible sorrow for his proud friend.

'She was entirely charming,' Frederickson went on, 'just as one would expect from such a lady, but she was also entirely adamant in her refusal. You ask why I will not return here? Because I would find it grossly embarrassing to continue an acquaintanceship which has proved so unwelcome to Lucille.'

239

'I'm certain you're not unwelcome,' Sharpe said, and, when Frederickson made no reply, he tried again. 'I'm so very sorry, William.'

'I can't possibly imagine why you should be sorry. You don't like the woman, so presumably you should be glad that she won't become my wife.'

Sharpe ignored the bombast. 'Nevertheless, William, I am truly sorry.'

Frederickson seemed to crumple. He closed his eyes momentarily. 'So am I,' he said quietly. 'I want to blame you, in some ways.'

'Me!'

'You advised me to pounce. I did. It seems I missed.'

'You pounce before you propose. For God's sake, William, can't you see that women want to be pursued before they're caught?' Frederickson said nothing, and Sharpe tried further encouragement. 'Try again!'

'One doesn't reinforce failure. Isn't that the very first lesson of successful soldiering? Besides, she was quite clear in her refusal. I made a fool of myself, and I don't intend to stay here and endure the embarrassment of that memory.'

'So go,' Sharpe said brutally, 'but I'll come with you.'

'Do you mean to hop to Paris? And what if Jane does come to the château? And how will Harper find you?' Frederickson threw down the cheroot and ground it under the toe of his boot. 'What I'm trying to tell you, my friend, is that I seek my own solitary company for a while. Misery does not make the best entertainment for others.' He turned and saw the elderly Marie carrying dishes to the table in the yard. 'I see supper is served. I would be most grateful if you attempted to carry a little more of the conversation tonight?'

'Of course.'

It was still a miserable supper, but for Sharpe, as for Frederickson, it had fast become a season of misery.

Harper had disappeared, Jane's silence was ominous,

and in the morning a moody Frederickson left for Paris. Madame Castineau stayed indoors, while, in the château's archway, Sharpe sat alone and scowling.

* * *

May had been warm, but June was like a furnace. Sharpe mended in the heat. Lucille Castineau would watch as he exercised his left arm, holding the great cavalry sword outstretched for as long as he could before the muscles became nerveless and, after a moment's quivering, collapsed. He could not raise the arm very high, but each day he forced it a fraction higher. He drenched himself with sweat as he exercised. He disobeyed the doctor by cutting away the brittle plaster from his right leg and, though he was in agony for three days, the pain slowly ebbed. He stumped doggedly about the yard to strengthen his atrophied thigh muscles. He had let his black hair grow very long so that the missing chunk of his left ear would be hidden. One morning, as Sharpe stared into his shaving mirror to judge the success of that vain disguise, he saw a streak of grey in the long black hair.

No news came from London, and none from Frederickson in Paris.

Sharpe looked for tasks about the château and took a simple pleasure in their completion. He rehung a door in the dairy, remade the bed of the cider press and repaired the kitchen chairs. When he could not find work he went for long walks, either between the apple trees or up the steep northern ridge where he forced his pace until the sweat ran down his face with the exertion and pain.

Lucille saw the pain on his face that evening. 'You shouldn't try to . . .' she began, but then said nothing more, for her English was not good enough.

Most of all Sharpe liked to climb up to the tower roof that Frederickson and Harper had mended, and where he would spend hours just staring down the two roads which met at the château's gate. He looked for the return of friends or the coming of his beloved, but no one came.

In late June he struggled to clear a ditch of brambles and weeds, then he repaired the ditch's long disused sluice gate. The herdsman was so pleased that he sent for Madame Castineau who clapped her hands when she saw the water run clear from the mill-race to irrigate the pasture. 'The water, how do you say? No water for years, yes?'

'How many years?' Sharpe was leaning on a billhook. With his long hair and filthy clothes he might have been mistaken for a farm labourer. '*Vingt, quarante?*'

Sharpe's French came slowly, but night by night, sitting awkwardly at the supper table, he was forced to communicate with Madame Castineau. By the end of June he could hold a conversation, though there were still annoying misunderstandings, but by the middle of July he was as comfortable in French as he had ever been in Spanish. He and Lucille now discussed everything: the late war, the weather, God, steam power, India, the Americas, Napoleon, gardening, soldiering, the respective merits of England and France, how to keep slugs out of vegetable gardens, how to grow strawberries, the future, the past, aristocrats.

'There were too many aristocrats in France,' Lucille said scornfully. She was sitting in the last of a summer evening's sunlight, darning one of the big flax sheets. 'It wasn't like England, where only the eldest son inherits. Here, everyone inherited, so we bred aristocrats like rabbits!' She bit the thread and tied off her stitches. 'Henri would never use his title, which annoyed Maman. She didn't care that I ignored mine, but daughters were never important to Maman.'

'You have a title?' Sharpe asked in astonishment.

'I used to have one, before they were all abolished during the revolution. I was only a child, of course; nothing but a little scrap of a child, but I was still formally the

242

Vicomtesse de Seleglise.' Lucille laughed. 'What a non-sense!'

'I don't think it's a nonsense.'

'You're English, which means you are a fool!' she said dismissively. 'It was a nonsense, Major. There were noble-men who were truly nothing but peasants who lived off beans, but still they were accounted aristocrats because their great-great-grandfather had been a viscount or a duke. Look at us!' She gestured about the farmyard. 'We call it a château, but it's really nothing more than a large and penniless farmhouse with a very inconvenient ditch around it.'

'It's a very beautiful farmhouse,' Sharpe said.

'To be sure.' Lucille liked it when Sharpe praised the house. She often said that all she now wanted was to live in the château for ever. There had been a time, she admit-ted, when she had thought that she would like to cut a dash in Paris, but then her husband had died, and her ambition had died with him.

One evening Sharpe asked about Castineau and Lucille fetched his portrait. Sharpe saw a thin, dark-faced man in a well-cut colonel's uniform which gleamed with gold aigulettes. He carried a brass helmet under his left arm and a sabre in his right hand. 'He was very handsome,' Lucille said wistfully. 'No one understood why he chose me. It certainly wasn't for my money!' She laughed.

'How did he die?'

'In battle,' Lucille said curtly, then, with an apologetic shrug, 'how do men die in battle, Major?'

'Nastily.' Sharpe said the word in English.

'Very nastily, I'm sure,' Lucille said in the same language, 'but do you miss it, Major?'

Sharpe pushed his black hair, with its grey streak, away from his forehead. 'The day I heard that peace was signed was one of the happiest of my life.'

'Truly?'

243

'Truly.'

Lucille paused to thread a needle. This evening she was embroidering one of her old dresses. 'My brother said that you were a man who enjoyed war.'

'Maybe.'

'Maybe.' Lucille mockingly imitated Sharpe's scowl. 'What is this *peut-être*? Did you enjoy it?'

'Sometimes.'

She sighed with exasperation at his obdurate evasion. 'So what is enjoyable about war? Tell me, I would like to understand.'

Sharpe had to grope for words if he was to offer an explanation in the unfamiliar language. 'It's very clear-cut. Things are black or white. You have a task and you can measure your success absolutely.'

'A gambler would say the same,' Lucille said scornfully.

'True.'

'And the men you killed? What of them? They were just losers?'

'Just losers,' Sharpe agreed, then he remembered that this woman's husband had died in battle, and blushed. 'I'm sorry, Madame.'

'For my husband?' Lucille instantly understood Sharpe's contrition. 'I sometimes think he died in the way he wished. He went to war with such excitement; for him it was all glory and adventure.' She paused in the middle of a stitch. 'He was young.'

'I'm glad he didn't fight in Spain,' Sharpe said.

'Because that makes you innocent of his death?' Lucille scorned him with a grimace. 'Why are soldiers such romantics? You obviously thought nothing of killing Frenchmen, but just a little knowledge of your enemy makes you feel sympathy! Did you never feel sympathy in battle?'

'Sometimes. Not often.'

'Did you enjoy killing?'

'No,' Sharpe said, and he found himself telling her about

the battle at Toulouse and how he had decided not to kill anyone, and how he had broken the vow. That battle seemed so far away now, like part of another man's life, but suddenly he laughed, remembering how he had seen General Calvet on the battlefield and, because it might help Lucille understand, he described his feelings at that moment; how he had forgotten his fear and had desperately wanted to prove himself a better fighter than the doughty Calvet.

'It sounds very childish to me,' Lucille said.

'You never rejoiced when Napoleon won great victories?' Sharpe asked.

Lucille gave a very characteristic shrug. 'Napoleon.' She pronounced his name scathingly, but then she relented. 'Yes, we did feel pride. We shouldn't have done, perhaps, but we did. Yet he killed many Frenchmen to give us that pride. But,' she shrugged again, 'I'm French, so yes, I rejoiced when we won great victories.' She smiled. 'Not that we heard of many great victories in Spain. You will tell me that was because we were foolish enough to fight the English, yes?'

'We were a very good army,' Sharpe said, and then, provoked by Lucille's continuing curiosity, he told her about Spain, and about his daughter, Antonia, who now lived with relatives on the Portuguese border.

'You never see her?' Lucille asked in a shocked voice.

He shrugged. 'It's being a soldier.'

'That takes preference over love?' she asked, appalled.

'Her mother's dead,' Sharpe said lamely, then tried to explain that Antonia was better off where she was.

'Her mother's dead?' Lucille probed, and Sharpe described his first wife, and how she had died in the snows of a high mountain pass.

'Couldn't your daughter live with your parents?' Lucille asked, and Sharpe had to confess that he had no parents and that, indeed, he was nothing but a fatherless son of a long-dead whore. Lucille was amused by his embarrassed confession. 'William the Conqueror was a bastard,' she said, 'and he wasn't a bad soldier.'

'For a Frenchman,' Sharpe allowed.

'He had Viking blood,' Lucille said. 'That's what Norman means. Northman.' When Lucille told him facts like that she made Sharpe feel very ignorant, but he liked listening to her, and some days he would even take one of her books up to the tower and try hard to read what she had recommended. Lucille gave him one of her brother's favourite books which contained the essays of a dead Frenchman called Montesquieu. Sharpe read most of the essays, though he frequently had to shout down to the yard for the translation of a difficult word.

One night Lucille asked him about his future. 'We'll find Ducos,' Sharpe answered, 'but after that? I suppose I'll go home.'

'To your wife?'

'If I still have a wife,' Sharpe said, and thus for the first time acknowledged his besetting fear. That night there was a thunderstorm as violent as the one which had punctuated Sharpe's long journey north through France. Lightning slashed the ridge north of the château, the dogs howled in the barn, and Sharpe lay awake listening to the rain pour off the roof and slosh in the gutters. He tried to remember Jane's face, but somehow her features would not come clear in his memory.

In the rinsed daylight next morning the carrier arrived from Caen with a letter addressed to Monsieur Tranchant, which was the name Frederickson had said he would use if he had news for Sharpe. The letter bore a Paris address and had a very simple message. 'I've found him. I will wait here till you can come. I am known as Herr Friedrich in my lodging house. Paris is wonderful, but we must go to Naples. Write to me if you cannot come within the next fortnight. My respect to Madame.' There was no explanation of how Frederickson had found Ducos's where-abouts.

'Captain Frederickson sends you his respects,' Sharpe told Lucille.

'He's a good man,' Lucille said very blandly. She was watching Sharpe grind an edge on to his sword with one of the stones used to sharpen the château's sickles. 'So you're leaving us, Major?'

'Indeed, Madame, but if you have no objections I would like to wait a few days to see if my Sergeant returns.'

Lucille shrugged. '*D'accord.*'

Harper returned a week later, full of his own happy news. Isabella was still in her native Spain, but now safely provided with money and a rented house. The baby was well. It had taken Harper longer than he had anticipated to find a ship going to Pasajes, so he had temporarily abandoned his plans for taking Isabella back to Ireland. 'I thought you and I should finish our business first, sir.'

'That's kind of you, Patrick. It's good to see you again.'

'Good to see you, sir. You're looking grand, so you are.'

'I'm going grey.' Sharpe touched his forelock.

'Just a badger's streak, sir.' Harper had been about to add that it would attract the women, but then he remembered Jane and he bit the comment off just in time.

The two men walked along the stream which fed the mill-race. Sharpe liked to sit by this stream with a horse-hair fishing line and some of Henri Lassan's old lures. He told Harper of Frederickson's letter. He said they would leave in the morning, bound first for Paris, then for Naples. He said he was feeling almost wholly fit and that his leg was very nearly as strong as ever. He added a lot more entirely inconsequential news, and only after a long time did he ask the question that the Irishman dreaded. Sharpe asked it in a very insouciant voice that did not in the least deceive Harper. 'Did you manage to see Jane?'

247

'So Captain d'Alembord didn't write to you, sir?' Harper had continued to hope that d'Alembord might have broken the bad news to Sharpe.

'No letter reached me. Did he write?'

'I wouldn't know, sir. It's just that he and I saw Mrs Sharpe together, sir, so we did.' Harper could not bear telling the truth and tried desperately to return the conversation to its former harmless pattern. He muttered that the cows across the stream looked good and fleshy.

'They don't give a bad yield, either,' Sharpe said with a surprising enthusiasm. 'Madame has her dairymaid rub butterwort on the teats; she says it gives more milk.'

'I must remember that one, sir.' Harper stripped a grass stalk of its seeds which he scattered into a drainage ditch. 'And would that be the sluice gate you rebuilt, sir?'

Sharpe proudly showed Harper how he had stripped the worm-gear of rust and smeared it with goose-fat so that the rebuilt blade would once again rise and fall. 'See?' The gear was still stiff, but Sharpe managed to close the gate to cut off the stream water.

'That's grand, sir.' Harper was impressed.

Sharpe wound the gate open again, then sat heavily down on the stream bank. He stared away from Harper, looking across the water towards the beech trees that climbed up the northern spur of the hills. 'Tell me about Jane.'

Harper still tried to evade telling the truth. 'I didn't speak to her, sir.'

Sharpe seemed not to hear the evasion. 'It isn't hard to explain, is it?'

'What's that, sir?'

Sharpe plucked a leaf of watercress from the stream's edge. 'I saw an eel trap once, and I was wondering whether I could put one down by the spillway.' He pointed downstream towards the mill. 'But I can't remember how the damn thing worked exactly.'

Harper sat a pace or two behind Sharpe. 'It's like a cage, isn't it?'

'Something like that.' Sharpe spat out a shred of leaf. 'I suppose she took the money and found herself someone else?'

'I don't know what she did with the money, sir,' Harper said miserably.

Sharpe turned and looked at his friend. 'But she has found another man?'

Harper was pinned to the truth now. He hesitated for a second, then nodded bleakly. 'It's that bugger called Rossendale.'

'Jesus Christ.' Sharpe turned away so that Harper would not see the pain on his face. For a split second that pain was like a red hot steel whip slashing across his soul. It hurt. He had more than half expected this news, and he had thought himself prepared for it, but it still hurt more than he could ever have dreamed. He was a soldier, and soldiers had such high pride, and no wound hurt more than damaged pride. God, it hurt.

'Sir?' Harper's voice was thick with sympathy.

'You'd better tell me everything.' Sharpe was like a wounded man aggravating his injury in the vain hope that it would not prove so bad as he had at first feared.

Harper told how he had tried to deliver the letter, and how Lord Rossendale had scarred him with his whip. He said he was certain Jane had recognized him. His voice tailed away as he described Jane's whoop of triumph. 'I'm sorry, sir. Jesus, I'd have killed the bugger myself, but Mr d'Alembord threatened to turn me over to the provosts if I did.'

'He was quite right, Patrick. It isn't your quarrel.' Sharpe pushed his fingers into the soft earth beside a water-rat's hole. He had watched the otters in this stream, and envied them their playfulness. 'I didn't really think she'd do it,' he said softly.

'She'll regret it, sir. So will he!'

'God!' Sharpe almost said the word as a burst of laughter, then, after another long pause during which Harper could scarcely even bear to look at him, Sharpe spoke again. 'Her brother was rotten to his black heart.'

'So he was, sir.'

'Not that it really matters, Patrick. Not that it really matters at all,' Sharpe said in a very odd voice. 'It's just sauce for the goose, I suppose.'

Harper did not understand, nor did he like to ask for any explanation. He sensed Sharpe's hurt, but did not know how to salve it, so he said nothing.

Sharpe stared at the northern hill. 'Rossendale and Jane must think I'm done for, don't they?'

'I suppose so, sir. They think the Crapauds will arrest you for murder and chop your head off.'

'Perhaps they will.' Not six months before, Sharpe thought, he had commanded his own battalion, had a wife he loved, and could have called upon the patronage of a prince. Now he wore a cuckold's horns and would be the laughing stock of his enemies, but there was nothing he could do except bear the agony. He pushed himself upright. 'We'll not mention this again, Sergeant.'

'No, sir.' Harper was feeling immensely relieved. Sharpe, he thought, had taken the news far better than he had expected.

'And tomorrow we leave for Paris,' Sharpe said brusquely. 'You've got money?'

'I fetched some from London, sir.'

'We'll hire horses in Caen. Perhaps, if you'd be kind enough, you'll lend me some so I can pay Madame Castineau for her services to me? I'll repay you when I can.' Sharpe frowned. 'If I can.'

'Don't even think about repaying it, sir.'

'So let's go and kill the bugger!' Sharpe spoke with an extraordinary malevolence, and Harper somehow doubted whether Pierre Ducos was the man Sharpe spoke of.

Next morning they wrapped their weapons and, in a summer rainstorm, left Lucille's château to find an enemy.

CHAPTER 12

If William Frederickson was in need of solace after his disappointment that Lucille Castineau had rejected his proposal of marriage, then no place was better provided to supply that solace than Paris.

At first he made no efforts to track down Pierre Ducos; instead he simply threw himself into an orgy of distraction to take his mind away from the widow Castineau. He wandered the city streets and admired building after building. He sketched Notre-Dame, the Conciergerie, the Louvre, and his favourite building, the Madeleine. His best drawing, for it was suffused with his own misery, was of the abandoned Arc de Triomphe, intended to be a massive monument to Napoleon's victories, but now nothing more than the stumps of unfaced walls which stood like ruins in a muddy field. Russian soldiers were encamped about the abandoned monument while their women hung washing from its truncated stonework.

The city was filled with the troops of the victorious allies. The Russians were in the Champs-Élysees, the Prussians in the Tuileries, and there were even a few British troops bivouacking in the great square where Louis XVI's head had been cut off. A prurient curiosity made Frederickson pay a precious sou to see the *Souricière*, the 'mousetrap', which was the undercroft of the Conciergerie where the guillotine's victims had been given their '*toilette*' before climbing into the tumbrils. The '*toilette*' was a haircut that exposed the neck's nape so that the blade would not be obstructed, and Frederickson's guide, a cheerful man, claimed that half Paris's mattresses were stuffed with the tresses of dead aristocrats. Frederickson probed the thin mattress in his cheap lodging house and was disappointed to find nothing but horsehair. The owner of the house believed Herr Friedrich to be a veteran of the Emperor's armies; one of the many Germans who had fought for France.

On the day after his visit to the Conciergerie, Frederickson met an Austrian cavalry Sergeant's wife who had fled from her husband and now sought a protector. For a week Frederickson thought he had successfully blotted Lucille out of his mind, but then the Austrian woman went back to her husband and Frederickson again felt the pain of rejection. He tried to exorcise it by walking to Versailles where he drowned himself in the château's magnificence. He bought a new sketchbook and for three days he feverishly sketched the great palace, but all the while, though he tried to deny it to himself, he was thinking of Madame Castineau. At night he would try to draw her face until, disgusted with his obession, he tore up the sketchbook and walked back to Paris to begin his search for Pierre Ducos.

The records of the Imperial Army were still held in the Invalides, guarded there by a sour-faced archivist who admitted that no one had informed him what he was expected to do with the imperial records. 'No one is interested any more.'

'I am,' Frederickson said, and at the cost of a few hours sympathetic listening to the archivist, he was given access to the precious files. After three weeks Frederickson had still not found Pierre Ducos. He had found much else that was fascinating, scandals that could waste hours of time to explore, but there was no file on Ducos. The man might as well never have existed.

The archivist, sensing a fellow bitterness in Herr Friedrich's soul, became enthusiastic about the search, which he believed was for Frederickson's former commanding officer. 'Have you written to the other officers you and he served with?'

'I tried that,' Frederickson said, but then a stray idea flickered into his thoughts. It was an idea so tenuous that he almost ignored it, but, because the archivist was breathing into his face, and because the man had lunched well on garlic soup, Frederickson admitted there was one officer he had not contacted. 'A Commandant Lassan,' he said, 'I think he commanded a coastal fort. I didn't know him, but Major Ducos often talked of him.'

'Let's look for him. Lassan, you said?'

The idea was very nebulous. Frederickson could now wander freely among the file shelves, but, before Napoleon's surrender, regulations had strictly controlled access to the imperial files. Then, any officer drawing a file had his name, and that day's date, written on the file's cover, and Frederickson had been wondering whether Ducos had discovered Lassan through these dusty records and, if so, whether the dead man's file would show Ducos's signature on its cover. If it did – the idea was very tenuous – the archivist might remember the man who had drawn that file.

'It shows an address in Normandy.' The archivist had discovered Lassan's slim file. 'The Château Lassan. I doubt that's one of the great houses of France. I've never heard of it.'

'May I see?' Frederickson took the file and felt the familiar pang as he saw Lucille's address. Then he looked at the file's cover. There was only one signature, that of a Colonel Joliot, but the date beside Joliot's name showed that this file had been consulted just two weeks before Lassan's murder. The coincidence was too fortuitous, so, rejecting coincidence, 'Colonel Joliot' had to be Pierre Ducos. 'Joliot,' Frederickson said, 'that sounds a familiar name?'

'It would be if you wore spectacles!' The archivist touched an inky finger to his own eyeglasses. 'The Joliot brothers are the most reputable spectacle makers in Paris.'

Ducos wore spectacles. Frederickson recalled Sharpe describing the Frenchman's livid anger when Sharpe had once broken those precious spectacles in Spain. Had Ducos consulted this file, then scribbled a familiar name on its cover as a disguise for his own identity? Frederickson had to hide his sudden excitement, which was that of a hunter sighting his prey. 'Where would I find the Joliot brothers?'

'They're behind the Palais de Chaillot, Capitaine Friedrich, but I assure you that neither of them is a colonel!' The archivist tapped the signature.

'I need to see a spectacle-maker anyway,' Frederickson said. 'My eye, Monsieur, is sometimes made tired by reading.'

'It is age, mon Capitaine, nothing but age.'

That diagnosis was echoed by Jules Joliot who greeted Captain Friedrich in his elegant shop behind the Palace of Chaillot. Joliot wore a tiny gold bee in his lapel as a discreet emblem of his loyalty to the Emperor. 'All eyes grow tired with age,' he told Frederickson, 'even the Emperor is forced to use reading glasses, so you must not think it any disgrace. And, Capitaine, you will forgive me, but your one eye is forced to do the labour of two so, alas, it will tire more easily. But you have come to the best establishment in Paris!' Monsieur Joliot boasted that his workshops had despatched spyglasses to Moscow, monocles to Madrid, and eyeglasses to captured French officers in London and Edinburgh. Alas, he said, the war's ending had been bad for business. Combat was hard on fine lenses.

Frederickson asked why a captured officer would send for spectacles from Paris when, surely, it would have been swifter to buy replacement glasses in London. 'Not if he wanted fine workmanship,' Joliot said haughtily. 'Come!' He led Frederickson past cabinets of fine telescopes and opened a drawer in which he kept some of his rivals' products. 'These are spectacles from London. You perceive the distortion at the edge of the lens?'

'But if an officer loses his spectacles,' Frederickson insisted, 'how would you know what to send him as a replacement?'

Joliot proudly showed his visitor a vast chest of shallow tray-like drawers which each held hundreds of delicate plaster discs. Joliot handled the fragile discs with immense care. Each human eye, Joliot said, was subtly different, and great experimentation was needed to find a lens which corrected any one eye's unique deficiency. Once that peculiar lens was discovered it was copied exactly in plaster, and the casts were kept in these drawers. 'This one is an eyeglass for Marshal Ney, this one for the left eye of Admiral Suffren, and here,' Joliot could not resist the boast, 'are the Emperor's reading glasses.' He opened a velvet lined box in which two plaster discs rested. He explained that by using the most delicate gauges and calipers, a skilled workman could grind a lens to the exact same shape as one of the plaster discs. 'No other firm is as sophisticated as we, but, alas, with the war's ending, we are sadly underemployed. We shall soon have to begin making cheap magnifying glasses for the amusement of children and women.'

Frederickson was impressed, but Frederickson had no way of discovering that the Joliot Brothers had never ground a lens in their lives, or that they simply supplied the same Venetian lens that every other spectacle-maker used. The plaster discs, with their promise of scientific accuracy, were nothing but a marvellous device for improving sales.

'Now,' Joliot said, 'we must experiment upon your tired eye, Captain. You will take a seat, perhaps?'

Frederickson had no wish to be experimented on. 'I have a friend,' he said, 'whose spectacles came from your shop, and I noticed that his lens suited my eye to perfection.'

'His name?'

'Pierre Ducos. Major Pierre Ducos.'

'Let us see.' Joliot seemed somewhat disappointed at not being able to dazzle Frederickson with his array of experimental lenses. Instead he took Frederickson into a private office where the firm's order book rested on a long table. 'Pierre Ducos, you say?'

'Indeed, Monsieur. I last saw him at Bordeaux, but alas, where he is now, I cannot tell.'

'Then let us see if we can help.' Monsieur Joliot adjusted his own spectacles and ran a finger down the pages. He hummed as he scanned the lists, while Frederickson, not daring to hope, yet fearing to lose hope, stared about the room which was foully decorated with large plaster models of dissected human eyes.

The humming suddenly ceased. Frederickson turned to see Monsieur Joliot holding a finger to an entry in the big ledger. 'Ducos, you say?' Monsieur Joliot spelled the name, then said it again. 'Major Pierre Ducos?'

'Indeed, Monsieur.'

'You must have very bad sight, mon Capitaine, if his lenses suited your eye. I see that we supplied him with his first eyeglasses in '09, and that we urgently despatched replacements to Spain in January of '13. He is a very short-sighted man!'

'Indeed, but most loyal to the Emperor.' Frederickson thus tried to keep Monsieur Joliot's co-operation.

'I see no address in Bordeaux,' Joliot said, then beamed with pleasure. 'Ah! I see a new order arrived only last week!'

Frederickson hardly dared ask the next question for fear of being disappointed. 'A new order?'

'For no less than five pairs of spectacles! And three of those pairs are to be made from green glass to diminish the sun's glare.' Then, suddenly, Joliot shook his head.

'Alas, no. The order is not for Major Ducos at all, but for a friend. The Count Poniatowski. Just like you, Capitaine, the Count has discovered that Major Ducos's spectacles suit his eyes. It frequently happens that a man discovers that his friend's eyeglasses suit him, and so he orders a similar pair for himself.'

Or, Frederickson thought, a man did not want to be found, so used another name behind which he could hide. 'I would be most grateful, Monsieur, if you would give me the Count Poniatowski's address. Perhaps he will know where I might find the Major. As I told you, we were close friends, and the war's ending has left us sadly separated.'

'Of course.' Monsieur Joliot had no scruples about betraying a client's address, or perhaps his scruples were allayed by the thought that he might lose this customer if he did not comply. 'It's in the Kingdom of Naples.' Joliot scribbled down the Villa Lupighi's address, then asked whether Captain Friedrich could remember which lens of Ducos's spectacles had suited his eye.

'The left,' Frederickson said at random, then was forced to pay a precious coin as a deposit on the monocle which Monsieur Joliot promised to frame in tortoiseshell and to have ready in six weeks. 'Fine workmanship takes that long, I fear.'

Frederickson bowed his thanks. As he left the shop he discovered that the passion of the hunt had meant that he had not thought of Lucille Castineau for the best part of an hour, though the moment he realized his apparent freedom from that obsession, so it returned with all its old and familiar sadness. Nevertheless the hounds had found a scent, and it was time to summon Sharpe to the long run south.

* * *

It was the ignorance that was the worst, Ducos decided, the damned, damned ignorance.

For years he had moved in the privileged world of a trusted imperial officer; he had received secret reports from Paris, he had read captured dispatches, he had known as much as any man about the workings of the Empire and the machinations of its enemies, but now he was in darkness.

Some newspapers came to the Villa Lupighi on the coast north of Naples, but they were old and, as Ducos knew well, unreliable. He read that a great conference would decide Europe's future, and that it would meet in Vienna. He saw that Wellington, newly made a duke, would be Britain's Ambassador in Paris, but that was not the news Ducos sought. Ducos wished to learn that a British Rifle officer had been court-martialled. He wanted to be certain that Sharpe was disgraced, for then no one else could be blamed for the disappearance of the Emperor's gold. Lacking that news, Ducos's fears grew until the Rifleman had become a nemesis to stalk his waking nightmares.

Ducos armed himself against his worst fears. He had Sergeant Challon clear the undergrowth from the hill on which the decayed Villa Lupighi stood so that, by the time the work was done, the old house seemed to be perched on a mound of scraped earth on which no intruder could hope to hide.

The villa itself was a massive ruin. Ducos had restored the living quarters at the building's western end where he occupied rooms which opened on to a great terrace from which he could stare out to sea. He could not use the terrace from midday onwards for he found that the brilliant sunlight reflecting off the sea hurt his eyes and, until the Joliot Brothers sent him the tinted spectacles, he was forced to spend his afternoons indoors.

Sergeant Challon and his men had the rooms behind Ducos's more palatial suite. Their quarters opened on to an internal courtyard built like a cloister. An old fig tree had split one corner of the cloister. Each of the Dragoons had his own woman living in the house, for Challon had insisted to Ducos that his men could not live like monks while they were waiting for the day when it would be safe to leave this refuge. The women were found in Naples and paid with French silver.

The eastern half of the villa, which looked inland to the olive groves and high mountains, was nothing but a ruined chaos of fallen masonry and broken columns. Some of the ruined walls were three storeys high, while others were just a foot off the ground. At night, when Ducos's fears were at their highest, two savage dogs were unleashed to roam those fallen stones.

Sergeant Challon tried to ease Ducos's fears. No one would find them in the Villa Lupighi, he said, for the Cardinal was their friend. Ducos nodded agreement, but each day he would demand another loophole made in some exterior wall.

Sergeant Challon had other fears himself. 'The men are happy enough now,' he told Ducos, 'but it won't last. They can't wait here for ever. They'll get bored, sir, and you know how bored soldiers soon become troublemakers.'

'They've got their women.'

'That's their nights taken care of, sir, but what use is a woman in daylight?'

'We have an agreement,' Ducos insisted, and Challon agreed that they did indeed have an agreement, but now he wanted its terms altered. Now, he suggested, the remaining Dragoons should only stay with Ducos until the year's end. That was enough time, Challon insisted, and afterwards each man would be free to leave, and to take his share of the gold and jewels.

Ducos, presented with the ultimatum, agreed. The year's end was a long way off, and perhaps Challon was right in his belief that by the New Year the dangers would be gone.

'You should enjoy yourself, sir,' Sergeant Challon said slyly. 'You've got the money, sir, and what else is money for?'

And Ducos did try to enjoy himself. One week, after a comet had been discovered, he fancied himself as an astronomer and ordered celestial globes and telescopes to be sent from Naples. That enthusiasm died to be replaced with a burning desire to write the history of Napoleon's wars, which project evaporated after four nights of feverish writing.

He devised a scheme for irrigating the high fields behind the village which lay between the villa and the sea, then he took up painting and insisted that Sergeant Challon fetched the prettiest girls from the village to stand before his easel. He obsessively worked at mathematical problems, he tried to learn the spinet, he found a fascination in maps on which he refought the campaigns of two decades and, in so doing, pushed the bounds of Empire further than Napoleon had ever done. He took to wearing the uniforms that had been in the Emperor's baggage, and the villagers spoke of the mad, half-blind French Marshal who paced his vast house dressed in gold braid and with a huge curved sword hanging by his skinny legs. Ducos might call himself the Count Poniatowski, and claim to be a sickly Polish refugee, yet the villagers knew he was as French as their own King who had once been a real French Marshal.

Sergeant Challon endured all the enthusiasms, for the benefits of indulgence were manifold. There truly was so much money to be divided that this temporary exile was endurable. Challon knew that Ducos could go on spending money like water and there would still be a fortune at the year's end. Even so, when Ducos insisted that more guards be hired, Challon felt constrained to offer a warning note.

'The lads won't be too happy to pay them, sir.'

'I'll pay them.' That generosity was easy to offer because Ducos had insisted that he himself guard the treasure which was stored in a great iron chest cemented to the floor in Ducos's rooms. Even Challon was not certain just how much money was in the box, though he knew down to the last sou just how much each man had been promised at the year's ending. Ducos, to keep faith with the Dragoons, only had to ensure that those shares were faithfully paid when the time came, and in the meantime the balance was his to spend. He knew, even if Challon did not, that the balance was an Emperor's ransom; more than even the greedy Cardinal might imagine.

Challon again tried to change Ducos's mind. 'There might be trouble, sir, between my lads and these new fellows.'

'You're a Sergeant, Challon, you know how to prevent trouble.'

Challon sighed. 'The new men will want women.'

'They may have them.'

'And weapons, sir.'

'Buy only the best.'

So Challon went to the waterfront at Naples and found twenty men who had once served as soldiers. They were scum, Challon told Ducos, but they were scum who knew how to fight. They were deserters, jailbirds, murderers, and drunks, yet they would be loyal to a man who could pay good wages.

The newly hired men moved into the half ruined rooms in the villa's centre. They brought women, pistols, sabres and their muskets. There was no trouble, for they recognized Challon's natural authority and were well rewarded for very little effort. They were not allowed on to the western terrace which was the private domain of their new employer who rarely appeared elsewhere outside the building for he said the sun hurt his eyes, though sometimes they would glimpse him strolling through the big internal courtyard in one of his magnificent uniforms. It was rumoured that he rarely had a woman in his rooms, though once, when he did, the girl reported that the Count Poniatowski had done nothing except stare north to where, far beyond the horizon, another imperial exile had his small kingdom in the Mediterranean. The newly hired guards opined that the Count Poniatowski was mad, but his pay was good, his food and wine plentiful, and he did not quibble when a village girl complained of rape. He would simply have the girl or her parents paid in gold, then encourage his men to practise with their weapons and to keep a good look out for strangers in the hot barren landscape. 'We should have a cannon,' he said to Challon one day.

Sergeant Challon, presented with this new evidence of Major Ducos's fears, sighed. 'It's not necessary, sir.'

'It is necessary. Vitally necessary.' Ducos had decided that his safety depended on artillery, and nothing would change his mind. He showed Challon how a small field gun, mounted in the villa's southern wall, would dominate the road which approached the hill. 'Go to Naples, Challon. Someone will know where a gun can be had.'

So Challon took the money and returned three days later with an old-fashioned grasshopper gun. It was a small field piece which, fifty years before, had been issued to infantry battalions in some armies. The gun was reckoned small enough for two men to carry, which only proved that its inventor had never had to march over rough country with the three-foot brass barrel roped to his shoulder. The barrel was fitted with four stout legs which served as a carriage and, when it was fired, the whole contraption leaped into the air; thus earning the weapon its nickname. Mostly it toppled over after each convulsion, but it could easily be set on its feet again. 'It's all I could get, sir.' Challon seemed somewhat embarrassed by the small and old-fashioned grasshopper gun.

Ducos, though, was delighted, and for a week the landscape echoed with the dull blows of the gun's firing. It took less than a half pound of powder for its charge, yet still it succeeded in blasting a two and a half pound ball over six hundred yards. For a week, solaced by his new toy, Ducos could forget his fears, but when the novelty wore off his terror returned and a green man again began to haunt his dreams. Yet he was fiercely armed, he had loyal men, and he could only wait.

*   *   *

On the day Sharpe left the château Lucille Castineau discovered a piece of paper behind the mirror on the chest of drawers in her room. Sharpe had scrawled Lucille's name on the paper which, when unfolded, proved to contain twelve English golden guineas.

Lucille Castineau did not wish to accept the coins. The gold pieces somehow smacked of charity, and thus offended her aristocratic sense of propriety. She supposed that the big Irishman had brought the money. Her instinct was to return the guineas, but she had no address to which she could send any draft of money. Sharpe had written a brief message in hurried and atrocious French on the sheet of paper which had enclosed the coins, but the message only contained a fulsome thanks for Madame Castineau's kindnesses, a hope that this small donation would cover the expenses of Sharpe's convalescence, and a promise that he would inform Madame Castineau of what had happened in Naples.

Lucille fingered the thick gold coins. Twelve English guineas amounted to a small fortune. The château's dairy urgently required two new roof beams, there were hundreds of cuttings needed if the cider orchard was to be replenished, and Lucille had a nagging desire to own a small two-wheeled cart that could be drawn by a docile pony. The coins would buy all those things, and there would still be enough money left over to pay for a proper grave-slab for her mother and brother. So, putting aristocratic propriety to one side, Lucille swept the coins into the pocket of her apron.

'Life will be better now,' Marie, the elderly kitchen-maid, who had elected herself as a surrogate mother to the widow Castineau, said to Lucille.

'Better?'

'No Englishmen.' The maid was skinning a rabbit which Harper and Sharpe had snared the previous evening.

'You didn't like the Major, Marie?' Lucille sounded surprised.

Marie shrugged. 'The Major's a proper man, Madame, and I liked him well enough, but I did not like the wicked tongues in the village.'

'Ah.' Lucille sounded very calm, though she knew well enough what had offended the loyal Marie. Inevitably the villagers had gossiped about the Englishman's long stay in the château and more than one ignorant person had confidently suggested that Madame and the Major had to be lovers. 'Tongues will be tongues,' Lucille said vaguely. 'A lie cannot hurt the truth.'

Marie had a peasant's firm belief that a lie could sully the truth. The villagers would say there was no smoke without fire, and mud on a kitchen floor spoke of dirty boots, and those snidely sniggering suggestions upset Marie. The villagers told lies about her mistress, and Marie expected her mistress to share her indignation.

But Lucille would not share Marie's anger. Instead she calmed the old woman down, then said she had some writing to do and was not to be disturbed. She added that she would be most grateful if the miller's son could be fetched to take a letter to the village carrier.

The letter went to the carrier that same afternoon. It was addressed to Monsieur Roland, the advocate from the Treasury in Paris, to whom, at long last, Lucille told the whole truth. 'The Englishmen did not want you to be told,' she wrote, 'for they feared you would not believe either them or me, yet, on my honour, Monsieur, I believe in their innocence. I have not told you this before because, so long as the English were in my house, so long did I honour their fear that you would arrange their arrest if you were to discover their presence here. Now they are gone, and I must tell you that the scoundrel who murdered my family and who stole the Emperor's gold is none other than the man who accused the Englishmen of his crime; Pierre Ducos. He now lives somewhere near Naples, to which place the Englishmen have gone to gain the proof of their innocence. If you, Monsieur, can help them, then you will earn the gratitude of a poor widow.'

The letter was sent, and Lucille waited. The summer grew oppressively hot, but the countryside was safer now as cavalry patrols from Caen scoured the vagabonds out of the woodlands. Lucille often took her new pony-cart between the neighbouring villages, and the old gossip about her faded because the villagers now saw that the widower doctor frequently served as the pony-cart's driver. It would be an autumn marriage, the villagers suggested, and quite right too. The doctor might be a good few years older than Madame, but he was a steady and kindly man.

The doctor was indeed a confidant of Lucille, but nothing more. She told the doctor, and only the doctor, about the letter she had sent, and expressed her sadness that she had received no reply. 'Not a proper reply, anyway. Monsieur Roland did acknowledge that he had received my letter, but it was only that, an acknowledgement.' She made a gesture of disgust. 'Perhaps Major Sharpe was right?'

'In what way?' the doctor asked. He had driven the pony-cart to the top of the ridge where it rolled easily along a dry-rutted road. Every few seconds there were wonderful views to be glimpsed between the thick trees, but Lucille had no eyes for the scenery.

'The Major did not want me to write. He said it would be better if he was to find Ducos himself.' She was silent for a few seconds. 'I think perhaps he would be angry if he knew I had written.'

'Then why did you write?'

Lucille shrugged. 'Because it is better for the proper authorities to deal with these matters, *n'est-ce-pas?*'

'Major Sharpe didn't think so.'

'Major Sharpe is a stubborn man,' Lucille said scornfully, 'a fool.'

The doctor smiled. He steered the little cart off the road, bumped it up on to a patch of grass, then curbed the pony in a place from where he and Lucille could stare far to the south. The hills were heavy with foliage and hazed by heat. The doctor gestured at the lovely landscape. 'France,' he said with great complacency and love.

'A fool.' Lucille, oblivious of all France, repeated the words angrily. 'His pride will make him go to be killed! All he had to do was to speak to the proper authorities! I would have travelled to Paris with him, and I would have spoken for him, but no, he has to carry his sword to his enemy himself. I do not understand men sometimes. They are like children!' She waved irritably at a wasp. 'Perhaps he is already dead.'

The doctor looked at his companion. She was staring southwards, and the doctor thought what a fine profile she had, so full of character. 'Would it trouble you, Madame,' he asked, 'if Major Sharpe was dead?'

For a long time Lucille said nothing, then she shrugged. 'I think enough French children have lost their fathers in these last years.' The doctor said nothing, and his silence must have convinced Lucille that he had not understood her words, for she turned a very defiant face on him. 'I am carrying the Major's baby.'

The doctor did not know what to say. He felt a sudden jealousy of the English Major, but his fondness for Lucille would not let him betray that ignoble feeling.

Lucille was again staring at the slumbrous landscape, though it was very doubtful if she was aware of the great view. 'I've told no one else. I haven't even dared take communion these last weeks, for fear of my confession.'

A professional curiosity provoked the doctor's next words. 'You're quite certain you're pregnant?'

'I've been certain these three weeks now. Yes, I am certain.'

Again the doctor was silent, and his silence troubled Lucille who again turned her grey eyes to him. 'You think it is a sin?'

The doctor smiled. 'I'm not competent to judge sinfulness.'

The bland reply made Lucille frown. 'The château needs an heir.'

'And that is your justification for carrying the Englishman's child?'

'I tell myself that is why, but no.' She turned to stare again at the distant hills. 'I am carrying the Major's child because I think I am in love with him, whatever I mean by that, and please do not ask me. I did not want to love him. He has a wife already, but . . .' she shrugged helplessly.

'But?' the doctor probed.

'But I do not know,' she said firmly. 'All I do know is that a bastard child of a bastard English soldier will be born this winter, and I would be very grateful, dear doctor, if you would attend the confinement.'

'Of course.'

'You may tell people of my condition,' Lucille said very matter of factly, 'and I would be grateful if you would tell them who the father is.' She had decided that the news was best spread quickly, before her belly swelled, so that the malicious tongues could exhaust themselves long before the baby was born. 'I will tell Marie myself,' Lucille added.

The doctor, despite his fondness for the widow, rather relished the prospect of spreading this morsel of scandal. He tried to anticipate the questions that he would be asked

268

about the widow's lover. 'And the Major? Will he return to you?'

'I don't know,' Lucille said very softly. 'I just don't know.'

'But you would like him to return?'

She nodded, and the doctor saw a gleam in her eye, but then Lucille cuffed the tear away, smiled, and said it was time they went back to the valley.

Lucille made her confession that week, and attended Mass on the Sunday morning. Some of the villagers said they had never seen her looking so happy, but Marie knew that the happiness was a mere pose which she had assumed for the benefit of the church. Marie knew better, for she saw how often Madame would gaze down the Seleglise road as if she hoped to see a scowling horseman coming from the south. Thus the warm weeks of a Norman summer passed, and no horseman came.

Part Four

CHAPTER 13

It proved a long journey. Sharpe still feared capture and so he avoided all livery stables, coaching inns and barge quays. They had purchased three good horses with a portion of the money Harper had brought from England, and they coddled the beasts south from Paris. They travelled in civilian clothes, with their uniforms and rifles wrapped inside long cloth bundles. They avoided the larger towns, and spurred off the road whenever they saw a uniformed man ahead. They only felt safe from their shadowy enemies when they crossed the border into Piedmont. From there they faced a choice between the risk of brigands on the Italian roads or the menace of the Barbary pirates off the long coastline. 'I'd like to see Rome,' Frederickson opted for the land route, 'but not if you're going to press me to make indecent haste.'

'Which I shall,' Sharpe said, so instead they sold the horses for a dispiriting loss and paid for passage on a small decaying coaster that crawled from harbour to harbour with an ever-changing cargo. They carried untreated hides, raw clay, baulks of black walnut, wine, woven cloth, pigs of lead, and a motley collection of anonymous passengers among whom the three civilian-clothed Riflemen, despite their bundled weapons, went unremarked. Once, when a dirty grey topsail showed in the west, the captain swore it was a North African pirate and made his passengers man the long sweeps which dipped futilely in the limpid water. Two hours later the 'pirate' ship turned out to be a Royal Navy sloop which disdainfully ghosted past the exhausted oarsmen. Frederickson stared at his blistered hands, then snarled insults at the merchant-ship's captain.

Sharpe was impressed by his friend's command of Italian invective, but his admiration only earned a short-tempered reproof. 'I am constantly irritated,' Frederickson said, 'by your naïve astonishment for the mediocre attainments of a very ordinary education. Of course I speak Italian. Not well, but passably. It is, after all, merely a bastard form of dog-Latin, and even you should be able to master its crudities with a little study. I'm going to sleep. If that fool sees another pirate, don't trouble to wake me.'

It was a difficult journey, not just because circumspection and Harper's shrinking store of money had demanded the most frugal means of travel, but because of Lucille Castineau. Frederickson's questions about the widow had commenced almost as soon as Sharpe rejoined his friend in Paris. Sharpe had answered the questions, but in such a manner as to suggest that he had not found anything specifically remarkable in Madame Castineau's life, and certainly nothing memorable. Frederickson too had taken care to sound very casual, as though his enquiries sprang from mere politeness, yet Sharpe noted how often the questions came. Sharpe came to dread the interrogations, and knew that he could only end them by confessing a truth he was reluctant to utter. The inevitable moment for that confession came late one evening when their cargo-ship was working its slow way towards the uncertain lights of a small port. 'I was thinking,' Frederickson and Sharpe were alone on the lee rail and Frederickson, after a long silence, had broached the dreaded subject, 'that perhaps I should go back to the château when all this is over. Just to thank Madame, of course.' It was phrased as a benign suggestion, but there was an unmistakable appeal in the words; Frederickson sought Sharpe's assurance that he would be welcomed by Lucille.

'Is that wise?' Sharpe was staring towards the black

274

loom of the coast. Far inland a sheet of summer lightning flickered pale above jagged mountains.

'I don't know if wisdom applies to women,' Frederickson said in heavy jest, 'but I would appreciate your advice.'

'I really don't know what to say.' Sharpe tried to shrug the topic away, then, in an attempt to head it off entirely, he asked Frederickson if he had tasted anything odd in the supper served on board that night.

'Everything on this ship tastes odd.' Frederickson was irritated by Sharpe's change of subject. 'Why?'

'They said it was rabbit. But I was in the galley this morning and noted that the paws of the carcasses had been chopped off.'

'You have a sudden taste for rabbit paws?'

'It's just that I was told that rabbit carcasses sold without paws are almost certainly not rabbit at all, but skinned cats.'

'It's undoubtedly useful information,' Frederickson said very caustically, 'but what in hell has that got to do with my returning to the château? I do you the distinct honour of asking for your advice about my marital future, and all you can do is blather on about dead cats! For Christ's sake, you've eaten worse, haven't you?'

'I'm sorry,' Sharpe said humbly. He still stared at the dark coast rather than at his friend.

'I have been thinking about my behaviour,' Frederickson now adopted a tone of ponderous dignity, 'and have decided that I was wrong and you were right. I should have pounced before proposing. My mistake, I believe, lay in treating Madame Castineau with too great a fragility. Women admire a more forthright attitude. Is that so?'

'Sometimes,' Sharpe said awkwardly.

'A very useful reply,' Frederickson said sarcastically, 'and I do thank you for it. I am asking your advice and I would be grateful for more substantial answers. I know your feelings about Madame Castineau . . .'

'I doubt you do . . .' Sharpe began the feared confession.

'You have a distaste for her,' Frederickson insisted on continuing, 'and I can understand that attitude, but I confess that I have found it impossible to exorcise her from my thoughts. I apologise profoundly if I embarrass you by raising the matter, but I would be most grateful if you could tell me whether, after I had left the château, she showed even the slightest attachment to my memory.'

Sharpe knew how very hard it was for Frederickson to reveal these private agonies, but Sharpe also knew it was time for him to make those agonies much worse with the admission that he had himself become Lucille's lover. He feared that his friendship with Frederickson would be irreparably damaged by such an admission, but it was clearly inescapable. He hesitated for a bleak moment, then seized his courage. 'William, there is something that you ought to know, something I should have told you much earlier, indeed, I should have told you in Paris, but . . .'

'I don't wish to hear unwelcome news,' Frederickson, hearing the despondency in Sharpe's voice, interrupted brusquely and defensively.

'It is important news.'

'You are going to tell me that Madame does not wish to see me again?' Frederickson, anticipating the bad news, was trying to hurry it.

'I'm sure she would be very happy to renew your acquaintance,' Sharpe said feebly, 'but that . . .'

'But that she would not be happy if I was to renew my attentions? I do understand.' Frederickson spoke very stiffly. He had interrupted Sharpe again in a desperate attempt to finish the conversation before his pride was lacerated any further. 'Will you oblige me by not mentioning this matter again?'

'I must just say, I insist on saying . . .'

'I beg you.' Frederickson spoke very loudly. 'Let the

matter rest. You, of all people, should understand how I feel,' which, oblique though it was, was Frederickson's first indication that he had learned the truth about Jane from Harper.

Thereafter neither Sharpe nor Frederickson spoke of Madame Castineau. Harper, oblivious to either officer's interest in Lucille, would sometimes speak of her, but he soon realized that the subject was tender and so ceased to mention the widow, just as he never spoke of Jane. The only safe topic of conversation was the Riflemen's mutual enthusiasm for the pursuit and punishment of Pierre Ducos.

Which pursuit and punishment at last seemed imminent when, on a hot steamy morning, the merchant ship came to Naples. The first evidence of the city's proximity arrived before dawn when a southerly wind brought the stench of faecal alleyways across the darkened sea. In the first light Sharpe saw the volcanic smoke smearing a cloudless sky, then there was the hazy outline of hills, and lastly the glory of the city itself, stinking and lovely, heaped on a hill in jumbled confusion. The bay was crowded. Fishing boats, cargo vessels and warships were heading to and from the great harbour into which, creeping against a sulphurous wind, three Riflemen came for vengeance.

*   *   *

Monsieur Roland had silently cursed the widow Castineau. Why had she not written earlier? Now the Englishmen, with all their precious information, had fled, and Roland himself must move with an unaccustomed alacrity.

He wrote an urgent message that was placed in the hollow handle of a sword-hilt. The sword belonged to a Swiss doctor who half killed six horses in his haste to reach the Mediterranean coast where a sympathizer carried him in a fast brigantine to Elba. The Royal Naval frigate, ostensibly guarding Elba's small harbour at Portoferraio, did not search the brigantine, and if she had her crew would merely have discovered that one of the Emperor's old doctors had arrived to serve his master.

The message was unrolled in an ante-chamber of an Emperor's palace that was nothing more than an enlarged gardener's cottage which stood in a grand position high above the sea. The Emperor himself was somewhere in the island's interior where he was surveying land that could be used to plant wheat. A messenger was sent to summon him.

That evening the Emperor walked in the small garden behind his palace. A man had been found among his exiled entourage who both knew Pierre Ducos and, by some fluke of good fortune that could hardly be expected to attend a fallen idol like Napoleon, had even met the two English Riflemen. 'You'll sail for Naples tomorrow, and you will take a dozen soldiers with you;' the Emperor ordered. 'I doubt that Murat will want to help me, but we have little time, so you will have to seek his aid.' The Emperor stopped and jabbed a finger into the chest of his companion. 'But do not, my dear Calvet, tell him that there is money at stake. Murat's like a dog smelling a bitch on heat when he scents money.'

'Then what should I tell the bastard?'

'You must be clever with him!' The Emperor paced the gravel walk in silence, then, realizing that his companion was not a subtle man, he sighed. 'I will tell you what to say.'

Yet, in the event, Joachim Murat, once an imperial Marshal, but now King of Naples, would not receive General Calvet. Instead, in subtle insult, Napoleon's envoy was sent to the Cardinal who, enthroned in his perfumed grandeur, was annoyed that this squat and battle-scarred Frenchman had not gone on his knees to kiss the Cardinal's ring. Yet his Eminence was well accustomed to French arrogance, and it was high time, the Cardinal believed, to punish it. 'You come on an errand,' the Cardinal spoke in good French, 'from the Emperor of Elba?'

'On a mission of goodwill,' Calvet replied very grandly. 'The Emperor of Elba is eager to live in peace with all his fellow monarchs.'

'The Emperor always said that,' the Cardinal smiled, 'even when he was killing the soldiers of those fellow monarchs.'

'Your Eminence is kind to correct me,' Calvet said, though in truth he felt the insults of this meeting deeply. Napoleon might now be diminished into being the ruler of a small and insignificant island, but even in his sleep the Emperor had been a greater monarch than the gimcrack ruler of this ramshackle statelet. Joachim Murat, King of Naples and the titular master of this fat Cardinal, had been nothing till Napoleon raised him to his toy throne.

The Cardinal shifted himself into comfort on his own throne's tasselled cushion. 'I am minded to expel you from the kingdom, General, unless you can persuade me otherwise. Your master has greatly troubled Europe, and I find it disturbing that he should now send armed men, even so few, to our happy kingdom.'

Calvet doubted the kingdom's happiness, but had no reason to doubt that the Cardinal would expel him. He made his voice very humble and explained that he and his men had come to Naples to search for an old comrade of the Emperor's. 'His name is Pierre Ducos,' Calvet said, 'and the Emperor, mindful of Major Ducos's past services, only seeks to offer him a post in his private household.'

The Cardinal pondered the request. His spies had not been idle during the months in which the Count Poniatowski had fortified the Villa Lupighi, and the Cardinal had long ago discovered Ducos's identity, and learned of the existence of the great strongbox with its seemingly inexhaustible supply of precious gems. Whatever General Calvet might claim about Napoleon wishing to offer Ducos

279

an appointment, the Cardinal well knew that it was money which had brought General Calvet to Naples. The Cardinal smiled innocently. 'I know of no Pierre Ducos in the kingdom.'

Calvet was too wily to accept the bland statement at its face value. 'The Emperor,' he said, 'would be most grateful for your Eminence's assistance.'

The Cardinal smiled. 'Elba is a very little island. There are some olives and shellfish, little else. Do mulberries grow there?' He made this enquiry of a long-nosed priest who sat at a side table. The priest offered his master a sycophantic smile. The Cardinal, who was enjoying himself, looked back to Calvet. 'What gratitude are we to expect of your master? A cargo of juniper berries, perhaps?'

'The Emperor will show his gratitude with whatever is in his power to give,' Calvet said stubbornly.

'Gratitude,' the Cardinal's voice hardened, 'is a disease of dogs.'

The insult was palpable, but Calvet steeled himself to ignore it. 'We merely ask your help, your Eminence.'

The Cardinal was becoming bored with this unsubtle Frenchman. 'If this Pierre Ducos is in the kingdom, General, then he has caused us no trouble, and I see no reason why I should help betray him to your master.'

Which was the moment when General Calvet played the Emperor's card, and played it very well. He feigned a look of astonishment. 'Betray, your Eminence? We don't seek Major Ducos for any reason other than to offer him employment! Though, in truth, we do know that the English seek Major Ducos, and are even sending men here to do him harm. Why they should wish that, I cannot tell, but on my master's life, it is true. The Englishmen may already be here!' Calvet doubted whether Sharpe had yet reached Naples, for Monsieur Roland had moved with an exemplary speed, but Calvet knew it would not be long before the Riflemen did arrive in the city.

There was a long silence after Calvet had spoken of the English involvement. The Cardinal might despise the fallen Napoleon, but he disliked the rampantly victorious English far more. He was forced to shelter their Mediterranean fleet and flatter their heretic ambassador, but the Cardinal feared their territorial ambitions. Their troops had taken Malta, and thrown the French from Egypt, and where else would the Redcoats choose to land on the Mediterranean's shores? Even now, as the Cardinal and the General spoke, there were no less than six British warships in the harbour at Naples. Their fleet used the harbour as if it was their own, and though they claimed they were only present to deter the scum of the Barbary Coast, the Cardinal nevertheless feared the English, though he would not betray those fears to General Calvet. 'The English have never expressed any interest in this man,' the Cardinal said instead, though in a much milder tone.

'Nor will they, your Eminence. They are insolent enough to believe they can ignore you. Nevertheless, on my honour, I do assure you that a party of Englishmen is either in your kingdom or on their way here.' Calvet was certainly not going to reveal that there would only be three Englishmen and that, far from being on official business, they were themselves fugitives.

'The Emperor has sent you to kill these Englishmen?' The Cardinal was beginning to wonder whether this bluff Frenchman might not, after all, be of some use to him.

'I am only here to dissuade them, your Eminence. I am not here to use violence, for the Emperor has no wish to disturb the peace of your happy kingdom.'

'But you are a man accustomed to death, General?'

'It's my only trade.' Calvet could not resist the boast. 'I learned it against the Austrians, who are easily killed, then perfected it against the Russians, who die very hard indeed.' Calvet had finished the war as a General of

Brigade, but had begun it as a common soldier. Calvet, indeed, was one of Napoleon's beloved mongrels; a veteran brawler and gutter-fighter who had risen from the ranks because of his ability to ram men into battle. He was not clever, but he was lucky, and he was as tough as a battered musket. In campaign after campaign Calvet had savaged the Emperor's enemies. He had even brought an intact brigade out of Russia because his men feared the peasant General more than they feared the Cossacks or the Muscovite winter. Indeed, Calvet had only known one personal defeat, and that was when his brigade tried to drive Sharpe's force of Riflemen and Marines from the Teste de Buch fort. It was Calvet's memory of that defeat which gave his present pursuit of the Riflemen a special piquancy.

The Cardinal ignored the belligerence. 'How will I recognize these Englishmen?'

Calvet had met both Sharpe and Frederickson once, and he had glimpsed Sharpe amidst the smoke of the Toulouse battlefield. He was not certain he would recognize either man again, but Monsieur Roland had also provided a full description of both Rifle officers. Calvet was too canny to give away the small advantage of those descriptions straightaway. 'Details of their appearance are being sent to me, your Eminence.'

The Cardinal allowed Calvet the point. 'And what do the English plan to do here, General?'

Calvet shrugged. 'To kill Major Ducos, but why, I cannot say. Who can explain the spleen of the English?'

Who indeed? the Cardinal thought, or who could not see through the clumsy lies of a French General? Yet, amidst the deception, the Cardinal could perceive a very real profit for himself and the kingdom. Clearly the English were after the Count Poniatowski's strongbox, as was the Emperor of Elba, but so, too, was the Cardinal. His spies in the Villa Lupighi had reported that Ducos and his men were planning to leave the kingdom at the end of the year and when they left, the strongbox would leave too. There would be no more lavish bribes from the Villa Lupighi and no more extortionate rents. The golden goose would fly north, but in the arrival of General Calvet the Cardinal saw a heaven-sent way of preventing that flight. He smiled on the General. 'Help us find the meddling English, General, and perhaps we might then discover that there is, indeed, a Pierre Ducos hiding in the kingdom.'

Calvet hesitated. 'And what happens when I do find them?'

'You shall bring them here, and we shall see whether a spell of Neapolitan prison life satisfies their curiosity.'

'And afterwards,' Calvet insisted, 'you will direct me to Major Ducos?'

'Yes.' The Cardinal spoke as though to an importunate child. 'I promise you that.' He sketched a vague blessing, then watched the short squat Frenchman leave. 'Do you think,' the Cardinal asked when the door was closed, 'that he believed me?' Father Lippi, the long-nosed priest, shrugged to suggest he could not answer the question. The gesture irritated the Cardinal. 'Do you believe the Frenchman's story then?'

'No, your Eminence.'

'You're not entirely a fool. So advise me.'

Father Lippi, whose whole career depended on the Cardinal's favour, shrugged. 'The Count Poniatowski is a valuable contributor to your Eminence's treasury.'

'So?'

Lippi rubbed long thin hands together as he nervously thought the matter through. 'So, your Eminence, the Count Poniatowski should be warned of his enemies. He will doubtless be grateful.'

The Cardinal laughed. 'You must learn cleverness, Father Lippi. The future strength of Mother Church does not always rest upon doing the obvious. What do you think will happen when General Calvet discovers these Englishmen?'

'He will hand them into our custody?'

'Of course he will not!' The Cardinal was irritated by Lippi's stupidity. 'The General is a man of war, not of diplomacy. He was not sent here to make peace, but to fight, and when he does find these English, if they exist, he'll endeavour to discover whether they know how to find Pierre Ducos. And if they do know, and tell him, then Calvet will abandon his promise to hand the Englishmen into our custody, but will attack the villa himself. His master is after money, Lippi, money! And when Calvet does attack the villa, what then?'

Father Lippi frowned. 'There will be bloodshed.'

'Precisely, and it will be our duty to arrest the malefactors and impound the evidence of their misdeeds. And if, by chance, the Count is killed by these criminals? Why, then, we shall be forced to give his fortune into the safekeeping of the church.' By which the Cardinal meant his own treasury, but it was almost the same thing. 'And if, by chance, this General Calvet fails to capture the Count Poniatowski, then we shall still arrest him for affray, which will please the Count and doubtless provoke the gratitude you mentioned. Either way, Father Lippi, the church will be the richer.'

Lippi bowed in acknowledgement of the Cardinal's subtlety. 'And the English? How do we find them?'

'By helping the General, of course. He will give us their description, but we shall still let him deal with them.' There would be the most pompous and threatening protests from London if Naples was to kill Englishmen, so it was better to let the foolish General Calvet run that risk. The Cardinal smiled. 'And once Calvet has dealt with the English, our forces will deal with General Calvet.'

Politics were so very simple, the Cardinal thought, just so long as a man believed no one, double-crossed everyone, kept a full treasury, and inveigled others into doing the dirty work. He waddled down from his throne, plucked his cape about him, then went for some supper.

*   *   *

The optician Joliot had betrayed Ducos's address to Frederickson, but the location of the Villa Lupighi still had to be found and it took Frederickson two whole days to discover that the building was not in Naples itself, and another full day to find a carrier who, for the last piece of Harper's gold, grudgingly offered Frederickson directions. The villa lay a day's march northwards, close to the sea and secure on a steep hill.

'It will be guarded.' Sharpe observed.

'Of course it will be guarded,' Frederickson snapped.

'So we'll approach by night,' Sharpe ignored his friend's short temper.

'And we leave when?' Harper hated the bitterness that he detected between the two officers. He spoke mildly, trying to be a peace-maker.

'Tonight,' Sharpe said. It was already evening. 'We should arrive at dawn, we can watch all day, then attack tomorrow night. Do you agree, William?' He asked the question only to placate Frederickson.

'It seems an obvious course of action. Yes, I agree.'

They left the tavern at nightfall. There was a nervous moment as they passed the slovenly blue-uniformed guards at the city outskirts, but none of the soldiers gave the three travellers a second's notice. Nevertheless Sharpe did not feel secure until they had long left the city's last houses and were alone in a sultry countryside. It was good to be marching again, to feel a flinty road beneath boot-soles and to know that a task awaited at the road's end. It was not a task confused by the demands of peace, but a soldier's task; something best done swiftly and brutally. And when the task was over, Sharpe thought, and his enemy was confounded, then he would have the confusing tasks to face. Jane and Lucille. The names echoed in his head to every scrape and crunch of his boots on the road. What if Jane wanted him back? Which woman did he want himself? He had no answers, only questions.

It was a warm night, cloudless and windless. A bright moon rose above Vesuvius. At first the moon was misted by the volcano's smoke, but soon it sailed clear across the sea to show the northern road as a white twisting strip against the darker fields. A thousand thousand stars pricked the sky, while a small white surf fretted at the beaches and broke bright about the tree-shrouded headlands. An owl passed close above the three men and Sharpe saw Patrick Harper cross himself. The owl was the bird of death.

An hour before midnight they left the road and climbed a hundred paces into the shelter of an ilex grove. There, in silence, they undid the bundles they each carried. At long last, after weeks of hiding, they could strip off their civilian clothes and pull on their green jackets. Sharpe had debated whether to make the change now, or to wait till the very eve of his attack, but wearing the green would force them to move as silently as ghosts through this strange countryside. He buckled on his sword, then scraped its blade free of the scabbard's wooden throat so that the long steel shone in the moonlight.

'It feels better, does it not?' Frederickson buckled on his own sword.

'It feels much better,' Sharpe said fervently.

Frederickson drew his blade and whipped it back and forth. 'I suspect I may have been somewhat fretful lately.'

Sharpe was immediately embarrassed. 'Not at all.'

'I do apologize. Upon my soul, I apologize.'

Sharpe felt a pulse of pleasure that the awkwardness between them was ending, but the pleasure was immediately followed by a pang of guilt about Lucille. 'My dear William . . .' Sharpe began, then stopped, because this was

286

certainly not the moment to make the feared confession. He could see the happiness on Harper's face that the bad blood between the two officers seemed to be drawn, and Sharpe knew he could not spoil the moment. 'I am certain my own behaviour has been aggravating,' he said humbly.

Frederickson smiled. 'But now we can fight. Our proper task in life, I fear. We're not meant for peace, so to war, my friends!' He saluted Sharpe by whipping his sword blade upright.

'To war.' And the battle-cry put Sharpe into unexpected high spirits. For a moment he could forget Jane, forget Rossendale, forget Lucille, he could forget everything except the work at hand, which was the oldest kind of work; that of punishing an enemy.

They left the ilex grove. They had to skirt a straggling village, though the village dogs must have caught their scent for the barking snapped loud as the three Riflemen flitted through an olive grove. Beyond the olive grove, in fields that went down to the sea, there were white marble pillars that Frederickson said had fallen in the days of the Roman Empire. Sharpe did not believe him, and the friendly argument took them well past midnight. The road ran through open country, but in the small hours, when the waning moon was almost beyond the western horizon, they came to the mouth of a ravine which was shadowed as black as Hades.

They stopped where the rock walls narrowed. 'A perfect place for an ambush.' Frederickson stared into the darkness.

Sharpe grunted. He had no idea how long it might take to go round the ravine. Such a detour would mean climbing the hills and scouting forward over rough ground. He was only sure of one thing, that to make the detour would take hours, and that the dawn would then find them stranded far from the villa. 'I say we should go through.'

'Me too,' Harper offered.

'Why not?' Frederickson said.

The rock walls closed on them. The ravine's slopes were not bare, but thickly covered with small tough shrubs. Sharpe tried to climb one flank to get a glimpse ahead, but gave up when the brambles tore at his hands. He could have saved himself the discomfort for, just around the next bend, a long view showed where the ravine ended two miles ahead. The road emerged from its rock walls to run gently downhill into a wide and empty lowland that was edged by the sweeping curve of a long moonlit beach. The sight of that empty landscape and their evident loneliness on the deserted road gave all three Riflemen a sense of safety. This was not Spain where an ambush might wait, but a sleepy southern country where they could walk in peace. Beyond the lowland, and dark on the northern horizon, were jagged peaks touched by the moon. Sharpe was certain that the Villa Lupighi must lie among the foothills of those peaks, and that thought made him point towards the far mountains. 'Journey's end,' he said.

Somehow the two words plunged all three Riflemen into a wistful mood. Harper, thinking of the ultimate destination of his travels, began to sing some sad lament of Ireland. Frederickson smiled privately to Sharpe. 'You think he'll be happy out of the army?'

'I think Patrick has the great gift of being content almost wherever he is.'

The two officers had fallen a few paces behind the tall Irishman. 'Then he's a fortunate man,' Frederickson said, 'because I sometimes doubt whether I'll ever find real contentment.'

'Oh, come! That can't be true,' Sharpe protested.

Frederickson grimaced. 'The pig-woman did, so perhaps there's hope for me.' He walked in silence for a few paces. Harper still sang, and his strong voice echoed eerily from the ravine's bluffs.

Frederickson shrugged the sling of his rifle into greater

comfort on his shoulder. 'Harper's happily married, is he not?'

Sharpe's heart plunged as he sensed the imminent conversation. 'They're very happy. Isabella's a tough little creature, despite her pretty face.'

Frederickson found the opening he wanted. 'Do you think Madame Castineau is strong?'

'Very.'

'My thoughts, too. It can't have been an easy life for her.'

'Lots have it harder,' Sharpe said sourly.

'True, but she's preserved that château despite all the deaths in her family. A very strong woman, I'd say.'

Sharpe desperately tried to change the subject. 'How far do you reckon till we're in open country? A mile?'

Frederickson glanced casually at the road ahead. 'Just under a mile, I'd say,' then, with much greater enthusiasm, he spoke of his plans for further journeys. 'I shall go to London to straighten my career, then, just as soon as I can, I'll return to Normandy. You don't abandon a siege just because the first assault fails, do you? I've been thinking about that a great deal.' He gave a short embarrassed laugh. 'Indeed I confess that is why my temper has not been of the best lately, but I cannot believe that I should fail a second time with Madame. She surely needs some proof of my seriousness? My first proposal was a mere statement of intent, but now I shall reinforce it with an assiduous devotion which must persuade her. Good women, like bad, do yield to siege warfare, do they not?'

'Some do,' Sharpe said drily.

'Then I shall renew my siege. Indeed, I confess that it is only my anticipation of success in that siege which offers me some prospect of future happiness. Perhaps I deceive myself. Lovers are very prone to that failing.'

The moment was inescapable. Sharpe stopped. 'William.'

'My dear friend?' Frederickson, euphoric with hope, was in an expansive mood.

'I have to tell you something.' Sharpe paused, overcome with horror at what he was doing. For a second he was tempted to forget his own attachment to Madame Castineau; just to abandon her and to let Frederickson ride to Normandy like Don Quixote trotting towards the windmills, but he could not do it.

'What is it?' Frederickson prompted.

'Women destroy friendships.' Sharpe sought a tactful way into a confession that could never be tactful, not against the high hopes that Frederickson was nurturing.

Frederickson laughed. 'You fear we will see less of each other if I am successful? My dear Sharpe, you will always be a welcome guest wherever I–' he paused – 'I hope wherever I and Lucille are living.'

'William!' Sharpe blurted out the name. 'You must understand that I . . .'

The gunshot startled them, blasting the night's peace with an appalling and sudden violence. Sharpe had a glimpse of a muzzle flash high on the ravine's right flank, then he was rolling to the right of the road. Frederickson had gone left. Harper, his singing so brutally interrupted, had unslung his volley gun and was peering upwards. The bullet had missed all of them.

A man, hidden from the Riflemen, laughed.

'Who's there?' Sharpe called in English. No one answered. 'Can you see the bugger, Patrick?'

'Not a bloody thing, sir.'

The hidden man began to whistle a jaunty tune, then, very carelessly, as though he knew he had nothing to fear from the three crouching soldiers, he stepped out from the shadows thirty yards ahead of Harper. The man wore a long cloak and carried a musket in his right hand. Harper immediately aimed the seven-barrelled gun at the stranger, but as he did, so a whole slew of dark shapes moved on the ravine slopes. Sharpe heard the clicks as their musket locks were armed.

'Bandits?' Frederickson suggested to Sharpe. Both officers had their rifles cocked, but each knew that a single shot would provoke an instant and destructive volley. Sharpe could not see exactly how many men opposed them, but there seemed to be at least a dozen.

'Bugger.' Sharpe had forgotten the threat of robbery. He stood upright as if to show that he was not frightened. 'Can you talk us out of this one, William?'

'I can try, but at best they'll still steal our weapons.' Frederickson looked at the single man barring the road and called out in Italian, 'Who are you?'

The cloaked man chuckled, then walked slowly towards the three Riflemen. He carried his musket loosely. He walked past Harper, ignoring the threat of the huge gun, and instead approached Sharpe. 'Do you remember me, Major?' He spoke in French.

Sharpe could not even see the approaching man properly and, besides, he was too startled by the odd greeting to think coherently, but then the cloaked man suddenly shrugged the swathing cape away to reveal an old blue uniform with shreds of tattered gold lace. '*Bonsoir*, Major Sharpe.' The man was short, barrel-squat, with a face as scarred as the backside of a cannon.

'General Calvet,' Sharpe said in astonishment.

'That's very good! Well done! I am indeed General Calvet, and you are the so-called soldiers who stroll through ravines as casually as whores looking for business. A troop of baboons could have ambushed you!'

Sharpe did not reply, though he knew Calvet was right. He had been careless, and now he must pay the price for that carelessness.

Calvet stepped close to Sharpe. The Frenchman slowly reached out, daring Sharpe to move, and pushed Sharpe's rifle muzzle to one side. Then, with an extraordinary quickness, Calvet slapped the Rifleman's face. Sharpe was so stunned by the sudden blow that he did nothing. Calvet sneered. 'That, Englishmen, was for the powdered lime.' Calvet was recalling the powdered lime that Sharpe had broadcast from the ramparts of the Teste de Buch fort. The powder had burned the eyes of the attacking Frenchmen, and turned their attack into a panicked retreat. The memory of it evidently still rankled with Calvet. 'Only an Englishman would use a bastard trick like that on a pack of soft-arsed lilywhite conscripts. If I'd had my veterans, Englishman, I'd have filleted you.'

Sharpe said nothing. He was still trying to work out how a French General he had last seen on a battlefield in southern France had turned up on this remote Italian road. He looked left and right, trying to count the General's companions.

Calvet laughed. 'You think I need help to kill you, Sharpe? I needed some help to find you, but not to kill you.'

'To find me?' Sharpe found his tongue.

'I was sent to find you. By the Emperor. I stayed loyal, you see. Not like all those other damned Frenchmen who are licking fat King Louis's bum. But it wasn't hard to find you, Major. A man in Paris wrote to the Emperor, who sent me to Naples, where a fat Cardinal wants me to arrest you. They're very clever, these Neapolitans. I told them you were coming and they followed you from the day you landed. And now,' Calvet spread his arms as though he was a host welcoming treasured guests, 'here we are!'

'Why did you want to find us?' Frederickson asked.

'The one-eyed monster has a tongue!' Calvet jeered. 'I have orders to kill you, that's why. They are the Emperor's orders. He wants you dead because you stole his gold.'

'We didn't steal it,' Sharpe said angrily.

'But you're going to!' Calvet suddenly laughed. 'You haven't stolen it yet, Major, but as soon as you find

Pierre Ducos you will!' Calvet turned scornfully away from Sharpe and shouted for his men to come out of their hiding places.

The French soldiers pushed their way through the brambles and stamped the cramp out of their legs on the road. They surrounded the three Riflemen, and Sharpe could see, despite the darkness, that all of these grinning men wore the moustaches of the Emperor's beloved veterans.

Calvet raised his musket so that the barrel was under Sharpe's chin. 'Put your rifle down, Major, and tell your two men to do the same.' He saw Sharpe's hesitation. 'You'd prefer my men to disarm you? It's all one to me, but if you wish to keep your swords like gentlemen, then I suggest you put down your guns.'

There was perhaps a shade more pride in grounding their own arms than having them forcibly taken away, and so the three Riflemen slowly stooped and ignominiously abandoned their guns on the white roadway. Calvet waited till Sharpe was standing again, then once more put his musket to the Rifleman's throat. 'Do you know where Pierre Ducos is, Major?'

'Yes,' Sharpe said defiantly.

'But I don't,' Calvet disarmingly confessed. 'So tell me.'

'Go to hell, General.'

'You're determined to die like a cornered rat, aren't you? You'll die snarling, full of defiance. Except I'm under the orders of a fat Cardinal to return you to Naples. Have you seen the prison in Naples? You might survive it, Major, but so crippled with disease and hunger and filth that you'll wish you'd never been born. But if you tell me what I wish to know, Englishman, then I'll consider letting you walk away from this miserable kingdom.' Calvet twitched the musket so that the cold barrel knocked against Sharpe's jawbone. 'Where is Pierre Ducos, Major?'

'I should have killed you at Toulouse,' Sharpe said.

'So that was you?' Calvet laughed. 'The Englishman who can kill me has not been born, Major, but I will shoot you down like a rabid dog if you don't tell me where Pierre Ducos is hiding.' He twitched the musket again to jar its foresight against Sharpe's chin. 'Tell me, Englishman.'

Sharpe stared into the Frenchman's eyes, then, with a speed that equalled Calvet's earlier quickness, he slapped the General's face. The blow sounded like a pistol shot.

Calvet's head was jerked to one side. He stepped back, brought the musket into his shoulder and aimed it between Sharpe's eyes. 'Bastard,' he snarled.

'Bugger off,' Sharpe said in English.

Calvet pulled the trigger.

Sharpe twisted away, reached for his sword hilt, and he had drawn a clear foot of the steel clear of the scabbard before he realized that the musket had not been loaded. Calvet laughed. 'You can stop pissing your breeches, Major, the gun wasn't loaded. So pick up your bloody rifles and take me to Ducos.' He turned away from Sharpe and ordered his men to fall in. The moustached veterans obediently made two ragged ranks, but the three Riflemen did not move. Calvet turned on them with feigned astonishment. 'Don't just stand there! Move!'

Still none of the three Riflemen shifted. 'You expect us to take you to Ducos?' Sharpe asked.

'Listen, you Goddamn fool.' Calvet, who was plainly enjoying himself, walked back and planted himself squarely in front of Sharpe. 'Why should I send you to the Cardinal? All he wants to do is steal the gold for himself. And the Emperor wants it back, and that's my task, Major, and to help me fulfil it I'm offering you an alliance. You tell me where Ducos is hiding, and I will let you live. Indeed, I will even offer you the greater privilege of fighting under my command. For a change, Englishman, you and I will be on the same side. We are allies. Except that I am a General of Imperial France and you are a piece of English toadshit, which means that I give the orders and you obey them like a lilywhite-arsed conscript. So stop gawping like a novice nun in a gunners' bath-house and tell me where we're going!'

'I don't think we have very much choice,' Frederickson observed drily.

Nor did they. And thus Sharpe was under orders again, back in an army's discipline, but this time serving a new master: the Emperor of Elba himself, Napoleon.

CHAPTER 14

'Of course the Cardinal wants the money, he's nothing but a tub of greed, but what high churchman isn't?' General Calvet spoke quietly to Sharpe. The two men were lying at the crest of a steep ridge from where they could observe the Villa Lupighi which lay on yet a higher hill a mile to the west. They were hidden and shaded by a thick growth of ilex and cypress. Frederickson, Harper and the General's twelve men were resting among the gnarled trunks of an ancient olive grove that grew in a small valley behind the ilex-covered ridge. 'And like every other churchman,' Calvet went on, 'the Cardinal wants someone else to do his dirty work for him. In this case, us.'

The Cardinal had done everything he could to make Calvet's task easier, except betray Ducos's hiding place. The Cardinal had provided a house in which Calvet and his men could wait for Sharpe's arrival in Naples. That arrival had been reported by the customs' officials who had been warned by the Frenchman to expect a tall, black-haired man and a shorter, one-eyed companion. The house where Calvet waited had been very close to the place where the Frenchman had ambushed the three Riflemen. A messenger had come from the city to warn Calvet that three, not two, Englishmen had left on the northern road, and it had been a simple matter for Calvet to wait at the ravine's northern end. 'You'll notice, though,' Calvet went on, 'that the Cardinal has left us alone now.'

'Why?'

Calvet said nothing for a few seconds, but just stared at

the Villa Lupighi through an ancient battered telescope. Finally he grunted. 'Why? So we conveniently kill Ducos, then the Cardinal can arrest us and keep the money. Which is why, Englishman, we shall have to outguess the bastard.'

Calvet's idea for outguessing the Cardinal had the virtues of extreme simplicity. The Cardinal must surely plan to waylay Calvet as he withdrew from the villa, and the likeliest places for that ambush would be on any of the roads leading away from the half-ruined house. So Calvet would not leave the villa by road. Instead three of his men would be detached from the assault and sent to the west of the villa where a small village lay on the sea-shore. The three men's task was to sequester one of the bright-painted and high-prowed fishing boats from the tiny harbour. Two of the three men had been sailors before the collapse of the French Navy had persuaded Napoleon to turn seamen into soldiers, and though their detachment meant sacrificing three precious men from the assault, Calvet was certain the ploy would outwit the Cardinal. 'We'll also attack at night,' Calvet had decided, 'because if that fat fool has sent troops, then you can be certain they're almost as useless as you are.' Raw troops were easily confused by night fighting, which was why, Calvet continued, he had not launched his brigade of conscripts against the Teste de Buch fort during the night. 'If I'd had my veterans, Englishman, we'd have gobbled you up that very first night.'

'Many French veterans have tried to kill me,' Sharpe said mildly, 'and I'm still here.'

'That's just the luck of the devil.' Calvet spotted some movement at the villa and went silent as he gazed through the glass. 'How did you learn French?' he asked after a while.

'From Madame Castineau.'

'In her bed?'

'No,' Sharpe protested.

'Is she beautiful?' Calvet asked greedily.

297

Sharpe hesitated. He knew he could deflect Calvet's impudent enquiries by describing Lucille as very plain, but he suddenly found that he could not so betray her. 'I think so,' he said very lamely.

Calvet chuckled at the answer. 'I'll never understand women. They'll turn down a score of prinked-up thorough-breds, then flop on to their backsides when some chewed-up mongrel like you or me hangs out his tongue. Mind you, I'm not complaining. I bedded an Italian duchess once, and thought I'd shock her by telling her I was the son of a ditch-digger, but it only made her drag me back to the sheets.' He shook his head at the memory. 'It was like being mauled by a troop of Cossacks.'

'I told you,' Sharpe lied with fragile dignity, 'that I didn't go to Madame Castineau's bed.'

'Then why should she try to protect you?' Calvet demanded. He had already confessed to Sharpe that it was Madame Castineau's unwitting letter that had alerted Napoleon to Ducos's treachery, and he now described how that letter had tried to exonerate the Riflemen. 'She was insistent you were as innocent as a stillborn baby. Why would she say that?'

'Because we are innocent,' Sharpe said, but he felt a thrill of gratitude at such evidence of Lucille's protective care. Then, to change the subject, he asked whether Calvet was married.

'Christ, yes,' Calvet spat out a shred of chewing tobacco, 'but the good thing about war, Englishman, is that it keeps us away from our own wives but very close to other men's wives.'

Sharpe smiled dutifully, then reached out and took the General's telescope. He stared at the villa for a long time, then slid the tubes shut. 'We'll have to attack from this side.'

'That's bloody obvious. A schoolboy with a palsied brain could have worked that one out.'

Sharpe ignored the General's sarcasm. He was beginning to like Calvet, and he sensed that the Frenchman liked him. They had both marched in the ranks, and both had endured a lifetime of battles. Calvet had risen much higher in rank, but Calvet had a devotion to a cause that Sharpe did not share. Sharpe had never fought for King George in the same fanatic spirit that Calvet offered to the Emperor. Calvet's devotion to the fallen Napoleon was absolute, and his alliance with Sharpe a mere expedience imposed by that forlorn allegiance. When Calvet attacked the Villa Lupighi he would do it for the Emperor, and Sharpe suspected that Calvet would cheerfully march into hell itself if the Emperor so demanded it.

Not that attacking the Villa Lupighi should be hellish. It had none of the defensive works of even a small redoubt of the late wars. There was no glacis to climb, no ravelins to flank, no embrasures to gout cannon-fire. Instead it was merely a ragged and fading building that decayed on its commanding hilltop. During the night Calvet and Sharpe had circled much of that hill and had seen how the lantern-light glowed in the seaward rooms while the eastern and ruined half of the building was an inky black. That dark tangle of stone offered itself as a hidden route to the enemy's heart.

The only remaining question was how many of that enemy waited in the rambling and broken villa. During the morning Sharpe and Calvet had seen at least two dozen men around the villa. Some had just lounged against an outer wall, staring to sea. Another group had walked with some women towards the village harbour. Two had exercised large wolf-like dogs. There had been no sight of Pierre Ducos. Calvet was guessing that Ducos had about three dozen men to defend his stolen treasure, while Calvet, less his three boat-snatchers, would be leading just ten. 'It'll be a pretty little fight,' Calvet now grudgingly allowed.

'It's the dogs that worry me.' Sharpe had seen the size

of the two great beasts which had strained against the chains of their handlers.

Calvet sneered. 'Are you frightened, Englishman?'

'Yes.' Sharpe made the simple reply, and he saw how the honesty impressed Calvet. Sharpe shrugged. 'It used not to be bad, but it seems to get worse. It was awful before Toulouse.'

Calvet laughed. 'I had too much to do at Toulouse to be frightened. They gave me a brigade of wet-knickered recruits who would have run away from a schoolmistress's cane if I hadn't put the fear of God into the bastards. I told them I'd kill them myself if they didn't get in there and fight.'

'They fought well,' Sharpe said. 'They fought very well.'

'But they didn't win, did they?' Calvet said. 'You saw to that, you bastard.'

'It wasn't my doing. It was a Scotsman called Nairn. Your brigade killed him.'

'They did something right, then,' Calvet said brutally. 'I thought I was going to die there. I thought you were going to shoot me in the back, and I thought to hell with it. I'm getting too old for it, Major. Like you, I find myself pissing with fright before a battle these days.' Calvet was returning honesty with honesty. 'It became bad for me in Russia. I used to love the business before that. I used to think there was nothing finer than to wake in the dawn and see the enemy waiting like lambs for the sword-blades, but in Russia I got scared. It was such a damned big country that I thought I'd never reach France again and that my soul would be lost in all that emptiness.' He stopped, seemingly embarrassed by his confession of weakness. 'Still,' he added, 'brandy soon put that right.'

'We use rum.'

'Brandy and fat bacon,' Calvet said wistfully, 'that makes a proper bellyful before a fight.'

'Rum and beef,' Sharpe countered.

Calvet grimaced. 'In Russia, Englishman, I ate one of my own corporals. That put some belly into me, though it was very lean meat.' Calvet took his telescope back and stared at the villa which now seemed deserted in the afternoon heat. 'I think we should wait till about two hours after midnight. Don't you agree?'

Sharpe silently noted how this proud man had asked for his opinion. 'I agree,' he said, 'and we'll attack in two groups.'

'We will?' Calvet growled.

'We go first,' Sharpe said.

'We, Englishman?'

'The Rifles, General. The three of us. The experts. Us.'

'Do I give orders, or you?' Calvet demanded belligerently.

'We're Riflemen, best of the best, and we shoot straighter than you.' Sharpe knew it was only a soldier's damned pride that had made him insist on leading the assault. He patted the butt of his Baker rifle. 'If you want our help, General, then we go first. I don't want a pack of blundering Frenchmen alerting the enemy. Besides, for a night attack, our green coats are darker than yours.'

'Like your souls,' Calvet grumbled, but then he grinned. 'I don't care if you go first, Englishman, because if the bastard's alert then you're the three who'll get killed.' He laughed at that prospect, then slid back from the skyline. 'Time to get some sleep, Englishman, time to get some sleep.'

On the far hill a dog raised its muzzle and howled at the blinding sun. Like the hidden soldiers, it waited for the night.

* * *

Calvet's infantrymen, like the three Riflemen, wore their old uniforms. The twelve Grenadiers were all survivors of Napoleon's élite corps, the Old Guard; the Imperial Guard.

Just to join the Imperial Guard a man must have endured ten years of fighting service, and Calvet's dozen Grenadiers must have amassed more than a century and a half of experience between them. Each of the men, like Calvet, had abandoned royal France to follow their beloved Emperor into exile, and they now wore the uniforms which had terrified the Emperor's enemies across Europe. Their dark blue coats had red turnbacks and tails, and their bearskins were faced with brass and chained with silver. Each man, in addition to his musket, was armed with a short, brass-hilted *sabre-briquet*. The Grenadiers, as they assembled in the olive grove, made a formidable sight, yet it was also a very noticeable sight for their white breeches reflected very brightly in the moonlight, so brightly that Sharpe's earlier proposal that the Greenjackets should go first made obvious good sense.

At midnight Calvet led the small force out of the olive grove, across the ilex ridge, and down to the valley at the foot of the villa's hill. The three men who would secure the fishing boat had already left for the small harbour. Calvet had threatened the three with death if they made even the smallest noise on their journey, and he reiterated the warning now to his own party which thereafter advanced at an agonisingly slow pace. It was thus not till well after two o'clock that they reached a stand of cypress trees that was the last available concealment before they climbed the steep, scraped hillside towards the villa's eastern ruins. The inconveniently bright moon shone above the sea to silhouette the ragged outline of the high building.

Calvet stood with Sharpe and stared at the silhouette. 'If they're awake and ready, my friend, then you're a dead Englishman.'

Sharpe noted the *'mon ami'*, and smiled. 'Pray they're asleep.'

'Damn prayer, Englishman. Put your faith in gunpowder and the bayonet.'

'And brandy?'

'That, too.' Calvet offered his flask. Sharpe was tempted, but refused. To have accepted, he decided, would be to demonstrate the fear which he had earlier confessed, but which now, on the verge of battle, must be hidden. It was especially important to hide it when he was being observed by these hardened men from Napoleon's own Guard. Tonight, Sharpe vowed, three Riflemen would prove themselves more than equal to these proud men.

Calvet had no qualms about displaying a fondness for brandy. He tipped the flask to his mouth, then, to Sharpe's astonishment, gave the Rifleman a warm embrace. '*Vive l'Empereur, mon ami.*'

Sharpe grinned, hesitated, then tried the unfamiliar war cry for himself. '*Vive l'Empereur, mon General.*'

The Imperial Guardsmen smiled, while a delighted Calvet laughed. 'You get better, Englishman, you get better, but you're also late, so go! Go!'

Sharpe paused, stared up the hill and wondered what horrors might wait at its black summit. Then he nodded to Frederickson and Harper, and led the way into the moonlight. The long journey at last was ending.

*   *   *

It was simple at first, merely a tough upwards climb of a weed-strewn hillside that was more trying on the leg-muscles than on the nerves. Once Sharpe stepped on a loose stone that tumbled back in a stream of smaller stones and earth, and he froze, thinking of the scorn Calvet would be venting in the trees below. Harper and Frederickson watched the great building above, but saw no movement except for the bats that flickered about the broken walls. No lights showed. If there were guards in the ruins they were very silent. Sharpe thought of the great wolf-like dogs, but, if the beasts waited, they too were silent. Perhaps, as Frederickson had dared to hope, they were nothing but pets which, at this moment, slept in some deep recess of the silent villa.

The three Riflemen pushed on, angling to their right so that they could take the greatest advantage of the building's mooncast shadow that spread its blackness a quarter way down the eastern slope. Still no one challenged them. They moved like the skirmishers they were; spread apart with one man always motionless, a rifle at his shoulder, to cover the other two.

It took fifteen minutes to reach the shrouding darkness of the building's shadow. Once in that deeper darkness they could move faster, though the slope had now become so steep that Sharpe was forced to sling his rifle and use his hands to climb. A small wind had begun to stir the air, travelling from the inland hills and olive groves towards the sea.

'Down!' Harper hissed the word from the left flank and Sharpe and Frederickson obediently flattened themselves. Harper edged his rifle forward, but left his seven-barrelled gun slung across his back. Sharpe pulled his own rifle free, then heard a scraping sound from the hilltop. The sound resolved itself into footsteps, though no one was yet visible. Very slowly Sharpe turned his head to stare down the long slope. He could see no sign of Calvet or his Grenadiers beneath the ink dark cypresses.

'Sir!' Harper's voice was as soft as the new small wind.

Two men strolled unconcernedly around the corner of the ruined building. The men were talking. Both had muskets slung on their shoulders, and both were smoking. Once they were in the shadow of the eastern wall the only sign of their progress was the intermittent glow of the two cheroots. Sharpe heard a burst of laughter from the two guards. The sound confirmed what the men's casual attitude had already suggested: that Ducos had not been warned. Men who expected an attack would be far more wary and silent. The two guards were clearly oblivious to any danger, but they posed a danger themselves for they stopped halfway down the eastern flank and seemed to settle themselves at the base of the ruined wall. Then, from somewhere deep inside the black tangle of ruins, a dog growled. One of the two guards shouted to quieten the animal, but in the ensuing silence Sharpe's fear surged like a great burst of pain in his belly. He feared those dogs.

Yet, despite the fear, he made himself squirm up the hill. He was on the right flank of the three Riflemen, furthest from the two guards, so he possessed the best chance of reaching the ruins unseen. He inched forwards, dragging himself painfully with his elbows. He estimated he was forty yards from the closest ruins, and perhaps sixty from where the two men crouched among fallen masonry. He ignored the two men, instead trying to see a route into the tangle of broken stone above. If he could work his way round behind the two guards then he might yet be able to silence them without the need to fire a shot. He had sharpened the big sword so that its edge was bright and deadly. The scabbard was wrapped in rags so that the metal did not chink on stone. He listened for the dogs, but heard nothing. His left shoulder was a mass of pain as it took the weight from his elbows. The joint had never healed properly, but he had to ignore the pain. He sensed that Frederickson and Harper were motionless. They would be hearing the tiny noises of Sharpe's stealthy movements, would have guessed what he planned to do, and would now be waiting with their rifles trained on the two glowing cheroots.

Sharpe could feel his heart thumping. The two guards were still talking softly. He pulled up his right leg, found a foothold, and gingerly pushed himself up. In two minutes, he estimated, he would be inside the ruins. Add ten minutes to stalk the two men, then Calvet could be summoned with the agreed signal of a nightjar's harsh call. He eased himself another foot up the slope, but then all his hopes of surprise, and all the pent-up fears of the night exploded in a lethal burst of noise.

The two dogs had caught the strangers' scent on the freshening breeze.

One second there had been silence on the hilltop except for the muttering of the two guards, then, with a horrid abruptness, two dogs howled their cries at the moon as they came scrabbling and desperate over the ruined walls. Sharpe had time for one foul glimpse of their ragged silhouettes as they leaped against the sky.

'Fire!' He shouted the order in panic.

Harper and Frederickson fired at the two sentries. The rifles' noise was startlingly loud; so loud that thousands of roosting birds shattered up from the ruined masonry. A guard shouted with pain.

The dogs were scenting their closest enemy: Sharpe.

He had just had enough time after his first glimpse of the beasts to rise to one knee and draw the big sword. He could not see the beasts in the dark shadows, but he could hear and smell them. He screamed as he swung the heavy blade. He felt the steel thump into a pelt, jar on bone, then slide free. The animal he had struck howled like a soul in torment. Sharpe knew he must have hurt it badly for it slewed sideways, but then the second animal came straight for him with its teeth bared. Sharpe's sword arm was unbalanced so he swung his left arm to ward off the attack. The dog's teeth closed on the green cloth of his old jacket, then the animal swung all its weight on the fragile cloth that ripped, but not before the impact of the attack had sent Sharpe tumbling down the slope. He was nerveless with fear. He knew how to fight men, but this feral violence was something he could neither anticipate nor understand. He lost both sword and rifle as he fell. The second dog had also lost its balance and spilt sideways on the slope. The first dog, bleeding from its flank and with a broken foreleg, lunged at Sharpe. He scrambled away from it and, in his desperation, sprawled on to his back, but then the second dog, with shreds of green cloth hanging from its teeth, sprang on to his belly. Sharpe smelt its rancid breath and knew the dog was about to rip his windpipe open.

Sharpe desperately lunged up with his right hand, caught the dog's throat, and squeezed. A musket fired from the hilltop and the dog's eyes reflected sudden and red in the muzzle's flash. Calvet was shouting orders at the foot of the hill. Saliva dripped on to Sharpe's face. The dog was a heavy mass of bone and muscle; nothing but a killing beast. It scrabbled for a foothold on Sharpe's chest and belly, shook its head to loosen the terrible grip on its sinewy throat, and thrust its weight down so that its teeth could flense the skin from Sharpe's face. Somewhere on the hilltop a man screamed. Another musket fired, but nowhere near Sharpe. He wanted to shout for help, but he needed all his strength to hold off the dog's lunges.

Sharpe twisted, heaved, and rolled the dog over on to its wounded companion. He still had his right hand hooked and clawed into the animal's throat. He screamed at it in impotent rage, then wrenched his grip as if he would tear the windpipe clean out. The wounded dog snarled at him. Another musket fired and in its burst of flame Sharpe saw the sheen of dark-light on his fallen sword blade. He picked up the weapon in his left hand, holding it by the blade, and stabbed it down. The force of the blow rammed his hand down the edge, slicing his palm open, but he hurt one of the dogs badly for it whined and Sharpe felt the steel jerk as the beast tried to twist free of the blade. He let go of the dog's throat with his right hand, seized the sword hilt, and stood up. Both dogs wrenched towards him, but he hacked down as if the sword was an axe, then went on hacking till there was nothing but bloodied pelts and butchered flesh.

'Sir!' Harper shouted from the ruins. 'Where are you, sir?'

'What's happening, for Christ's sake?'

'Two dead 'uns here, sir.'

'Get into the ruins!' Sharpe clenched his slashed left hand to stem the blood that poured from his palm. His right leg and left shoulder were hurting like the devil. Beneath him he could see Calvet's men desperately climbing towards the ruins. Sharpe could not see his rifle. He knelt again and felt around the slope, finally discovering the weapon's stock beneath the still warm gobbets of dogflesh. He dragged the blood-sticky weapon free, then limped up to the hilltop.

Frederickson found him there. 'Harper shot one man, I killed the other. Are you all right?'

'No, I'm not. Bloody dogs.' Sharpe still shivered with the remembered fear of the dogs. He ripped a scrap of torn cloth from his left sleeve and wrapped it round his cut hand. A man shouted from the villa's corner, telling Sharpe that other picquets had come to join the fight. He would ignore them. Calvet's Imperial Guardsmen could suffer and deal with their threat because the important thing, the only thing, was to get deep inside the building. 'Come on!'

Harper had already found a way across the outer broken wall and now waited for Sharpe in the crumbling remains of an old courtyard. In some places the ancient masonry reached up two storeys, while in others it was just a few weed-grown feet high.

'Quick! Move!' Sharpe was hissing with pain, but it had to be suppressed. Surprise was gone, so now the attack must lunge like a blade as fast and deep as it could before the enemy rallied. He led the two Riflemen into a maze of broken walls and collapsed arches, dodging from shadow to shadow, always heading west towards the intact part of the house. At every step Sharpe expected a musket's muzzle blast as greeting, but each corner turned and each wall jumped revealed nothing but silence and motionless ruin. Stone columns lay fallen over roofless corridors, and beams were half buried in fallen walls. It was a place for birds, lizards, snakes and silence.

'This way!' Harper called. He had found an undamaged cloister that seemed to offer a way through to the western end of the building. Sharpe followed the Irishman. One of Calvet's men shouted from behind, but Sharpe ignored the call. Muskets suddenly crashed from the eastern face of the ruins. Sharpe stumbled on a broken piece of masonry, then fell into the deep shadow of the intact cloister. Frederickson followed and the three Riflemen, temporarily hidden, stopped to draw breath.

'Is everyone loaded?' Sharpe asked.

All three rifles were charged. Sharpe sheathed his sword and cocked his own rifle. His left arm and hand were ripped with pain, but he had to forget that agony if the night was not to end in ignominious defeat. The cloister was pitch dark. It led west to where, surely, Ducos must be waiting. Sharpe expected Ducos's men to appear at any moment and pointed his rifle towards the threatening dark shadows.

'Major!' Calvet roared from the eastern wall. 'Where the hell are you, you bastard?'

Sharpe was about to reply, but any sound he might have made was drowned by a new explosion of musketry. It seemed to come from the sky, and Sharpe sidled to the cloister's edge and looked up to see a dark mass of men crowning the intact wall which marked the edge of the ruined part of the building and the beginning of the living quarters. They were firing down at Calvet's men who now sought desperate shelter among the broken stones.

Sharpe raised his rifle.

'No!' Frederickson hissed.

'No?'

'The bastards probably don't know we're this deep in the building! Come on!' Frederickson felt his way down the black cloister. Calvet's men were returning the fire now, but the musketry duel was dreadfully one sided. Ducos's men were hidden by the roof's parapet and could plunge their fire down into the ruins, while Calvet's men could only fire blindly upwards.

'Major!' Calvet bellowed again. 'Where in Christ's name are you?'

Sharpe had reached the cloister's end, and found it blocked by a heavy timber door. Frederickson, crouching at the door's foot, calmly produced his tinder box, struck flint to steel, and blew on the charred linen to make a tiny flame. The small light revealed ancient blackened timber. The door was constructed from five vertical baulks, studded with iron nails, but the long years and the desiccating heat had shrunk the wood to leave finger wide gaps between the heavy timbers. There was a rusted latch which, try as he might, Frederickson could not shift. 'Bastard's locked.'

'Give me room.' Harper pushed the two officers aside, then rammed his bayonet's stout blade into one of the gaps. He levered the steel, grunting with the effort, and Sharpe was certain that the thick blade would snap before the ancient wood gave way. The noise of the muskets drowned any sounds Harper made.

Frederickson blew on the tinder's flame to keep it alight as Sharpe drew his sword and rammed the blade alongside Harper's. He twisted the sword so that the strain would be taken from edge to edge, then added his weight to the Irishman's. The feeble flame went out, then, with a crash and a gout of dust, the timber cracked and split. Harper ripped the board away, then used Sharpe's sword to attack the next heavy timber. The fire from the rooftop was persistent while that from the eastern ruins was sporadic, suggesting that Calvet's men were trapped among the fallen stones.

'We're through!' Harper had made the hole large enough, and now pushed the sword back to Sharpe. The Irishman went first through the gap, Frederickson followed, and Sharpe went last. They went into an utter darkness, bereft of stars, and it seemed to Sharpe as though they had stumbled into some capacious dungeon with a smooth stone floor, sheer stone walls, and a high echoing ceiling. Sharpe groped his way forward. The sound of the musketry was muffled now. The villa's defenders doubtless believed they were winning the battle, but were still unaware that one tiny group of attackers had managed to reach deep into the huge building.

'Door!' Frederickson had found the way out of the dark room and, miraculously, the new door was unlocked. It grated and squealed as Frederickson thrust it ajar. It led into a passage that was suffused with the faintest pre-dawn light from north-facing windows. No enemy waited in the passage, only a black cat which hissed at them, then fled.

A winding stairway climbed from a jet black arch in the passage's left wall. Sharpe knew this was no moment to be cautious, speed was all, and so he hefted his bloodied sword and climbed. He did not try to be silent, but just blundered up the winding stair two steps at a time. The stairway opened into a stone-walled room where a flickering tallow candle revealed two terrified girls clutching each other in the remnants of their beds. Men's clothes were on the floor, though doubtless the men themselves were among the defenders on the roof. One of the girls opened her mouth to scream and Sharpe instinctively threatened her with the sword. She went very still.

Harper pushed past Sharpe, saw the girls, and aimed his rifle on which his bayonet was now locked. The girls shook their heads, as if to show that they would not make any noise. Frederickson appeared in the room. He had prepared for battle in his usual way by stowing his eyepatch and false teeth in his ammunition pouch, and he thus presented a fearsome sight which made one of the girls draw breath to scream. Harper rapped the side of her head with the edge of his blade. She froze. The blanket dropped away to show that she was naked.

'Kill the bitches.' Frederickson came into the room last.

'Tell them that if they make a noise we'll kill them both,' Sharpe ordered. Frederickson seemed disgusted at this display of weakness, but obeyed. One of the two girls nodded to show that she understood, and Sharpe plucked a blanket from the floor and tossed it over their heads. 'Come on!'

A second winding stairway led from the room. Sharpe again climbed it first. The sound of musketry was much louder now, betraying that the Riflemen were close to Ducos's men. At the top of the stairway was a half-open door which Sharpe knew would lead on to the flat roof from which Ducos's men poured their fire down on to Calvet's soldiers. Sharpe remembered a moment like this on the Portuguese border when he and Harper had climbed just such a stair in the certain knowledge that the enemy waited at its top. He felt like a rat in a barrel, and the fear slowed his step. Through the half open door he could see the sky. There was a high wisp of cloud, lit silver grey against the dark.

'Move yourself, sir.' Harper unceremoniously pushed Sharpe aside to take the lead. He had slung his rifle and bayonet on his left shoulder so he could use his favourite weapon; the big seven-barrelled gun. The Irishman licked his lips, crossed himself, then pushed the door fully open.

Harper froze. He could see the enemy and Sharpe could not. Frederickson tried to push on, but he could not get past Sharpe.

'God save Ireland,' Harper whispered, and Sharpe knew that the big man, like himself, was scared. There was a hard knot in Sharpe's belly, put there by the certainty that death waited beyond the open door.

'How many?' he whispered to Harper.

'At least a dozen of the bastards.'

'For Christ's sake!' Frederickson sounded angry. 'Calvet's being crucified!'

'*Vive l'Empereur!*' Sharpe said fatuously, and the erstwhile enemy's battle cry seemed to propel Harper through the open door.

'Bastards!' The Irishman screamed the word as his own battle cry. Men turned to stare at him, astonishment on their faces, then Harper pulled the trigger and the flint sparked fire into the chamber behind the seven barrels. The gun hammered like a small cannon and two of Ducos's men were snatched clean off their feet to tumble, screaming, to the broken stones below.

Sharpe had followed Harper on to the smoke-wreathed roof. He carried the rifle in his clumsily bandaged left hand, fired it, did not wait to see if his bullet hit, but just ran forward with the sword in his right hand. The blade was matted thick with dog blood and hair. Frederickson flanked Harper's right. A musket hammered at them, but the three Riflemen were moving too quickly and the ball whined harmlessly between Sharpe and Harper.

The surprise of their small attack was absolute. One second Sergeant Challon's men had been firing down in comparative safety, and the next they were being violently assaulted from their left flank. Those men nearest to the Riflemen had no time to escape. One man tried to twist out of Sharpe's way, but the big sword caught him on the backswing to flay his throat back to the spine. Sharpe's scream of triumph would have curdled a devil's blood. Harper was using the butt of the big gun like a club. Frederickson shot a man, discarded his rifle, then elegantly skewered another with his sword. Sharpe was past his first victim, hunting another. The fear had gone now, washed away by the old exaltation of battle. The enemy was running. They were desperately jostling towards a doorway on the roof's far side. These men had no belly for this fight, all except one man who had the tough face of an old soldier.

The moustached face was framed with the pigtails of the élite Napoleonic Dragoons. The man wore the remnants of his green uniform on which was the single stripe of a Sergeant. He lifted his straight sword towards Sharpe, feinted, then lunged at Harper. He did not finish the lunge, but stepped back and swung the blade towards Frederickson. The man was cornered, his companions had abandoned him, but he was making a professional cold fight out of his desperate position.

'Give up,' Sharpe said in English, then corrected himself by giving the command in French.

The only response was a sudden and savage attack. Sharpe parried so that the two swords ran like a bell. The other enemy had disappeared down the far stairway, and now the French Sergeant retreated after them, but never turned his back on his three opponents. Frederickson edged round to threaten his right flank and the Dragoon Sergeant's sword slithered towards the new threat, but Harper was even faster. He moved to the Sergeant's left, reached out, and seized his belt to pull him off balance. The Sergeant tried to reverse his blade, but Harper contemptuously ripped it from his hand and sent it spinning over the parapet. He then hit the French Sergeant on the head so that the man slumped down in dazed agony. 'You were told to give up,' Harper said patiently, then hit the man again. 'You stubborn bloody bastard.'

'Major!' General Calvet was standing in the ruins below.

'Go right!' Sharpe pointed to where they had broken through into the passage. 'Hurry!'

'Englishman! Well done!'

Sharpe laughed at the compliment, then essayed an elaborate bow to the Frenchman. As he bowed, so Harper screamed a sudden warning, and Sharpe abandoned his courtesy to fall ignominiously on his face as a small cannon split the dawn apart with its sudden noise. The ball thumped over Sharpe's head.

'Ducos!' Frederickson had spotted the enemy.

Sharpe looked where Frederickson was pointing. Beyond this roof was another courtyard, this one intact, and on its far side Sharpe saw an open full-length window on an upper floor. The room had a balcony that billowed with smoke. Men moved in the lantern light behind the balcony, then the small wind shifted the obscuring smoke and Sharpe at last saw his enemy. He recognized the round lenses of the spectacles first, then he saw the thin face and he saw, too, with astonishment, that Ducos was in the uniform of a French Marshal. For a second Ducos looked straight into Sharpe's eyes, then he twisted away. Two other men took his place. Between them they carried a strange brass object which they stood in the window. For a second Sharpe thought it was a small misshapen table, but then Frederickson recognized the four-legged gun. 'A bloody grasshopper!' he said scornfully, but he still dropped flat as the linstock touched fire to the charge. This time the small gun had been loaded with multiple shot that whistled harmlessly overhead.

A scream sounded below, and Sharpe knew Calvet's men must have entered the second courtyard. The sound of musketry began again, rising in a snapping crescendo, but this time the deadly sound came from deep inside Ducos's fastness. The dawn was already lightening the eastern sky with a pale silver wash and Sharpe knew this battle was half won, but still not complete. An enemy had to be trapped and taken alive. He loaded his rifle, wiped blood off his blade, and went back to the fight.

CHAPTER 15

Sergeant Challon lay disarmed and unconscious on the roof, but Pierre Ducos could not know of his loyal Sergeant's predicament. Instead he cursed the Sergeant for abandoning him, just as he cursed the hired men who now scrambled desperately from the villa to run away into the night's remnant. Only a handful of Dragoons had stayed with Ducos, not out of loyalty, but with the demand that Ducos now open the great strongbox and let them flee with their plunder.

Their greed was interrupted by Calvet's men who began storming the lower corridors. Women and children screamed as they tried to escape the vengeful Guardsmen, and the screams served to remind Ducos's Dragoons of their predicament. They slammed doors shut to cut the strongbox off from the attackers, then axed loopholes in the doors so they could keep Calvet's men at bay. The grasshopper gun fired once more at the far roof, but the three green uniformed men seemed to have gone and the gun was brought down into the curtained archway that faced towards the sea. From that position it could slaughter any enemy who tried to outflank the loopholed doors by crossing the paved and balustraded terrace. 'If we just hold long enough,' Ducos urged his six remaining men, 'I promise we'll get help.'

Ducos loaded two gilt-chased pistols that had been gifts from the Czar of Russia to the Emperor of France before the two nations fell into enmity. He carried the pistols to the window facing the courtyard and fired them both at the place where he believed he had seen Sharpe. No one could be seen on that far roof now, so Ducos merely shot at phantoms. He was trying to persuade himself that Sharpe's appearance had been just that; a phantom sprung on him by his over-heated fears and made more palpable by the dawn's bad light. Yet he could hear that the men in the corridors outside the locked doors were no phantoms; they were fellow Frenchmen, come for a treasure that Ducos would not surrender.

Some of the products of that treasure were now used to barricade the archway where the grasshopper gun stood. A celestial globe was heaped on top of a japanned chest of drawers. A green silk covered chaise-longue made a breastwork, while beneath it an ebony table with a surface of inlaid silver and ivory was stacked as a shield for enemy bullets. Cushions, curtains, rugs and bedclothes were crammed between chairs to make the barricade yet more formidable. Only the heavy green curtain which shielded the deep alcove where the strongbox was hidden was left in its place. Two men crewed the grasshopper gun in its cushioned embrasure, while the other four Dragoons took it in turns to fire through the two loopholed doors. Ducos, his gaudy uniform hanging from him like finery draped on a scarecrow, paced between the three positions and spun a fantasy of imminent Neapolitan rescue.

The two loopholed doors were old and tough. A musket bullet could not penetrate the wood. At first the fire from the corridors was frightening in its intensity, but the Dragoons soon learned they were safe, and soon discovered they could drive the attackers away by firing from the loopholes. They had made a fortress within the villa, and the only entrances into the fortress were through the two doors or across the terrace that would prove a killing ground for the small brass gun. The Dragoons missed Sergeant Challon's reassuring presence, but they felt safe enough now and even found a grim enjoyment in their successful defiance. Ducos made himself useful by loading every spare musket, carbine and pistol so that any determined attack could be met by an unrelenting fire.

'Pity about the women,' one Dragoon muttered.

'They'll come back.' His companion fired through one of the splintered loopholes and his bullet ricocheted down the dark corridor. The attackers had taken cover from the fire, and their answering shots were as ill-aimed as they were infrequent. The man who had fired stepped back and glanced scornfully at Ducos. 'First time I've seen a Marshal of France loading a musket.'

'We'll drive these bastards off,' his companion muttered, 'then we'll kill the little runt and take the money home.' It had only been Sergeant Challon's stubborn loyalty that had prevented such a desirable solution before, but Challon was now gone. The man fired through the door again, stepped back, then glanced up as an odd sound attracted his attention. He gaped at the high ceiling, then grabbed a loaded musket which he pointed directly overhead and fired. The fortress within a fortress was not quite as safe as it might have seemed.

*　　*　　*

The musket bullet buried itself in a floorboard beneath Harper's feet, but struck with such force that the heavy board seemed to quiver beneath him. Dust jarred up along the timber's formidable length. Harper wrenched at a crack between the boards with his bayonet. 'I need a bloody axe.'

'We haven't got a bloody axe,' Frederickson said curtly, then jumped back as three more gunshots thumped into the floor. 'Why don't we just set the bloody place on fire?'

Neither Sharpe nor Harper answered. Both had stouter blades than Frederickson's slim sword, and both were levering at the old thick timbers. They had made their way around the villa's roof to find this dusty attic directly over the enemy's inner sanctuary. Sharpe had knocked tiles from the roof to get into the dusty space where bat droppings lay thick on the floor.

'It's moving!' Harper alerted Sharpe who went to the other side of the heavy floorboard. Sharpe slid his sword under the wood and levered. Both men were crouching back from their work. Bullets were slamming noisily into the underside of the floor, and Sharpe feared that one would strike the tip of his sword and break the steel. He stood upright, put his foot on the hilt, and shoved downwards so that the timber creaked and heaved along its whole length. The far end of the board was still held fast by ancient nails and the consequent tension threatened to snap the timber back like a spring until Frederickson jammed his rifle beneath to hold the raised end firm. Ducos's men were shouting below. One musket bullet found the gap and smashed a tile not a foot from Frederickson's head.

Harper found his seven-barrelled gun, poked it under the raised timber, and fired blindly down. The noise was huge in the confined space, but even so the Riflemen could hear a scream from the room below as the seven bullets ricocheted wildly from its stone walls and floor. Sharpe fired his rifle into the gap, then both men stepped back to reload. Frederickson crouched to fire Harper's rifle into Ducos's lair. 'Like shooting rats in a barrel,' he said grimly, then suddenly all the Riflemen were deafened and Frederickson, the rifle still unfired, fell back.

The raised board seemed to have exploded and jumped up at him. The attic was filled with a rending and splintering crash, beneath which sound and mixed with it, was the vast echoing report of the small grasshopper cannon. The gun had been placed upright, balanced on its hind legs and breech, then fired upwards. Its roundshot had mangled one of the attic's floor timbers, then splintered on up through the tiles. Frederickson lay motionless. His face was bleeding from a score of splinters, but Sharpe could find no other wounds. The closeness of the cannonball's passage must have literally knocked him out. Sharpe had seen men similarly felled by a buffet of a roundshot's air. Frederickson would live, but within a few hours his face would be one huge bruise.

'He'll live,' Sharpe told Harper, then, vengefully, he picked up the unfired rifle and fired it down through the hole torn by the roundshot. Harper was grimly loading his seven-barrelled gun and, at the same time, counting the seconds it would take for the men below to reload the small cannon. Frederickson groaned woefully. One of the splinters had lodged in his empty eye-socket that was now filling with blood.

'Mind yourself, sir,' Harper warned. He was guessing that the grasshopper gun was reloaded. The two Riflemen went very still. If the men below had any wit they would not fire at the same place, but would blast the shot into an unbroken part of the ceiling. Sharpe felt the fear of utter helplessness, knowing that at any second a cannonball could drive up beneath his feet.

'Fire, you bastards!' he muttered.

The gun fired. The men below had guessed wrong and the shot smashed through the attic's far end. Dust and noise billowed about the confined space while broken tiles clattered down the roof and smashed themselves in the courtyard.

As the cannon's noise still echoed in the attic, Harper moved with the speed of a scalded cat to the first hole. He peered down, rammed the seven barrels through the ragged gap, then pulled the trigger. He had only had time to charge five of the barrels, so much of the gun's force was wasted through the two empty muzzles, but the grass-hopper's crew was only fifteen feet below him and the five bullets had enough force to kill both men. Sharpe fired his own reloaded rifle through the newer hole, then went to help Harper who was levering at the tensioned floorboard. Frederickson moaned, rolled on to his side, then lay still. The floorboard, weakened by the cannonball's strike, snapped, and Sharpe and Harper could at last peer down at their enemy.

Two men lay dead beside the fallen grasshopper gun which, because it had been placed on its butt to fire upwards, now had two bent back legs. A third wounded man lay in a puddle of blood by the far door. The other Dragoons had taken shelter in the corners of the room. One of them raised a carbine and both Sharpe and Harper ducked back.

Sharpe reloaded his rifle. Frederickson was breathing hoarsely now. There was silence from below. Ducos and the remaining Dragoons feared the awesome destructive power of the seven-barrelled gun and none of them dared step into the room's centre to retrieve their small cannon, and so they shrank back into corners and stared in fear at the broken ceiling. They were still staring as Calvet's men came to the loopholed doors and thrust their muskets through.

'Non! Non!' one of the Dragoons shouted.

Sharpe took one of the rifles and worked at the board beside the broken one. It had been loosened by the two cannon blows and came up with surprising ease. He saw the Dragoons with their hands up, and he saw the muskets protruding from the doors, but he could not see Ducos. 'General!' he shouted.

'Major?' Calvet's voice was muffled.

'Wait there! I'll open up!'

Harper tried to stop Sharpe. 'You'll break your bloody legs, sir!'

But Sharpe wanted Ducos alive. Sharpe wanted to capture the small cunning enemy who had dogged his footsteps from the Portuguese border to this broken house in Italy, and Sharpe, this close to his old enemy, would not be denied. He lowered himself through the gaping hole, hung for a second by his hands, then dropped.

The height from ceiling to floor was fifteen feet. Sharpe had shrunk that distance by hanging from the broken boards, but he still dropped the best part of nine feet. The fall jarred him. He spilt sideways on the stone floor and a pain shrieked up from his right ankle to his newly mended thigh. He screamed with the pain, rolled to the right, and snarled at the Dragoons to stay still. He expected a bullet at any second. Harper was above him, threatening the room with his rifle. None of the Dragoons fired. They just stared at the blood-streaked, savagely scarred man who had dropped from the roof and who now struggled to stand upright. There was no sign of Ducos. The room was lit by the pale grey wash of the lightening sky. Sharpe drew his sword and the sound of the scraping blade made one of the Dragoons whimper and shake his head.

'Where's Ducos?' Sharpe asked in French.

One of the Dragoons gestured towards a heavy green curtain.

Sharpe knew he should have unlocked the doors to let Calvet's men into the room, but he was too close to his enemy now, and he had travelled too far and suffered too much to let this man escape him. He limped towards the curtain, flinching each time the weight went on to his right leg. He stopped a half dozen paces from the heavy green cloth. 'Ducos! You bastard? It's Major Sharpe!'

A pistol exploded beyond the curtain and a bullet plucked at the green cloth. The pistol ball tore a ragged hole, went a foot to Sharpe's right, then buried itself in the ebony and silver inlaid table.

Sharpe stepped two paces closer to the curtain. 'Ducos! You missed!'

Another bullet twitched the heavy curtain. This one went to Sharpe's left. The curtain quivered from the bullet's passing. The new ragged hole had scorched edges. The

Dragoons stared at the limping madman who was playing this insane game with death.

Sharpe stepped so close that he could have reached out a hand and touched the green curtain. 'You missed again!' He could hear the Frenchman breathing hoarsely beyond the curtain, then he heard the click as another weapon was cocked. Sharpe sensed from the sound that Ducos was standing well back from the green material and must be firing in blind panic at its heavy folds. 'Ducos? Try again!' he called.

The third bullet jerked the cloth. It went to Sharpe's right, but so close that it could not have missed by more than a sword blade's thickness. Dust sprang from the curtain's thick weave to drift in the silvery dawn light. Sharpe laughed. 'You missed!'

'Open the door!' Calvet roared angrily through one of the loopholes.

'Ducos?' Sharpe called again, and once again the hidden Frenchman fired one of his stock of pistols, but this time the shot was not greeted by Sharpe's mockery. Instead the Rifleman screamed foully, gasped in awful pain, then moaned like a soul in sobbing torment.

Ducos shouted his triumph aloud. He ran to the curtain and snatched the heavy cloth aside. And there, at the moment of his personal victory, he stopped short.

He stopped because a sword blade flashed up to dig its point into the skin of his throat.

An unwounded Sharpe, with dog-blood lining the scars on his powder-stained face, stared into Ducos's eyes.

The Frenchman held a last unfired pistol, but the huge sword was sharp in his throat and the eyes that stared into his were like dark ice. '*Non, non, non.*' Ducos moaned the words, then his gun dropped on to the floor as his bladder gave way and a stain spread on the white silk of his French Marshal's breeches.

'*Oui, oui, oui,*' Sharpe said, then brought up his left knee

323

in a single, savage kick. The force of it jarred Ducos's spectacles free, they fell and smashed, and then the Frenchman, clutching the warm stain on his breeches, fell after them and screamed a terrible moaning scream.

And the long chase was done.

Sharpe limped to the door to let in an irate General Calvet. The dawn was full now, flooding the limpid sea with a glitter of silver and gold. The villa was thick with smoke, but oddly silent now that the muskets had stopped firing. It was the silence after battle; the unexpected and oddly disappointing silence when the body still craved excitement and there was nothing now to do but clear up the wounded and dead, and find the plunder. Calvet's men tramped into the room and disarmed the broken Dragoons. Harper carried Frederickson downstairs and tenderly laid the officer on to a chaise-longue taken from the dismantled barricade. Two of Calvet's men had been wounded, one of them badly, but none had been killed. The wounded Grenadiers were laid beside Frederickson whose wits were slowly coming back. His face was already blackening and swelling in a vast bruise, but he managed a wry smile when he saw the ludicrously uniformed Pierre Ducos. The Frenchman still gasped from the pain of Sharpe's kick as Harper tied his wrists and ankles, then pushed him scornfully into a corner of the room to join the captured Dragoons.

General Calvet ripped down the alcove's curtain. Beyond it, and deep shadowed at the end of an otherwise empty recess, was a great iron box. The keys for the box were found in a pocket of Pierre Ducos's gaudy uniform. The locks were snapped open, and the lid was lifted on an Emperor's fortune. Calvet's men stared in an awed silence. The gems were so bright in the shadowed alcove that it seemed as if they generated their own dazzling light. Sharpe edged past a Grenadier and gazed down at the splendour.

'It all belongs to the Emperor,' Calvet warned.

'I know, but Ducos is mine.'

'You can have him.' Calvet stooped to pick up a handful of pearls. He let them trickle through his stubby fingers so that they glittered like scraps of starlight.

'Sir?' Patrick Harper's voice was oddly subdued. He had not gone to see the treasure, but had instead cleared a passage through the barricade and now stood on the terrace, staring southwards. 'Sir?' he called more loudly. 'I think there's something you should see here, sir.'

Calvet crossed to the terrace with Sharpe. '*Merde*,' Calvet said.

A battalion of infantry was approaching the villa. Behind them, and still shadowed by a stand of trees, was a squadron of cavalry. The head of the small column was half a mile away, still on the coastal plain, but only a few minutes from the hill on which the captured villa stood. The battalion's shadow stretched towards the sea, and the dawn's clear light showed that its marching was a shambles, its demeanour unprepossessing, but it was nevertheless a complete battalion of infantry with at least six hundred muskets, and its arrival explained why the Cardinal had given Calvet his free rein.

Because Calvet and Sharpe had done the Cardinal's dirty work, and now the Neapolitans had arrived to reap the work's reward.

'*Merde*,' Sharpe said.

*   *   *

Ducos overcame his pain to crow a vengeful triumph. His friends had come to rescue him, he said, and Sharpe and Calvet would now suffer for their temerity. Harper slapped him to silence.

'We can escape,' Calvet said glumly, 'but not with the fortune.'

'We can take a good deal of it,' Sharpe suggested.

'The Emperor wants it all.' Calvet scowled at the

325

Neapolitan battalion which now spread itself into a line of three ranks at the foot of the villa's hill. The cavalrymen behind the battalion spurred their horses past the infantry. Clearly the Neapolitans planned to surround the hill. There would be a few minutes before that manoeuvre was completed, and Calvet had rightly guessed that those moments would just be sufficient for his small band to scramble northwards into the hills, but they would be forced to travel light and they would doubtless be pursued mercilessly through all the long hot day. They would be weighed down by the treasure they carried, by their wounded, and by their prisoner.

The battalion of Neapolitan infantry waited on the parched grass. So far they had ignored the small village where Calvet's three men should be guarding a boat, but that did not signify, for the Italian infantry now lay between the villa and Calvet's seaborne escape. Three of the Neapolitan officers stood their horses a few yards in front of the resting infantry and Sharpe guessed that an envoy would soon be sent up the hill to demand the surrender of the villa's occupants.

'Ignore the bastards.' Calvet, seeing no solution, turned away and ordered his men to fill their packs, cushion covers and any other receptacle they could find with the Emperor's treasure. Harper joined the Frenchmen and marvelled at the slew of rubies, emeralds, diamonds and pearls. There were a few bags of gold heaped at one end of the iron chest, and a tangle of candlesticks at the other, but most of the great box was bright with gems. They lay a foot deep in the box, which was itself three feet high, suggesting that much of the treasure had already been squandered. 'How much did you waste?' Calvet snapped at Ducos, but the thin-faced Frenchman said nothing. He was waiting for his salvation.

Which salvation appeared to be in the hands of the three Neapolitan officers who spurred their horses up the hill's steep southern flank. Dust drifted from their hooves towards the sea.

'Bloody hell,' Harper had rejoined Sharpe on the terrace, 'the buggers look as if they're going to their first communion.' The Irishman spat over the balustrade. His disgust was at the uniforms that the officers wore. Neither he nor Sharpe had ever seen uniforms so splendid or so impractical. All three officers were in pristine and dazzling white. Their elegant cutaway coats were faced with cloth of brightest gold, while their cuffs and epaulettes were similarly arrayed with gold cloth that was dangling with gold chain. They wore black riding boots topped with gold turnovers, and on their heads were tall snow-white bearskins with gold chains looped from the crests to the blood-red plumes. 'What are we supposed to do,' Harper said, 'fight the buggers or kiss them?'

Sharpe did not reply. Instead he limped to that part of the balustrade closest to the approaching officers. All three were sweating because of the weight and constriction of their white fur hats. Their leader, whose rank Sharpe could not recognize, curbed his horse and gave the Rifleman a curt nod. 'Are you French?' the man asked in that language.

'My name is Richard Sharpe, and I am a Major in His Brittanic Majesty's army,' Sharpe said in English.

'My name is Colonel Pannizi.' Pannizi must have understood Sharpe's reply, though he still spoke in French. He waited, as though expecting Sharpe to offer him a salute, but the filthy, bloodstained Englishman did not move. Pannizi sighed. 'And what is an English officer doing in the Kingdom of Naples?'

'Visiting a friend.'

Pannizi was a slim, handsome man. He wore a razor-thin moustache that curled up into sharp waxed tips. Gold tassels hung from his bearskin's plume, while a tiny gold and silver cuirass hung beneath the high stiff lapels of his white and gold coat. He momentarily closed his eyes in apparent exasperation at Sharpe's insolent answer. 'Is General Calvet with you?'

'I am General Calvet. Who the devil are you?'

Pannizi bowed in his saddle towards the stocky Frenchman who now stumped on to the terrace. 'My name is Colonel Pannizi.'

'Good morning, Colonel, and goodbye.' Calvet had clearly decided that defiance was the best course of action.

Pannizi touched a white-gloved finger to a tip of his moustache. His two companions, both much younger, sat with impassive faces. Pannizi quietened his horse that jarred away from an insistent fly. 'You are trespassing upon the property of a prince of the Church.'

'I couldn't give a bucket of cowshit whose house it is,' Calvet said.

'The house and all its contents,' Pannizi went on with remarkable equanimity, 'are hereby placed under the protection of the Kingdom of Naples, whose warrant I hold. I therefore request that you leave the villa immediately.'

'And if I don't?' Calvet challenged.

Pannizi shrugged. 'I shall be forced to arrest you, which will cause me extreme pain. The bravery of General Calvet is legendary.'

The flowery compliment plainly pleased Calvet, but could not persuade him. There was a fortune at stake, and even if Calvet himself did not receive a groat of the treasure, he was determined that his master would be denied none of it. 'To arrest me,' he said, 'you will have to fight me. Not many men have lived to say they fought General Calvet.'

Pannizi gave a flicker of a smile. He drew his sword, but very slowly so as to demonstrate that he meant no threat. He pointed the shining blade down the hill to where his men sat slumped on the grass, then sheathed the blade again. The gesture was eloquent. Pannizi controlled six hundred bayonets, and must have known that Calvet had scarcely more than a dozen. 'Your bravery, as I said, is legendary.' Pannizi was hoping to flatter Calvet into surrender.

Calvet glanced at the Neapolitan battalion. Their colours had been unfurled, though the wind was not strong enough to lift the heavy fringed silk. Beneath the two flags the men appeared dispirited and flaccid. 'You have the stomach for a fight, Colonel?' Calvet challenged Pannizi.

'I have the orders for a fight, General, and I am a soldier.'

'A good answer.' Calvet scowled down the hill. He knew better than anyone how hopeless this fight was, yet he was a soldier too, and he also had his orders. 'And if we surrender to you now?' he asked with evident distaste for the question.

Pannizi looked shocked. 'My dear General, there is no question of your surrendering! You are invited to be the guests of the Cardinal, the most honoured guests. Consider my regiment to be nothing more than an escort sent to conduct you with due honour into the city.'

Calvet had the grace to smile at the outrageous description. 'And if we choose not to be the Cardinal's guests?'

'You are free to leave the kingdom, all of you.'

'Free?' Calvet probed.

Pannizi nodded. 'Entirely free. And you may take with you your uniforms and personal weapons,' he paused, 'but nothing more.'

The threat was in those last three words. Pannizi knew what treasure lay in the villa, and he did not care what became of Calvet, Sharpe, or their men, so long as the treasure became his.

Calvet turned abruptly to stare north. The Neapolitan horsemen had cut off that escape route. He turned back. 'You will give us fifteen minutes to consider our position, Colonel?'

'Ten,' Pannizi said, then drew his sword again. He saluted Calvet with the shining blade. 'And you will do the honour of breakfasting with my officers, General?'

'Only if you have bacon,' Calvet said. 'I have a great liking for fat bacon.'

Pannizi smiled. 'Bacon will be found for you, General. You have ten minutes to anticipate its taste.' The Neapolitan Colonel sheathed his sword, nodded a summons to his two companions, then galloped back down the hill.

'*Merde, merde, merde,*' Calvet said.

* * *

'Lime!' Calvet snarled at Sharpe. 'I had you trapped in a fort and you escaped with powdered lime. So tell me what foul trick you have this time?'

Sharpe did not reply immediately. He was staring downhill at the dispirited Neapolitan infantrymen who, in anticipation of the ten minutes' expiry, were being ordered to their feet. 'Will they fight?'

'Of course they'll bloody fight,' Calvet said. 'That bastard Pannizi is telling them that there's a battalion of whores and a king's ransom in this place! Any minute now and they'll be raring to fight! They smell plunder.'

'So give it to them,' Sharpe said abruptly.

'What?'

'Give them the damned gold! It weighs too much anyway. Take the stones and give them the bags of gold.'

Calvet stared at the Rifleman. 'You're mad.'

'On the contrary, General. We haven't got lime, but we can blind them with gold. Showers of gold! Gold dropping from the heavens!' Sharpe was suddenly enthusiastic. 'For God's sake, General, how much is this treasure worth to you? Would you rather crawl back to your Emperor with nothing? Or would you rather buy your way out of this trap with a little gold?'

Calvet turned to look at the somnolent battalion. 'So

what do I do, Englishman? Go down there and haggle like a shoemaker? Don't be a fool. If we offer a little gold they'll want it all, and once they have it all, they'll want the stones, and once they have the stones, we have nothing.'

'We don't offer it to them,' Sharpe said, 'but we give it. How good do you think their discipline is?'

Calvet snorted. 'They're a shambles! I've seen men reeking with drink who made a better show than that.'

'So we test their discipline by appealing to their greed.' Sharpe grinned at Harper. 'I want the grasshopper. And some powder.'

Harper carried the brass gun, a powder keg and a bag of quick-fuse on to the terrace. Sharpe placed the weapon butt down, balanced by its bent rear legs, so that it could fire high into the air like a mortar. Sharpe did not want to blow a swathe of death through the Neapolitan battalion which waited a quarter mile away, he only wanted to swamp it with greed, and so he would literally make the gold of heaven rain from the sky.

Two of Calvet's men fetched the bags of gold coins while Sharpe ladled a minuscule amount of powder into the gun. He tamped it down. He dared not charge the gun fully, or else the coins would be blasted across empty miles of countryside. He poured a small fortune of gold into the brass barrel, then pushed a length of quick-fuse into the touch-hole. 'General?'

Calvet had been sulking at the prospect of losing even a small amount of his master's treasure, but now he brightened at the prospect of firing the first golden volley. The gun was aimed so that the golden shower would fall to the east, away from the sea. Before he fired, Calvet glanced to make certain that his men were ready to make their bid for escape.

Harper was supporting the still dazed Frederickson, and had Ducos tied to a length of rope. He had cut the Frenchman's ankles free so Ducos could run. Calvet's men, all but for the two wounded Grenadiers, were laden with their bags and packs of gems. The prisoners, all but Ducos, would be abandoned. 'We're ready,' Calvet said, then gleefully touched the glowing end of a cheroot to the stub of quick-fuse.

There was a brief hiss, a coughing dull explosion, and a spew of dark smoke. The gun jarred backwards, then toppled, as Sharpe had an impression, nothing more, of a gouting of bright gold that glittered almost straight into the air through the acrid billow of smoke. Then, a second later, it seemed that a patch of the sky twinkled as though fragments of the sun itself were shattering in the upper air. Sharpe knew he watched the coins at the top of their arcing flight, but then they disappeared. He waited, and suddenly Harper whooped as the shards of light bounced and scattered and winked on the ground just beyond the Neapolitan battalion's right flank.

Sharpe righted the fallen gun, ladled in another scoop of powder, then rammed yet more coins on to the charge. He glanced downhill and saw the movement as men turned in the infantry's ranks. He rammed another length of quick-fuse home, then touched Calvet's cheroot to its tip.

Another shower of gold sparkled high, then fell to earth in a glitter of greed.

'They're trying to hold the buggers!' Harper reported gleefully.

A third charge, then a fourth, and now Sharpe was adding a half ounce to the charge so that the gold was spreading itself in a bright swathe that led away from the sea. He touched the cheroot on the fifth charge and this time, as the gold shattered the dawn sky into a thousand bright sparks, the battalion below broke their ranks, cheered, and stormed the empty fields to make their fortunes. The three Neapolitan ranks had dissolved like men hit by canister. Their sergeants and officers could not hold them and the men scattered like a chaotic mob to the

332

countryside. They threw away their packs, muskets and shakoes as they fought and scrambled for the coins. They plucked the golden harvest and constantly watched the sky for yet more of the wonderful goldfall.

Sharpe gave them a last heavy blast of gold, this one from a barrel almost fully charged so that the thick coins glittered a full half mile inland as they fell. For the last time he watched the brightness tumble, then he turned and hobbled after Calvet's men.

It was a race now. The infantry had been taken from the equation, but there were still the cavalry and Pannizi's mounted officers. Calvet's men, weighed with their prize of precious gems and their two wounded comrades, stumbled down the steep hill. Harper forced Ducos on, while Sharpe helped Frederickson. 'I'm all right,' Frederickson protested, but as soon as Sharpe let him go, he stumbled as if drunk.

'Ware left!' Harper warned.

Pannizi and three officers were spurring to cut off their retreat. Sharpe dropped to one knee, aimed, and put a bullet across their path. The crack of the Baker Rifle sounded very purposeful and the spurt of dust in front of Pannizi's small group was more than enough to check their ardour.

Sharpe ran on. One of Calvet's men was watching the right flank, from where the cavalry might appear, but the hill had hidden those horsemen from the fall of gold and they were still ignorant of what happened to their south. Far off to Sharpe's left a rabble of infantrymen still rooted through the grass, olive groves and stubble. Some officers and sergeants tried to whip the men back to their duty, but the lure of the gold had turned the battalion into a mob. Some of the lucky Neapolitans were finding more money in five minutes than they could have expected to make in a lifetime.

Sharpe stumbled through a dry watercourse, scrambled

up its far bank, and half carried Frederickson through patches of tall, thick leaved plants that had saw-like edges. The village lay to their left, its harbour just beyond. Lieutenant Herguet, who had led Calvet's small band down to the harbour, jumped up and down on the quay. The cavalry had still not appeared, and Pannizi's infantry were scattered to uselessness. Sharpe was limping badly, but Frederickson, his one good eye almost closed by the swelling dark bruise, found new strength. Harper kicked Ducos on. Calvet was suddenly enjoying himself; he whooped his men through the village, past the barking dogs, and on to the sharp flinty quay. They ran past drying nets and wicker pots, down to where Herguet guarded a bright-painted boat on which two disconsolate crewmen cowered beneath his men's two guns.

'Cavalry!' Calvet's man warned. But the cavalry was too late. They burst over the hill's shoulder, they drew their swords, they spread out in fine array, but Calvet's men were already aboard the fishing boat, Harper was slashing at the stern line with his bayonet, and the dirty sail was already catching the dawn's land breeze to drive the high-prowed craft out into the bay.

Ducos, with his hands still tied, was pushed to the bottom of the fish hold. He stared myopic hatred at Sharpe, but then Sharpe closed the hatch to leave his enemy in a stinking darkness. The Grenadiers were laughing with the pleasure of victory. It might not have been Jena or Wagram or Austerlitz, but it was still a victory for an Emperor who all the world thought was past winning victories.

Calvet embraced Harper, then the foully bruised Frederickson, and lastly Sharpe. 'I forgive you for the lime, Englishman, and I will say that, for a man who is not French, you fight with a reasonable skill.'

Sharpe laughed. 'Be glad, General, that you will not have to fight me again.'

'Who knows?' Calvet's voice was mischievous. 'If I can

bring the Emperor enough gold then perhaps he can raise an army again?'

The mischievous remark reminded Sharpe of Major-General Nairn's wistful dream of one last great battle, one climactic killing in which the Emperor would be arrayed against the world, but Nairn was dead, his old bones flensing in a French grave. Sharpe smiled. 'No, General, there'll be no more battles.'

'You're right.' Calvet sounded miserable as he made the admission. 'You and I are finished, my friend. The world's at peace and we're useless now. We're the hunting dogs, but rabbits rule the earth now.' Calvet turned to watch the Neapolitan cavalry curb their horses on the far quay. 'But I tell you, my friend, that within a year, you and I will be wishing for battle again.'

'I won't,' Sharpe said fervently.

'You wait.' Calvet turned away from the land, and stared out to sea where two sails showed on the hazy horizon. 'So what will you do now, my friend?' he asked Sharpe.

'Take Ducos to Paris and present him to Wellington. After that he will be given to the authorities.'

'Which authorities?'

'The ones who will execute him for the murder of Henri Lassan.'

Calvet offered Sharpe a mocking smile. 'That small crime worries you?'

'It worries Madame Castineau.'

Calvet still smiled. 'And why should Madame Castineau's concerns be of any interest to you?'

Sharpe turned away because one of the Neapolitan cavalrymen had fired a carbine at the fishing boat. The ball splashed uselessly a hundred yards astern. None of the boat's occupants even bothered to raise a weapon in reply.

Calvet fished in his pouch and brought out a handful of gems. He sorted through them with a grimy finger, then

335

selected one flawless, blood-red ruby. 'Give that to Madame Castineau, for, even if unwittingly, by writing her letter she did a great service for France.'

Sharpe hesitantly took the jewel. 'For France, General? Or for Elba?'

'Napoleon is France, my friend. If you tied him in chains and dropped him to the ocean's deepest pit, he would still be France.' Calvet folded Sharpe's hand over the precious jewel. 'I will give you nothing more, Englishman. Does that hurt? That you must go empty-handed from a fight where we filled a morning sky with gold?'

'I lived,' Sharpe said simply.

'And you left empty-handed.' Calvet smiled. 'So you see, Englishman, the French won after all!'

'*Vive l'Empereur, mon General.*'

'*Vive l'Empereur, mon ami.*'

An hour later they accosted a Piedmontese merchant ship which, for a handful of imperial gold and under the threat of a dozen muskets, agreed to take the soldiers on board. Calvet would go to Elba and Sharpe, with his prisoner, would seek a Royal Naval ship. Thereafter they would be unwanted hounds in a kingdom of rabbits, but they had lived when so many had died, and that, at least, was something. Thus, in their separate ways, they sailed towards peace.

EPILOGUE

Pierre Ducos died in a fortress ditch, shot by a firing squad from France's royalist army. No one mourned him; not even those soldiers in the firing squad who were still secretly loyal to the exiled Emperor. Ducos had betrayed Napoleon, just as he had betrayed France, and thus he was shot like a dog and buried like a suicide in an unmarked grave beyond the fortress glacis.

In London an aide-de-camp to the Prince Regent heard of Ducos's death and, as a result, suffered sleepless nights. The Frenchman's execution was a triumph for a Rifleman who had come from ignominy to regain his reputation, and any day now that man would cross the channel. Lord Rossendale contemplated flight to the remnants of his family's Irish estates, but his pride forced him to stay and show a bravado he did not feel. Each morning he went to a fencing master in Bond Street and each afternoon he shot with long-barrelled duelling pistols at targets in the yard of Clarence House. He claimed he was just honing his military skills, but all society knew he was practising for the ordeal of grass before breakfast. 'He's left Paris,' Rossendale told Jane one autumn morning.

Jane did not need to be told who 'he' was. 'How do you know?'

'A courier came from the Embassy yesterday. All three of them rode for Calais.'

Jane shivered. Beyond the window rain swept in grey curtains across the park. 'What will happen?' she asked, though she well knew the answer.

337

Rossendale smiled. 'It's called grass before breakfast.'

'No,' Jane protested.

'He'll call me out, I'll choose the weapons, and we'll fight.' Rossendale shrugged. 'I imagine I shall lose.'

'No.' Jane remembered the terrible arguments that had preceded Sharpe's duel with Bampfylde. She had lost those arguments, but now she would lose the man she had come to love.

'I'm not a swordsman,' Rossendale said ruefully, 'and I'm a rotten shot with a pistol.'

'Then don't fight!' Jane said fiercely.

He smiled. 'There's no choice, my love. None. It's called honour.'

'Then I'll go to him!' Jane said defiantly. 'I'll plead with him!'

'And where's the honour in that?' Rossendale shook his head. 'You can't cheat honour,' he added, though he had done little else for months, which only proved that honour could be cheated, but that the price of it would still have to be paid before breakfast one wet, drab morning.

Thus Lord Rossendale and Jane could only wait, for honour would not let them run away, while the man for whom they waited came to Calais.

Sharpe and Frederickson had been reinstated, then reassured that their honour was still bright and their ranks inviolate. Apologies had been made, and now, in Calais, they breakfasted in the private room of a harbour tavern. Their plates were heaped with mutton chops, eggs, garlic sausage and black bread. 'You'll go to London first, of course?' Frederickson poured coffee.

'Will I?' Sharpe asked.

'Unfinished business,' Frederickson said grimly. 'Or shouldn't I mention it?'

'You mean Lord Rossendale.' Sharpe sipped the newly poured coffee. 'I'm to kill him?'

'Stop being obtuse. Of course you're to kill him. I'll be

your second, if you'll let me have that honour? Naturally the duel will have to be secret. We both have our careers to think of now.' Frederickson smiled. His face was still darkened by the bruise, though the swelling had long subsided. 'I assume you're no longer contemplating a Dorset retirement?'

Sharpe leaned back in his chair. Through the window he could see the packet boat loading by the quay. The ship would leave on the tide in two hours time, and, if he chose, it would take him to the foul mess of an unfaithful wife and pistols at dawn. 'And Jane?' he asked Frederickson. 'What am I to do with Jane?'

'Give her a damned good thrashing, of course, then cast her off. If you can't bear to face her, then I'll gladly tell her myself. You can give her a pittance, if you must, but don't be too generous. She can become a governess or a companion.'

Or a whore, Sharpe thought sadly, but he did not say as much. 'You're very kind, William.'

Frederickson shrugged away the compliment, then mopped up his egg yolk with a hunk of bread. 'You're surely not still thinking of retiring to Dorset, are you?'

'The countryside has a certain appeal.'

'For God's sake, Sharpe! You heard the Duke! There's restitution to be made. My God, man, you could have a battalion!'

'In peacetime?'

Frederickson grimaced. 'We don't have much choice, do we? We can hardly order another war for our own convenience.'

'No.' And indeed the Duke of Wellington was going from his Paris Embassy to a great congress at Vienna to ensure that there would not be another war. The Duke, Sharpe allowed, had been kindness itself in Paris, even after his Embassy had been invaded by three fugitive Riflemen bearing the bruised and terrified Pierre Ducos. The French royalist authorities had been perturbed that General Calvet had taken a fortune to Elba, and the Neapolitan Embassy had made a stiff protest about uniformed thieves disturbing their kingdom's peace, but the Duke had scornfully ridden down such diplomatic carping. All was forgiven. There was even an implicit promise of promotion for Sharpe and Frederickson, though it was difficult to see how such a promise was to be kept with no battles to create vacancies.

'So London first,' Frederickson planned their joint future with relish, 'then we'll demand a battalion of our own. You'll be in command, of course, though I shall be senior Major and can assure you I'll be demanding a spate of leave just as soon as we're settled.'

'Leave?' Sharpe smiled. 'So soon?'

Frederickson looked very coy. 'You know very well why I want leave. You might be despairing of marriage, but I haven't abandoned all hope. Far from it! I'll establish myself first, of course. Promotion perhaps, a spot of money, and a new uniform.' He smiled, as though the accretion of those things would guarantee the success of his courtship. 'I know you're not fond of Madame Castineau, but in many ways she's ideal for me. A widow, you see, so I don't suppose she'll expect too much from marriage, and once I can persuade her to live in England I'm sure she'll be very happy. Mind you, I can't say I'm averse to her property. That'll be worth a tidy sum in the future.'

'No,' Sharpe said brutally.

Frederickson frowned. 'No?'

'No,' Sharpe said again. He had somehow persuaded himself that Frederickson had abandoned his hopes of Madame Castineau in the excitement of these last days, but instead his friend was betraying these hopeless dreams which would now have to be cruelly shattered. It was time for Sharpe to say the thing that should have been said weeks before. It was time to break a friendship, and Sharpe flinched from the deed, but knew he could not hold back.

'I'm not going to England.' Sharpe looked up at his friend. 'Patrick took my luggage off the boat an hour ago. I'm only here to see you safe on your way, William, but I'm not going with you. I'm staying here.'

'In Calais? That's a very bleak choice, if you'll forgive me.' Frederickson frowned suddenly. 'My God! It's your damned pride, isn't it? You fear to go to England because of Jane and that wretched man? You think you'll be mocked because you've been cuckolded?' Frederickson scorned the fear with a dismissive flick of his napkin. 'My dear Sharpe! Kill the man in a duel and no one will dare mock you!'

'No.' Sharpe hated saying it, but it had to be said. 'It's nothing to do with Jane, and I'm not staying in Calais. I'm going back to Normandy.'

Frederickson stared at Sharpe for a long long time. And, for a long long time, he said nothing, but then, and as though it took a great effort, he finally found his voice. 'To Lucille?'

'To Lucille,' Sharpe confirmed.

'And she?' Frederickson hesitated. There was real pain on his bruised face, evidence of just how hard his dreams were breaking into misery. 'And she will consent to your arrival at the château?'

'I believe she will.'

Frederickson briefly closed his one eye. 'And may I ask whether you have grounds for this belief?'

'Yes,' Sharpe spoke very quietly, 'I do.'

'Oh, God.' Now it seemed there was nothing but hatred in Frederickson's gaze. Or else he felt a pain so deep that it could only show on his face as hatred.

Sharpe tried to explain. He heard himself stammering as he told the old story; of how a dislike of the woman had turned into a friendship, and then how the friendship had turned into love, and he remembered, but did not tell Frederickson, how on that black night of sky-breaking thunder he and Lucille had met in the passageway and

341

not a word had been said, but she had come to his room and afterwards, as she slept, and as Sharpe had listened to the rain pouring from the gutters, he had thought that never before had he known such peace. 'I should have told you weeks ago,' he said miserably, 'but somehow . . .'

Frederickson broke Sharpe's words off by abruptly standing and turning away. He walked to the fireplace and stared down at the coal fire which sputtered damply in the grate. 'I don't want to hear any more.'

'I didn't want to hurt you,' Sharpe said lamely.

'God damn you!' Frederickson turned on Sharpe in a sudden blind fury.

'I'm sorry.'

'I don't need your bloody pity! God damn you! How many damned women do you want?'

'William . . .'

'Damn you! Damn you! Damn you! I hope she breaks your bloody heart like the last one did!' Frederickson was still holding his napkin which, in petulant anger, he threw towards Sharpe. Then, saying nothing more, he snatched up his greatcoat and sword, then stormed from the room.

Sharpe stooped, retrieved the crumpled napkin, and smoothed it on the table. He thought of following Frederickson outside, but he knew it would do no good. Instead he sat for a long time, empty-eyed, watching the sea.

Harper came very quietly into the room, looked at Sharpe, then held his hands towards the feeble fire. 'So you told him, sir?'

'I told him.'

'God save Ireland,' Harper said of nothing in particular, then he stooped and shoved at the coals with a poker made from an old French bayonet. 'It wouldn't have worked, of course,' he said after a while, 'but I suppose he'd never be convinced of that.'

'What wouldn't have worked, Patrick?'

'Mr Frederickson and Madame. He doesn't like the women, you see. I mean he likes them well enough, but he'd never make a woman into a friend now, would he? It isn't enough to take them to your bed. You have to actually like them, too.'

Sharpe smiled. 'Is that so, Mr Harper?'

'It is Mr Harper now, isn't it?' Harper laughed. In his pocket the Irishman had his discharge papers, signed by the Duke of Wellington himself. Mr Harper was a free man now, going to England where he would catch a fast ship for Spain, after which, with Isabella and the baby, he would go home to Ireland. Home for good, he said, home to where the rain fell on thin fields from which a poor people scratched their daily bread.

Sharpe stood and led the Irishman out to the quayside. There was no sign of Frederickson on the packet's deck, though his luggage, along with Harper's heavy pack, lay stacked beside an open hatchway. Sharpe turned away from the gangplank and walked with Harper to where the packet boat's bowsprit reared tar-black against the sullen clouds. 'I don't know what to say, Patrick.'

'Nor me, sir,' Harper spoke softly, 'but we've had some good times, sir, so we have.'

'We've had some bloody terrible ones, too,' Sharpe laughed. 'You remember that day you fought me in the snow?'

'You cheated, sir, or else I'd have split your skull wide open.'

'I'd never have beaten you without cheating.'

They fell silent. A slew of gulls shrieked and tumbled above the fish quay. Rain fell in a sharp stinging slant.

'If you're ever in Normandy?' Sharpe suggested.

'Of course, sir. And if you ever take yourself to Donegal then you'll know there's a rare welcome for you. Go to Derry, keep going west, and someone will know where the big fellow back from the wars will be.'

'Of course I'll come. You know I'll come.'

Harper thrust his hand deep into the pocket of his fine civilian greatcoat. 'You're all right for the money, are you now?'

'You know I am.' Sharpe had pocketed some of the gold coins as he had loaded the small grasshopper gun, just as Harper had filched a few handfuls of gems from the big strongbox. 'I owe you money anyway,' Sharpe said.

'Pay it when you come to Ireland,' Harper said.

The packet's bosun shouted for the last passengers. A headsail was already being hoisted, and it was time for Harper to leave. He looked at Sharpe and neither man could find anything to say. They had marched all the soldiers' miles together, and now their ways parted. They would promise reunion, but such promises were so rarely kept. Sharpe tried to say what he felt, but it would not come, so he gave his friend an embrace instead. 'Look after yourself, Patrick.'

'I'll do that.' Harper paused. 'It is the right thing you're doing, sir?'

'Not for Mr Frederickson, it isn't.' Sharpe shook his head. 'I don't know, Patrick. I wish I did.' Going back to Normandy was like the roll of a dice, or the whim of an action in battle. There was no rationality to it, but life did not yield to reason, only to instinct. 'I think it's the right thing. I want it very much, if that's any answer. And I'm not certain I want to live in England. They'll never accept me there. To them I'm just a bastard upstart who can use a sword, but in peacetime they'll spit me out like a speck of rotten meat.'

'And if they want your sword again?' Harper asked.

Sharpe shrugged. 'We'll see.' Then the bosun bellowed his impatient summons again, and the last passengers broke from their farewell embraces and hurried towards the gangplank. Sharpe gripped Harper's hands. 'I'll miss you, Patrick. You were an awkward bugger, but by God I'll miss you.'

'Aye.' Harper could not find the proper words either, so he just shrugged. 'God bless you, sir.'

Sharpe smiled. 'God save Ireland.'

Harper laughed at Sharpe's mimicry. 'I'll come and find you, sir, if you don't come and find me.'

'I hope you do. Maybe we'll meet halfway.'

Harper turned and walked away. Sharpe watched the Irishman board the packet, he waved once, but then Sharpe turned away so that the parting would not be prolonged. He heard the flogging sound of the wind catching the great mainsail as it was hoisted.

Sharpe hurried back to the inn and paid his bill. He strapped the saddlebags on to his new horse, paid the ostler, and swung himself into the saddle. He wore a coat of brown homespun over black breeches, but at his side there hung a long trooper's sword and on his back there hung a rifle. He touched the spurs on his new plain boots to the animal's flanks. The packet boat was clearing the harbour, but Sharpe did not turn back to watch. He rode away from the sea, away from England, going into the enemy's country to where a woman watched an empty road. It was there, Sharpe decided, that his future lay; not in Dorset, not in a peacetime army, but with work on a Norman farm and perhaps, one day, there would be a French-speaking son to whom he and Lucille would bequeath an old English sword and a ruby stolen from an Emperor.

He clicked his tongue and urged the horse into a trot. He felt dazed. There was no more war, no more soldiers, no more fear. No more Emperor, no more Harper, no more gunsmoke skeined above a field of blood. No more closing of ranks, no more miles of pain, no more skirmish chain. No more cavalry in the dawn and no more picquets in the dusk. There was only Lucille and what Sharpe thought was a love sufficient for both their lives. He rode on into France, his back turned on all he had fought for, for now it was all gone; the wars, a marriage, a friendship, and an enemy; all gone in Sharpe's revenge.

HISTORICAL NOTE

Napoleon's baggage was lost, though not in Bordeaux. The loss of that baggage was just a small part of the chaos that engulfed France after the Emperor's surrender. The battle of Toulouse was fought after that surrender, but such was the speed of travel that the news did not reach Wellington till two days after he had trounced Soult.

The battle happened much as described in the novel. Today it is chiefly remembered for the tragic Spanish assault which, launched early and unsupported, was bloodily repulsed. The battlefield is now entirely built over, just an anonymous part of the city's sprawl.

In northern and southern France the Imperial armies were disbanded, ejecting on to the roads of Europe a startling number of vagabonds and highwaymen. The era of the soldiers, it seemed, was over, for the long, long war was finished. Wellington's army, perhaps the best that Britain has ever possessed, had won the Peninsular Campaign and now, in the spring of 1814, that army was no longer wanted. Its men were dispersed about the globe, while its women, who had so loyally supported their men, were callously sent home to Spain or Portugal. The fate of those abandoned women is accurately recorded here. They disappear from the history books, and their anguish can only be surmised. A few British soldiers did successfully evade the provosts to go back to Spain with their wives, but they were very few.

Wellington, before going to the Congress of Vienna, was appointed Britain's ambassador in Paris where, on behalf of the government, he bought the house of Napoleon's sister, Pauline. It remains the British Embassy to this day. Many other British officers resigned their commissions. Doubtless, like Sharpe, they believed they could hang up their swords, and none, surely, could have foreseen that Napoleon's restless ambition would soon lead to a shallow valley on the road to Brussels; a valley where Wellington would sorely miss his Peninsular veterans.

But Waterloo is another story.